1

Sergei froze suddenly, and put his face to the window.

Here we go, Andriy thought.

"Andriy, look!" He pointed astern, "they're coming at us!"

"What are you talking about?" Andriy said, trying his best to sound concerned and put his face to the glass.

"Hijackers!" Sergei swiftly moved and pressed the alert button that set off the sirens throughout the ship's quarters. On a normal day, it would simultaneously alert nearby harbors and ships, sending out distress signals. However, Andriy had disabled it three days ago. Unbeknownst to Sergei, no such signal went out.

Wings

THE PIRATES OF ADEN

by

Daniel Rasic

A Wings ePress, Inc.

Suspense/Thriller novel

Wings ePress, Inc.

Edited by: Jeanne Smith
Copy Edited by: Joan Powell
Senior Editor: Jeanne Smith
Executive Editor: Marilyn Kapp
Cover Artist: Trisha FitzGerald

Wings ePress Books
http://www.wings-press.com

ISBN 978-1-61309-992-6

Published In the United States Of America

April 2011

Wings ePress Inc.
403 Wallace Court
Richmond, KY 40475

Dedication

For Ewa, always.

I would also like to thank Mama and Tata for all their support; Baka, Nivez, Aleks, Andrzej, and Robert for their valuable help; Deda for teaching me how to tell stories. To Maya and Luka for providing inspiration

One

U.S. Black Site, Ethiopia, 1999

The sun descended behind Mount Entoto, casting a shadow over the metropolis of Addis Ababa. Traffic swirled through the city and yellow streetlights dotted the darkening cityscape. At the foot of the mountain, twenty-three miles past the outer reaches of the city, surrounded by overgrown eucalyptus trees, a lone black sport utility vehicle was parked in front of a one story concrete structure with broken windows. At one point in history, the building had served as a schoolhouse.

On this day, it was a torture chamber.

Inside, Dr. Marshall Ramsey led two large men in black leather jackets as they dragged the prisoner through the front door, down a short hallway and into the main room of the schoolhouse. He carried a black briefcase in one hand and a battery-operated lantern in the other, which cast a bluish-white light against the crumbling interior walls. As soon as Ramsey turned the corner into the main schoolroom, illuminating the set-up inside, the prisoner went rigid, but was powerless against the brute force the two men used to lift and then slam him against the pine board. While one of the men leaned over the prisoner to stop him thrashing about, the other threw leather restraints around his legs, torso and forehead, fastening him to the plank. The prisoner now lay prone, balanced between two sawhorses, his feet elevated slightly above his head. They wrapped a black cloth around the prisoner's head, covering his face.

Ramsey clicked his briefcase open, removed a pulse oximeter and placed the probe on the prisoner's middle finger. It was the only finger with the nail bed still intact, the others had been plucked (or 'manicured' as the men referred to it), one each day, until he cooperated with the interrogation. Nine days later, he still hadn't spoken a word.

The oximeter beeped and displayed a blood oxygen saturation of one hundred percent and a normal pulse of sixty-three. *The bastard's not even anxious,* Ramsey thought.

The older of the two men in leather jackets, the team leader Staff Sergeant Steve Sidwell, tightened the strap around the prisoner's torso with a good, solid yank and looked up at the doctor. "We good to go?"

Ramsey nodded and watched as the other man, FBI Agent Bruce McCormick, stood a digital audio recorder on the floor. He then placed a towel over the prisoner's face and poured a steady stream of water from a red watering can onto the towel. Ramsey kept his eyes on the oximeter as water saturated the towel and then the cloth covering the man's face. Water dripped off the towel and onto the floor.

The three men waited for the moment when the prisoner would no longer be able to hold his breath and exhaled, after which a deep inhalation would inevitably follow. The damp cloth would block air from entering the oxygen-starved airways like a massive wet mitt clamping down on the mouth and nostrils. Instead of sucking in air, water would seep into his nasal passages, down his throat and into his lungs, triggering a powerful gag reflex, which no matter how hard his mind tried, it could not interrupt, and more water would be swallowed. It was controlled drowning and Dr. Ramsey was the controller. He was there to bring the prisoner to the brink of drowning—so that the prisoner *believed* he was dying—but to intervene before irreparable damage to the body tissues occurred. The magic number was seventy. *Never let a prisoner's* O_2 *go below 70,* was the protocol. That's when they start dying.

For eleven months, the team had one mission: to bring those responsible for the planning and execution of the U.S. Embassy bombings in Nairobi and Dar es Salaam to justice. They were part of the larger FBI/U.S. army task force assembled as a response to the attacks. Eleven months of reviewing surveillance tapes, following leads, interviewing witnesses and questioning suspects had led them to this man: Kadar Hadad. The amount of evidence they had accumulated was enormous: photos placing him at the embassy hours before the explosion, connections to Al-Fawari—bin Laden's associate in East Africa, audio recordings of him calling for the ousting of the U.S. from Africa, and extensive military training in demolition.

But none of that would lead to an indictment.

They needed a confession.

A poor audio recording retrieved by a CIA case officer in Kenya one month earlier was the closest thing they had to direct evidence linking Hadad to the embassy bombing. Through the static, Hadad was heard saying—presumably to a group of associates—that *the next target will castrate the United States.* The fact that he had said "*next* target" implied that there had to have been a previous one, didn't it? It was enough evidence for them, but not enough to cover the gap between what makes intuitive sense and what gets a conviction in court.

But the very idea that there even was a *next target* gave the entire mission more urgency. They needed to find out what the next target was, and if it was already planned. Hadad's choice of words—*castration*—led the three men to speculate what he was referring to. Ramsey's mind had immediately jumped to an economic "castration" and thought of the attempted World Trade Center Bombing in '93. Could Hadad be planning to bomb the towers again? McCormick assumed that meant a military target, and mentioned the Pentagon. Sidwell, perhaps the most concrete thinker of the three, took the castration reference the most literally; he shared his thought that Hadad would go after the Washington Monument. His idea was met with laughter but he did not back down: *Can you think of something that looks more like a penis?* The truth was that they had no idea, but had to find a way to get Hadad to speak.

Dr. Ramsey's role on the team was to: (1) monitor the health status of the prisoner, (2) ensure the prisoner survived the interrogations, and (3) identify potential vulnerabilities in the health status of the prisoner that could be used advantageously during interrogation. It was the last point that had troubled Marshall. It was not that using one's own health against them was contrary to the Hippocratic Oath that bothered him, as monsters like Kadar Hadad did not qualify for the graces of ordinary ethics. It was that three weeks of investigation had not turned up any vulnerability. He was physically and psychologically healthy. And they were running out of time.

They had been holding Hadad in a prison in the center of Addis Ababa since he had been arrested trying to cross the border from Kenya into Somalia. For two weeks, Hadad was in a four-by-four foot cell, cold at fifty degrees and chained by his neck to the ceiling to force a standing position. At one point, he had stood for thirty-eight hours before his legs gave out. In spite of all that, he did not speak.

Not one word.

But then, Marshall had noticed something in one of the transcripts of interviews with Mohammed Al-Nadir, a childhood friend of Hadad's. Rebels had drowned Al-Nadir's parents in a river during a civil war in Sudan. He ended up in an orphanage where he had befriended Hadad. And then he had added, almost teasingly, *Maybe we were friends because our parents died the same way.*

And then the vulnerability was obvious.

Ramsey looked at the oximeter, which was now beeping quickly and flashing an oxygen saturation reading of seventy. Sidwell and McCormick quickly removed the straps, unwrapped the cloth and lifted Hadad up to a sitting position, but as soon as they let him go, he collapsed onto the floor on all fours, coughing rhythmically and spitting a white foam onto the concrete. He heaved and vomited a small amount of water before he looked up at his interrogators, his eyes red and filled with tears. Then, almost imperceptibly slowly, his lips parted so that his teeth became visible and it turned into a smile. He spoke his first words. "That was not very nice of you." But Marshall then realized he wasn't smiling at *them*, he was smiling at *him*.

A long moment passed, and then three men stared back at Hadad, not so much stunned at what he had said, but rather that he had said something. Sidwell, the team leader, reacted first and spoke. "You're right, that was not nice." Sidwell crouched in front of Hadad, who was still on all fours. "But you need to realize that we will not stop until we have a chat about the Nairobi bombing."

Hadad nodded, and sat back against one of the sawhorses. "I will say that what happened in Nairobi was a travesty."

"Two hundred and twenty four people died."

"Yes, but the travesty is that one thousand survived."

"You fuck—" McCormick pounced forward and kicked Hadad squarely in the face, the force sending him backwards, knocking the sawhorse over. Sidwell placed a hand on McCormick's chest and pushed him back, telling him to calm down.

Hadad got up slowly, his eyes narrow, the grin still there, beaming. "Officers, you can torture me as much as you want. Hit me as many times as you want. You cannot kill me because then you will not have justice, will you?"

"It would be justice enough for me," McCormick said.

"But he won't let you," Hadad pointed at Ramsey, "even though he wants to kill me, wants me dead, maybe more than you." He didn't break eye contact with Ramsey. "But killing me will not bring Dennis back, will it?"

Ramsey stared back at him, the words not registering in his mind initially. He felt unable to break free of Hadad's gaze. The grin on Hadad's face widened, seemingly taking pleasure in the surprise his words had evoked in Ramsey. Had he just spoken Dennis's name? It seemed impossible; surely he had misinterpreted what was just said. But his mind wouldn't let it go.

The images in the embassy flashed through Ramsey's mind. They walked through the main foyer wearing their finest suits (maybe the only one Dennis actually owned), towards the main auditorium where their audience waited for them to deliver their presentation on setting up a joint psychiatric-medical clinic for children affected by war to treat both physical and emotional scars. It was a cutting edge proposal and Ramsey's mentor through medical school, Dr. Dennis Hamilton's brainchild. The clinic would be up and running within two years and would treat one thousand children annually. The final stage was approval of the international community, whose representatives sat in the Embassy's main theatre.

Before they had the chance to get out of their seats and make their way to the podium, the building shook. Before anything else, any noise or smells, the ground shook. Next, they followed the mass of officials and delegates running through the hallways. Fire enveloped the walls and concrete chunks rained down from the ceiling. Tarry black smoke rolled in like a thick fog and lingered. The side exit came into view and the crowd filed out of what was left of the building when Ramsey heard a crash and groan behind him. He turned and saw Dennis on the floor, his lower body crushed beneath a concrete slab. When he turned back, the ground shuddered and flames burst out behind Dennis. Ramsey stopped and stared. The heat radiated. It was too hot. It was too late, wasn't it? He didn't have time to turn back, did he? No, Ramsey pushed the thought out of his mind again, it was the explosion that killed him. It killed all of his plans for children in Africa with him. It was this man, *this devil*, in front of him that killed Dennis.

"What did you just say?" Ramsey whispered.

Hadad's response was a grin. That stupid grin. Nothing else.

"Listen, Kadar," Sidwell said and stepped in between Ramsey and Hadad, "we're looking for those responsible. It's our job to do this. But we want to find those that are actually responsible; we're not interested in forced confessions," he exhaled. "But we have evidence that implicates you. We are interested in a confession but we would like to know who else you're involved with."

"I have four wives and two girlfriends, they keep me busy enough. I have no time to be involved with anyone else," Hadad waved his hand in the air.

McCormick stepped forward again with his fists balled, but Sidwell stepped in front of him, which seemed to temporarily defuse the Irish-American's temper.

Sidwell rested his right hand on his chin, the sleeve of his jacket slipping to his elbow, revealing a detailed forearm tattoo of a spider web. A remnant of his early, pre-military days, he had told Ramsey. He turned. "Dr. Ramsey, can I talk to you for a minute?"

Ramsey followed Sidwell out of the room and into the dark hallway.

"How far can we take this thing?" Sidwell said.

"Excuse me?"

"The fucker knows we can't hurt him, that we need him alive. And he's smearing that shit in our faces every chance he gets." Sidwell pounded the bottom of his fist against the concrete wall. "We need to make him think we'll kill him if we need to. So, I need to know how far you'll let me take this."

Ramsey swallowed. Sidwell was right, enhanced interrogation only worked if the prisoner believed he could die. If they *believed* the interrogators would let them die. Dennis hadn't thought he would die; he had no idea. No one in the Embassy had. But they did. And now there could be more targets? More good people killed? They had to find out more, and there was only one way to do it. Ramsey clenched his jaw and spoke through his teeth, "Take it as far as necessary."

Sidwell slapped the wall in approval and Ramsey followed him back into the room.

Ramsey watched as Sidwell and McCormick laid Hadad on the plank and fastened the straps again. Ramsey placed the oximeter probe on Hadad's finger and stared at Hadad, whose grin never left his face. Even when the black cloth was wrapped around his head, Ramsey swore he could still see the outline of the grin through the folds of the fabric. *He has no idea what's in store.*

As McCormick poured the water over the towel covering Hadad's head— slowly, as though he were watering a delicate flower—Ramsey kept his eyes on Hadad's face.

O_2: 92%

Hadad's head thrust forward, his neck muscles straining impotently against the leather strap and then his head recoiled with an audible thud against the pine board.

O_2: 80%

His skinny arms tensed against the leather strap around his torso and his forearms twitched. Ramsey imagined Hadad's eyes widening beneath the towel,

O_2: 72%

not of surprise, no, of shock,

O_2: 70%

at how the doctor could let this happen,

O_2: 65%

because the doctor is supposed to stop it by now,

O_2: 55%

but he wants you dead more than anyone else.

O_2: 44%...

Two

32 Miles off the coast of the Puntland, Somalia, 2008

Samatar 'Sami' Al Jelle couldn't help but think this was the way his life was supposed to be. At least he wished it were. Sami sat on a bench at the stern of his fishing boat, holding a fishing rod in one hand and a half smoked cigarette in the other. The calm turquoise water surrounding the boat looked like glass, broken only by the bobbing of his flaccid fishing line. A small tape player beside him played Somali pop music, filling the stifling air with strong beats and soft melodies. Yes, this was how he was meant to live: fishing, smoking and sunbathing.

Sami owned one of the largest fishing boats in Puntland. Most fishermen managed with fifteen-foot wooden, paint peeling, undecked boats fitted with small outboard motors. Sami's vessel, a twenty-five foot boat with a rusting metal hull, large outboard engine and cabin space was gigantic by comparison. He had a seven-man crew aboard with him, so while most other fishermen relied on their family members to help drag in the nets, Sami had over half a dozen young, strong, skilled workers.

The boat was passed on to him by his father, but it was in the family long enough that Sami considered it an heirloom. And while this large rusty boat had been in his family for fifty years, fishing was in the family blood. He had worked on the boat since his father and grandfather had taken him out on the sea for the first time when he was nine years old. He remembered what seemed like an endless supply of tuna spilling out from their nets and onto the deck and playfully clubbing them with a broom. It all happened on this deck, on this boat.

But that was then, and it had been a long time since the nets were full.

When Sami's father, Abdi Al Jelle, was on his deathbed being suffocated by tuberculosis, he made his final wishes clear in what had become a rare lucid moment for a man who spent months in a feverish delirium. Minutes before his death, with his entire family surrounding him and the sweat drenched mattress he laid on, Abdi announced that the fishing boat would go to his youngest son, Sami. His father's dark eyes then filled with intensity and squared on Sami's and he said, *The boat has kept this family from hunger for fifty years, you must ensure that it continues to do so.* And then his eyes became glassy again, his breathing shallow and groaning and then it stopped. The image of his father's eyes was so deeply engraved in Sami's mind that he saw them each time he stepped onto the boat. The old man had made his point.

For several years, Sami fished daily, the only exception being during Karan, the heavy rains in the springtime. Year by year, the amount of tuna he caught became less.

At first, he was unable to turn a profit at the local market in Bosasso. The problem then worsened; he could no longer make enough money to fill the massive engine with diesel and as a result, his boat was beached. He purchased several goats and sheep to feed his wife and four young daughters. His father's final words, once comforting, began to haunt him. *You must ensure it continues to do so.* But he couldn't and his family was hungry.

Explanations for the declining fish population off the coast of Somalia ranged from pollution to disease to algae blooms. But Sami always suspected, and he was not alone in his suspicions, that the area was over-fished. Not by Somalis, of course, but by huge commercial boats coming from the Arabian Peninsula, Europe and India. Somalia was too busy in civil war to have a coast guard to protect its waters. Fishing off the coast was a free-for-all.

But that didn't change his situation.

The boat has kept this family from hunger for fifty years, you must ensure that it continues to do so...

Sami took a long hard drag on his cigarette and tossed it into the water where it fizzled out. He turned and looked at his crew pulling in empty nets from the calm blue waters. The rusty pulleys creaked as they collected the nets into neat piles on the deck. He imagined for a moment that the nets were full of fish, flopping around on the deck and a smile broke his stern expression.

Yes, this is how it was supposed to be: simple and uncomplicated.

The cell phone in his pocket vibrated, breaking him from his trance. He opened the phone and read the text message.

SHIFT CHANGE - 10 MINUTES.

Sami tapped out another cigarette from the carton he had in his shirt pocket, lit it and inhaled deeply. Three weeks ago, a man who claimed to have information on a ship coming through the Gulf of Aden contacted him. Sami had received tips from this man on three previous occasions, and each time the information was exact and led to successful hijackings. The man would not give any more information regarding the details of his affiliations. The man refused to meet in person but delivered on his promise. The detailed manifest and shipping route coordinates of a Ukrainian cargo ship were placed inside the pages of a Somali-translated copy of *Moby Dick* in the library in Bosasso just as they had discussed. According to the manifest, the ship was full of military weapons, from guns to tanks, heading for Nairobi. A man would be on the inside, working as a watchman. All Sami would have to do was board it. The ship was a sitting duck.

For four days Sami and his men had floated around off the coast of Puntland, waiting to cross paths with the ship. Some of the men began to doubt the accuracy of the information, but Sami only needed to remind them of the booty. If the manifest was accurate, the weapons were worth over $80 million and this would trigger a huge bidding war amongst the warlords and clan leaders of their fragmented nation.

Sami walked along the deck and entered the open wheelhouse, a claustrophobic six-by-six foot room, which consisted of the boat's steering wheel, a small folding table, a tiny humming fan and a GPS device. Sami spread a nautical map on the table, looked at the set of coordinates scribbled on a piece of paper from his pocket and traced a line using a parallel ruler. He fanned the cigarette smoke away from his face with his hand and glanced at the screen on his GPS and compared his current coordinates—11.17, 52.51—to those on the map. Their position was perfect. The cargo ship was going to pass right by them, almost running them over.

Sami stepped out of the wheelhouse, scanned the horizon and barely made out the shape. The hull was a sliver against the orange backdrop of the dusk sky. She seemed small to him now, but Sami knew the true enormity of the *Stebelsky*. More importantly, he knew how quickly she would arrive. He bounced back into the wheelhouse, turned off the boat's engine and prepared to drop anchor. They didn't need to go any farther.

Sami ran out to the deck as quickly as he could without tripping on a loose deck board. His men sat along the bow's outer ledge, talking and laughing loudly.

"Is this what I pay you to do?"

"What do you want us to do… fish?" one of his men sneered and this resulted in laughter throughout the group.

"At least pretend to," Sami dragged a small crate along the deck and sat in front of his men who had formed a semi-circle around him. He leaned in, "I want to tell you all a story, an English story called *Moby Dick*."

His men sat with furrowed brows. Ali, the youngest man in the group and Sami's nephew spoke up, "I've heard this story."

"What is it about then, professor?" one of the men who wore fluorescent board shorts said, waving his hand dismissively.

"A whale."

"Not quite," Sami rose from his seat and walked with deliberate steps to the edge of the deck. "It is actually about the biggest catch in the sea." Sami kept his expression serious, raised his hand in dramatic fashion and pointed out towards the horizon. "I call her *Stebelsky*."

The men followed Sami's finger and saw the rapidly approaching cargo ship. The hull smashed through the calm waters, leaving a foamy wake behind her. Along the deck, stacked boxcars towered above the waterline. She moved quickly; moments earlier she had been a sliver against the sky, now she was dominating it. Soon she would be on their doorstep. They had to move quickly.

The men jumped up and smoothly descended below deck through a small square opening on the deck's surface. As they moved, their lean, sinewy muscles under their black skin became obvious. All the men were ex-military and had fought alongside Sami during the clan wars in the 1990s. Two of them had fought the Americans in Mogadishu in 1993 and worked that into any conversation they could. But for the last two years, the only military operations of any sort in which these seven men had participated started on this boat.

Sami stayed on deck and took in the enormity of the cargo ship. Ali approached Sami from behind and wrapped his powerful arm around Sami's shoulder. "Uncle, we have made it," his smile beamed.

"This is the beginning of the mission, Ali," Sami didn't break his gaze with the *Stebelsky*, "we still have to complete it."

"I know," Ali nodded. The ends of the black bandana on his head began fluttering in the developing evening wind. "But I know we'll succeed."

Ali was young, nineteen years old. Although Sami knew Ali was only a nephew, Ali felt much closer than that. Ali's parents, Sami's brother and sister-in-law, were killed in a roadside bomb when Ali was eight and Sami had raised him. Although Sami did not have a son, he felt that if he ever did, he would want him to be like Ali. The young man was strong, disciplined, perhaps a bit brazen but not reckless. And he couldn't ignore the fact that Ali was a fantastic shot. For a year following his eighteenth birthday, Ali had begged Sami to join his crew out on the seas, taking ships for ransom, but Sami resisted. It was too dangerous for a young boy. But his father's words again came into his mind again, *the boat has kept this family from hunger for fifty years, you must ensure that it continues to do so...* Ali was the next generation in the family, after all, so Sami gave in.

Sami went below deck where the crewmen were assembling weapons. Sami stepped down the ladder and ducked his head because of the low ceiling. Assault rifles leaned against one wall in neat rows. Against the other, boxes containing hand held pistols, plasticuffs and nylon rope were stacked up. He opened a bag sitting in the middle of the floor, removed a set of black military fatigues and boots and slipped them on. He lifted a pistol out of one of the boxes, snapped on the magazine, loaded the barrel and slotted the gun in his hip holster.

The crewmen who had been in fluorescent shorts, but had since changed into dark fatigues, brought Sami his rifle, his M-16. It was the only one on board; the other men had to settle for AK-47s. He had been using it since his second hijacking and he knew it well. Sami knew that it shot three degrees to the left and he could feel the millisecond delay from the time he pulled the trigger to when the bullet left the barrel.

"I was going to use it today," the crewman smiled.

"Don't take Sami's gun, he'll kill you," another chimed in while slipping on black boots.

"Sami, why don't you use an AK?" Fluorescent Shorts asked.

"This has been my gun for two years."

"A good soldier can use any gun," he laughed.

"In two years, I've been on eight missions. Every one was a success. And you know how many men have been hurt?" Sami curled his index finger and thumb together, "Zero."

He quickly grabbed the gun out of the crewman's hand and pointed it at the group, slowly moving it along. "Does one of you want to be the first? Because I can take care of that right now."

The men kept their eyes on the ground as Sami stared intensely without retracting the gun.

"Okay, you keep it," the crewman raised his hands.

Sami lowered the gun and boomed a laugh, slapping the man on the shoulder. Sami started up the ladder to the deck.

"You superstitious bastard," he called up after Sami, smiling.

The *Stebelsky* was more visible now, despite nighttime descending, and Sami could make out her name painted against the side of the hull. From what Sami could gather, her trajectory would miss them by about 500 meters in fifteen minutes. The wind had picked up and the glassy surface of the water had become choppy and waves slapped against the side of Sami's boat.

"Let's prepare the boats," Sami said to Ali, referring to the fifteen-foot long fiberglass skiffs-tied against the sides of his rickety old fishing boat.

Three

The thirteen-man crew of the *Stebelsky* was congregated below deck for dinner. Two flickering bulbs overhead provided light for the small dining hall and the men divided themselves between two small tables. They took turns telling jokes and stories from their home countries in an assortment of Slavic languages. They rarely understood each other as something almost always got lost in the translation, but they laughed hysterically all the same. Between jokes, they slurped the piping hot fish stew in front of them.

They had been at sea for only eight days so far. The trip from Odessa, through the Black Sea and Bosporus, the Mediterranean and the Red Sea, had been entirely uneventful. The only complication had been a leaky fuel line, which made below deck smell even more of diesel, but that was quickly fixed.

But now they were in the Gulf of Aden. Modern day Pirate Alley.

Most of the men, even the most junior of officers, had passed through these waters more times than they could count. An actual hijacking was a rare event, like a plane crash. But ever since passing into the Gulf of Aden each one of the crewmembers had thought about the possibility of a hijacking. When they were on deck, they each took an extra long look on the horizon for any approaching boats. But none of them would dare bring up the topic of pirates at the dinner table. That would be a bad omen.

~ * ~

Above deck, on the bridge of the *Stebelsky*, which housed the ship's navigation systems, Andriy Simonov, the night watchman, stared at the green radar screen in front of him. A few blips were visible, which were likely small boats slowly drifting away from them. Andriy rubbed his eyes and looked out the window in front of him. Although the *Stebelsky* was considered a small sized cargo ship, she still looked massive to him. The bow of the ship extended like a rail yard. Two rows of metal boxcars stacked thirty feet high flanked three cranes that stood on the middle of the deck. In that moment, Andriy wondered what it was inside the boxcars that was so valuable. He was paid handsomely for his services, up front. He wished he had asked the man who had handed him a briefcase full of American bills two weeks earlier what was aboard the ship. But then again, maybe he was better off not knowing.

Andriy looked at the radar screen again. Two sporadic blips flashed. He knew that represented hijackers rapidly approaching from astern. They were likely using low-lying, high-speed fiberglass boats. These small vessels were ideal for approaching slow moving merchant vessels. The wake of large cargo ships like the *Stebelsky* blurred their radar footprint. Despite the sophisticated security technology on the ship, these boats were undetectable, or at least easily overlooked, even by the most vigilant watchman. Andriy turned and looked behind him to the stern of the ship and could see the two small boats quickly approaching the vessel. They were barely perceptible, especially given the darkening sky. His job was done. Soon they would board the ship and take it for ransom. They would float around for a few days until either the trading company that owned the ship or the Ukranian government paid the ransom. Then he would be able to take his mother to Germany for her medical needs and buy an apartment for himself. No one could possibly know of his involvement, could they? Would people question how he had overlooked the approaching boats? He doubted it, but even so he thought it was wise to have an alibi.

Andriy lifted his massive frame out of his chair and stretched, partly to look casual, but more so to calm his trembling nerves. He walked next door, where Sergei, the steersman, sat at the ship's navigation station eating dinner. The stew dripped onto his beard from the spoon. He didn't seem to notice. Andriy handed him a cigarette and lit it for him before lighting one for himself.

"Night shift for you, too?" Sergei said without looking up from his stew.

"I can sleep during the day and I like to think during the night."

"Andriy, you think too much."

"I have a lot to think about… My mother is sick at home. She cannot pay for her medicine. I try, but it's hard." Andriy sat up on the windowsill, and stared over the bow of the ship, trying to forget about what only he knew was happening at the stern.

"Doctors are the biggest criminals, Andriy, not the mafia," Sergei opened the drawer next to him and passed over a flask of whiskey. Sergei's reddened face and large belly showed that he was no stranger to a drink. Andriy welcomed the opportunity to calm his nerves, and knocked a big gulp down. The pirates had to be near the ship.

"What about your family?"

"No family, Andriy. All I have is this ship."

Andriy grunted, unsure of how to respond but took another long swig of whiskey.

"I like it that way, I never miss anything or anyone," Sergei said.

"Maybe you need a woman."

"I'll have one when we land."

"I mean one you don't have to pay for," Andriy laughed, perhaps too forced, he thought. Where were the hijackers? Time seemed to be moving very slow.

"Show me a woman that is free. I was married and she took half," Sergei stood up abruptly and took a few steps towards the window overlooking the stern. "Never get married, Andriy, it's no good."

Sergei froze suddenly, and put his face to the window.

Here we go, Andriy thought.

"Andriy, look!" He pointed astern, "they're coming at us!"

"What are you talking about?" Andriy said, trying his best to sound concerned and put his face to the glass.

"Hijackers!" Sergei swiftly moved and pressed the alert button that set off the sirens throughout the ship's quarters. On a normal day, it would simultaneously alert nearby harbors and ships, sending out distress signals. However, Andriy had disabled it three days ago. Unbeknownst to Sergei, no such signal went out.

Four

By the time Sergei had seen the pirates and activated the (disarmed) alarms aboard the *Stebelsky*, it was too late. Just as the cargo ship had passed by, Sami and his men had divided themselves into the two high-speed fiberglass skiffs that were tied against the sides of his fishing boat. They piled AK-47s (and Sami's M-16), handheld pistols, rope, machetes and more plastic handcuffs than they could possibly need into the well of each skiff. Initially it was a game of catch-up as the vessel chugged away from them, but they easily matched and surpassed the *Stebelsky's* 20 knots and were on her heels within a few minutes. The pirates crouched and held on tight to the sides as the skiffs skipped through the ship's massive wake. If all went as planned, they would be on the bridge of the ship before anyone knew they were there. Everything — from the now black starry sky, the approach from the stern, the dismantling of the alert system aboard the ship, the dark fatigues, even their dark skin — made them almost undetectable. Almost as if they were worried that a peep would suddenly alert the crew aboard the *Stebelsky*, the pirates kept silent, even though the cargo ship's roaring propellers chopping through the dark water were deafening. From this point on, all communication was strictly for tactical purposes.

While one of the skiffs went to the starboard side of the ship, Sami's skiff kept close to the ship's stern. Sami rose to his feet but quickly lost his balance as the skiff rocked violently in the large wake made by the ship's two propellers. The momentum nearly threw him overboard, but as his feet hit the water, he grasped the skiff's edge, held on and managed to stop himself from being swallowed by the wake. Sami crawled back over into the skiff, dug into one of the backpacks and removed a grappling hook, which was attached to a length of rope. He stood on one knee and looked up at the back of the *Stebelsky*. The ship was huge this close up; the black hull rose like an iceberg out of the sea. He lifted the grappling hook and launched it over the poop deck on the back of the ship. It sailed and gripped firmly to the safety rails on the edge of the ship. He tied the ladder to the end of the rope attached to the grappling hook and fed the line through so the ladder now hung off the back of the ship.

"Go, go, go!" he could barely hear his own voice over the sound of the roaring propeller.

His men skillfully climbed the swinging ladder towards the deck of the ship. Their dark fatigues made them look like moving shadows against the dark hull of the *Stebelsky*. Only the occasional glitter of the AK-47s or the machetes they had strapped to them gave them away.

Sami saw movement on the deck of the ship. The crew was out. He could barely make out the sound of the ship's alarm siren over the crashing waves but someone had definitely sounded it. The crew was likely out just to see what was happening, to see a hijacking up close. But they couldn't risk a crewmember putting up resistance and trying to save the ship.

Sami motioned for his men who were hanging on the rope ladder on the back of the ship, to hold their positions and reached for his machine gun. He searched the bottom of the skiff but all he found was a lone AK-47. Someone had taken his M-16. Bastards. He grabbed the machine gun and peppered a series of bullets towards the crew, aiming high enough to miss them but close enough to show them they were serious. The figures then disappeared, likely ducking for cover.

Sami checked his watch. By this point, the men from the other skiff were likely boarding the ship on the starboard side. The men from his skiff had reached the deck and waved all clear, so Sami threw the AK-47 around his shoulder. Fluorescent Shorts steered the skiff in close to the *Stebelsky* so Sami could reach the rope ladder. His defined forearm muscles tensed as he climbed the unstable ladder. As Sami reached the top, Ali offered him an arm over the rail and greeted him with a grin as if he were saying: "We have done it, Uncle, we are rich beyond our wildest dreams." Sami didn't take Ali's arm, nor did he reciprocate his smile. They still had work to do. Sami refused to relax until the bridge was secure and all of the *Stebelsky's* crewmembers were in handcuffs.

Sami had learned this lesson from an incident aboard the *Hercules*, a private German yacht two years earlier. They had boarded the ship and already taken control of her navigation. They had radioed in their ransom demands. All the civilians aboard were locked in the yacht's quarters below deck. Or so they thought. Eighteen hours in, the teenage son of the yacht's owner burst out of a storage closet in the wheelhouse swinging a butcher knife, narrowly missing Sami's head. It took three men to subdue him and put him in handcuffs. That was his one slip-up. Fate would not allow any more.

In front of him, the ship's tower rose three stories above the ship's deck. A series of emergency steel staircases that connected to platforms on each story ran along the outside of the tower, which led up to the bridge, the ship's navigation center. Lights were on inside the bridge, which looked like a beacon against the dark sky. Sami hoped his contact was inside, as was agreed upon, waiting for him to take control of the ship.

Sami's men had already divided into three teams and were securing the crewmen. He figured that most of the ship's men were below deck, so he sent two teams downstairs. Sami and Ali were the third team and their objective was to secure the bridge.

They moved along the deck between the rows of stacked metal boxcars. At each corner, Ali crouched in a low position while Sami stepped in a wide arc watching for an ambush at a corner. It was precautionary; cargo crews were trained to surrender, not cause a fuss and wait for support on the ground to come to their rescue. But every once in awhile, someone would try to be a hero.

They arrived at the foot of the tower, directly below the bridge of the *Stebelsky*. As they approached the tower, the ship's continuously blaring alarm became louder. Ali walked up the steps leading to the first platform. Sami took a position covering his blindside as Ali moved upwards, the sound of his footsteps drowned out by the ship's siren. Ali scanned the area on the platform just below the bridge and raised his fist, signaling 'Clear' for Sami. Sami moved up the steps, continuing the procedure, knowing that they had at least one man on the inside that wouldn't be hostile.

The final stairway that led up to the bridge was more of a vertical ladder than a stairway and it led through an opening the size of a manhole. Sami looked up through the opening, his gun pointed and finger on the trigger and waited a long moment, at least 5 seconds, to satisfy himself that it was clear of any hostiles. He edged up the stairs, one hand on the rails, the other on the machine gun.

Rat-tat-tat-at!

Bullets ricocheted through the metal framework of the platform. Sami fell backwards down the four steps and onto his back. He rolled as soon as he hit the deck and scurried for cover behind a support beam. Then the gunfire stopped.

"Where is he?" Sami mouthed to Ali, who had also taken several steps back.

"Upstairs to the right."

Sami looked down at his intact body. How was he not hit? How was he still alive? He looked over at Ali, who was staring at Sami, his mouth half open as if asking the same questions. A long moment passed that seemed much longer than it actually was and then they exhaled in unison, pushing the questions from their mind.

Sami refocused and thought as quickly as he could. There was only one gun, definitely not two. The man had been waiting for them to enter his trap the entire time. They had to secure the bridge soon, before a distress signal could be radioed in. But there was no way they could get up this way without both of them dying.

Sami looked up through the perforations in the metal platform above him, trying to visualize his assailant. A shadow, a figure, anything. Surprisingly, the man hadn't moved. Paralyzed by fear? Or lying in wait.

Sami turned gradually, mindful of being silent despite the intermittent siren blaring. He scanned around and noticed a second ladder about ten yards from his position that connected the platform they were on to the bridge. There was no way that their assailant could cover both entries.

Ali had noticed the second ladder at the same time and motioned that he was moving there. Sami walked back to the foot of the first ladder. Ali peered upwards through the floor and motioned to Sami, 'All clear.'

Sami took several deep breaths and waited until the siren blared and stepped right under the manhole cover and fired off several rounds up the hole in the platform. Ali seized the opportunity that the assailant was distracted and ran up the back stairs. A series of rounds went off above and Sami waited for the call from Ali. He waited a long time. Each passing second seemed slower than the last. The flesh on his arms began to creep and the hairs on his neck were becoming stiff. He thought he heard himself yell for Ali, but his mouth hadn't moved. His mind kept yelling, screaming for Ali, his nephew, his son.

Suddenly, he heard footsteps and grunting above him and felt the blood return to his brain. He kept his eyes up the hole. A dark limp body was dropped through the hole just missing Sami. He looked at the body, the dark fatigues and the dark skin. It was Ali. Sami held Ali's body in his lap, wanting to comfort him but he immediately felt his soaked clothing. Blood. Oozing—no pouring—from somewhere in his chest. The momentary relief Sami had felt was now replaced with fear and guilt. Why had he agreed to bring Ali with him? He was too young, too inexperienced.

Ali opened his eyes, staring into Sami's. His breaths were short and choking. "Uncle, we almost made it."

"No, it is okay, we will put pressure on it. Come with me."

Sami slung Ali's arm over his back and they climbed down the stairs to deck. He dragged Ali behind a stack of crates and a pile of ropes. He tore Ali's shirt open and ran his fingers across his chest. There were two bullet holes on the right side of his chest and another hole in his back. Two shots, one still lodged in his chest cavity, one went right through.

Sami took his own shirt off and pressed it under Ali's back. A small amount of air flowed in and out of the wound. Untreated, the lung would collapse and the air pressure would constrict his aorta, causing death in minutes.

"Ali, you have two shots, one is still inside your chest."

"I think that's it, Uncle." Tears formed in his eyes.

"No, we will get a doctor."

Sami removed the adhesive tape on the handle of his machete and tore a small square. He placed it around the exit hole and pressed it on three sides creating a one-way valve, preventing external air from entering his chest.

"You will breathe better. But I must get this ship under control."

Sami didn't elaborate but he knew Ali was lucky the bullets hit the right side of his chest. But without medical attention soon, he would certainly die. He had to get ashore. To do that, he had to take control of the ship. The only way he could do that was to kill the hostile man on the bridge.

Sami poked his head out from behind the crates to see if he could see the hostile crewman on the well-lit bridge. Just as he turned, a figure stepped in front of the light and bullets screamed past his ear. He had been spotted. Sami crawled towards a pile of ropes beside the crates. He tied a length of rope to the handle on one of the crates and then moved back behind the ropes. He removed his handheld gun and clicked it back. Sami pulled hard on the rope, pulling a crate over and as he expected, a barrage of bullets reduced the wooden crate to splinters. He had created the diversion. Sami popped out from behind the ropes and saw the assailant's shadow on the bridge. He took aim and fired off two rounds. The dark figure collapsed to the ground.

Sami emerged from his position and walked up the stairs to the bridge. Meanwhile, his men were lining up the crewmen on deck their hands bound by plasticuffs.

Andriy crouched over Sergei's body with his mouth gaping. Sami came up from behind, grabbed his collar and lifted him so they faced each other.

"You're Andriy?"

Andriy did not respond.

"Are you Andriy? I said."

"Yes."

"Put these on," Sami handed him the black plasticuffs.

"No one was supposed to be harmed," Andriy put them around his hands and fastened them with his teeth.

"That's correct. And maybe if you had stopped this fat man from shooting at us, that would be the case. You will be lucky if you survive yourself." Sami raised his gun and put it to Andriy's forehead. "You will go and sit with your crew, and maybe you will live."

Sami's men led Andriy below deck.

Sami and another of his men entered the navigation room on the bridge.

"Steer the ship to Bosasso to unload," Sami said. The only thing on his mind was saving Ali's life.

Five

Bosasso, Autonomous Republic of the Puntland, Somalia

The first shipment of foreign aid to reach Puntland in nearly six weeks arrived the next morning. A lone military truck pulled up in a dusty clearing, off the main highway, on the outskirts of the city of Bosasso. Word that a convoy had passed into Somalia from Eritrea had spread quickly amongst the foreign aid workers in the region and a large group had congregated at the usual drop spot hours before the truck pulled in. They had all engaged in the usual basic chatter about lack of supplies, their experiences with the militias, about what they hoped would come on the truck be it medical supplies, food, books, computers or plumbing equipment. The one common thread in their conversations was that they needed more.

Before the flatbed truck came to a complete stop, the crowd of foreign workers—of all sorts of races, black, Indian, Arab, a few white—had already converged at the truck's heels, rubbing elbows, hoping to be first in line and pick up their supplies. One tall Somali man with a machine gun slung on his shoulder stood guard at the edge of the truck to deter any overenthusiastic workers from jumping on.

It wasn't only that few supplies made it through to Somalia, past checkpoints where cargo would be combed through and anything of value taken as "toll" by the multitudes of militia that controlled every region. It was that even the aid that did get through and into the hands of the aid workers was still in jeopardy. They were all aware of the potential for a Jeep packed with militia to have followed the convoy truck and declare the shipment property of (insert clan name here). Or, even if they were handed their boxes of supplies and loaded them into their own vehicles, they still had to drive through Bosasso, through any number of checks where the supplies could be taken.

While the crowd tightened up around the truck, one man stood several meters back and put his fourth cigarette of the morning out underneath his foot. He stuck out from the rest of the crowd, partially because he barely spoke a word to anyone for the forty-three minutes he was standing there and partially because of the scowl that seemed tattooed on his face. He had been in Somalia for a long time, too long, and that was emphasized by his sun-bleached graying hair and bronzed skin.

The man stared out at the scene in front of him and squinted slightly, which accentuated the fine wrinkles around his eyes. The morning sun was particularly bright and reflected off the landscape of sand, dust and rock around him. He smirked just a little bit at the displays of enthusiasm of the other aid workers, who thought that being first in line meant something.

The guard walked to the edge of the flatbed and pointed at the man who had just put out his cigarette. "Doctor Alban," he yelled, and motioned for the man to come forward.

The man nodded and then his smirk grew and became more obvious as he weaved through the crowd and stopped in front of the guard. He ignored the looks of indignation on the faces of a few of the workers who had fought their way to the front of the line moments earlier. He smiled up at the guard. "What have you got for me this time?"

"Two boxes. What will you give me for them?"

The doctor rolled his eyes at the request. "I have a gun, you know."

"A gun is no good if you can't pull the trigger," he laughed.

"I can't help it if I'm a pacifist."

"You know what they call a pacifist in Somali? A chicken."

"I'd be surprised if you knew where the trigger was on that thing."

The guard lifted his trigger finger and flexed it.

"Quit wasting my time and just give me the boxes before I really get pissed off." The doctor smiled, took the two boxes the guard passed down to him and walked back through the crowd.

It had been ten years since Dr. Paul Alban had left his home, stepped off an airplane in Ethiopia and hopped on a bus to enter Somalia's sweltering heat. He had planned on staying eight weeks, which turned into one year, then two, then five and another five. Ten years. A decade. More than a fifth of his life. He had been young and energetic when he started, but the wrinkles on his face had accumulated and there were more grey hairs on his head now than blonde ones.

Paul was one of a handful of physicians in the Puntland region of Somalia. Most came for a short stint and then went back home, thanking everyone for the wonderful experiences, and leaving with a backpack full of souvenirs and 5 gigabytes of photographs. They all said they would come back the second they got the chance, but that 'chance' never seemed to materialize.

But it was because of that very reason that all of the other workers, while polite and orderly, had to look on as Paul was the first to hold his medical supplies. Seniority.

Paul crossed the clearing and piled the cardboard boxes into the trunk of his dusty forest green Jeep SUV. He leaned against the bumper and flicked the keys in his hand. He glared across the parking lot, trying to catch Ellen's eye, but she was immersed in some meaningless conversation with a Kenyan nurse who worked in a clinic on the opposite side of Bosasso. Her hands waved as she was in full storytelling mode, a funny story judging from the other woman's bursts of laughter. Paul guessed she was telling her about her recent adventure home to Montreal, where she was interrogated at a stopover by customs at JFK airport. Having an Arabic last name and living in Somalia tended to raise eyebrows with Homeland Security. Or maybe customs officials couldn't fathom how a beautiful, exotic young woman could possibly be traveling alone without her partner. What kind of man would let her out of his sights? Paul could tell from her gestures that she wasn't even at the halfway point of her story. And it was a long story. He considered closing the trunk, firing up the engine and slowly pulling away until she chased after him, but he thought better of it. It wasn't worth the argument that would inevitably ensue.

Instead, he turned and opened an X-acto knife from the breast pocket of his khaki vest and cut the tape on one of the boxes. He rummaged through its contents—saline bags, syringes, I.V.s, bags of penicillin, packs of gauze, suture trays—and then folded the box back up. Paul had heard that less than ten percent of all aid actually reached its desired recipients, but lately he came to realize that was a generous estimate. Everyone took their cut; hospitals in western countries donated leftover supplies while workers swiped what they felt they couldn't part with. The items that were left went to shipyards where boxcars disappeared. The portion that made it onto a ship and arrived in a destabilized region would first be rummaged through by the powers that be, leaving the scraps for the people for whom they were intended in the first place. That is, of the shipments that weren't blocked by pirates. And in Somalia, the pirates were taking more and more.

Paul glanced over his shoulder at Ellen, who unsurprisingly hadn't noticed him waiting by the Jeep and kept on with her conversation. The other aid workers loaded their supplies into their vehicles and a few pulled onto the highway towards Bosasso.

Paul picked up each of the other three boxes one at a time and gave them a shake, until he heard the jangling of glass against glass in one of them. He tore open the box, ignoring the X-acto knife that sat on the floor of the trunk. Inside he found exactly what he was looking for. He dug through the bottles of chloroquine—the treatment for malaria, almost everyone who came into the clinic whether it was for pneumonia, delivering a baby or a headache was first treated for malaria—and then found what he was looking for. Forty-eight vials of 10 cc's of morphine or, ninety-six hits. Paul let out a deep breath and swirled a vial between his fingers.

He looked behind him, at Ellen hugging the other worker and then walking away from her towards the Jeep. She smiled at him, as if to say: *Sorry, I was talking non-stop for the past hour and a half, and I did see you there waiting, but I was so excited to talk to someone other than you, I hope you're not mad.* But he wasn't mad. He was relieved that she was finally done and they could get back into the city.

He didn't smile back. Instead, he swiveled back towards the morphine vials, turning his back to her, and placed a handful of the vials inside each pocket of his vest. He worked quickly, and then put the remaining vials back into the box and shut it, just before Ellen was at the Jeep.

"Sorry about that. You know how blabby I get," she said, touching his shoulder. Paul grunted; nothing new. "Did we get anything worthwhile today?"

"Not great," he waved his hand towards the boxes. "Bandages, sutures, casts, IVs, antibiotics—"

"That *is* great," she smiled and her dark brown eyes met his. She wasn't kidding, he could tell that from the way she nodded slightly and how she bit the corner of her lip whenever her mind worked. She was already thinking about all the patients at the clinic she could treat. The leg ulcers she could debride, the pneumonia she could eradicate and broken bones she could repair.

It was her genuineness that had attracted Paul.

Ellen Al-Hamadi had arrived in Somalia two years ago as a locum physician. Paul had initially dismissed her as another wide-eyed humanitarian, out to save the world. But Ellen was different. She was pragmatic and self-assured. Yet totally idealistic.

He had ignored her for days after she had arrived at the clinic, until Ellen confronted him in front of a dying patient.

Do you totally not care or do you just act that way?

Excuse me?

I've been here eight days and you haven't acknowledged me. She glared at him. *I'm here to learn, but I can't if you don't teach me. And I can't help anyone if you don't let me.*

Who are you going to help? He pointed at the patient. *This man? He's dying.*

Her mouth opened, at a loss. She gathered herself. *Help isn't all about saving lives, you know.*

You can't change the world.

But maybe if I try, it will mean the world to him.

It was the look in her eye. The slight tear that formed on her lower lid showed Paul that this wasn't about her. She wasn't in Africa to collect pictures to show her family and friends.

And he had seen that look many times since, and it was that same look in her eye at that moment, while she looked at the first medical supplies they had received in weeks.

They hopped in the Jeep and Paul turned on the ignition, pulled his sunglasses on and started up the barren dirt road toward the city. The Jeep rattled as it rolled over the bumpy, pot-holed road. On either side of the road, empty desert punctuated by dry shrubs stretched far into the distance. To one side, the foothills of the Cal Madow Mountains rose out from the flat desert. They slowed down slightly as they passed a family marshalling a group of goats along the side of the road. Behind the goats in the distance, a cell phone tower stood in the middle of the desert. Towers like these had sprung up throughout East Africa, and telecom had become a major industry in Somalia.

Bosasso sprawled out ahead of them. They were headed for the clinic, which was on the far end of the city, and Paul considered cutting through the eastern district, but remembered that a roadblock had been put up there several days earlier so he elected to drive straight through the city center. It was a slower route, and traffic would be heavier, but a roadblock could take hours.

The air conditioner in the Jeep had conked out the week earlier, so they had the windows rolled down, but it did little to cool them down. Sweat had already accumulated around Paul's neck. Ellen turned on the radio and Bob Dylan's *Forever Young* played.

"I love this song." She turned the volume up.

"American rock classics in the Puntland, what's next?"

"This song reminds me of my childhood. My dad sang to it all the time."

"A Syrian immigrant singing Bob Dylan," he laughed. "That makes for a great visual."

She smacked his shoulder.

"Come on, Paul, you must have had some song your mom sang to you when you were a kid."

Paul stared straight ahead. "No, nothing."

"Something about love, amour," she pursed her lips.

"Nothing, we didn't really sing over there." He stared straight at the road ahead and gripped the steering wheel. He hated when she pried, especially about that. He had told her about it already, hadn't he? She knew about his father's death and then about his subsequent move to France with his mother. She didn't need to know more. But she always *wanted* to know more.

Ahead Paul saw a red rusted pickup truck parked sideways across the road, blocking any traffic going either way. There was just enough space for a vehicle to pass by without slipping into the ditch, but truck tires were stacked in that space, making it impossible to pass. Four men, who couldn't have been a day over sixteen and wore shorts and military boots, patrolled the area holding semi automatics.

"Ah, damn. Another checkpoint," Paul said at the sight of the blockade. He said it with as much disdain as he could muster but he actually felt relieved that they would get off the topic of his family.

"These checkpoints are getting ridiculous." Ellen leaned her head against the half opened window.

One of the soldiers approached the Jeep with a machine gun cradled in his hands. He was chewing on a leafy substance, khat. The active ingredient in the leaves was an amphetamine, and many soliders used it. Not only did it keep them awake and reduced their appetites, but it reduced fear. Judging by the size of his pupils, he had been chewing a lot of it. The soldier took a quick look at Paul and Ellen, and then leaned in the window scanning the backseats. He held out his hand. "Identification."

Paul handed the man—although technically he was still a boy, but perhaps manning a road blockade with a machine gun qualified as a rite of passage to manhood—his passport and MSF I.D. The boy examined it carefully, but Paul was pretty sure he couldn't read a lick of Somali, let alone English or French.

"It's Doctors without Borders," Paul said, doing little to disguise the annoyance in his voice.

"Doctor?"

"Yeah, I'm a doctor. Can I get through?"

The boy stared at Paul blankly for a moment before his eyes turned towards Ellen, scanning her up and down slowly, resting momentarily on her breasts.

"Very nice, doctor," the boy said to Paul, amused, referring to Ellen.

"Just keep your eyes on my I.D."

The boy flicked the ID in his hand momentarily before he turned and walked to the truck. He spoke to someone through the window, pointing at the ID. The boy was likely unsure of what to make of them.

Paul reached across Ellen's lap into the glove compartment and lit up a cigarette. Hold ups like this could take awhile. He probably shouldn't have given the kid attitude, Paul thought.

"Smoking will kill you, you know," Ellen piped in, silent up to this point.

"So will living here."

The truck door opened and a tall heavyset man who wore military fatigues and a beret came towards Paul's Jeep. A handgun was holstered on his hip. He was at least twice the age of the other soldiers, likely a sergeant of some sort, in some sort of army. He handed Paul his identification and passport.

"How are you, Doctor Paul? I am Colonel Sayyid."

"I'm doing well, Colonel. Just trying to get back to the clinic," he put his cigarette out in the ashtray.

"Of course. I'm running this security point today." He leaned on the windowsill. "What were you doing in the eastern quarter?"

Paul hesitated only a brief second, but the colonel noticed. "Picking up supplies. A shipment."

The man smiled, showing his missing teeth. "Hello, Dr. Ellen."

Ellen lifted her hand, barely a wave.

"Okay, doctor, you can pass," he motioned to his men to move the tires blocking the path. Paul put the Jeep into gear. "But first, I need to check the shipment for contraband."

"It's in the back," Paul sighed, and got out of the car. He motioned for Ellen to stay quiet. She had a habit of exploding in situations like these. The colonel, of course, was not checking for contraband at all, he wanted to see whether there was anything of value in the medical shipment. In particular he was looking for narcotics. More powerful than a pound of khat, and worth more than a kilo. But Paul doubted these boys were interested in selling it—they likely wanted a downer to balance out the stimulant they had in their systems. They walked around the car and Paul opened the trunk. He looked and saw Ellen staring out the front window. He opened the box, rummaged through the contents and handed the man a vial of morphine.

"There are four of us, doctor."

"You know, that's getting greedy," Paul whispered.

"It's a toll."

"It's fucking blackmail," he said as he handed him three more vials. He looked up at Ellen, still looking ahead, listening to the radio.

"And supplies, doctor."

He reached in the box and handed the colonel a syringe.

"Four of us, doctor?"

"I need these for my patients, you can share with your men."

He stared at Paul for a moment, his face serious. He fingers slowly moved to the gun in the holster.

"If you shoot me, Colonel, you won't get any more morphine."

The colonel considered for a moment. "Go ahead."

Paul hopped in the driver's seat and rolled through the blockade. He waved to the militiamen as he passed and they nodded back. He hadn't looked at Ellen. He knew she wouldn't have given up the morphine to them, that she would have stood by her principles. Sure, they would have felt good about themselves, but they'd probably be dead, too.

The cellular phone rang on the dashboard and Paul answered it. As he listened to Abedi, a nurse, a normally unflappable person, relay the patient history to him in almost hysterical fashion, his expression changed and his stomach turned. His mind worked fast to try and keep up with her.

"Okay, start an IV, wide open and tie a tourniquet tightly around his thigh. We'll be there in a couple of minutes."

Paul closed the phone, tossed it on the dash and stepped on the gas pedal.

"What's the situation?" Ellen said.

"Two kids stepped on a mine," he turned to her, "they're unstable."

Six

The Jeep parked with a screech in front of the clinic. Paul and Ellen burst out of the vehicle's doors and ran towards the entrance. Only a small wooden panel that hung over the double doors with the painted Somali words *Bosasso Medical Centre - Northern District* identified the clinic. Paul cut his way through the line of locals, which looped around the long, one story grey concrete building. By this point in the day, noontime, the lineup to be seen by anyone was four hours. And by two in the afternoon, people would be turned away.

As he pushed the doors open, the story he had heard from the nurse on the phone ran through his mind repeatedly like a bad dream. Two boys, brothers, aged 6 and 8 chased a stray dog out into an open field near their home outside the city limits. The younger of the two tripped and fell, and the older one came to offer him a hand and stepped on the mine. If his foot had been two inches to the right or left, they'd still have legs. Paul inferred from the panic in the nurse's voice that having legs wasn't even part of the equation at this point—if they left with their lives it would be a miracle.

Ellen ran ahead and into the clinic. Paul was right behind her until a man in line grabbed his arm, the momentum swinging Paul around. The man was a local, not one he recognized, who was several inches taller than Paul's six feet and younger, too.

"Are you the doctor here?"

"Yeah."

"I've been waiting for four hours," he pointed at his foot. "I fell down the stairs at work, I think it's broken."

"And you're in line, you'll be seen."

"I can't wait any longer," he pleaded, "I need you to look at it."

Paul clenched his teeth. It crossed his mind to hit the man, either in the stomach or a slap across the face. Or perhaps it would have been more tactful to walk away and not respond to the man's pettiness. But Paul didn't do either.

"Really?" Paul said, "Come with me then." He took the man by the elbow and led him into the building.

Paul dragged the man into the clinic and walked at an unnaturally quick pace, which induced a grimace on the man's indignant face with each painful step. The inside was a hollow auditorium—prior to having been transformed into a clinic, the building was an abandoned gymnasium. They passed the rows of patients who lay in cast iron beds, most of them with I.V. poles standing next to them. Ceiling fans created a constant hum in the building and dampened the patients' groans and occasional wretches. They avoided the nurses buzzing around the room, hovering over patients. They passed through the huge canvas curtain that divided the room in two. On the other side were the ten-bed intensive care unit and the two surgical suites.

Within seconds of laying eyes on the scene in front of him, Paul realized it was probably too late. Maybe if the boy's family lived inside the city, they could have arrived in time, or maybe if they had lived closer to the clinic he would have had a chance. Or maybe if someone had been watching the boys more carefully. Fuck, maybe if no one had buried the mine there.

Three nurses surrounded the boy, who looked like he was the six year old. Two nurses pressed blood drenched blankets around the boy's stump, the third was checking his blood pressure. Blood dripped off the table and had already formed a pool on the floor. A thin attractive lady—even given this scene, he noticed she was attractive—who looked about the right age to be the boy's mother, wept in the corner.

Paul then realized that his grip on the man's arm had tightened to the point that his hand ached, but the man, whose mouth was gaping at the scene in front of him, didn't seem to notice.

"So do you want me to see you before this boy who's lost one of his legs?" Paul said. "Or his brother, who's lost both?"

The man's mouth moved but no sound came out.

"Get. The fuck. Out of here."

The man backed out of the room, forgetting to limp.

Paul scrubbed his hands with soap in a bucket of water in the corner. He snapped on a pair of latex gloves and approached the boy.

The mother's weeping turned to wailing, repeated wailing. As he bent over the boy, he caught her eye briefly and saw that she, too, thought it was too late. The woman was grieving. To her, her sons were already dead. This woman—who had come in with two sons—was going to go home alone, or at most with legless sons. Perhaps she was thinking about how they wouldn't be able to run out in the fields anymore, or kick a homemade soccer ball against the outside walls of their house. Maybe she was crying because they wouldn't be able to throw their arms around her anymore, or worse, that she would not have anyone to hug when she needed it. *No. The boy was still breathing, he wasn't dead... yet.*

"Okay, first thing, the mother has to leave," Paul demanded and pointed towards the exit.

"Let me look at the leg," he pushed his way in between the nurses and removed the blankets covering the boy's leg. Blood pulsated out of the stump that was below the knee. His blood pressure was low and his extremities were cold and the skin was becoming pale.

"Okay, it's below the knee, but the tibial artery's been cut. I'll have to repair it. His pressures are down, we have to give him more fluids. Start another IV and pour the fluids in. And get me a suture tray," he motioned to the boxes he had put on the table.

He tore the blanket into small strips and tied it around the boy's leg just above the knee, using his entire bodyweight to tighten it. That slowed the blood loss to an ooze. He set up the suture tray and grabbed the forceps that were still warm from having been boiled for sterilization. The clinic's autoclave had broken down two months ago and they were still trying to get another.

He took the forceps and searched through the mangled mess of tissues for the tibial artery. He steadied his hand on the edge of the table. He grabbed the end of the severed artery and tied it closed with the sutures. He untied the tourniquet and blood barely oozed from the wound. He threw his gloves in the garbage.

"Put a dressing on there, keep the IV going and we'll monitor him. Tell the mother he'll be okay. I'll be back to check on him in a bit."

Paul poked his head through the curtain to the next surgical table where Ellen was working. She was alone in the room, standing over the patient with her back to Paul. She was motionless and so was the patient. Blood dripped down from the patient's bed and onto the floor. Paul came up behind her and placed his hands on her delicate shoulders.

"How's the other brother?" she asked and placed a hand on Paul's.

"He'll make it."

"I couldn't stop the bleeding." She wiped the tears slipping down her cheeks. "I just couldn't…"

Paul looked into the older brother's vacant eyes staring back at him. He inhaled deeply and ran his hand along the boy's face, closing his eyes. "You did what you could."

"Maybe if I had been able to tie a good tourniquet. The artery kept slipping away from me."

"It's not your fault," he covered the boy with a white blanket. "Things were decided for him before he came through that door."

Ellen removed her gloves, threw them out and sat on a stool. Her white shirt was blood-stained. "How do you do it, Paul?"

"How do I do what?"

"Deal with all this. Child after child dying. People killing each other. Being alone."

He stared at the boy for a long moment.

"I just… do my job. I'm here to fix what I can. I don't have time to worry about those I can't help. " He placed his hand on her cheek. "The alone bit?" He smiled, "You've helped with that."

She managed a slight smile.

"Why don't you go home, get some rest. I'll finish up the work here," Paul said.

Seven

Nine hours and forty-five minutes later, Paul had finished his day's work. By the time he tossed the last pair of latex gloves of the day into the trash, he had sutured nine lacerations, prescribed eighteen courses of chloroquine, four courses of amoxicillin, examined fourteen people with infectious diarrhea and admitted one person with tuberculosis.

His legs felt heavy as he walked up the darkened aisle towards the exit and it struck him that he had not sat down the entire day. It was strange to him how the body could seemingly go on forever when the mind was preoccupied and only when faced with the prospect of rest did the accumulated fatigue come into conscious awareness.

Most of the patients were asleep in their beds, but a few sat up and waved at him, to which he responded with a nod. One man, an elder in a nomadic tribe who likely had cholera, dry heaved rhythmically in the far corner of the clinic as he had been doing most of the day. At the entrance, a nurse wearing a crisp white scrub top sat at a small desk, holding the *Puntland Post* under a small desk lamp. He said goodnight to her, and she didn't look up immediately, but instead held her finger up as she finished her sentence. When she did, the initial apologetic expression on her face turned to concern.

"You look sick."

"Excuse me?" he was certain he hadn't heard her correctly.

"You're pale and you're shaky," she looked at him like he was green, "and you're sweating."

Paul hadn't noticed that his arms were shaking. In fact, he was vibrating and suddenly a wave of cold ran along his sweat-covered skin like a cold draft. His heart, too, was beating quickly. He thought of the boy who stepped on a mine for some reason he wasn't sure of. The boy was alive, conscious and stable and most importantly, he would survive. But the picture of his mother crying kept rising in his mind. It bothered him that she was alone. The whole night she had been the only person next to the boy, holding his hand. His father—who for all Paul knew may not have been alive—was not there. He was not there to hold the boy's hand, or console the mother, or to grieve the death of their elder son. The image of Paul's own father came up then, his bearded face mashed against the hardwood floor, his eyes glazed over and empty, looking at him.

"Dr. Alban?" the nurse was standing in front of him, looking at him sideways. "Are you feeling ill?"

Paul jolted upright as her words dragged him back into the present. "I'm fine. Just a bit tired…and hungry." That weak explanation hadn't changed her expression, so he forced a smile to try and reassure her that he was okay. "If you need anything, I have my cell with me."

Paul turned abruptly and walked out of the clinic across the parking lot to his Jeep. Only the crunching of his hiking boots along the gravel-paved lot broke the dead silence of early nighttime. The small incandescent security lamp that hung above the clinic entrance did just enough to illuminate Paul's path. He pulled out his keys—there were a lot of them and he had been meaning for years to throw away the unnecessary ones—from his short's pocket and held them up to the light, struggling to find the one to the car.

Then he clasped the keys in his hand to stop the jangling and cocked his head to one side. The small hairs on his neck rose and he held his breath. The sound he heard was initially distant, but became close. There was a vehicle approaching, quickly. His palm seemed to instantaneously become wet and his fingers became uncoordinated as he flicked through the keys. All he could focus on was the roar of the engine. Gunmen and bandits patrolled the roads after dark and he couldn't be sure if they would drive right past him, or come asking for some sort of payment.

He found the key (always the last one on the chain) and inserted it in the lock. He looked up and saw a black truck rounding the corner, complete with a machine gun mounted in the back. Two men were sitting in the cab. He left the key in the lock. It was too late.

The truck skidded to a stop beside him and the driver, a dark skinned man of about twenty, looked at Paul through the open window.

"Are you the doctor?" the driver said, and Paul instantly noticed the hypertrophied scar that ran along his throat. It had likely been slit at some point in time and somehow the man survived.

"Yeah, but the clinic's closed, if that's what you're asking," Paul responded in nearly flawless Somali.

"It's an emergency."

"Then you should go to the main hospital."

The driver looked at the man in the passenger seat who was at least ten years his senior. The way the driver immediately deferred to him told Paul the passenger was in charge. The passenger stared unflinching at Paul for a moment and ran his hand through his beard. He then said something to the driver that Paul couldn't make out.

"No hospitals," the driver then said, as if translating for the passenger.

"Then I'm afraid I can't—" Paul stopped himself mid-sentence and looked through the window at the two men sitting in the truck. It was the sight of the two AK-47s that were propped up on the seat between them that made him stop. The driver looked anxious, but the passenger was calm and staring out the window. But what bothered Paul was that he didn't see any physical problem with them. He immediately thought of the militia he gave the morphine to. *Word must be out about the French doctor handing out narcotics*, he thought.

"What's the emergency?"

"His nephew in the back. He's been shot."

Both the driver and the passenger threw open the doors and led Paul towards the box of the truck. Lying on the bottom of the box, Paul saw something he had already seen that day. A person he thought was going to die. A young man in dark military fatigues stained darker by blood lay motionless. Had it not been for his rapid and wheezy breaths, Paul would've thought he was already dead. His glassy eyes stared up at the night sky and for a moment, Paul thought they might have focused on him. Paul touched the dying man's chest and felt his ribcage rise and fall a small amount each time. Under his palm, he felt the crustiness of dried blood on the man's shirt. This man had already been bleeding for hours. Somehow he was still alive.

"We have to get him inside."

The driver held the young man's legs while the uncle held the young man under the armpits and they carried him to the clinic door. Paul knocked loudly and the nurse opened the door. Paul thought he heard her gasp a little bit when she saw the young man. They carried him towards the back of the clinic. A few patients sat upright in their beds, looking to see what the commotion was.

The two men lay the man on the surgical table and then stood against the wall. Paul noticed that the two men were in good shape. Their muscles popped through their shirts. If anything, the older one was the more muscular.

The nurse entered. She had gathered herself from her initial shock.

"Dr. Alban, do you need me to bring anything?"

"If you could set up a tray of—"

"Not her," the uncle cut in, "Just you, doctor."

Paul was about to correct the man and tell him that in his clinic, he would decide who works on patients, but the man's serious demeanor told him there would be no negotiating.

"It's okay, I can take care of this alone."

A wave of relief spread across the nurse's face and she quickly left the room. The uncle motioned for the driver to leave as well.

"You know I can take care of this more quickly if I have a nurse assisting me," Paul said.

"You have me."

Paul walked past the man, scrubbed his hands in a metal bucket of soapy water and snapped on a pair of gloves.

"Then bring that over," Paul pointed towards the oxygen tank and mask in the corner of the room. The uncle unbuttoned his black shirt and threw it into the corner, wearing only a tank top that showed his sinewy muscles. It was warm in the clinic, and sweat had beaded on Paul's forehead as well. While the uncle walked over to get the tank, Paul checked his patient's blood pressure. He then slid the oxygen mask over the young man's face and opened the valve.

He cut the man's shirt open with a pair of scissors and removed it. He examined his chest. Two holes on the right side of his chest oozed blood. The wounds were not fresh, at least twelve hours old, Paul figured, judging by the amount of dried blood on their edges. How had this man survived that long? He turned the man over and saw one hole, likely an exit wound, covered with a bandage. It was taped on three sides and called a flutter valve, which prevented air from entering the chest cavity and collapsing the lung.

"You put that on?" Paul said.

The man nodded cautiously.

"That probably kept him alive."

"So he will live?" It was the first sign of emotion that Paul had seen in the man: hope.

"I said it kept him alive. I didn't say he'd stay that way."

Paul didn't look up to notice the uncle hunch down onto a stool holding his head in his hands. If Paul had not been preoccupied caring for the dying man, he would have seen tears welling in his eyes.

Instead, Paul continued working on the young man, listening to his chest with his stethoscope and examining the rest of his body. Paul walked past the uncle, grabbed a saline bag and tried to start an IV several times. He was unable to thread the IV needle into the man's vein on four separate tries (once in each hand, then the pit of the elbows) as the man was profoundly dehydrated and his veins had collapsed.

Paul threw the needle onto the ground in frustration. "When did he get shot?"

"O-o-one hour ago."

"But he's got dried blood all the way down his leg. I don't understand how the bleeding has stopped in under one hour."

"There was a lot, but we were able to stop most of it." The man ignored Paul's implication.

"In an hour, that's impressive."

Paul grabbed a chest tube and made a small incision through the skin and then through the space between his ribs and into his chest cavity. The patient didn't react. He inserted the chest tube and attached it to a suction apparatus. A small amount of blood dripped off the tube.

"He's lost a lot of blood. I can't even get a vein to start an intravenous." Paul looked at the uncle, who stared out into space and didn't react to Paul's suggestion. "How did this happen?"

"We were practicing shooting and he was caught in the crossfire."

"Bullshit," Paul said under his breath.

Paul threw open a drawer and found an intraosseous needle that he needed to start an intravenous. He rolled up the patient's pant leg and twisted the needle into the man's shinbone. The uncle winced as he saw what Paul was doing.

"What are you doing?"

"Like I said, I can't get an intravenous started, so I have to do this."

The man stared blankly as though he were waiting for an explanation.

"Or he'll die," Paul looked up. "He's lost a lot of blood, more than anyone could in an hour without dying. He's got two bullets in his chest from an Uzi, a machine gun that is rare in Somalia. I've been here for over a decade, so I'm not fucking stupid, okay? So cut the bullshit already and give me some straight answers 'cause you're a horrible fucking liar."

Paul calmed down after taking a few huffing breaths and stared at the man. Only then did he regret what he said. Here he was with a young man with bullet holes in his chest who had come in with two men with a truck full of weapons and ammunition and he was telling them how to run the show. *Not smart, Paul,* he thought. But the bearded man didn't become angry or defensive. Instead, he stood up and paced.

"Last night. It happened last night." He looked at Paul and sighed. "You must know what we do. Pirates? Hijackers?"

Paul nodded and listened while he continued working on the man. He attached the saline and let the fluid run. He opened a suture tray, removed the forceps and began digging in the holes in the man's chest. He removed a piece of shrapnel that clanged as it dropped on the metal tray.

"We were on a ship last night," the man continued. Paul nodded. "On the ship a man, a big Russian man, shot at us and shot my nephew. I thought Ali was killed. But somehow, he has survived. I killed that Russian man with two shots. I thought it would feel good, Doctor, getting revenge, but all I thought about was my nephew. I could not bear him dying because of this hijacking. You must save him."

~ * ~

Paul tied the final suture, closing the man's chest wound. The third bag of saline was dripping into the man's veins. His blood pressure had improved and the vacant look in his eyes was now more of a glossy stare. The man would probably live, provided he didn't develop a major infection. The bearded man sat in the corner observing and puffing away on his tenth cigarette. He hadn't moved from the stool during the past two hours.

Paul washed the man's chest with a wet cloth in a circular motion. Then his weakness returned. His vision became blurry and his legs became rubber. The entire room seemed to spiral around him and he fell onto his backside.

"Are you okay?" the uncle hopped up and grabbed him, helping him to a stool.

"Yeah. Just weak," Paul said.

The man dipped a cloth in a bucket of water and handed it to Paul. Paul placed it on his forehead.

"Thanks."

He offered Paul a cigarette. Paul thought about saying no but instead pulled the cigarette from the package and lit it up.

"Do you think he will be okay?" the uncle asked.

"I think so. He's stable now. He'll have to stay here for awhile, there's a risk of infection."

"You saved his life, Doctor."

"You can call me Paul," he said, ignoring the compliment.

"I am Sami."

Sami stared at his nephew, whose breathing had slowed to a gentle rhythm and then placed his palm on his nephew's forehead. He leaned in and whispered something in his nephew's ear that Paul couldn't quite make out. Then he looked up at Paul. "Do you have a family?"

Paul shook his head and started cleaning the suture tray that rested beside his patient's body. Perhaps because he had seen two young men almost die that day and had seen the reactions of their families, Paul then said something to Sami he had not said to anyone he had met in Somalia. "I used to. I had a son."

"I have four daughters, no sons. But Ali has become my son." Paul detected a slight quiver in Sami's voice. "And I almost lost him today. I can see that you know how that feels, losing a son."

Paul half shrugged, turned and focused his attention to collecting the bloody sheets that surrounded the hospital bed. He wet another cloth, dropped it on the floor and moved it around with his foot, cleaning the blood that had dried.

"When his parents—my brother—died, he was supposed to go to England to live with my sister," Sami continued. He placed a hand on Ali's forehead and shook his head slowly. "But I insisted he live with me. If I had let him go, his life would be different today. Better." He looked up at Paul, tears filling his eyes.

"Maybe," Paul considered, "but sometimes you can't do anything but live with the choices you make."

Sami smiled a bit at that, then turned his head to the side and furrowed his brow. "They say you are French, but your accent isn't French," Sami said.

"Who's they?"

"People, in town, they know you."

"I'm a French citizen. But I lived in America as a child."

"I lived here my whole life."

"How long of that have you been a pirate?"

"Too long," he stood up and placed his palm on the young man's forehead. "Paul. You're a good man. You saved my nephew's life," He extended his hand. "If you ever need someone to help you with anything, you can count on us."

Paul didn't ask how these men who had hijacked a ship the previous evening were now on land less than twenty-four hours later. Most hijacked ships floated around in the Gulf of Aden until a ransom request was met, which usually took months. Had he bothered asking, Sami would have made up some story about them hauling Ali off the ship and into a lifeboat to get medical attention. He would not have told Paul what had actually happened: that they had docked the ship at the port in Bosasso and were unloading the cargo.

Instead, Paul shook Sami's hand and nodded slightly, recognizing that having these men on his side could come in handy some day. He checked Ali's blood pressure one more time to reassure himself that the improvement in his condition was not due to his imagination. He then said goodnight to Sami and told him that he would be back in the morning but that the nurses could monitor Ali overnight. Paul then staggered out of the room, stopping only to place his hand on a table briefly to steady himself. He was trembling all over and he felt nauseated.

He passed by the young boy he had worked on earlier that night. Paul only glanced at him for a second, just enough to hear the boy snoring. The mother was sleeping next to him, hunched over in a wooden chair. He thought of finding a blanket and covering her, but a wave of nausea came over him so he kept moving.

Paul continued down the aisle to the entrance, trying to keep his eyes from going out of focus. He briefly gave the nurse orders for monitoring Ali through the night and then pushed through the doors of the clinic and out into the parking lot.

When he reached the Jeep, he saw that he had left the keys in the door lock the whole time. He turned the handle and hopped in and closed his eyes. He replayed the scenes of the day in his head but kept coming back to the same one. *You know how that feels, losing a son,* Sami had said. He wished he had responded differently. *I do know what it's like, but you don't. 'Cause I just saved your son, nephew actually, you don't even have a fuckin' son.*

Neither do you, another part of his mind responded immediately, *and thanks to you he doesn't have a father, either.*

Paul's breathing was quick and his heart raced and he realized what was happening. He was having an anxiety attack. He closed his eyes, but the nausea kept coming and he felt like he was floating. He needed sleep, that was all, a good night's sleep.

Paul reached in the pocket of his khaki vest, removed a vial of morphine and held it between his fingers for a moment. Then he opened the backpack resting on the seat next to him, removed a syringe and a rubber tourniquet and tied it around his calf. After removing his shoe and sock, Paul drew up a vial of morphine into a syringe and injected it into the vein on the back of his foot. A small amount of blood dripped from the injection site and he dabbed it with his white sock.

The morphine felt warm as it traveled up his leg and into his arms and then head. The tension left his body and his breathing slowed. He fumbled for the seat lever and reclined the seat back, turned the music up and closed his eyes.

Eight

The port in Bosasso was quiet at this hour of night. Red, orange, blue and maroon metal shipping containers sat on top of each other in rows. The constant buzzing of orange overhead lights almost completely drowned out the gentle slapping of waves against the docks. Towering overhead, rusted ship-to-shore cranes stood dormant in a line along the shore. Since there was very little shipping in Bosasso, there was very little need for shipping cranes. Years of sea spray combined with no oil on their decaying gears had rendered the cranes useless and the port almost dead. The port averaged one ship every two and a half weeks. Fewer and fewer ships had come through the port over the years. First, it was because of the clan wars that lasted a decade (and which continued to this day), then it was because of economic collapse, and most recently it was increased piracy that deterred trading to the ports in the Horn of Africa.

A black pickup truck with a patchwork of rusted holes in its exterior sped along the tarmac between the rows of containers. Inside, a husky bearded man pressed the gas pedal in his old truck to the floor. He kept one hand on the wheel and held a cigarette in the other, puffing away. The smell of smoke mixed with the smell of oil from an oily rag that lay in the passenger foot well. A thin layer of dust, the kind in which you could write a message like 'Wash Me' with your finger, coated the dashboard and radio dials. Beside him on the grimy, faux-leather passenger seat sat an orange hardhat and a badge that identified him as Nadif Yusuf, Port Supervisor.

He drove to a fenced-off area at the far end of the port which bustled with activity. Razor wire coils ran along the top of the twenty-foot chain link fence. Lookout posts broke the fence every one hundred meters. No intruder could get in unharmed, and if they did, they certainly wouldn't leave.

Through the fence, Nadif saw the docked *Stebelsky*. The three cranes on its deck lifted containers off the ship and stacked them on the dock. He stopped the truck at the entrance which was being guarded by three men with machineguns. He stuck his head out the window.

"I'm the Super tonight. I'm looking for Abu."

One of the guards leaned on the window.

"He's over by those containers," he pointed with an outstretched gun. "He's been asking when you would be here." The young man looked at Nadif with his eyebrows raised. "It sounds like there's something special on that ship. I've never seen him so anxious."

Nadif ignored the young man's indirect request for information.

"Can you let me through?"

The young man made a motion with his arm and the other two pulled up the bar blocking the entrance. Nadif drove through, thinking about what could possibly be on the ship that had led Abu to call him at three in the morning. Nadif was one of the most experienced longshoremen in the Puntland. He had worked the docks for over thirty years and was now the port supervisor. However, Abu was only a few years his junior, so he would only call with good reason. All Abu told Nadif over the phone was that there was a new ship in port, and he needed him to come in.

He drove to the area where the cranes placed the containers and spotted the tall figure of Abu with a hardhat on, directing the cranes. He parked the car, leaned over and opened the glove box, removed a small flashlight, placed the hardhat on and got out.

"Abu," he yelled over the clang of metal on metal from the containers, "Abu!"

Abu noticed Nadif, yelled out some instructions to another man in a hardhat and jogged lightly over to him carrying a clipboard.

"Nadif, what took you so long?"

"I was sleeping. Now what is going on here?"

Abu led Nadif away from the cranes.

"Yesterday this ship was brought in by a group of hijackers. It is a Ukranian ship, registered to a private company."

"This ship is hijacked?" the cigarette almost fell out of Nadif's mouth. "Are you crazy? When they realize the ship is missing, we are going to have a hundred NATO bombers flying overhead turning Bosasso into another Baghdad. And not to mention the police, they must be on the way. Turn the ship back out to sea, Abu."

"Relax, Nadif, relax."

"How can I relax? This ship is stolen property and you're unloading it."

"Nadif, the ship was in Somali waters. We can call it a security check, the same as any other nation would do."

"Any other nation would board the ship, check the papers and let them pass! Not hijack it and unload the cargo."

"We can send the ship back out to sea tomorrow, Nadif. Today, we can take some of the cargo. There is some precious cargo on this one."

"How precious?"

"Weapons."

Nadif rubbed his palm against his beard and shook his head. The military in the Puntland was starved for weapons of any kind. They were in constant battles with insurgents trying to gain a foothold in the country. Military weapons were worth a lot of money.

"Colonel Atto is coming in the morning. He is interested in a deal." Abu stared at Nadif, who shook his head. "There are no bombers, Nadif, they will not come tonight." Abu stared up at the heavens and smiled. "All we have to do is unload a few boxes and wait for the colonel to come."

Nadif rubbed his eyes and let out a sigh. "Unload a few boxes, then send the ship back out."

A smile broke across Abu's face, showing several gaps in his teeth.

"How many crew aboard?"

"We counted twelve. They're still on the ship."

"All are safe?"

"One was killed in the raid, the others are all fine," Abu paused and his smile faded. He put his hand on Nadif's shoulder. "But there is something strange about this ship, Nadif. It only has weapons. Not one container has anything else."

"A private ship? That is strange." He lit up another cigarette and offered one to Abu who refused. "What kind of security did it have?"

"Almost nothing. SAS was the only system, but it was disabled. My guess is that they were trying to make the ship inconspicuous."

"Maybe. Or they wanted us to get it. Where was its destination?"

"The captain says Nairobi. But the crew doesn't know anything about the shipment. We have had men questioning them for hours."

"This is common." Nadif knocked his fist against one of the containers. "They do not want sailors to know what they are transporting. It makes the selling of information less likely."

"But Nadif, there *was* a sailor who informed Sami of their position."

"Does he know anything?"

Abu frowned. "He says he was promised ten thousand pounds to inform Sami when he was on duty. He was the watchman and he allowed them to get on the ship."

"So you're saying that Sami knew about the ship beforehand? That this hijacking was set up somehow?"

"For money, people will do things they shouldn't. He probably does not know anything more. But we'll put pressure on him to make sure."

"This seems like it was too easy. Something is not right here."

"What is the problem? Someone anonymously contacted Sami and gave him the ship's manifest. He had a man working on the ship and they've brought it here. It's not the first time there has been a tip on a ship."

"But he never met them. He doesn't even know who gave him the information."

"This ship was delivering arms from Odessa to Nairobi," Abu said. "A private arms dealer, most likely. Someone didn't want that deal to happen, so they got Somali pirates to intercept the ship. So what? Nadif, there are thousands of people who don't want arms deals to happen. Rebels, governments, other businessmen. I don't know who gave this information." He put his hand on Nadif's shoulder, looking him in the eye. "But I know that we will never find out. Our job is to unload this ship and keep the cargo safe until we can transfer it to the military."

Nadif rubbed his forehead. This situation was not sitting well with him. He looked at Abu who bit his lower lip and then looked over his shoulder. "There's more, isn't there?" Nadif sighed.

"I need to show you something."

Abu led Nadif through the dark rows between the containers. They stopped in front of one of the containers where two guards stood holding machine guns.

"This must be an important one," Nadif laughed. "*Two* guards with guns."

Abu showed Nadif the clipboard. "This manifest is very detailed."

"And so it should be."

"Every single item in every single container was accounted for…" he handed the open book to Nadif and pointed at the container with his flashlight. "Except this one."

Nadif stamped his cigarette out on the ground and examined the side of the container. The flashlight illuminated the white print on the side of it. *R-EX 030862*. He scanned through the long list of cargo, holding a small flashlight in his teeth.

R-EX 030860, R-EX 030861, R-EX 030863…

He cleared his throat and flipped through the other pages, searching for the misplaced entry. Abu put his hand over the book, grabbed it and put it under his arm.

"I've looked through it three times. It's not in there."

Nadif took a breath in, and offered an explanation, "It does occasionally happen, that a container is accidentally forgotten in a manifest."

Abu shook his head. "I don't think anyone would forget this one."

Abu pushed between the guards and swung the container door open. Nadif and Abu shone their flashlights inside the darkened container and stepped inside. A palate of wooden boxes was centered inside the container, with a space just wide enough between the palate and the inner wall for a man with a belly the size of Nadif to squeeze by. Nadif noticed that two of the boxes on top of the stack were open and Abu reached inside.

"When I was told about the container, I came to examine it myself." He pulled a pistol from inside a crate in front. "But nothing strange here. Guns."

They walked around the side of the crates to the back of the container. Nadif had to suck in his gut to get around the stacks of boxes. "But what is at the back is what I called you about."

On the other side of the palate at the back of the container, Abu aimed his flashlight and tracked it across stacked aluminum trunks, the size of medium rolling suitcases. Nadif flicked his flashlight on and pointed it at the metal boxes. He counted a dozen, four stacks three boxes high.

Then he stopped, nearly dropping the flashlight. He couldn't believe his eyes. Plastered around the edges of the suitcases were the unmistakable yellow stickers with three black semicircles.

Radiation.

Nuclear.

"Is? Is… this?" Nadif could barely make words.

Abu nodded and heaved one of the trunks off of the stack and placed it on the ground. He flicked the clasps and lifted the top open. He reached inside, lifted a metal canister that looked like an artillery shell and held it in front of Nadif. "Nuclear weapons."

Nine

Paul woke up four hours after he had caved in to his craving for morphine. A mosquito—or perhaps several mosquitoes, Paul couldn't quite tell—had entered through the open window of the Jeep sometime through the night and the buzz in his ear had caused him to reflexively swat at the side of his face. He opened his eyes slowly, squinting to try and keep out the blinding early morning sun. Everything hurt, even light hitting the retinas. As he adjusted the seat back up, the pressure around his temples intensified so that now he was squinting not only because of light but of pain, too. Ringing in his ears accompanied the headache. The car radio was cranked up too, playing static.

He rubbed his eyes with his index finger and then turned and focused them on the clinic parking lot, which was empty. He looked at his watch and saw that it was 6:00 AM, which meant that it wouldn't stay empty for long. Nurses came in at seven and Ellen would be there by eight. She was probably still sleeping.

He dug into his shorts pocket and found the keys, turned the car on and cleared his throat. He adjusted the rearview mirror and caught a glimpse of himself. The first thing he saw were dark circles, not just under his eyes, but around them. A crease ran along his right cheek, and his graying hair looked as though it had not had a comb run through it in weeks.

He decided he needed to go home to have a shower and some more rest. As he pulled out of the parking lot and onto the road, he searched between the car seats with his free hand and retrieved his cell phone. Paul opened it and saw that he had three missed calls, all from Ellen. He flipped the phone shut and tossed it onto the passenger seat without listening to the messages. He didn't need to because he already knew what was on them. They were always the same. *Where are you? Why aren't you answering?* And Paul's personal favorite: *I'm worried.* Why was it that she always said that when she was angry? When what she really meant was *What the hell have you gotten yourself into... Again.*

~ * ~

The rattling of Paul's Jeep pulling up to the metal gates of his home broke the early morning silence. It was located just off a main road in the eastern quarter of Bosasso, several blocks from the clinic, on what most people in town considered a quiet street. Paul though, found it was far too close to the main drag and the houses were too close together. Tall trees around the perimeter of the property endowed the two-story home with some privacy and shade. Orange sunlight filtered through the leaves of the trees and reflected off the white concrete walls of the building. Grapevines climbed up the front walls to the second floor balcony that overlooked the short driveway.

He stepped out of the vehicle and left the car running. He unlocked the padlock that chained the red painted metal gates and pulled the chain off. He dragged one of the gate doors open, which creaked horribly—Ellen had been asking him to put oil on the hinges for weeks. He stared up at their open bedroom window on the second floor to see if the noise had woken her. Satisfied that it didn't, he quickly looked around the sides of the house.

"Raza?" he whispered, "Raza?"

There was no answer. He only heard the rustling of the palm trees overhead. Paul had hired Raza three years ago to guard the house during the nighttime. He stayed within the parameters of his job description. At the crack of dawn, Raza was always gone.

Paul drove the Jeep through the open gate and up the short driveway to the front of his house. The gate clanged as he pushed it closed and then chained it shut. He walked up the tiled walk to the side of the house where a set of stairs led him to the second floor. Paul unlocked the deadbolt and then slowly turned the doorknob and slipped inside as quietly as possible. He slid his hikers off on the Turkish rug inside and walked lightly towards the bedroom along the cool, red tiled floor. He stopped at the long walnut bookcase that ran along the wall and placed his keys on a glass ashtray that sat on one of the shelves. More pictures than books filled the shelves of the bookcase. And most of them were Ellen's.

The photos read like a picture book that chronicled her life. Pictures of the places she had lived adorned the top shelf. It was a collage of framed 4 x 6 photos of her time working in a village in Nicaragua, smiling beside school children she had taught in India, arms interlocked with her fellow tree planters in British Columbia, and casting a leg in a desert in Sudan. The pictures on the shelves at eye level—in noticeably larger frames—were dedicated to her family. The photo of Ellen in her medical school graduation gown standing next to her father wearing an impeccable double-breasted suit and black tie was larger than all of the rest. His nose was slightly raised and he hung on to his lapels, beaming with all the pride that would be expected of an immigrant who came to Canada with no money and was witness to his only living child becoming a doctor.

It was the same look Paul had seen when her father, Kazim Al-Hamadi, had first laid eyes on him exiting the gates of Terminal 1 in Charles De Gaulle airport. It was three years into their relationship when Ellen had arranged for Paul and Kazim to meet in Paris for several hours before they each took their respective connecting flights in opposite directions. Except at that time, Kazim's pride seemed to dissolve into arrogance as the "meeting" Ellen had hoped for turned into an interrogation. *What is your background? What are you doing in Somalia for so long? Where is your family from? Why doesn't a man of your age have a family?* and so forth. The encounter lasted all of thirty minutes before Paul excused himself to check the flight tracker on one of the overhead screens and then did his best to appear genuine when he lied to Kazim about how disappointed he was that his connecting flight was early. It was the last time Paul had seen him. Paul assumed that Kazim was as unimpressed with the company that day as he was because Ellen had never tried to arrange another meeting between them.

While the other photos were there for Ellen to remember, Paul always sensed the small Polaroid in a wooden frame was one she wanted to forget. A young Ellen, thirteen maybe, being carried on the shoulders of her older brother. He had died weeks later, hit by a taxi driver at a crosswalk. Ellen could go on for hours when a guest came to the house for the first time, telling detailed stories to accompany each picture but she always skipped over the one with her brother.

Paul's eye was drawn away from Ellen and her brother to the photo next to it, the only one of his in the house. He remembered the moment it was taken. They were at Crane Beach, near their home and he and his father had just completed a sandcastle, with six turrets, one for each year of Paul's life—it was his birthday. His mother had collected shells to decorate the walls of the castle. The photo captured the three of them, his mother and father with their arms interlocked around him, crouched beside the castle, smiling. Everyone has those moments, Paul thought, where they wish life paused, where they were truly happy. Beside the photo sat one of those white seashells that he had saved and he ran his finger slowly across its ridges.

After his brief foray into the memory banks, Paul shook his head to bring himself back into the moment. He walked towards the bedroom at the end of the hall, unaware that he was walking on the balls of his feet. He turned his head slightly and listened for Ellen's snoring (which if you ever asked her about she would deny). After a brief moment of silence, he turned back towards the entrance and realized that his shoes were the only ones there. And his keys were the only ones in the glass dish. Had he missed her already? It was only 6:45 in the morning.

Paul pushed the bedroom door open with the pads of his fingertips and poked his head inside. The bed was empty. Sunlight filtered through the wooden shutters on the window, casting shadows against the crisp white linen on the perfectly made bed. Paul then shoved the door open completely so that it slammed against the wall behind it.

"Ellen?"

No answer.

"Sorry I'm late. It was really crazy at work. A gunshot wound."

Silence.

He opened the bathroom door. It was clean; there was no fog on the mirror and the tub was completely dry. Their towels hung in the exact same spot as they had been the day before. Paul ran the taps, splashed cold water on his face and stared at his reflection in the mirror. He hadn't shaved in days, his hair was greasy and he could tell that his breath stunk. His eyes were a bit bloodshot, and he still felt a little high.

And he was in trouble.

Ellen always waited up for him except when she thought he was shooting up. Paul figured that she probably called the clinic and asked if he was still there, found out that he had left hours ago and put two and two together. Then she would go for a run. Ellen always went for a run when she was angry, and this definitely would have made her angry.

Paul sat on the edge of the bed and chewed his fingernails. All of a sudden he felt sober. His mind searched for an excuse to offer Ellen, because she would expect one. Three months ago, Paul had picked up a shipment, a big shipment compared to the one today, and was on his way to the clinic when he was stopped at a roadblock for four hours. A roadside bomb had gone off near the road and there was no way through. Traffic was at a standstill. He waited for over an hour and decided to turn around and drove to a nearby beach with his stockpile of narcotics. He sat on the secluded beach for eight hours, injecting the next dose of morphine before the last one wore off. The morphine eventually accumulated in his system and he passed out. The next morning, a local boy found him half conscious and covered in sand, and ran to get his father who carried Paul to the clinic. Ellen worked on him and supported him through the withdrawal. Three days of the worst diarrhea, vomiting, fevers, headaches he had ever experienced led him to vow to never use again. When the withdrawal was over, Ellen just said one thing to him.

This is your last chance.

Nothing else was said. The distance in her voice and her sullen expression echoed in his mind.

He had blown it.

Paul's right hand began shaking and he couldn't quite tell if it was the morphine leaving his system or nerves about the impending blowout. He reached into his vest pocket, removed his half smoked cigarette package and lit up a cigarette. He took a long drag, fell back onto the bed and closed his eyes.

~ * ~

Paul awoke several hours later (or it could have been minutes, he wasn't quite sure) from his drug-induced slumber to the sound of tires skidding on the gravel road in front of his house. At first he thought the sound was part of a dream that he couldn't remember and scrunched his eyelids together to try to fall back asleep but it was quickly followed by several car doors slamming. *Ellen's home*, Paul assumed, forgetting that he had determined earlier that she had gone out for a jog, without her car.

Paul rose out of bed, picked up the ashtray on the nightstand and dumped the ashes into the toilet and flushed. He opened the bedroom window shutter, which overlooked the front of the house. What he saw caused him to freeze instantaneously. Perhaps because he was in shock, or because he was too focused on what was going on in front of his house—within spitting distance—he didn't realize that the glass ashtray had slipped out of his right hand and shattered on the ceramic floor.

A white van with tinted windows idled in front of the house. Two men in military fatigues with scarves wrapped over their faces holding assault rifles snapped the chain on his front gates with bolt cutters and burst through. Another masked gunman emerged from the van and the three ran onto the property and scattered with purpose. Two of them went to the lower floor and one went up the side stairs to the second floor. Paul could hear the gunman's steps approaching the front door.

He didn't know why gunmen were invading his home, but he recognized them. The black-checkered pattern on the white base of their scarves helped to identify them but something a man he had treated for a non-life-threatening gunshot wound had told him settled it. The man was a bodyguard for a prominent judge and the two were entering the courtroom when a truck with three gunmen opened fire on them, killing the judge and wounding the guard. He said they were from the Asabiyyah Resistance, a newly formed secular terrorist group (or freedom fighters, depending on one's perspective) responsible for a number of attacks in the Puntland. The next morning, Paul had seen a blurred photo of the gunman spraying bullets at the courthouse on the front page of the newspaper and saw the distinctive pattern on their scarves. The article had said that the group's mission was to stop what it felt was Western influence in the government. What wasn't clear to Paul was why they were now on his doorstep.

Paul slid down under the windowsill, and out of sight. He wasn't sure if they had spotted him. His hand fell on the glass, gashing part of his palm open. He rubbed the blood on his pants and crawled on his elbows along the floor around the bed to the nightstand. He crouched with his back to the bed and then turned his head slowly, looking just over the mattress towards the open door. He had at most a few seconds before the man was in the room. Paul slid the drawer of the nightstand open, and felt around the bottom. He pulled a dusty seven-chambered revolver from inside, and felt blindly around the bottom with his fingers, looking for the cartridges that he heard rolling along the bottom of the drawer. His fingers found two cold cylindrical cartridges and he clenched them between his sweaty, trembling fingers. He had fired a gun a half dozen times in his life and it taught him that he was a lousy shot. His medical training had not prepared him for a standoff.

The gunman's heavy footsteps approached the bedroom. Paul's hand shook and he fumbled sliding the rounds into the revolver. One of the bullets slipped out of his hand and rolled along the floor and under the bed. He managed to slide one into the chamber and shut the revolver.

The gunman was at the door. Paul held his breath, and slowly lowered himself prone onto the ground, hearing the bones in his wrists crack a bit. All he saw through the six-inch space between the bed frame and the floor were the gunman's scuffed black boots. The gunman stood momentarily at the door and then stepped into the room and walked along the edge of the bed opposite Paul. Whatever else might happen, Paul knew that once the gunman's feet rounded the corner of the bed and walked towards him, it would be too late. If his one bullet was to have a chance against the assault rifle in the gunman's hands, he had to strike first. He never took his eyes away from the man's scuffed, dusty boots. His finger tensed around the trigger.

Then, the gunman's feet turned away from Paul and towards the bathroom, so that Paul could see his heels. The gunman's back was turned, not five feet away. Paul pushed off his fingertips and in one fluid motion pointed the gun at the back of the gunman's head where he expected to see a dot of red enlarge along the white and black-checkered scarf.

Click.

Chamber empty.

Click, click.

Fuck.

The gunman swiveled around and pointed the assault rifle at Paul. The surprise that Paul had expected to see in the eyes of a man who had just survived a round of Russian roulette was absent. The gunman's eyes were steady.

"Put your gun down."

Paul tossed the revolver.

"Hands up high."

Paul stretched his arm up.

The gunman walked over to the bedroom window and yelled something in Arabic out the window. The two other gunmen, who were nowhere near as calm as the first, ran into the bedroom within seconds and yelled at Paul to get on the floor.

"I don't know what you want, but I think you've got the wrong guy."

"Doctor Paul Alban?" one of them said.

"Yeah."

"You are the right man."

"Money?"

There was no answer. The men were busy tying his hands tightly behind him with nylon rope that burned his wrists. It happened quickly, and now they spoke at him from behind.

"If you want money, I'll get it for you. How much am I worth?"

"We don't want money."

"What is this?"

"We're taking you in for questioning."

"What? Why? For what?"

"Conspiracy."

And before Paul could say anything more, a dark hood was placed on his head and he was led out of the house.

Ten

The gunman herded Paul down the exterior stairs of the house by jamming the muzzle of the assault rifle deep into the small of Paul's back. A combination of the dark hood over his head and the awkwardly painful position his hands were tied behind his back made him unsteady. He nearly lost his balance and tumbled down the stairs when the gun muzzle was jabbed into his back again but he righted himself at the expense of twisting his ankle painfully. He thought to yell for help as loudly as he could manage, but his neighbors suddenly seemed too far away. Even if they heard him, would they think anything of it? Could his scream be blood curdling enough to cause them to step outside and see him being kidnapped by three masked men with machine guns? The impulse to yell dissipated immediately as the muzzle nudged him forward, a reminder that any gesture might cause the muzzle to stop nudging and fire.

He heard the van door slide open and then one of the men forcefully put his hand on Paul's head and shoved him into the backseat. Two of the gunmen sat on either side of him. The door closed and the van began to move.

It was stifling inside and underneath the hood beads of sweat tracked down Paul's face.

"Who are you people?" were the first words that came out of his mouth even though he had already concluded that these men were members of Asabiyyah.

There was no answer. Instead, the men spoke softly to each other in Arabic and the radio was turned up so that Arabic music muffled their voices. Paul craned his neck in an attempt to hear what they were saying, but even at the best of times, his Arabic was weak.

"Who are you?" he raised his voice, "where are you taking me?"

"We are a security force," a man up front spoke in heavily accented English, "and you are under arrest."

"What kind of security force invades a person's private residence, places a bag over their head and rushes them off in a van? Your security force sounds like a bunch of terrorist —"

Whack!

An object struck him square in the face with enough force that it caused his head to snap back so that it was parallel to the floor. He wasn't sure what the object was, but it was too hard to be a fist, and too soft to be the butt of a gun. At first his eyes watered and tears ran down the sides of his nose. The streams became warmer when they dripped onto his lips. Only a moment later did Paul notice the salty metallic taste on his tongue and realize that his nose was bleeding.

"You will not speak, unless we ask you to. Okay?" the man beside him said.

"Are you asking?"

Whack!

Paul was pretty sure that one broke his nose. An intense heat pulsated under the skin of his face, making the skin feel taut. He ran his tongue along his upper lip where more blood had accumulated. Part of him wanted to make another anger-fueled comment, but it was overshadowed by the fear of another blow to the head and a fascination at what these men wanted with him.

The van sped up, and turned a hard corner, the momentum pressing Paul against the shoulder of the man to his left. In a vain attempt to have the ability to retrace his steps should he miraculously escape his captors, Paul had tried to keep track of the turns they had made (eight so far). But the speed of the van, the throbbing on his face, the mélange of forty-five degree bank turns and ninety degree turns disoriented him. Waves of nausea coursed through his body, and with each turn, he felt like he was going to vomit.

For nearly half an hour, they drove around like that. Varying speeds, constant turns, with each one nearly knocking Paul over. No one spoke. All he could hear was the blaring radio and the acceleration of the van engine. The hood made everything pitch black, and Paul couldn't tell whether there were three men in the van, or ten. He had no idea where he was. They were driving for a long while, but with all of the turns, he couldn't tell if they were two blocks from his house, or on the other side of the city.

Then the van stopped.

Nothing happened for an uncomfortably long moment, and Paul's face tightened underneath the hood, unsure of whether the stop would herald another blow to the head, or worse, a bullet through his skull. Were the guns pointed at him? Could a sudden motion cause a nervous gunman to pull the trigger? *No, if they wanted you dead, you'd be lying facedown on your bedroom floor beside sprayed flecks of bone and chunks of your brain.* Paul pushed aside his conjectures about what his kidnappers were doing. He had no control over his fate anyway. It was easier to just sit there and not think, not even about his aching nose and cheekbones. It was easier to ignore the thoughts about what his face looked like now, and whether his nose was straight. It was easier to not think about having heard that some members of the Asabiyyah Resistance had been recruited by Al-Qaeda to interrogate and torture lawmakers that were unsympathetic to their cause. It was easier not to think about the rumors of de-nailing, beatings, and watching them torture family members.

Then some part of Paul's mind was activated, one that at once triggered both horror and anger, and he realized that they could have Ellen. He had assumed she left the home in the morning after realizing he had been injecting drugs, and that she went for a jog to burn off the tension. But something was wrong with that. His mind flashed back to the perfectly made white linen on the bed at home. Ellen had never been able to fold the sheet's edges at the corners of the mattress that perfectly; that had been the maid's work from the previous day. The bathroom had been pristine, fresh towels were on the towel racks and she wouldn't have had time to replace the linen that early in the morning. These images led him to conclude that Ellen never made it home that day, that these men had ambushed her, and that he was about to see her tied to a chair, her face bruised and cut, being used as leverage to get some sort of information from him. What he couldn't figure out was what it was they wanted to know.

The van engine turned off, the door slid open and a hand that seemed to envelop the top of his head pushed Paul out of the van. He stumbled onto the ground and another pair of hands picked him up and led him forward, their feet crunching along a gravel path, and then down a set of stairs.

He heard a door open and was led through it.

It was only a few degrees cooler through the door but it was enough to cause gooseflesh to rise on his skin. He heard several men talking to each other a fair distance ahead of him, but he could not make out what they were saying. He only heard male voices, not one female, not one that was Ellen's. He heard the legs of chairs, or tables, being moved around and the occasional squeak of the legs scratching the floor. Footsteps filled the room.

He heard a loud clang that sounded, at least to him, like a gunshot and his whole body tensed up before he realized that it was the door slamming behind him. It was louder than any door slamming he had heard before. He knew that deprivation of one sense (like sight) could heighten others (like sound). But expecting the next bang to signal *lights out* tended to make one hyper-vigilant too.

The man beside him had a tight grip on his shoulders and pushed Paul down onto a cold metal chair. A thick rope was tied around his midsection, fastening him to the chair. He tried to take a deep breath but the rope limited the expansion of his chest. His legs were bound to one another. The relief of his sore hands being untied was short-lived, as they were bound again on his lap.

He immediately recognized the next sound he heard and it created a chill that crept up his spine all the way to the hairline on the back of his neck. It was a sound he had heard countless times. The high-pitched ring of fine metal instruments being unwrapped on top of a metal tray. Surgical instruments.

Paul's toes curled reflexively and his hands clenched into little balls as footsteps approached. The hood over his head was untied and slipped off.

Light.

Paul squinted as bright sunlight came through a small window near the ceiling, reflecting off the bare grey concrete walls, burning his eyes. He slowly scanned the room, taking in his surroundings, giving his eyes time to adjust. He was in a dingy cellar, tied to a chair against a wall of the small room, on the opposite side of the one door. Water dripped from a ceiling pipe in the far corner into a puddle on the concrete floor.

The other men he had heard must have left because only two men with scarves covering their faces, wearing green military fatigues, sat across from him. One of them was preoccupied with mounting a small video camera on top of a tripod in the far corner of the room, beside the door. Wires ran from the camera to a laptop placed on a long folding table. Beside the laptop, covered in a layer of sawdust, sat a high-powered circular saw.

The other man, who was noticeably shorter and slighter, paced back and forth holding his arms crossed behind his back just a few feet in front of Paul. Beside him, just out of reach, the surgical instruments were lined up on a metal tray. The red record light on the camera began flashing and the smaller man abruptly turned and dragged a chair from against the wall and sat down, not six inches away from Paul.

"Welcome," he began, "your medical work has helped our poor nation very much, Dr. Alban and we thank you for that."

The man's English was near perfect, tainted by only the slightest hint of an accent. Sitting above the scarf covering his face, the man's dark brown eyes looked like bricks in a massive, unwavering wall. The expression in them was so piercing that they caused Paul to lower his head and look down, so that only the whites of his eyes were visible. They were the eyes of a man who was familiar with his captive, and was there only to confirm his suspicions.

"We need to work with you. We want what *you* want." The man paused and let his words hang in the air.

"I doubt that," Paul muttered.

"I'm sorry, Dr. Alban, I could not hear you." The man leaned forward and turned his head to the side, trying to meet Paul's downward stare. "What can we do for you?"

"You can let me out of here, for one."

"Then we have a common objective." The corner of the man's eyes puckered a bit, and Paul assumed that meant there was a smile underneath the scarf. "You have my word that if you cooperate with us today, you will leave this basement unharmed. That is the agreement."

Paul's eyes drifted upwards, without moving his head, to the surgical instruments on the metal tray. The blade of the scalpel reflected the sunlight coming in through the window. Paul thought of the layers of body tissue a single, swift swipe of the blade could penetrate. Outside the cellar window, cars honked intermittently, and Paul wondered whether they would hear his screams.

The man noticed Paul looking at the tray and waved his hands over the instruments like a magician performing a trick. "These should not be necessary. I will only use them should the cooperation part of our agreement become difficult."

A hopeful wave of relief caused Paul to let out a sigh and then a nod.

"Please state your full name." The man motioned for Paul to speak towards the camera.

"What's with the camera?"

"It is for documentation purposes only. Now state your full name."

"Paul Marcus Alban."

"And what are you doing here in Somalia?"

"I am working at the Bosasso Medical Clinic as a physician."

"And when did you come to Somalia?"

"I don't know, ten years—"

"The date please."

Paul shook his head. "Who are you guys? Immigration?" As the words left his mouth, Paul thought he should've kept his mouth shut. But then again, he reminded himself, these men completed an orchestrated abduction to have the opportunity to interrogate him. Dissent was expected. His interrogator was calm, but maybe he was calm because they had stuck to his agenda, because Paul hadn't veered off the path, yet. And Ellen was nowhere to be seen. If they had her, she surely would have been dragged into the room by now, centered in front of the camera, tied up. His initial impression was probably the most accurate; she had gone for a run.

"You can consider us," the man leaned back and thought for a moment, "a police organization."

"Not the ethics police, I assume."

"Should you be commenting on other people's ethics, Dr. Alban?"

"Should you be calling yourself police?"

"Enough." The man raised his hand just off his lap. "We are interested in who you are."

"You know me. We've established who I am. I'm Dr. Paul Alban, a French physician, working for a humanitarian organization in a fucked up country where masked men can kidnap and interrogate innocent people for no reason."

The interrogator nodded, stepped away from the chair and crouched in front of Paul. He leaned in so that his face was only a few inches from Paul's. The man's calm stare suddenly disappeared and in its place a fiery rage took hold. Paul moved his eyes away again, but the man clenched a bunch of Paul's hair in his fist, and jerked Paul's head so that he was looking directly into the man's eyes. "What confuses me, Dr. Alban is why you, an *innocent* foreign worker, would provide a group of pirates detailed information about a Ukrainian cargo ship." He uncoiled and struck Paul open palm in the face with his free hand. "Now why would an innocent doctor do that?"

The pain of being hit in the face did not stun Paul the way his interrogator's words did. His body's reaction betrayed the façade he tried to maintain with his next words. His mouth gaped and he let out a little gasp. His eyes darted around the room, and the room started to feel small, very small. But his mind reacted differently, trying to push away what he had just heard. "I, I don't… know what you're…"

"Do not lie to us." The man motioned to the camera. "Tell us where you obtained the information about the *Stebelsky*."

Somehow, these men had information connecting him to a vessel hijack. The interrogator stood over Paul, taking in deep huffing breaths. Paul's mind was spinning. How could they have connected him? He had been so careful. He had followed protocol exactly: never meet in person, never use your real name, arrive at the drop-point at least twenty-four hours before you say you will. He had left the manifest in the book as he said he would. No one had seen him enter, or exit the library. But things were becoming strange. First, the man, Sami, that he had left the manifest for, came to the clinic that day, after having hijacked the ship. Sami didn't let on he knew Paul was the one who had provided him the *Stebelsky*'s sea route and manifest. He couldn't have known. Could he? And now these men somehow knew about the manifest. Could Sami have told them? No. Why would he? Sami, Paul had learned, worked alone, with no associates. He hijacked weapons and sold them to the military in Somalia. No ideological connections. He would never work with the Asabiyyah resistance, assuming that's who these people were. But they needed confirmation from him, that's what the camera was for. They needed him alive.

The interrogator leaned in again and put his hand on Paul's shoulder. "Say who you work for. Then we can all go home."

"Doctors without..."

"No. That is not true." The interrogator turned abruptly and sat in the chair. He glanced towards the larger man behind the camera and made a gesture with his head towards Paul. The man, who was several inches taller and thicker, took several determined steps towards Paul.

"Your turn now?" Paul said. "You the bad cop?"

The large man did not speak, and instead clenched his hands into balls, took three swift steps towards him and landed a punch directly in Paul's solar plexus, pushing the wind out of his lungs. The force was enough to send Paul and the chair skidding backwards several feet along the ground. Paul sat hunched forward, wheezing and straining for air.

He caught his breath enough to raise his head. The large man towered over him with his hand raised. Before Paul could even flinch, the back of the man's hand came down against the right side of Paul's face, knocking a molar loose.

"You're definitely the bad cop," Paul said, rocking the tooth with his tongue.

The man raised his leg and kicked him in the chest with the sole of his foot, tipping Paul over backwards in the chair, sending him sliding along the ground towards the back wall. Paul lay sideways on the floor, still bound to the chair. The side of his face rested on the cool concrete floor, and blood drained out of his mouth and into a small puddle around him. The interrogator crouched in front of him. “Are you ready to speak now, Dr Alban?”

Paul nodded, his face rubbing against the floor. The interrogator sat Paul back up, and paced in front of him. “The pirates docked and unloaded the ship.” He walked towards the window and stared outside, pausing, “No ransom. To me that means there is something of value aboard.”

Paul nodded slightly.

“What was aboard?” he asked.

Paul looked down, avoiding eye contact. The interrogator knelt down and met Paul’s eyes. “Weapons?”

Paul licked the blood dripping down his lips. He took a deep breath and exhaled. “Yeah,” he nodded, “yeah, it was weapons.”

“Good, Dr. Alban. Very good. You’re doing well.” He seemed to be smiling, or sneering Paul couldn’t tell. “Do you see how we can work together?”

Paul nodded. “Are we done yet?”

“Soon,” the interrogator said. “Now tell us how it happened. How did you get this manifest? Why did you give it to these hijackers?”

“No,” Paul shook his head. “If I tell you that you’ll kill me. You’ll have no use for me.”

“We just want the information, Doctor Alban, that is all.”

“You first,” Paul said. “Why do you care about hijackers?”

The man laughed. “We are men who are bringing peace to this country,” he began. “Somalia has been in turmoil for almost two decades and we are here to stabilize it, to bring order and hope. Paul, these hijackers are pawns of the corrupt governments and warlords that are ruining this country. The hijackers sell them weapons to fight us, and then the government keeps draining the country of all its resources."

"Asabiyyah?" Paul nodded.

"Yes, we are. The warlords have become the de facto government and corruption is everywhere. We fight them for what is right: peace and prosperity," he said. "But Paul, the United States supports them, gives them weapons, even though they were the people who started these wars. The United States fought against those same warlords that they now support. But now, they fight us, and call it a war on terror. Why?" The man shrugged dramatically. "Maybe so U.S. companies can drill for oil in our deserts."

"That's not true," Paul said, "the U.S. has nothing to do with Somalia. They got out in ninety-three and that's it."

"But they have secret agents in Somalia, providing the warlords and pirates with intelligence," he smiled knowingly, "don't they?" Paul glanced at the metal tray one more time. "We know everything," the interrogator said.

"I can see that," Paul conceded.

"Tell us, who provides you with the information?"

Paul's breathing became shallow and quick. These men knew everything about him already. Somehow. And it was clear they would go as far as they needed to get him to confess to everything. The cover was blown.

The interrogator stood over him and stared intently. "Do you work for the United States government?"

"Yes," Paul said under his breath.

"Do you work for the National Clandestine Service?"

"Yes."

"Are you an undercover operative working in Somalia?"

"Yes," Paul's voice was louder now, more confident.

"Was the passage of information about the *Stebelsky* part of your work as an undercover operative?"

Paul waited a long moment. He took a breath in. "Yes."

Paul exhaled deeply and the tension left his body. He had spent ten years in Somalia, constantly looking over his shoulder, watching people for suspicious activity, part of him always waiting for someone to put a bullet in the back of his head. For a decade he had to lie about who he was and what he was doing. He had to lie to Ellen, keep her at a distance because of this. For it to be over was somewhat of a relief. But was this it? He had given them the information they were looking for, and they really had no use for him. But part of him clung on to the hope that they would let him leave as they promised.

"Thank you, Dr. Alban." The interrogator bowed slightly.

"Can you untie my hands?" Paul said.

"Goodbye, Doctor Alban."

Paul watched as the two men walked out of the room, the door clanging shut behind them. The red record light on the camera continued to flash.

"Hey!" Paul said, "Come back! Untie me!" He pleaded, trying to wiggle fitfully out of the ropes that tied him to the chair. No one came. The room felt silent, too silent, despite the occasional sounds of cars passing by outside.

His gaze shifted around the cellar, where everything was very still, almost slowed down. The initial urge to run faded as Paul began to realize that he was alive and that they had left him that way. It must have been minutes since they had left, and the place was completely silent. He even thought he heard the van pulling out of the driveway.

He relaxed and began to chuckle nervously but tears flowed out as well, so that he wasn't certain whether he was experiencing massive relief or shock at what had just happened. But he was alive, and he hadn't heard any footsteps, or talking, or even a throat clearing.

Then, as Paul started formulating a plan to untie himself from the chair and leave the cellar, the clang of the door latch opening echoed off of the walls. Paul jumped a little and saw a tall man wearing a balaclava enter the room. He stood, arms crossed, examining Paul from a distance, without saying a word.

While Paul's heart picked up at the realization that he would now likely not escape, the feeling did not compare to what he experienced when the man removed his balaclava. Although his eyes saw a familiar long thin black face with a thin nose with a long, hypertrophied scar that ran through the man's eye and a crafty grin, his mind refused to recognize it. Instead, he stared for a long time. He felt immobilized as the disbelief slowly gave way to fear and he recognized the man in front of him.

Kadar Hadad.

The Devil.

Hadad spoke. "Hello, Dr. Ramsey."

Eleven

A woman with dark chestnut hair raced through the rows of cubicles on the top floor of the CIA headquarters' North Building, taking care not to twist an ankle on her high-heeled shoes. The men inside the cubicles were too busy hovering over the morning spreadsheets and written briefings to notice the young and petite woman juggling a stack of dossiers under one arm and a black leather briefcase and bottled water in the other.

This was the National Clandestine Service.

The suits that passed through the three security checkpoints every day to come to work in the NCS, a department that occupied the top three floors of the one million square foot Langley, Virginia complex coordinated undercover overseas operations. Most of the men in the department had worked here when it was known by its pre-9/11 name: the Directorate of Operations.

Just as the woman stopped in front of the closed office door with a nameplate that read *J. Crilley - Executive Officer of Operations* engraved, the dossiers spilled out from under her arm onto the grey carpet. She sighed, bent down and gathered the papers, taking care to arrange them in the exact order she had placed them in before. She stood up straight and adjusted the collar on her dark suit jacket with her free hand, looked at the time on her digital watch, gave a courtesy knock and opened.

"Bailey, sit down please."

Bailey entered the small office and looked over the paper stacks on the oak veneered desk at Jim Crilley, her boss. He was leaning back in his leather chair with his shirt cuffs rolled up showing his hairy grey arms, reading the day's sports section. She glanced out the window behind him, noting that it was still raining. Two family pictures of Crilley, his wife and two awkward looking adolescent sons hung beside the window. Judging from his wife's satin shirt and puffy hairdo, the picture was at least five years old.

Crilley was one of the oldest, longest serving operations officers in clandestine ops. He was well past his pension date. Bailey had heard rumors that Crilley was sucked into a sophisticated Ponzi scheme in the mid-1990s, losing his kids' education funds and his own retirement investments. In the midst of the scheme, Crilley flaunted his apparent earnings to anyone who would listen and even bought himself a top of the line Cadillac. When he lost it all (people whispered that in the end he had dumped over $325K into it), he became an office joke. He was in charge of stopping terrorism but couldn't sniff out an obvious Ponzi scheme. While his colleagues had moved on to fancy retirements in South Florida or cottages on the Great Lakes, he was stuck working to earn back his losses.

Bailey put her water down on a small piece of desk not occupied by files and looked around for a spot to sit, both visitors' chairs being covered in files.

"Good morning, sir."

He didn't respond immediately, rather he finished reading his sentence and tossed the paper down. "Just shove those aside." He dropped a couple of stacks of papers from his desk to the ground and Bailey followed suit.

"Behind on paperwork, sir?"

"Just a little bit," he raised his hand, "sorry I was late today, traffic through the causeway was horrible."

Bailey shrugged, suggesting it was no problem. She had gotten used to their morning debriefings being at least an hour late. She didn't mind, though, it gave her more time to prepare the previous day's intelligence summaries for her boss.

"You live in the district, don't you?"

"Yes sir, but I don't have to take the causeway," she lied. If she told him the truth, that she took almost the exact same route to work that he did, it would mean that he was lying.

"You're lucky," he took a sip from his mug, "'cause the traffic is horrible."

"That's what I hear."

Crilley looked across the desk at Bailey, half smiling, barely showing his teeth. She avoided making eye contact and shuffled through the papers in her lap. She didn't understand why he always smiled at her like that, but it made her uncomfortable. She handed him a few printed pages.

"Here's today's summary."

Crilley put his gold-rimmed aviator reading glasses on the tip of his red bulbous nose and perused the sixteen-page document, spending a few token seconds on each page, sipping his coffee loudly. Bailey already knew that he didn't read any of it and only pretended to look it over for her benefit. She had proofread her work three times that morning, scouring the text for any spelling errors and getting the margins just right. She couldn't afford any mistakes with her new boss. Crilley was referred to as "The Bull" among the low level NCS analysts. And, it was warranted, four years ago he fired eleven collection management officers on the spot when they failed to recognize a systematic error in the intelligence reports about trade across the Kyrgyzstan-Tajikistan border. He even sent the officer that recognized the error packing because he hadn't noticed it "soon enough."

"Looks good," he looked at her over his glasses, "very good there, Officer Clark. Very thorough."

"Great," she let out a sigh of relief. "I'll send that out before the team meeting." She took the document back and placed it in the folder.

"Anything else happening?" he reached for his newspaper.

"There is one thing that didn't make it into the briefing," she waited for Crilley to look up. "I'm not sure if you're aware or not, but we received a report of a missing container ship."

"No, I haven't heard anything about it." He folded his glasses into his shirt pocket. "What are the details?"

"It was passing through the Gulf of Aden and went off the grid about fourteen hours before it was noticed missing."

"Fourteen hours?" he laughed. "Let me guess, the Maritime Police were tracking it?"

She nodded. The International Maritime Police was the developed world's response to the rise in piracy in South-East Asia and Africa. Comprised of a few basic radar stations that tracked ships through hot spots of pirate activity, their mandate was to identify ships that were veering off course, notify their owners, and coordinate efforts to recover the ship. In practice, however, the IMP was poorly coordinated and rarely identified any ships in actual danger. Since its creation, pirate attacks had risen.

"I think we need a police to police the Maritime Police." Crilley shook his head in disbelief. "What's this, the eleventh hijacking in the Gulf this year?"

"Twelfth, actually."

Crilley patted his round belly and made a sound, which was like more of a grunt than a chuckle.

"It was a heavy weapons transport between Ukraine and Kenya," she continued, "but right now we don't have any details as to what was actually on the ship."

"How much do the pirates want?"

"We don't know, sir. There has been no contact with the crew or pirates."

"No ransom request?"

"I'm not sure that that's what they're looking for."

"Well then, what do they want?"

Bailey unfolded a blurry satellite photo and handed it to Crilley, who sat up straight, squinting at the photo. The image showed an arial view of the *Stebelsky*, docked at the port in Bosasso.

"We think its being unloaded in Somalia."

Crilley brushed his hand on his bald head and exhaled slowly. "What do the Ukrainians want?"

"Nothing," Bailey furrowed her brow, "I mean, they haven't contacted us."

"How are they responding to this?"

Bailey shrugged and shook her head slightly, then pushed her hair from her eyes.

"How did the pirates do this?" he scowled. "A heavy weapons transport that they've been able to dock without anyone getting wind of it? It doesn't make sense."

"It seems that's what's happened, sir."

Crilley rubbed his hand on his chin. "And no word from the Ukrainians."

Bailey shook her head slowly. She wondered why Crilley seemed so interested in this. Illegal weapons transfers were commonplace, the intelligence summary itself highlighted several other likely transfers; ones in Columbia and Indonesia.

"This is a problem." Crilley lifted himself from his chair and looked out the window, holding his coffee mug in his hand. "A hundred bucks says they're looking into this. And they want to know if we're involved."

"But we're not." Bailey looked at Crilley who gave her his half smile again, "are we?"

"As far as we know," he took another loud sip, "but they'll assume we are."

Bailey shifted in her chair, noting Crilley's knowing smile. She knew better than to pry, but he seemed to be waiting for her response. "Why would they assume that?"

Crilley smirked as though he were hoping for that question. He sat back down, his frame filling the chair, and began finger pecking on his computer keyboard. He was from the pre-computer generation, Bailey thought. He motioned for Bailey to come around and look at his screen. "How long have you been working here now?"

"Four years, sir."

"No, not for the agency, I mean here with NCS."

"Two months."

"I think its time, Officer," he looked back over his shoulder, "that I give you a bit of an orientation as to how things work here."

Bailey nodded, arms behind her back, and stared at the computer screen. She had applied for the position as assistant to the Executive Officer of Operations while still a data analyst for the paramilitary division on the pretext that it was a career building position and that she wanted to gain greater understanding for operations. That she wanted to understand "the big picture." It was common for data analysts to complain about not understanding the significance of their work as each of their contributions was only a component of a whole, like pixels on a television screen, and only case officers had access to the whole.

The truth was that Bailey loved data analysis. She was good at it. Piecing together data from intelligence reports into a coherent story was painstaking work but Bailey found it exhilarating. And in time, the data always told a story. And Bailey would sift and sift through the numbers until the truth revealed itself. Perhaps the only drawback was that she couldn't let a problem rest until it made sense in her mind.

Long before she had graduated near the top of her class in statistical science and had been recruited to work at the Central Intelligence Agency, Bailey learned she had a knack for numbers. Mr. Waters, her grade 11 math teacher, had recognized her talent and entered her in a statewide math competition. The winner received a full scholarship to Cornell. A way out of her home. Away from her father. That was all the motivation she needed to spend every night at her desk, working through formulas and problems.

Working in Operations meant that she would have contact with operatives. For most analysts, this would be an exciting prospect, but Bailey worried it would remove the objectivity she had looking at numbers. The human relationship was fraught with subjectivity.

But Bailey knew that she had really applied for the promotion to get away from the people at paramilitary. To run from the rumors, the stares, the judgments. Maybe she had brought it on herself as her old boss, Roger Blake (who looked strikingly similar to Crilley) had told her. *Don't be a tattletale. No one will believe you,* were his exact words. And no one did.

She had been working late one night, as she always did, and the office had emptied slowly. An inebriated Blake emerged from his office at the end of the hall, staggering a bit as he approached Bailey. He sat on her desk and began grabbing her, laughing the whole time. It was a game to him. When she tried to get up to leave, he pushed her down, and then things happened quickly, very quickly. Maybe her skirt was too short. Maybe her shirt was too tight. Maybe she should have said something earlier. Maybe then people would have believed her. Maybe then her (now ex) fiancé's response would have been something other than *if you didn't want it, why didn't you tell me sooner?*

Crilley continued and Bailey nodded. "The United States is in two wars right now and we can barely handle it. The problem is, there are a lot more threats to our interests than ones that come from those two countries. That's where we come in."

Bailey shifted her weight as she had heard this speech before, stopping the threat before it occurs etc, etc.

"We've been in Somalia before, remember that? It was a total fucking disaster, both from a military and political standpoint. We bailed before the job was done. But does that mean the threat is gone?"

Bailey opened her mouth, unsure if he expected an answer or if it was rhetorical.

"No," he continued, "the threat is still there. And that's where we come in. And we do it quietly, with the most discreet means possible."

"Intelligence."

"Bingo." Crilley opened a file on his computer, entitled *Strategic Objectives: Horn of Africa.* "Somalia's a hotbed for terrorism Clark, there's been no real government for decades, and warlords run the country…it's anarchy. For the past ten years, not only have fundamentalist groups been making serious inroads into Somalia and destabilizing it, so has a secular one."

"Asabiyyah." Bailey nodded her understanding.

"Exactly. But we can't wage war, it would be political suicide. So we do the next best thing."

"What's that?"

"We help those fighting them already."

"The warlords?"

He nodded.

"But they've caused it all, they plunged the country into anarchy."

Crilley raised his hands as if to say '*Oh well.*' "They were, but now, they're a potential solution. If we help them fight these extremists and stabilize the country, things could settle out. This is the future of warfare."

One of Bailey's eyebrows rose, showing her skepticism. There were constant news reports questioning policy makers' judgment in cases of former U.S. allies now orchestrating terrorist attacks against the United States.

"But we could never do that openly, public opinion is against it." Crilley clicked open news stories over the past several years of pirates' ransoms. "Instead we give them information."

"You give them information on ships?"

He nodded.

"But then?"

"They either get the cargo or a ransom. And then they can use the ransom to buy weapons to fight the insurgents."

Bailey stepped back and exhaled. "How do—"

"—we do it?" He opened another window on the computer. "We have a man inside Somalia."

Bailey looked in closely at the profile on the computer screen in front of her. In the top left corner was a small passport photo of a handsome middle-aged man. Next to it was his demographic information and name: *Paul Alban*.

"He's a doctor?"

"Correct."

"But, U.S. law dictates that operatives cannot pose as doctors, lawyers…"

"I know," he pointed at the screen, "but he's technically not American, he's French."

Bailey stepped back and put her hand on her chin. How many hijackings had the U.S. set up? What about robberies at military armories in the former Soviet Union? How many seemingly random acts were coordinated by the intelligence community?

"So we gave this man the information on this Ukranian ship and he gave it to the pirates?"

"Well," Crilley turned off his computer monitor, "we didn't have any information on this one."

"So?"

"We have to find out what happened."

Twelve

Kadar Hadad seemed to revel in the moment. He rubbed his beard with his palm, and smiled at Paul the way someone would after unexpectedly running into an old friend at the airport. He walked past the camcorder and sat on the table between the laptop and dusty circular saw. He cracked his bony knuckles one at a time. His legs hung off the edge of the table and he swung them back and forth rhythmically, playfully.

If one could overlook the scene around him—the man tied to a chair with blood dripping down his lips, the surgical instruments splayed out on the tray, the camcorder beside him, the dingy cellar—one would think Hadad was waiting at a bus stop.

While Hadad seemed prepared for this reunion, Paul felt disoriented and confused. Was he dreaming? Or was he dead? No, not yet. But he felt like he was looking at a ghost. He closed his eyes, part of him hoping that when he opened them, Hadad would be gone, and he could chalk it up to some strange *déjà vu* experience.

But he was still there, grinning at Paul. That stupid grin.

How was Hadad still alive? Two-and-a-half years after the disaster in Addis, Paul had heard on the local radio that Hadad was killed in a roadside bomb in Afghanistan. To be certain, he looked up news reports online and the *Washington Post*, *New York Times*, even *Time* were reporting *terror suspect Kadar Hadad confirmed dead in Kabul*. But he hadn't been killed; he was here, in front of Paul.

"You seem surprised to see me," Hadad began, "Dr. Ramsey."

In his mind, Paul saw Hadad strapped to the wood plank, his head covered in the water-saturated towel, his neck muscles tense and his abdominal muscles jerking. The oxygen saturation reading dropping until Hadad stopped moving and lay motionless on the board. He felt for the carotid pulse, but there was none. Hadad was dead. But then he ordered the men to take the leather restraints off his body and began chest compressions. Twenty compressions followed by two mouth-to-mouth breaths. Hadad was dead for three minutes before he coughed up a mouthful of foamy water, gasping for air. And he had brought him back to life.

And it was all for nothing. No confession. No indictment.

Hadad went free and the three interrogators (or *torturers* as the *Vanity Fair* exclusive had labeled them) were charged. Their lives ruined. Marshall Ramsey's life destroyed.

"It's Paul," he said through his teeth.

"Of course," Hadad gave an exaggerated nod, "because Marshall Ramsey died in prison." Hadad hopped off the table and walked up to Paul and untied his hands. "Because Marshall Ramsey would never leave his wife and child, leave his homeland, turn in his friends." Hadad shook his head, patronizing. "No, never, not Marshall Ramsey, he's dead."

Hadad reached out towards the surgical instruments and let his hand hover over them momentarily. He picked up the pair of forceps and clicked them open and closed several times, never taking his eyes off Paul. Instead of feeling anger at the accusation, Paul considered what Hadad had said in a way that he never had before. To an outsider, it would seem that he had taken the easy way out. The facts were that he had taken a deal in exchange for his testimony against his fellow interrogators. It resulted in one successful indictment against agent Bruce McCormick. It would have led to a second, but Steve Sidwell had disappeared, and was never charged.

But if it were not for McCormick's love of cheap whiskey, the entire investigation wouldn't have fallen to bits. If he hadn't bragged about Kadar Hadad's interrogation to the skinny blonde thirtysomething (and had he not been drunk he would have realized she was out of his league) that he had met in the bar who turned out to be an undercover reporter, the story wouldn't have made it to the press. An internal investigation wouldn't have been launched. Charges for *heinous interrogation techniques and prisoner abuse* wouldn't have been laid. Kadar Hadad wouldn't have been set free.

"And certainly," Hadad continued, waving the forceps as he spoke, "Marshall Ramsey would never torture anyone." Hadad planted the hand holding the forceps on the back of Paul's neck and pulled Paul's head forward. His other fist met Paul's face, sending blood from Paul's mouth spraying against the wall behind him. "You would never allow someone to be chained in a frigid room, choking all day long. You would not allow someone to almost drown on a table, over and over again, would you?"

Hadad released his grip on Paul's neck and stood in front of Paul with his fists clenched by his side, exhaling through his teeth. He stared at Paul, waiting for him to engage.

"If they were you?" Paul spoke softly, "I would."

Hadad took a deep breath and his muscles relaxed, his shoulders lowered. "You did do it."

"And I would do it again. You're a terrorist who's killed thousands of innocent people."

"And who are you?" Hadad said, "Someone who tortures people, and is so sick of himself that he has to change his identity and escape, so that he can forget about what he has done?"

Paul shook his head "No." He pointed at Hadad, "I did what I had to do. Finding out who blew those people up was necessary."

"And you would have done anything to have revenge for your friend's death," Hadad said quietly. "I read about him, Dennis Hamilton. He seemed like a good man."

"A great man."

"He was like a father to you."

"Something like that."

"Then you must realize," Hadad said, "that there will be collateral damage in operations like the one in Nairobi."

Paul shook his head. He had the urge to lunge forward, wrap his hands around Hadad's head and twist, but it dissipated when he took a breath and felt the rope dig into his chest reminding him that he was still tied to the chair. The idea that Dennis' death could be dismissed as something like collateral damage infuriated him.

"And as a result of these operations, there are investigations to bring killers like you to justice."

"And an opportunity for people like you to get revenge."

"Sometimes revenge can be justice."

"So imagine my excitement when I learned you were in Somalia."

"How did you find out?"

Hadad ignored this, and flicked the forceps in his hand. The grin returned to his face, and he called out a name, *Islam*, and the large man that had been behind the camera came back into the room. He stood beside the camcorder, his arms folded in front of him.

"So what? You work with Asabiyyah now?"

Hadad shrugged. "I go where there is work to be done."

That's what the file on Hadad had said, too. A contract worker. He had worked with six terrorist groups by the time Marshall had read the file in 1999. Groups with conflicting ideologies. By all accounts, Kadar Hadad did not subscribe to any ideology.

Hadad produced a latex glove from his pocket and snapped it onto his left hand. He pulled a towel off of the metal tray with surgical instruments and dropped it on Paul's lap. He dragged a chair from the corner of the room and sat down squarely in front of Paul. "I've been waiting for this day for a long time."

"What are you doing?"

"A manicure." Hadad spread his fingers wide apart and held the back of his hand in front Paul's face. At the end of each finger, a gnarled mass of yellowish tissue lay on the nail bed. "Don't worry, they grow back."

Before Paul could react, the man behind the camera, Islam, had a firm grip on both of his wrists and pressed them onto Paul's knees. Paul let out a shout and tried to withdraw his arms, but Islam was too powerful. He clenched his hands tightly and tucked his fingernails into his palms. Hadad dug his finger into Paul's left fist and pulled out Paul's index finger, extending it. Hadad held Paul's finger so tightly that Paul saw his finger turn white. He clamped the forceps down on the end of the nail and locked it in place. Now any attempt to withdraw his hand would only result in pain and the nail being pulled out.

Hadad gripped the forceps and wiggled it side-to-side forcefully. Paul screamed long after the nail was ripped right off the nail bed. Blood seeped out of the end of his finger, and pain ran through his hand so his entire hand felt inflamed, pulsating. If he hadn't looked down at the mangled mass of tissue, he wouldn't have been able to say whether the nail was plucked or his whole finger pulled out.

"What do you want from me?" he pleaded, his eyes closed.

Hadad wrapped the towel around Paul's finger and tied it in a tight knot, red slowly soaking through the white towel. He leaned in and whispered in Paul's ear, "We need access to the ship."

"What?" Paul winced. "I don't have access to it."

"We know that, but you have access to someone who does. Samatar al Jelle."

"Sami?"

Hadad nodded.

"Why don't you find him yourself?"

Islam slapped him in the back of the head but Hadad held up a hand. "These pirates are hard to find. And even when you do, they travel in groups."

"And you think I can find them?"

"You can call him and arrange a meeting." Hadad looked at Paul, who was already shaking his head at the idea. "You are his contact, correct?"

"I won't do it," Paul said.

"Yes, you will, Marshall, trust me."

"It's Paul."

Hadad turned abruptly and walked to the table at the far end of the room. He placed his hand on the circular saw, ran his hands along the power cord and then plugged the end into an extension cord. Hadad motioned to Islam who turned Paul over onto his side in the chair.

Paul thrashed his head side-to-side, like a bull avoiding a lasso. Islam placed his hand on the side of Paul's head and pressed down with all his weight, mashing Paul's head into the concrete floor, making it feel like it was going to explode. Paul shifted his eyes towards Hadad, who held the circular saw and revved it several times, making a screeching sound that reverberated off the walls. Rust coated the tips of the saw's teeth.

Hadad knelt in front of Paul. "I'm serious, Marshall."

Paul stared silently at Hadad, whose face was inches from his own. Thin beads of sweat rolled down Hadad's face and a smudge of blood, which Paul recognized as his own, ran down Hadad's cheek. Hadad's dark eyes initially seemed to penetrate right through Paul, but suddenly they seemed sympathetic, as though to say, *Please don't make me do this, Marshall.*

But the look quickly faded, and Hadad lifted the saw and placed it on Paul's neck. Three of the saw's teeth penetrated through the skin under the weight of the saw. A sharp lance of pain. He could feel the warm liquid drain down his neck from underneath the saw. Then Hadad pressed down on the saw, the teeth digging in further, biting

Paul's eyes shifted up towards Hadad's, hoping for the soft eyes he had seen briefly. Instead, he only saw determination and Hadad seemed to be looking through him.

"This is your last chance," Hadad said.

Paul saw the tendons in Hadad's hand tense slightly around the saw's trigger. "Okay, okay. I'll do it."

The saw made a loud clang as Hadad threw it onto the floor beside him. "Thank you." He exhaled, and Paul thought he heard more relief in Hadad's voice than disappointment.

Islam tilted Paul and the chair upright and untied the ropes around Paul's torso. Hadad handed Paul the cellular phone. "It's blocked, don't worry."

Paul looked at the phone in his hand and dialed the number.

Thirteen

Under different circumstances, Paul would have found it to be a good day to sit at a café in downtown Bosasso. A light breeze coming up from the harbor made the ninety-six degrees more bearable. The chatter of locals mixed with the noise of car horns as crowds overflowed into the streets. With no division between sidewalk and road, car traffic, pedestrian traffic, bicycle traffic, and even a couple of donkey-pulled carts competed for space between buildings. At the foot of the buildings, shoppers with sweat-drenched brows bargained with street merchants over the cost of items such as tomatoes, seafood, colorful fabrics and burned DVDs. Others sat under the shield of umbrellas at restaurants and cafes that lined the street. Men with fanny packs around their waists held wads of bills high in outstretched arms, announcing their exchange rates to the passing crowds. In a few hours, the merchants would pack up their stands and traffic would trickle down, leaving the streets nearly empty.

Paul sat at a plastic table in front of a building with a turquoise facade two blocks from the Bosasso harbor front across from the Hotel Huruse. A sign with blurry spray-painted letters that hung above Paul read *CAFÉ AMERICKA*. Men in colorful linen shirts and jeans sat at the other dozen or so tables, talking loudly. Paul waved at flies buzzing around his steaming black tea and took small sips; the smell of cloves opening his blood-congested sinuses. He had ordered a second one for Sami.

Three days ago, he and Ellen had sat in the very same café, one table over, drinking Cokes after finishing their grocery shopping. She had brought up the idea that they plan a vacation to the south of France to see where he had grown up. He had skipped over the suggestion—as he always did—a skill he had developed after years of secrets and lies. He was able to lie without a twinge of guilt. There were long periods where he forgot all about Marshall Ramsey, like a distant figure in his past who died and who he vaguely remembered on anniversaries and holidays. But now it seemed like Marshall Ramsey was always there, lurking in the shadows. But what could he say to her now? Where would he even begin? *There's something you should know about me.* What's that? *Well, for starters, my real name is Marshall Ramsey.* What? *Oh, and all that stuff I told you about my past, most of it's a lie, a cover story, you actually don't know the first thing about me. I'm a pretty convincing liar, don't you think?* You sure are. *Do you still want to go on that trip to France?*

He sat back, aware that his clothes were sticking to him, drenched from sweat. Not from the heat though; the sweat was the product of panic, terror. He touched the saw marks on his neck and then rubbed his fingers together, feeling for blood. The scars had dried up. One of Hadad's men had bandaged Paul's left hand and a small dot of red was visible soaking through the dressing. Paul let his hand hang by his side, out of sight. He ran his hand along his nose and it felt puffy and tender to touch. Even blinking too hard sent a shockwave of pain through his nose.

Paul looked out of the corner of his eye at the white van parked across the street in the shade underneath one of the balconies of the Hotel Huruse. Inside, Hadad and two of his men waited with a trunk full of machine guns. They waited for Sami to appear. As instructed by Hadad, Paul had called Sami and asked for an immediate face-to-face meeting to discuss distribution of the weapons on the *Stebelsky*. Sami did not protest. The meeting time was 3:45 p.m. at *Café Americka*. Paul looked at his watch, *three minutes away*.

As far as Paul knew, Hadad's plan was to lure Sami to one of the busiest areas in Bosasso, drag him to the van and then somehow blackmail Sami into giving up the weapons on the ship. *Have him sit down and speak with him for a few minutes*, Hadad had instructed him. *We will take care of the rest*. Paul had no idea how Hadad planned to get out of the downtown once they had kidnapped Sami, given the swarms of people and cars in the street — which looked more like a parking lot at a carnival than a city street.

He looked at Islam, who sat two tables over, pretending to read the newspaper. Hadad had said that Islam would stay nearby in case Sami tried to run, but Paul realized he was also there in case he, too, tried to make a break for it. Had Islam not been so close he could have run and slipped into the crowd and gone several blocks before the men in the van would have noticed him missing. And there was no question he was faster on foot than Islam, but that would only matter in an all-out sprint. Weaving through a packed crowd, they were likely the same speed; perhaps Islam's linebacker physique gave him the advantage of being capable of mowing people over in the event of a chase.

Then it struck Paul that the location gave a specific advantage to Hadad. The chaos in the street was so great that even if Sami suspected a set-up, he would likely not notice the van, or the large man reading the newspaper beside Paul. But once he got close enough and if Paul informed him of their location, the density of the crowd would keep him in. Once he got in, he would not get out. And Hadad would only have to wait like a patient spider. Paul hoped that Sami remembered what he told him when he had first anonymously contacted him several years ago: *we never meet face-to-face, if I ever ask for that, assume that something's wrong.*

Suddenly, a bearded man with a fanny pack sat in the chair across from Paul. He hammered several wads of Somali shillings down on the table and smiled. Paul rolled his eyes as peddlers and moneychangers accosted him every time he ventured downtown. They assumed he was a tourist or a journalist and could make an easy buck off him.

"I'm not interested," Paul said holding up his hand. "I'm waiting for a friend."

The man's smile disappeared and he leaned in across the table. "I'm with Sami," he spoke quickly. "Where are they?"

"What? How did you—"

"Where is Hadad waiting?" he commanded. "Hurry before he knows."

Paul swallowed hard. "Across the street," his eyes darted, "white van."

"Good," he smiled. "Sami will be here shortly." He pushed a stack of bills inches from Paul's nose. "Push me away now, like a beggar."

Paul played the part and made an exaggerated wave and the man retreated down the street. Paul sat back down and ran his hands through his hair feeling somewhat relieved. Sami had figured it out and seemed to have a plan. At least he had men with him.

He half stood, looking up and down the street for Sami. He caught Islam's eye as he did so. He hadn't told the man about Islam waiting there to grab Sami. Paul stood up, looking over the mass of people down the street for the moneychanger, but he had disappeared into the crowd.

Then he saw Sami coming towards him, weaving through the crowd. Islam must have spotted Sami too, since he folded up his newspaper, straightened in his seat and cocked his head to the side as though he was cracking his neck.

Sami was two tables away, grinning. "Doctor," he waved.

Islam pushed his chair back and stood. Across the street, the van door slid open and one of the men wearing a balaclava and holding a machine gun emerged. A crescendo of screams and shouts spread through the crowd. A clear line of sight developed between the van and Paul as people scattered in either direction away from the gunman like a flock of birds. Islam moved in Sami's direction.

Paul grasped the two steaming mugs of tea, sprung out of his chair and splashed them in Islam's face, sending him back against a table, clutching his face.

Without hesitation, Paul ran up the street after Sami, who was already in a full sprint, twenty yards ahead. The crowd dispersed in front of him. All he could see ahead were people's backs. Paul sped up and entered the sea of bodies, so that there were bodies between him and the gunmen. He pushed himself harder, darting between bodies. He kept his attention focused ahead on Sami who weaved effortlessly through the crowd.

He passed two more buildings before he finally caught up with Sami and at an intersection they turned the corner. They took cover at the corner of the building marked *Pharmacy*. Paul peered around the corner towards the van. The street behind them was nearly deserted. Two of the masked gunmen ran in his direction, holding their guns, taking aim. Paul jumped back around the corner and laid face down, interlacing his fingers behind his head as they fired a series of rounds at him. The shots hit the corner of the building, chipping off chunks of concrete debris onto Paul's head. Sami grabbed his arm and pulled him up and they started up the street.

A black pickup truck with two gunmen crouching in the box sped past them towards Hadad's men, kicking up a cloud of dust as it fishtailed around the corner. Paul recognized one of them as the moneychanger he had seen moments earlier. He kept running, trying to keep pace with Sami, and heard an exchange of fire *crack-crack-crack* around the corner.

Sami pulled car keys from his pocket and tossed them to Paul. "You drive." He pointed at green SUV parked up ahead.

"Me?" Paul fumbled with the key, trying to keep stride. "What are you going to do?"

Sami reached for his belt, pulled out a handgun and clicked back the chamber. "I'll protect us."

Paul unlocked the SUV and they jumped in. He shifted into gear and floored the gas pedal, spinning the wheels and they tore up the street.

"What the fuck is going on, Sami?"

"I wonder the same thing." Sami was almost completely turned around in the passenger seat, looking through the rear window.

"I just got tortured by these guys," he held up his bandaged hand, "because they wanted you."

"Why did you not tell me you were the one who called me with the manifest?" Sami looked both ways as they raced through an intersection.

"Because," Paul braked hard and swerved avoiding a parked car, "no one's supposed to know! But they found out. How the fuck did they find out? I need some —" He saw the white van approaching in the rear view mirror. "Shit, they're behind us."

Sami looked back. "Go faster." He climbed into the back seat.

They were now several blocks away from *Café Americka* and the streets were again congested with pedestrians. Paul steered the car through the crowds and braked hard to avoid rear-ending the parked cars that seemed to emerge from nowhere in the crowd. He had no idea where they were going, but knew they had to get away from there fast.

Bang! The rear window spider-webbed around the hole of a gunshot. Paul looked in his side mirror. One of the Hadad's gunmen hung out of the van's passenger side window with a gun aimed at them.

"Swerve," Sami turned, "don't let them get the tires."

"Well, you shoot them then." Paul turned the wheel hard at another intersection causing the truck to fishtail, the bumper scraping against the side of a building.

The momentum of the turn sent Sami smashing against the door of the van. He righted himself, took aim through the rear window and fired. Paul startled as he heard the rear window shatter and glanced at the side mirror. The top half of the gunman's body was slumped, hanging out of the window.

"Nice shot." Paul turned.

"Just drive."

Paul looked ahead and slammed on the brakes with enough force that he felt as though he were putting his foot through the floor of the SUV. The momentum threw Sami and wedged him in the space between the driver and passenger seats. It was a dead end. Ahead, the road simply ended in a sea of red umbrella-topped merchant stands. The outdoor market. The SUV shuddered as he kept his foot down on the brake, but the vehicle kept skidding relentlessly forward. Dust from the road and smoke from the brakes rose around the van. He cranked the steering wheel to the right, sending the SUV skidding sideways, but more slowly, until it stopped mere feet from the nearest vegetable stand.

He threw his head back against the headrest and exhaled a relieved sigh. Somehow he had survived.

Then, Paul looked out the open passenger window and saw Hadad's white van drive through the crowd of people thirty feet away. It accelerated; he could hear the engine straining, about to ram the side of the SUV. Paul reacted quickly and shifted the SUV into gear and pressed on the accelerator.

Paul would swear that the gearshift locked on him as the SUV didn't move. At that point, he was only vaguely aware of Sami yelling *go, go, go* because his attention was focused on the imminent collision. The sound of metal scraping against metal was the first thing he noticed. Then, a split second later, the entire passenger side of the SUV bent inwards around the front of Hadad's van, the interior plastic finish cracked and sent splinters flying through the interior. The force sent Paul's head through the driver's side window. He thought he heard screams outside from the crowd.

He turned around and saw Sami pull himself out from between the seats, raise his gun and fire several shots through the window towards the van. Blood ran from Sami's nose, and Paul could tell from the glassy look in his eyes that he had probably hit his head, too.

Paul found the door handle, swung the driver's side door open and hobbled out of the SUV. Sami came out of the rear driver's side door, and fired a few more aimless rounds at the van. Sami held the gun high and pointed it towards the van as he walked carefully around the SUV towards the mangled mass of busted metal on the other side. Paul followed closely behind, limping with each step. Steam and smoke rose up from the van's hood. The engine made a sizzling sound. There was no movement in the van. Sami swung the driver's side door open. The driver's head lay sideways on the steering wheel with streaks of blood running down his face. His eyes darted between Sami and Paul. Sami leaned in and glanced inside.

"Where are the others?" he held the gun to the man's head.

The man lips moved slowly, and he barely managed to form a word: "Gone."

Paul stepped in front of Sami, and pulled the man by the hair, knocking his head back into the headrest. "Hadad," he said through his teeth, "he was with you." Paul kept a firm grip on the fistful of man's hair. Sami kept the gun pointed.

"He suspected," he took a deep breath, "that you told him." He motioned towards Sami with his eyes.

"So where is he now?" Paul commanded.

The man closed his eyes and pursed his lips. Paul slammed his head into the steering wheel. "I'm serious," his face was inches from the man's bloody face, "tell me where he is."

The corners of the man's mouth curled upwards into a wry smile. "The shipyards," his eyes brightened, "to get the weapons."

Paul let go of the driver's head and turned to Sami.

"A distraction?" Paul said. "Why is he going through all this trouble?"

"Because," Sami put a finger in front of Paul's face, "your manifest was wrong."

"What are you talking about? There's weapons on the ship, isn't there?"

"There are weapons," Sami paused, "but not the kind that were on the manifest you gave me."

"What are you talking about?"

"One of the containers has nuclear explosives, small ones, one a man can carry himself."

"That's impossible; something like that would have been on the manifest."

"Unless someone didn't want anyone to know about it."

"You've seen them? The bombs?"

Sami nodded. "All thirteen."

"What did you do with them?"

"They are still at the port. In the container."

"It's guarded?"

Sami nodded. "I have several men guarding it," but then shook his head, "but we may not have enough. We knew that Asabiyaah would try to take them and we had heard they hired Kadar Hadad. So when you called, I came with half of my men, and we planned to take them out here, rather than fight them at the port."

"He's probably there by now. You have to stop him. You have to go to the port."

Sami nodded. "We're short on men, you're coming, too."

Fourteen

The needle passed 80 miles per hour as Paul pressed down on the gas. The low brush on the sides of the highway was nothing more than a blur. The car jarred over each pothole and crack in the crumbling road. The shocks creaked like an old bedspring and gravel clinked in the wheel well. Sami sat in the passenger seat beside him with a knapsack on his lap.

They borrowed the puke green 1985 Mercedes-Benz from a man Sami called uncle. The designation did not provide any real information on the man's relationship to Sami, as 'Uncle' could refer to anyone from one's mother's brother to the grocery store clerk, provided they were older than you. They had abandoned the crumpled SUV at the market and run to the uncle's home two blocks away. He wasn't home, but his car was parked outside, so Sami had shown Paul how to hotwire the Mercedes. *First try to shove a screwdriver into the ignition; if that does not work, open the steering column and connect the red wires*. Method one didn't work, but when they connected the red wires, the car groaned awake. But the car felt like it could stall at any minute.

Paul downshifted as the port came into view ahead of them. Sun glistened off the light blue harbor water. Four story cranes lifted containers off two docked ships and stacked them on the ground. Paul strained to see if one of the ships was the *Stebelsky*, but couldn't make out the names painted on the ships' hulls from his distant vantage. Forklifts beeped as they unloaded crates from inside the containers while dockworkers loaded the crates into canopy trucks. A chain link fence ran along the perimeter. Paul saw no sign of Hadad, no gunshots, no smoke and no carnage. Just business as usual at the port. Maybe Hadad hadn't arrived at the port yet, or maybe he was already gone.

"Turn left up there," Sami pointed at the upcoming intersection. "The ship is at the end dock. Drive slowly."

Paul made the turn and the Benz groaned as it climbed the steep incline towards the far dock. They drove a few minutes up the road, which traversed a ridge lined with palm trees, and was wide enough for only one car. Luckily, Paul realized, there was no traffic on this road. If they came upon another car, one would have to reverse all the way back down. The ridge overlooked the dock several hundred feet below. This area had razor wire running along the top of the fence, a much taller fence than the other dock. Through a clearing in the palm trees, he saw the *Stebelsky*, which looked much smaller from that distance than its true size.

"Stop here," Sami said.

He parked the vehicle and stepped out. A gust of wind slammed the car door closed. Sami stepped to the edge of the ridge and looked at the dock through a pair of binoculars he had removed from the knapsack. Paul stepped right to the edge, spilling a few pieces of gravel over, and looked down. The dock was at least three hundred feet down, he figured. An army-green canopy truck stood idling at the entrance while several figures loaded boxes into it.

"Is that your truck?"

Sami shook his head and said, "Hadad."

"I thought you had men guarding it."

Sami held the binoculars to his eyes for a long time before he turned and handed them to Paul without saying a word.

Paul scanned the docks. Because of the commotion, he couldn't tell how many of Hadad's men were loading the canopy truck, maybe four, but he recognized one of them as Islam. He did not see Hadad. Forklifts were parked, and the cranes seemed dormant. What he saw on the tarmac in between the rows of container caused him to freeze. Six bodies, men in fatigues, lay motionless in the center of pools of blood. Machine guns lay next to them. He put the binoculars down.

He looked at Sami, who stared unflinchingly down at the scene without blinking. An uncomfortable feeling came across Paul as he stared at Sami's sullen face and realized that Sami was going to cry. They were *his* men after all, Paul thought. The man had almost lost his nephew and now had lost at least six men, friends of his.

"I'm sorry about your men," Paul said, and meant it, although he didn't think it came out sincerely.

Sami blinked and then seemed to come back to the moment. The sadness on his face had left, hidden behind a stern and resolute expression. He unzipped his knapsack, removed a handgun and held it out to Paul, handle first.

"No, no," Paul raised his hand. "I don't really know how to use guns."

Sami raised an eyebrow at that. "What kind of CIA agent are you?"

Paul considered for a moment. "A bad one. One who gets his cover blown."

"How did that happen? How did they find you?"

"I don't know. It doesn't make any sense."

"Did you tell anybody about what you do?"

"No one. Not a soul. I've been careful."

Sami slowly shook his head. "If it wasn't you, then it was somebody else."

Paul heard what Sami said, but didn't absorb it. Instead, he looked down at the truck idling at the entrance to the dock. Hadad's men. "We have to get down there before they take off."

Over the ridge was a dropoff of about ten feet or so, at the bottom of which a steep hill led down to the dock. To call it a rocky hillside would be an understatement; the entire surface of the hill was bare, composed of soft white rock and gravel. It was as if the entire dockyard had been dynamited out of the rock. "We have to find a way to get to them."

Sami pointed down, over the ridge.

"What?" Paul said. "They'll shoot us halfway down. There's no cover."

"Do you have a better idea?" Sami grabbed Paul's hand and slapped the gun into his palm. "You point it and then pull the trigger. You don't have to shoot anyone, just shoot *at* them. I will do the rest."

Paul hesitated and stared at the gun in his hand. He had only used a gun in basic military training on a handful of occasions. And that was enough to teach him that he was a lousy shot.

He glanced at Sami, who still looked down at the docks. "Why are you doing this?" That caused Sami to look at him and cock his head to the side asking for clarification, "Trying to stop them. You don't need to. I mean, they're leaving most of the cargo; you can still sell it, make money. No sense risking your life."

Sami looked at Paul and spoke gently, but unwavering, "I do not need money. I have more than I will ever need. I used to think if I had enough, I would be able to live with my family in peace. But you cannot buy peace and security. Not in this place. Not in a place where people like this, like the Asabiyyah and Kadar Hadad promise the people peace but only bring chaos. I've sold the cargo we hijack to the authorities here, at a very low price, hoping it will make a difference by improving security forces, police forces, but it doesn't. There's too much corruption. I even thought to leave, to take my family and move to another country. But where? This is my place. And I am not a coward, I do not run. So I think maybe I can do something to make it better, if not for me than maybe for my family. And now these men may have a nuclear weapon. So if I can help stop them, then I will."

Paul opened his mouth to say *who's to say you can stop them*, but before anything came out, Sami removed the gun from his belt holster, turned and without the slightest hesitation jumped over the ridge.

It crossed his mind to turn around and hop in the car, drive home and sleep. Pretend that it was all a bad dream. It wasn't his job, after all, was it? Could he even stop them? But Sami's gently delivered words stung deeply: *I am (not) a coward.* His chest felt heavy. But Paul pushed it down, and the impulse to jump overtook his body and by the time he recognized what he was doing, he was already over the edge.

He landed ten feet below on the steep slope. His feet dug in deep into the gravel and it spilled around them like a waterfall. He tried to shift his weight onto his back, but the momentum from the fall carried him forward and he tumbled into a somersault. He focused his concentration on not letting the gun slip out of his hand. As he came out of a full somersault, he dug his heels ankle deep into the fine pebbles and leaned back, dragging his hands through the gravel. He slowed to a stop. The burning from the abrasions in his hands and elbows started to set in. A cloud of dust settled around him, and he could feel grains of sand on his tongue.

He looked ahead and saw Sami already halfway down to the base of the slope, traversing the decline by skillfully slaloming side-to-side. The knapsack strapped to his back and the handgun he held outstretched didn't seem to put him off balance one bit.

Paul scrambled to his feet and followed in the same way, trying desperately to keep up. He hit a rhythm, bounding side-to-side, using gravity to go faster than he thought possible. A strange sense of exhilaration coursed through him and he thought he could now understand why people jumped out of airplanes. Then, his right foot caught a large rock and again sent him tumbling head over feet again, but with more torque. His face smacked and then sunk into the gravel before his whole frame flipped him back upright. He stretched his arms out wide, begging for traction to slow his fall but the momentum made him fall faster.

Uncontrollably fast.

But he did stop. Halfway down the slope, he crashed into a boulder that jutted out from the hill. His chest absorbed the full impact of the collision. He tried to right himself, dizzy from the fall, and looked down. The gunmen had seen his fall and taken cover around the truck. They took aim with their machine guns. Paul crouched behind the boulder and reached in his belt for the gun but only felt air.

He'd lost his gun in the fall.

Crack-crack-crack!

Paul kept his back to the boulder as a series of gunshots ricocheted around him, making a thud as they penetrated the hill's gravel surface. Then he heard more shots, and looked to his left, where Sami was firing back at them from behind another boulder about forty feet away.

A bright light shined into Paul's eye and he recognized it as the sun's reflection off the metal surface of his handgun. Ten feet over, in the open, his gun was embedded in the gravel. He slowly raised his head to look at the men down below. Three gunmen exchanged fire with Sami, and seemed to have temporarily forgotten about him. Paul leaned back against the boulder and took several deep breaths and then lunged out towards the gun.

Crack-crack-crack!

Gunfire sent dust flying all around him and he grabbed the gun's handle, turned back and dove behind the boulder again. He glanced at Sami who made a motion, first pointing at Paul and then at the gunmen down below.

Paul poked out from behind the boulder and fired two shots in the direction of the truck. He had no idea where they landed, as he recoiled when the gunmen returned fire almost instantly. He saw Sami fire several shots and then heard two groans down below. Paul looked out and saw two gunmen face down.

Paul fired two more rounds at the truck. But this time there was no exchange. All of a sudden, it felt quiet. A gust of wind sent dust flying into Paul's eyes. Then, he heard the truck engine gear up and he looked up and saw it moving out of the fenced off area and onto the road. He fired at the truck again but it started up the road and out of sight. Then, *Bang! Bang!*

Those shots sounded different, louder, closer. He realized they came from above. Paul swiveled around and as he did so he caught the image of Sami collapsing backwards onto the boulder he had been using for cover. His back arched over the rock and he fell, making only the slightest thud. Paul looked up at the ridge and saw one of the gunmen holding an outstretched gun pointed at Sami.

Paul stood up and ran towards the gunman, holding the gun up and taking aim. He held the trigger as he ran towards him, firing ten rounds before the man was able to turn. Two of them hit the mark, and he collapsed.

Paul tossed his gun and ran to Sami. He picked him up from the rock and cradled him in his arms. All he needed was the one-second it took to look into Sami's vacant eyes to know he was dead. But Paul still checked for a pulse, and did one set of twenty chest compressions. With each pump, he prayed that Sami's eyes would open again.

Paul leaned back, fell onto his backside and stared at Sami's body. The whole world seemed to slowly fade into darkness around him, so that only he was left, sitting on that hill. He placed the heel of his hands on his temples and pressed.

Fifteen

Stuttgart, Germany

Major General Robert Kaczmareck kept talking on his cell phone even though the black limousine had stopped at the destination in downtown Stuttgart five minutes earlier. Rows of cars honked as they passed by the illegally parked limo, which effectively narrowed the congested street from four lanes to three. The driver grew impatient, rolled down the window divider and gave a polite nod, to which the general responded by pressing the button that rolled the divider back up.

"So it's been taken, good." He put the phone to his chest, leaned forward, knocked on the divider and motioned for the driver to open his door for him. He put the phone to his ear. "Now listen, do not call me on this number again."

He turned the phone off, stepped out of the open door and walked right past the driver, without so much as a nod of acknowledgment. He adjusted the lapels on his olive green military suit, which was specially tailored to make his round frame appear more of a "V." He adjusted the four rows of ribbons above his breast pocket and checked the alignment of his medals. He looked at his watch and realized he hadn't adjusted it to Stuttgart time, which meant that he was late.

General Kaczmareck entered the main doors of the half-moon shaped skyscraper that housed the centre of the United States Africa Command Centre, or AFRICOM as someone had mercifully shortened it. The interior was just as grand as the outside. Daylight shone through the tall glass façade, reflecting off the gray-blue granite floors and walls. He stopped at the security desk, checked in, emptied his pockets and walked through the metal detectors to the elevators.

He went up to the fourth floor. AFRICOM spanned floors four through seven, but the important meetings happened in the fourth floor boardroom. The monthly meetings brought together the leaders of various task forces and humanitarian organizations to coordinate U.S. efforts on the continent. This was where the United States Department of Defense made decisions regarding operations in Africa. Usually wrong decisions, as far as Kaczmareck was concerned.

Two years ago, he was appointed to run the Combined Joint Task Force - Horn of Africa division. He was an ideal candidate for the position; decorated, confident and had experience on the ground level in the Horn. He was a commander in ninety-three in Mogadishu, and received a bronze cross for his work there, but he never wore it. The mission was a failure in his mind.

He had watched in the news Somalia destroy itself for a decade, but his appointment to the Task Force presented his chance to effect change. Two years into the job, the only changes he saw were ones for the worse. Al-Qaeda had made inroads to all countries in the Horn, especially Somalia. Their influence stretched through most of the terrorist groups who had taken over half of the devastated country, including the capital. One movement in particular, the Asabiyaah, was most troubling. He pleaded with the department of defense, the defense secretary and anyone who would listen that ground forces were needed to stop the spread of radicals, but no changes were made. The reason? Opinion polls. *Americans still remember what happened in Mogadishu and would never support an invasion,* the Secretary of Defense told him. Her solution? Support internal resistances within the country, the warlords they had previously fought against. *Short-sighted*, he thought. *Don't they even remember what happened in Afghanistan in the eighties*?

The general opened the doors to the boardroom and walked inside. A dozen senior members of AFRICOM sat around a long impressive table. Three wore formal military attire, the rest were in black and navy suits. At the head of the table, a large screen projected the face of the Defense Secretary, Janet Carter. Neither she, nor the rest of the talking heads at the table, who had all turned as soon as they heard the door slam behind him, seemed pleased to see him. He gave a quick nod and moved towards the only empty chair.

"General, so glad you could join us," Secretary Carter said.

"Glad to be here, Madam Secretary." He sat down in his chair and leaned back.

He picked at his nails as she continued on the topic she had been on before he had sauntered in. It was the same old thing: Sudan's humanitarian crisis, Sierra Leone's rebuilding and droughts in Ethiopia. The politicians (the ones that wore suits) around the table said the occasional, well-rehearsed line about working with local governments to develop new water sources, schools and to establish programs to remove landmines. Everyone talked about the *progress* they had been making and they reframed failures with the standard *we're still working towards [blank]...*

"Major General Kaczmareck," the Defense Secretary spoke. "I didn't receive your written report."

He awoke from his daze. "Sorry about that, but I didn't think there was much need for a new one as there's been no changes. But if everyone takes a look at last month's, you'll be up to date."

Nervous laughter spread through a few of the people around the table. They managed to bottle up their giggles when they saw that Secretary Carter's face, several times normal human size on the projected screen, stayed serious. Kaczmareck leaned back in his chair and flashed a wry smirk and a wink at the projection. He swore he saw her right eyelid twitch slightly before she continued.

"What is our progress in Somalia?"

"Well, I'd have to say there isn't any *progress*. But what I can confidently say is that in many areas we've *regressed*."

"Such as?"

"Two roadside bombs three weeks ago with forty-four dead. Ongoing fighting on the Ethiopian border. People are starving to death and estimates indicate that less than five percent of aid is getting to the intended recipients. Radical militias have control of eighty percent of Mogadishu and have taken over four towns in the southwest portion of the Puntland region." He crossed his arms, "and people are welcoming them with open arms."

"So what is our…"

"I'm not done," he leaned forward and raised his voice. "Piracy is at its worst. The Gulf of Aden is one of the busiest commercial waterways in the world, and pirates operate freely. And if you haven't heard already, another ship was captured yesterday."

The Secretary leaned back in her chair and exhaled. "I've heard about the ship. It was a weapons transfer. But I've heard that the weapons are at the port in Bosasso in the hands of the governing body there."

"You mean the warlords."

"They are the governing body right now. And they are fighting the radicals. So for now, they are on our side."

"For now," he said, "but they weren't a year ago and they certainly won't be five years from now, either."

"What are you suggesting, General?"

"The same thing I always do. We need ground forces, American ground forces to go in and stabilize this region. I have drawn up plans and would need less than fifteen hundred troops to —"

"That is just not possible," her voice went up a little.

"Of course not," Kaczmareck shook his head and flicked his hand in the air. He put his hand to his face and chuckled. He glanced around the room. The suits sat like wooden mannequins, avoiding any gesture that could be construed as agreement.

"We are involved in two large and very unpopular wars right now, General, and while I can see that the conditions in Somalia are far from ideal, we have to concern ourselves with real, concrete and immediate threats."

"What does that take?" he gritted his teeth, "a group of Somalis crashing a plane into a skyscraper? Is that when this government will act? I'm sorry, Janet, but a reactionary military will never keep our country safe."

"We do not have time for these kinds of discussions, Bob. We do not have the resources, nor for that matter do we have due cause to risk American lives to engage in a battle on another front."

"It's a hotbed for terrorists. If we do not act now, we *are* risking innocent American lives."

The Secretary shook her head; Kaczmareck knew he was getting to her. They had butted heads on more than one occasion. He knew she was doing what she thought was right, but she was a politician. She had never worked on the ground, looked in the opponent's eyes and seen their determination. She didn't know what it took to win a war. And this was war.

"People still remember Mogadishu," she continued. Kaczmareck rolled his eyes. *Here it comes*, he thought. "No one will support a deployment there."

"So we're letting the media and opinion polls dictate our foreign policy now? Your government was elected to make the tough decisions."

"I am making a tough decision, General," she softened her tone, "staying out of Somalia is a tough decision because with adequate resources and positive public opinion we could make a difference. But the reality is that we can't. Not now."

Kaczmareck sulked in his chair, pulled a handkerchief from his pocket and wiped his glasses. "Maybe one day," he smiled as though he was daydreaming, "when a threat is more imminent."

Sixteen

Paul drove the Benz back to the clinic. The line-up looped around the building as usual. He only noticed a few casual glances from patients sitting up in their beds as he walked in. The clinic workers all seemed preoccupied. He saw Ellen sitting alone at a desk at the back of the auditorium past the surgical stations and walked towards her.

"I have nothing to say to you."

Ellen didn't look up at Paul. She kept writing in a patient chart. She pressed the pen down on the paper hard enough to make the tips of her fingers white. Dark circles had formed under her eyes and her hair was pulled back. She only pulled it back when she was exhausted. Perhaps from waiting for him overnight. Worried.

"Okay, you don't have to say anything, just listen for a second."

But Ellen didn't listen. There was no trace of the worry that Paul had assumed had kept her up to the early hours of the morning. No, she was angry, incensed. "Listen to what, Paul?" her voice rose to a volume that Paul hadn't heard before. A level that caused the elderly man in the bed fifteen feet away to startle. "Listen to another one of your excuses? Your bullshit?"

"Ellen—"

"There's nothing to say." She still didn't look up. "While you were out getting high, or, or shooting up or whatever, I was here. Managing this clinic, by myself," her voice trembled, "You didn't call, you didn't leave a note, nothing. We had a deal, Paul. That was your last chance and now that's it, it's over. But let's face it, it's been over for awhile."

Paul stood still while her words sunk in. He often wondered what kept her with him for so long. He assumed it was companionship. Living in a place so far from home, maybe he provided her with a certain familiarity and comfort level. Why else would a young, beautiful woman with an insatiable wanderlust get involved with a graying middle-aged man who was stuck in a place like this? He half suspected that she had been waiting to have an excuse to end their relationship. And he just handed it to her.

But Hadad would almost certainly come looking for him. And they would come across her. She was involved by proxy. Letting her stay was letting her die.

"We have to leave now," he said, steady and commanding.

"No, we don't," she said and slammed the pen on the desk. She looked up at him and her eyes initially glowered, but that was displaced by a look of bewilderment when she took in his image. "Jesus, what happened to you?"

Paul looked down and saw what caused Ellen's mouth to hang open. Raw, weeping scrapes ran up both of his forearms and stung when the sleeves of his tee-shirt rubbed against them. His light colored vest was now a patchwork of well-worked-in grime and dark bloodstains, Sami's blood. Stiff dried blood clung to his upper lip. His bandaged hand throbbed more than his nose did and blood had soaked through the bandage.

He stared at her, not sure of what to say. Not sure of where to begin.

"I'll explain later," came out, and he turned and started walking up the hallway towards the door.

"No," she stood up but didn't move from her spot behind the desk, "you explain it now, I deserve that much."

"Yesterday morning I was kidnapped. Kidnapped and then interrogated." Paul put a hand on her arm. "They tortured me, Ellen, but I escaped. But they're going to come looking for me, and they'll probably come looking for you, too. And it's only a matter of time before they come looking for me here, so we have to leave now."

Tears streamed down her cheeks and she trembled as she wiped them away with her fingers. "I'm so sorry. I, I didn't know. I thought you were off—"

"It's okay. Let's go."

Ellen took his hand and they walked quickly out of the clinic. He pointed at the Mercedes and they got in. Ellen buckled her seatbelt and took deep breaths while tears continued to flow. She noticed the gun lying on the dashboard and that caused her to stop sobbing momentarily and stare questioningly at Paul.

"Paul, what's happening?" her lip quivered. "Who are you running from?"

"People from Asabiyaah, they're the ones who kidnapped me."

"Why did they kidnap you?"

He thought to lie. He imagined taking time to formulate an eloquent, well-delivered fabrication. Tell her they wanted him for ransom. He had lied to her about who he was hundreds of times and it was easy. A gift, a talent.

But it all seemed forced now. The lies that used to flow so naturally had suddenly dried up. The charade had ended hours ago and even then it was well overdue. He sighed. "Because they thought I'm a spy."

"Are you?" Ellen said. If Paul hadn't been preoccupied thinking about the flood of follow-up questions that the discussion would inevitably lead to and if his chest didn't feel constricted, he would have found it strange how quickly Ellen asked that question, in that way.

Paul took a deep breath. "Yes."

Ellen looked at Paul with a combination of shock and disdain and then she turned her head and stared out the window. In the reflection, he saw the wound his admission had opened. She didn't look at him. They were strangers now, weren't they? All the moments they had shared, the times they had camped seaside, the grief she shared with him when her mother died of a sudden heart attack, the heated political debates they had over tea, had been tainted. She had shared them with a stranger.

But she had known that in some way, hadn't she? Ellen had complained that he was shut down, that he never let her into his world. She wanted to know more about him, about his childhood, about his parents, but he knew he could never tell her. It was his duty. It was his burden.

Maybe on some level, even when their love blossomed, she knew the relationship was doomed. Maybe the best solution was for Paul to let her walk out. But his secrets and his past now threatened her. Because of him, her life was in danger. *Just get her to safety*, he thought, *then let her walk out on you.*

Paul spoke. Initially the words formed slowly but then flowed freely. "You need to hear this, Ellen. I know this is painful for you, but you need to hear it. And it's not an excuse but it is an explanation. I've tried to keep it from you, but there's no use now. I'm a U.S. government operative. I've worked in Bosasso for the past ten years doing that. The work I do is mainly information sharing between the U.S. government and various organizations in the Puntland. Lately, a lot of it has been feeding shipping information to pirates. They do this so U.S. friendly security forces here that fight terrorist groups like the Asabiyaah can use the ransom money or cargo. I wasn't able to tell you because I'm sworn to secrecy. But everything's changed. The last ship I gave the pirates information on was one carrying weapons from the Ukraine. They hijacked it two days ago and they docked it and unloaded it. But they found something I had no idea was on it, and I don't think that anyone knew about it in the U.S. either. Ellen, there were nuclear weapons on the ship and the Asabiyaah have stolen them and I don't know where they've taken them."

Ellen didn't flinch at what he told her. She closed her eyes and inhaled deeply through her nose. Paul looked at her, waiting for her eyes to open and look at him again.

But she didn't. She kept staring out the window, pain etched on her face.

"My real name is Marshall," Paul continued, guessing that Ellen was hoping for more. The words flowed out, like an abscess that had been opened. "Ten years ago, I was working a case searching for the Nairobi embassy bombers. We found the prime suspect. His name was Kadar Hadad. We interrogated him for a long time and my role was to monitor his health through the interrogation. I watched as they used all sorts of techniques to get him to talk," Paul paused for a moment and then nodded. "We basically went too far. Word got out and next thing we knew, we're under investigation for prisoner abuse. And the authorities let Hadad go. So I did what I thought I had to do. I confessed, in exchange for getting the charges dropped. They used my confession to convict the others, but I thought it was worth it since they were the main interrogators anyway. But I had to do it, this Hadad, he's well connected and he, or someone connected to him, would find me. In exchange for the confession and the testimony, we faked my death and I moved here to a new post. I still get to be a doctor, help people. I had to do it, though. Ellen, I had a family. A wife and six-year-old son. If Hadad thought I was alive, they would have done anything to get to me, including hurt them. I had to do it. But now, Hadad is back. He's the one who interrogated me. Somehow he found out that I'm here in Somalia and he found me. And now he's stolen nuclear weapons. I have to find a way to stop him."

Ellen turned and Paul felt a sudden distance develop between them, a chasm. It struck him that this distance had always been there, but now Ellen was made aware of it. She didn't look at him, but through him. Her eyes had dried, but the sparkle that had lived there had faded. They were partners now, nothing more. If she opened the car door and left, Asabiyaah would undoubtedly pick her up. And she had nowhere to run.

"So what do we have to do?"

Paul turned the ignition. "There's another agent in Garowe who I work with. You see, when they send me information about a ship, it's an encrypted document. Then he'll send me the decryption code. Only he can send it to me because the SIM card on my cell phone only recognizes his phone's signature. So the only documents I receive can be ones sent from the agency."

"Why would they want you to give nuclear weapons to pirates?" Ellen shook her head.

"I don't know, but I have to find out."

"Can you call someone, let them know?"

"He's the only person I have direct contact with in the whole agency, so we have to go meet him."

Seventeen

"So let me get this straight," Agent James Wright said. "There were nuclear weapons aboard the ship?"

Paul nodded, tapped a cigarette out of the box and placed it in his mouth.

"No smoking in here," James smiled, masking an irritation below the surface, "Agency policy."

Paul placed the cigarette down on the glass table and looked up at James, who poured a glass of mineral water for himself and sipped loudly. Ellen sat across from him fixated on her interlaced fingers resting on the table. During the whole two-hour car ride from Bosasso to Garowe, Paul felt a massive pressure to make things right. To explain himself. But he couldn't do it. Every time he had the impulse to speak, his tongue bound up and his throat felt constricted. Instead they rode in silence, under constant tension.

Before they entered Wright's fourth floor apartment three blocks from the presidential palace, a fair-skinned guard wearing an ugly tan Hawaiian shirt searched through their bags, frisked them and took away Paul's gun. Two other guards stood outside. At first glance, the place seemed like a standard two bedroom flat with next to no décor, but James explained its safety features. Three layers of insulation within the concrete walls made the apartment soundproof, a steel insert in the wooden door and a keypad entry lock decreased the chance of break-ins and the windows were bulletproof. The west-facing windows provided a fabulous view of the city and overlooked the apartment complex's charming garden terrace three floors down, where rows of planters encircled a small swimming pool.

James stood six foot six with sparse graying hair and he was balder than Paul recalled. In Paul's experience, people of that size usually fit into the category of gentle giants but after their initial meeting, he decided that James Wright was a self-important prick. James, an environmental engineer by trade, came to work in the Puntland two years earlier as a governmental advisor on resource management. His covert job was to collect intelligence on government dealings and to liaise with other field operatives. James had had similar assignments for the agency in Sri Lanka and Indonesia. Shortly after arriving at his new post in Garowe, he made the trip to Bosasso to meet with a clan elder to discuss instituting new technology for treating contaminated groundwater. Afterwards, he had dinner with Paul to discuss what he referred to as 'ground rules' for communication. *First off,* he began after they exchanged initial pleasantries, *you don't contact me by phone under any circumstances, communication only goes one way: from me to you.* Even after Paul nodded his understanding James continued, *I'm serious about that, I don't know you from Adam so I can't trust that you keep your phone lines secure. Last thing I need is a cowboy blowing my cover.*

But Paul didn't really care about that anymore. The fact was that thirteen nuclear bombs were in the hands of terrorists. Certainly, James hadn't expected a crisis like that to arise when he was busy reading Paul the riot act. And Paul didn't have direct connection with Langley but James did. This was employed to keep more than one degree of separation between the National Clandestine Service and their field operatives should an operative be discovered. James openly worked as a government official and so he had ongoing contact with Langley.

James sat down cross-legged at the table and stroked his chin. "And the weapons are now in the hands of Asabiyaah."

"That's right."

"How do we know this?"

"What?"

"That they have the weapons."

"I saw them take them," Paul said. "They tried to kill me when I was there. And they killed my contact, shot him point blank."

Paul glanced at Ellen who had remained motionless the whole time. He thought it was odd that she did not react at all.

"Where were they going?" James continued.

"I don't know, they don't brief me."

"So you don't know. Any idea?"

Paul shook his head.

James rubbed his cheek, scratching his stubble with his palm. "So our manifest was wrong. That means that the intel on the ship was bogus, whoever gave it to Langley in the first place."

"Or someone could have put them on the ship unofficially."

"No, nuclear weapons are always flagged. Our intel was bad."

"I thought that all information coming to me is verified."

"Should be."

"Well, you texted me the decryption code. That's not supposed to come through until the information is verified."

"Yeah, you're right," James said, with a slight hesitation and then abruptly stood and walked over to the window, swirling the glass of water in his hand, "it was verified."

Whenever case officers gathered intelligence, they sent it back to the agency, where analysts would verify the information. The most common way was through a process called triangulation, where analysts would utilize algorithms to check the accuracy of the data against known information related to the intelligence topic. Only after data was triangulated within an acceptable margin of error was it then verified and disseminated to field operatives.

"You have to call Langley," Paul pushed his chair back and met James by the window. "We know that there's thirteen missing nuclear warheads and we know where they were less than five hours ago. This is our best chance to get them."

James stared at Paul blankly, not reacting.

"The United States gave information to pirates about a ship which led to nuclear weapons getting in the hands of terrorists," Paul pointed his finger in James' face. "If they trace it back to us, it'll be an international incident."

"Well," James took a sip of water and raised his eyebrows, "officially *you* gave the information to the pirates."

Paul pressed his forehead against the window and looked down at the swimming pool below. James was right. Paul was an unofficial covert operative; if anything were traced back to him, the United States would deny any relationship to him. He, too, was supposed to deny any affiliation to the United States government.

"Call them," Paul said.

"Okay, okay." James uncrossed his arms, removed a cell phone from his pocket and held it up. "I'll take this in the other room."

Once James left, Ellen got up slowly and walked up to Paul beside the window. She put one hand gently on his shoulder and the other on his hand. He turned and faced her. He saw tears forming in her eyes and she bit her lower lip.

"Paul," her voice was barely a whisper, "I need to confess something."

Eighteen

Bailey Clarke's desk phone rang, snapping her out of her daze. She sat in her cubicle on the chair that squeaked every time she moved, hovering over stacks of intelligence printouts related to shipping in the Gulf of Aden. Paul Alban's file rested beside leftover crusts from a tuna salad sandwich and a browning apple core. She had been through the documents a dozen times but couldn't connect the dots. She had left eight phone messages with security officials in Somalia and Ethiopia that could potentially have information on the *Stebelsky*. Crilley's instructions had seemed straightforward enough, *figure out what's going on with that ship*, but she was ready to give up. She hadn't moved in six hours. She couldn't move and she couldn't go back to Crilley empty handed. In her daze, she daydreamed. She was eleven, standing on the front steps of her parents' colonial with Sherri Banks, the best jacks player at Piedmont Elementary. Sherri was on foursies and scooped the jacks up, did a standing pirouette and still managed to catch the ball. Then the front door flew open and Bailey turned her head and saw her father holding her spelling test with the letter C scrawled across it in red. Before she could react, he had her by the hand and dragged her into her bedroom. He pushed her down into the chair, and slapped the test on the desk in front of her. *Little girls who can't spell 'knowledge' can't play games either*. She could still smell the Johnny Walker on his breath. But she sat there, sat there all night, until she wrote the word one thousand times like he instructed. Even when he passed out on the bed, she kept going. She thought of how her eyelids had started to feel like they were sticking together.

That was when the phone rang and she jumped in her chair. She fumbled with the phone a little bit but she managed to get the receiver to her ear.

It was the NCS operator. "An Agent Wright is on the line asking for James Crilley. He says it is an urgent matter."

Bailey's eyes widened and she suddenly felt awake. She recognized the name from Paul Alban's file. "Transfer him to Crilley's office."

She snatched Paul Alban's file from the desk, knocking a half empty bottle of water onto the floor, turned and ran as fast as she could in heels to Crilley's office. She didn't bother knocking this time and walked right in. Crilley looked up from his desk, startled. He had his feet up on the desk, reading from a folder perched on his belly. Before he could say anything, Bailey sputtered out, "James Wright from Somalia is being patched through to your line right now."

Then the phone rang and Crilley lifted himself out of the chair and motioned for Bailey to sit. "You can take this one. Part of the training."

Bailey placed Paul's file down, walked apprehensively to the chair and sat down. Her heart galloped. She had no idea what to say. She looked at the phone in the cradle for another two rings and then slowly pressed the button for speakerphone. By the time Wright's voice came through, her palms were clammy. She turned her head to find Crilley's intense gaze looking down at her as he paced behind the desk.

"You're online, Agent Wright." Bailey leaned over the speaker.

"Hello," his voice came in through static, "I have something urgent here."

"Tell me you know something about this Ukranian ship," Crilley jumped right in, leaning over Bailey's shoulder.

"I do. It's docked at the port in Bosasso and the cargo has been unloaded."

"What was on the ship?"

"Military weapons."

"Shit," Crilley slapped his hands together and continued pacing.

"But sir, there's more to it," James said, "there were nuclear weapons aboard." Bailey snapped her head around and exchanged glances with Crilley. "What did you just say?" came out reflexively.

"Man portable nuclear warheads."

"And where are they now?"

"That's the thing. They've been taken by members of Assabiyaah." Then a whoosh sound came through on the speaker and Bailey couldn't tell whether they lost the line or Wright was letting out a massive sigh. "I don't know where they are right now."

No one said anything. Crilley stood still with his arms crossed. Bailey chewed her fingernails. She knew what this meant. Her mind was already doing the calculations. Man portable nuclear weapons exploded with the power of one kiloton of TNT. A single blast could wipe out a radius of four city blocks leaving a hundred foot deep crater. The number of casualties depended on how many people lived in those four city blocks. Ten thousand roughly? And a detonator could be fashioned by an engineering school dropout. The possibility of a nuclear blast on U.S. soil had been giving homeland security officials cold sweats ever since a 1999 *Frontline* investigation reported that Russian General Alexander Lebed admitted that one of his assignments was to track down 132 missing suitcase-sized nuclear weapons the Soviet Union had manufactured in the eighties. He only found 48. Although a few Soviet officials supported his claims, most discredited them. The Russian Atomic Energy minister assured the United States that *all these devices are registered and it is impossible for them to find their way into terrorists' hands*. But in intelligence circles, *possibility* never entered the equation, as anything was possible. Probability meant something. Following the controversy, a confidential CIA report stated, *while it is very likely that the former Soviet Republics have man portable nuclear weapons, the likelihood of them falling into possession of hostile groups is low.* The facts now stared them in the face. The likelihood of them being in the hands of terrorists? 100%.

"H-ow did these weapons get on the ship?" Bailey pushed her hair out of her eyes.

"I have no idea."

"What about our man in Somalia," Crilley broke out of his trance, "have you had contact with him?"

"I have," James said, "he's here with me right now."

"How did you find him?"

"He found me, sir. And he's here with a woman. I think she's his girlfriend."

Bailey and Crilley exchanged glances again.

Crilley motioned for Bailey to speak. She cleared her throat. "Is he aware of what happened there?"

"You could say that."

"No need for cryptic remarks, Mr. Wright," Crilley said authoritatively. "What did he say?"

"He said he gave them the manifest."

"What?"

"I don't know how this happened, but he definitely gave the manifest to the pirates and he saw Assabiyaah take the warheads from the ship."

"How is that possible?" Bailey shook her head in disbelief. "Where did he get the manifest?"

"That's the thing. He thinks it came from us."

"What? Like the same channels?"

"That's what he says. He says he downloaded the manifest after he received the decryption code, which he thinks I sent him."

"How did he react when you told him that we didn't send it?"

"Well, I just didn't tell him anything."

Crilley stepped forward and pulled at his belt, lifting his pants up a bit. "How do we know that's how he got the manifest? Is there any proof?"

Fine static on the other end. No whoosh sound this time, just static. Bailey turned her head to the side and pursed her lips. A rush of cold swept down her neck. She hadn't considered this possibility. And it seemed Wright hadn't either. But it wasn't perplexity that she felt. She felt something, something heavy enter the room and slowly expand. Suddenly everything felt tight, swollen.

"There's no proof," James said, "but I mean, why would he come find me and tell me all this if it wasn't true?"

"I don't know," Crilley said, his voice rising, "to save his own skin? Maybe he sold the manifest to the pirates, the whole thing got botched somehow, and now he wants us to fix his mess."

"Or maybe" Bailey looked at Crilley incredulously, "he's been set up."

Crilley chuckled. "There's checks and balances for that. The only person who can send Alban the decryption code is Wright. And he didn't send it. So what's more likely? That this guy, Alban, who we know can be a manipulative son of a bitch, is trying to play us, or that the National Clandestine Service has been compromised by some sort of conspiracy that bypassed three different security measures?"

Bailey wanted to say something. She wanted to argue. But when she looked up at Crilley, who glared at her with eyes alight like fiery coals, she felt bound up. All the anger she felt at his assumption that Paul Alban somehow set this up quickly hid behind the shadow of fear. In spite of the convenience of Crilley's explanation, she just didn't believe it. If Paul Alban was smart enough to sell nuclear weapons to terrorists, why would he then walk into Wright's apartment and admit to it all? But Bailey turned away and sunk in her chair a couple of inches. She got back to chewing on her fingernail.

"So how do we figure this out?" James finally came through on the speakerphone.

"What is there to figure out?" Crilley snapped. "We know he gave them the manifest, he's contacted you so now he's connected with the United States government. It's time we nip this in the bud."

Whatever she had felt swelling in the room had just burst. The words struck her like a spray of ice water. She watched Crilley lumber around the table, but everything suddenly seemed slowed down. Yet, she could not stop it. She swore she saw the corners of his mouth curl up a little below his moustache. *Is he smirking?*

"Sir?" James Wright asked.

"It's an order, Wright," Crilley said, "he doesn't leave alive. And neither does the girl."

Nineteen

While James Wright ended his call with Bailey Clarke and Jim Crilley, Paul stood by the window overlooking the terrace and swimming pool holding Ellen's hand. She squeezed his hand so tight that a shot of pain went up to his elbow. Tears tracked down her ashen face and dripped onto her lips. She had twice opened her mouth to speak but nothing came out. Paul's initial thought was that she was afraid. Afraid because her life was in danger. But then he noticed a flicker of fear in her eyes. She lowered her head submissively and her hair fell over her nose and mouth. She had said she needed to confess something. Then he realized that she was indeed afraid—of him.

"What's wrong, Ellen?"

She took a deep stuttering breath and licked the tears on her bottom lip. "You have to leave."

"What?"

"You have to leave now." She let go of his hand and touched his chest with the pads of her fingers, "It's not safe here."

"Listen," Paul reached for her hand but she withdrew it, "it's not safe in Bosasso. But these people will help us. We'll get through this."

"They're not going to help you, Paul," she shook her head, "he's lying to you."

"What are you talking about? Who's lying to me?"

"James, he didn't give you the code."

"Yes, he did," Paul corrected her.

Ellen kept shaking her head, and took two steps backwards. Her jaw quivered and she put her hand to her mouth as if to stop it. She spoke through her fingers, "He didn't, Paul. I know he didn't. He's lying."

Her face crumpled together and she wept. Paul felt confused and suspicious at the same time and he had the urge to take her by the shoulders and shake her and scream *tell me what the fuck is going on here!* Instead, he reached out, placed a hand around her waist and the other behind her head, and gently pulled her face to his chest. Her sobbing slowed down. Her face felt warm on his skin. He closed his eyes.

Suddenly, she threw her arms up and broke from his embrace. She put her hands to her temples and shook her head. The fear in her eyes returned.

"What is going on here, Ellen?" Paul raised an eyebrow.

"I'm sorry, I'm so sorry…" Her voice trailed off.

"Ellen," Paul's voice rose, "speak to me."

"James couldn't've sent you the decryption code."

"No one else could," Paul said. "I explained that to you."

"I know, but I know it wasn't him," she pressed her lips together, "because I switched the SIM card on your phone."

Paul didn't say anything. He stared.

"Two months ago, I was at the market and this man came up to me at *Café Americka.* He said he was from INTERPOL, he showed me his badge. He told me you were aiding terrorists, that you were involved in weapons transfers. He said they were trying to catch you for years, but couldn't get enough evidence. He had pictures, Paul, he showed them to me. Pictures of kids blown up, with no legs. Pictures of militias transferring weapons across borders. He said you were involved. I couldn't believe it." Ellen put her hand over her mouth. "But then I followed you one day, and I saw you go to the library and I thought that was strange, because you never go to the library. And I saw you put some papers in a book. When you left, I opened it and I saw it was a shipping manifest. Then I started believing him. And I just couldn't live with myself, thinking you caused those people to die. He said he wanted to set you up by giving you fake information and gave me a SIM card to put in your phone. I told them I would ask you about it, confront you, but he said you would probably kill me if I did. I was so scared —" her voice broke off and she crouched down on the floor. "I didn't know you were working for the CIA."

For the decade that he lived the lies of Paul Alban, he never once considered that someone he trusted, someone he loved so much could lie to him. His mind reeled. He had always loved her sincerity, her honesty. But did it even exist? Could love that was built on a foundation contaminated by secrets and betrayal exist? He looked down at Ellen on the floor and realized she wasn't simply crouching but cowering. Her entire body trembled and she held her arms rigidly by her side as though she expected retribution for a sin. But he didn't feel anger or rage. He felt weak, like all strength had been sucked out of his muscles.

He pressed his palm on his sweaty forehead to try and slow his mind's spinning. He tried to process what she had just said. "So James didn't know about the manifest."

She shook her head and then shifted herself over so that she leaned against the window.

"He's playing along."

She nodded without looking at him.

"Fuck, Ellen," he threw his arms up and half turned before he looked back at her, "why didn't you ask me?"

"Because I was scared." Ellen looked up and Paul saw the smeared mascara around her eyes.

"Scared." Paul repeated, "Who was this INTERPOL agent?"

"I didn't get his—"

"You didn't get his name?" Paul shouted and stepped towards her. A surge of power ran through his hands and he lifted her by her armpits and pressed her against the window so he looked right into her eyes. He didn't notice the pain in his hand. "A man asks you to frame me and you don't bother getting his name?"

"You're hurting me," she twisted uncomfortably and he released his vise-like grip. "I didn't know what to do."

Paul took three steps backwards and breathed deeply as the fury left his body. She leaned against the window, rubbing her shoulders as though they were sore and stared blankly at him.

"Do you know anything about this person who gave you the SIM card?" he said evenly.

"He told me he worked with a general, a U.S. general."

"A name?"

"No."

Footsteps clicked along the hallway and Paul looked over his shoulder expecting James, but instead saw the guard in the tan Hawaiian shirt poking his head around the corner. "Is everything okay here?"

"We're fine," Paul said and then glared at Ellen who forced a smile.

Paul watched as the guard stared at them for another moment, gave a slight nod and walked back up the hallway to his chair beside the door. When he saw him sit down, Paul looked at Ellen again. "What else do you know?"

"That's it." She looked into his eyes "That's all I know."

"I'm serious. Tell me everything."

"I have."

Paul held her eyes, but they didn't waver. A hope lived inside her, hope that he would forgive her. But how could he? Yes, he had lied to her, but he did not betray. No, she had done that. But now she had told the truth. If she had switched the SIM card in his phone, then the manifest couldn't have come from James. He thought back to his interaction with James. All of James' movements seemed stiff and rehearsed. He had sat back and listened, letting Paul give him all the details of the operation. He hadn't shared anything himself. And then Paul realized that he was the only U.S. connection, the only loose end. No one else knew about the operation. There's no way they were letting him leave. He had to escape.

Paul scanned the room and remembered how James had explained the five-foot thick soundproof walls and bulletproof windows. The only way out was through the front door. Paul looked around the corner at the guard in the chair leaning against the door. The guard held his arms by his side and through his loose-fitting Hawaiian shirt Paul saw a bulge.

"I have to get out of here," he whispered to Ellen, "but I need your help."

"Can I go with you?"

"They'll keep you safe, it's me they want."

Ellen nodded her head slowly, resigned. "What do you want me to do?"

"When I say, call the guard over."

Paul grabbed one of the metal framed dining room chairs and crouched around the corner of the hallway, just out of the guard's view. He made a motion with his hand and Ellen called the guard. He felt hot suddenly and his heart fluttered. *What the hell are you about to do, Marshall?* But before he could answer that question, the guard's footsteps clicked quickly towards him and he raised the chair high above his head. He saw a flash of the guard's shaved head — enough to see the guard wince and try and raise his forearm to block the blow — before he swung the chair down on top of the guard's neck. That sent the guard crashing to the floor on all fours. A line of red appeared on the back of his head and then it spread.

Paul tossed the chair onto the floor and pressed his knee deep into the guard's upper back. He mashed the man's face into the floor with his bandaged hand. The guard writhed and grunted underneath Paul's weight, but Paul only pressed his knee harder into the guard's back until he heard a crunch. He ran his free hand up the guard's shirt along his back until his fingers found the holstered handgun.

Paul leaned forward and whispered in the man's ear, "Stay on the floor."

The guard grunted and Paul loosened his grip. He stood up and kept the gun aimed at the guard, who lay face down with his hands and fingers splayed out on the linoleum floor. Paul walked backwards up the hallway and put his ear to the door James had gone through earlier. He only heard whispers. Soft chatter. He pressed the side of his face to the door and squinted as though that would suddenly make his hearing supersonic. Then he heard the cellphone beep and click closed. Footsteps approached the door.

The door swung open and in the split second before James saw the gun in Paul's hand, he wore a smirk on his face. That look infuriated Paul. The idea that James was getting some strange pleasure out of this sent his stomach spinning. But when Paul pointed the gun directly in James' face, James reflexively recoiled his head as though he had been punched.

"Step outside," Paul said, "give me the phone."

James handed Paul the cell phone, raised his bony hands and stepped into the hallway. "I was just getting things sorted out for you."

"Bullshit."

"Why bullshit?" James said, still holding his hand feebly beside his head. "Don't you want to hear what we can do?"

"No."

In the corner of his eye, Paul saw the guard rise to his knees. Paul curled his finger around the trigger and then fired three rounds into the ceiling. The kickback twisted his wrist painfully. Paul swiveled around and snarled, "Stay down, I said!"

The guard flopped back down on his belly and stretched his hands out in front of him on the floor. Satisfied that he had been subdued, Paul pointed the gun at James again. "Give me the phone."

James clenched his jaw, reached into his shorts' pocket and passed it over.

"I need you to let me out the front door."

James shook his head. "I can't do that."

"Let me out." Paul touched the gun's muzzle to James' forehead. James went cross-eyed as his eyes followed the gun's trajectory.

"I can't," James pulled his head back a few inches, "but put the gun down and maybe we can figure this out. What's the problem?"

"I know you didn't give me the manifest."

"What?" the edges of James' mouth turned up anxiously and he let out a nervous laugh, "what are you talking about?"

"You lied to me. The decryption code didn't come from you." Paul shoved the gun in James' face, pressed it against his nose.

"Where else could it come from, Paul?" James's voice had become slightly nasal because the gun had plugged one of his nostrils.

"Me." Ellen seemed to materialize in front of Paul, placed her hand on the gun and lowered it. She looked him directly in the eye and he saw no trace of fear or panic. She nodded slightly as if to say *I'm sorry for what I've done, but I'm going to make this right* and turned towards James. "I switched the SIM cards."

James boomed a laugh. "You did?" he looked over Ellen at Paul. "Your girlfriend has got you in a lot of trouble."

James sneered and Paul felt the anger build inside of him. For some reason, he thought of Hadad's grin. He felt as though two massive hands clenched and squeezed him like a wet cloth. His insides twisted. Things became smaller and smaller until all he saw was James. James wearing Hadad's grin. That stupid grin. Paul squished his eyelids together to make the image disappear and in that instant James lunged forward, grabbed Ellen and spun her around. A gun suddenly appeared in his hand and he had it pressed to her head. James's face sat a full foot higher than Ellen's.

"Put the gun down, Paul," he commanded.

Instead, Paul raised his gun and pointed it at James' face.

"You don't want her to die, do you?"

"To tell you the truth," Paul shrugged, "at this point I don't really care."

He purposely kept his eyes on James. He couldn't look at Ellen and see the pain his comment had caused. But part of him had meant it because it was all over now, wasn't it? There was no going back to the way things were.

"Just go, Paul," Ellen said looking up at him while biting her lower lip, "Just go."

James' giant-like grip enveloped her tiny frame. He wanted to leave. She had caused this, after all. If she hadn't believed the man posing as an INTERPOL agent and switched the SIM cards, they wouldn't be here. They would still be in Bosasso. She would still love him.

Then he realized.

He wasn't the only loose end.

Ellen had heard everything about the CIA involvement in Somalia. She had seen the faces and knew the identities of several undercover operatives. There was no way they would let her live. Letting her stay was letting her die.

He didn't think about it, it just happened. Before he realized his finger had wrapped around the trigger and tightened, James' head snapped back and a thick red spray burst out of his face onto the wall. The bang echoed off the floors. James' body slammed against the wall and slid down, leaving a smeared track of blood.

Paul looked at James' corpse, entranced. James' eyes had crossed slightly and didn't stare up at him; they stared at nothing really. But it was the only feature on his face that was still recognizable. The rest was an explosion of bone and tissue. Paul had to remind himself that was his work.

Ellen wiggled out of James' limp hold and swept her hands down her arms as if she were covered in some toxic substance. Paul finally pulled his eyes away from James and gave his head a slight shake.

They ran past the guard into the dining room. The guard reached down, drew a pistol from a leg holster, scrambled to his feet and took cover around the corner. His head popped out and he fired two shots that narrowly missed Paul's head and instead thudded into one of the bulletproof windows, creating a small chip.

Ellen slithered along the floor on her elbows and took cover underneath the glass dining table while Paul took cover behind an armchair by the window. He took a deep huffing breath and stared at the black molded plastic gun clutched between his hands that had killed James Wright. For a moment, he thought of how in one day he had already fired a gun more times than in his entire life. And then he realized he had already killed two men and was now in a firefight with a third.

Another two shots whistled past, tearing holes in the armchair's fabric, inches away from Paul's hip. The bullet hit the window, cracking the glass slightly. Paul turned and fired another two shots towards the guard.

Paul looked at the window and noticed that the shots had cracked the glass part of the way through with only two shots. He knew that bullet-*proof* glass really only meant bullet-*resistant* and enough impact could break it. And getting past the guard seemed impossible. And even then, the front door was locked by a keypad. He had to get out through the window.

He placed the forearm of his free hand over his eyes and fired five shots at the window four feet from him.

Each bullet thumped against the window like a fist, and a fine white lace fanned out around each bullet hole.

He kept firing. *Thump, thump, thump.*

Crack.

The fine cracks merged and a thick white line ran diagonally through the window.

He stood up and fired a barrage of bullets towards the guard, but hit the wall instead, sending chunks of plaster and dust spraying. Then Paul stood up and swung the butt of the gun into the window. The glass separated at the crack and the glass fell down to the terrace below, opening a large hole in the window. A gust of wind entered, sending shards of glass tinkling on the floor.

Paul turned and saw the guard aiming his weapon and took cover behind the armchair. He glanced at Ellen lying prone under the glass table and waved for her to come over. As she slid out from under the table, Paul fired at the guard again. She sprinted across the living room and slid into him behind the armchair.

"We have to jump," he said, leaning his head over the armchair, looking at the guard. He saw the front door open and two men holding pistols ran in. More guards. "Now!"

They interlaced their fingers and before they could look down, their feet had already left the ledge. They fell and to Paul it felt much longer than the split second it took to hit the pool. They ripped through the water. Paul's heels smashed into the pool's floor, his knees buckling. Chlorine burned through his sinuses. He looked up at the sunlight penetrating the water's surface. He heard shots zip through the water. Ignoring the pain in his feet, he pushed off the bottom and pulled at the water with his arms. He broke through the surface, heard a shout and looked up. Two guards stood in the open window, aiming their pistols at them.

Paul pulled himself out of the pool and coughed up a good amount of water. He looked over and saw Ellen climbing out as well, her white shirt now transparent and clinging to her body. Paul took her hand and they raced towards the glass door leading back into the apartment building. Shots rang out. Sprays of cement and dust exploded behind them as they ran. Ellen opened the door and ran inside. Paul turned and looked up at the window again. He had seen two guards enter from outside just before they had jumped out of the window. But he didn't see the guard with the Hawaiian shirt and he could pick that ugly shirt out from any distance.

"Wait," Paul grabbed Ellen's elbow spinning her around. "One of the guards isn't up there. They're expecting us to go into the building. He's probably coming down here right now."

"Where else are we going to run?"

Paul scanned the terrace. Behind the rows of terracotta planters and padded lounge chairs, a waist-high concrete ledge ran along the perimeter. He looked at Ellen. "We jump."

They counted to three and ran back out to the terrace. A barrage of bullets swirled past them, smashing two pots and busting up the concrete floor. The shots didn't stop; they seemed to be coming from all angles. Paul looked back at the doorway and saw the guard in the Hawaiian shirt firing at them. They sprinted to the ledge and, without breaking their stride and without looking down, they fell.

They landed hard on the gravel parking lot below. Paul fell forward, landing on his palms and skidding forward. Ellen tumbled over onto her side. Paul scrambled to his feet and lifted Ellen up just above her elbow. They rounded a corner, out of the guard's line of sight.

He saw the Benz parked there. They ran to the car, aware that the guards were likely sprinting down the stairs to stop them before they pulled out. Paul closed his eyes as he touched the two frayed red wires together, praying that the Benz would start. It did. Paul threw the car into gear and accelerated out of the parking lot and onto the road.

He didn't see the guards exit the building, which meant he had a head start. They would certainly try to follow him, so he knew that the farther he could get mixed into city traffic, the easier an escape would be. He pulled onto a main road and immediately passed two cars. Traffic swelled. Paul took a corner, and another. He continually checked his rear view mirror and saw no sign that he was being followed.

They eventually turned onto the main road leading out of the Garowe towards Bosasso. He increased the speed and still saw no one following them. They had gotten away.

Paul and Ellen exchanged a tired glance, then let out a sigh.

Twenty

A crumbling, potholed road spanned the one hundred eighty-five miles of desert between Garowe and Bosasso, but that didn't stop Paul from keeping the accelerator to the floor. The car shuddered and twisted as he maneuvered the steering wheel through the cracked pavement. As they passed the town of Qardho, which marked the halfway point between the two cities, Paul thought the dry, rocky landscape had become sufficiently dim that he flicked on the high beams. He checked all three of his rearview mirrors one more time, but saw no sign of pursuers. In fact, he hadn't seen another vehicle in over thirty minutes.

Had the guards given up the chase? He knew it was impossible, but he clung to the glimmer of that unreasonable hope. Hope that he and Ellen could return to Bosasso, fall asleep in each other's arms and then start work in the morning like nothing happened. Put it all behind them: James' murder, Kadar Hadad, Marshall Ramsey. He had thought it was behind him for the better part of a decade and each day that passed that notion became more and more of a distant memory.

But putting it behind them wasn't possible anymore. The guards would have immediately notified Langley of James Wright's death. They would then notify security at airports and border crossings that a dangerous fugitive was on the loose. They would send men to his home, the clinic and anywhere else they estimated Paul could go.

They would block highways, too, wouldn't they? But now, over an hour away from James Wright's destroyed fourth floor apartment, he saw no sign of a pinch. But he couldn't relax. His eyelids begged to come together and rest, but he couldn't get his mind off of what had happened. He had been set up, he must have, but by whom? Someone posed as an INTERPOL agent and convinced Ellen to change the SIM card in his phone. They gave him a tampered manifest. Suitcase nuclear weapons were in terrorist possession. Kadar Hadad's possession.

He felt something, an unrelenting, invisible force. It curled around his arms, pulled and directed him, pulled everything that had happened today. In some way, those strings pulled the trigger that blew James' face apart. But from whose hand did the strings hang?

In the passengèr seat, Ellen reclined her seatback and closed her eyes. Her tee-shirt was still damp and she shivered slightly and rubbed her arms. He thought of his ex-wife. She wouldn't have been quiet. Joan hated being cold. She would have immediately cranked the heat up and rubbed her hands together in front of the vent even though it was barely a touch below room temperature inside the car. And the nausea. Joan would have held the back of her hand on her forehead and closed her eyes initially, but after two minutes or so, she would have jumped up and complained that he was driving too fast and making her carsick.

And he would have slowed down, even if it meant he was going to be late for his shift in the emergency room at the General. But then she would say he took the turn too fast and he would ask her, not politely, if she wanted to drive. And she would say *of course not, because you criticize my driving too much.*

He noticed that the left headlight had burned out. The working headlight shone on half of the road, turning it a soft blue. The other half of the road receded into the darkening desert landscape, so that no division was visible between the road and the starry sky. If the headlight hadn't burned out, he likely would have seen the Labrador retriever-sized hole in the concrete instead of driving right into it.

The tire thudded up into the wheel well and a high-pitched clattering sound vibrated through the car. He heard a loud *pop*! before the Benz lurched forward and swerved to the left. Ellen shot up in her seat and braced herself with one hand on the dashboard and the other on the window frame. She screamed something Paul couldn't make out over the wailing of the tires. Paul jerked the wheel to the right and that made the tires squeal desperately. The momentum sent the side of his head into the window frame and he saw twinkling blue dust before his eyes. All he could think to do was brake and he thrust his heel into the pedal.

The car slowed and then bounced up and down with each rotation of the flat driver's side tire. It came to a stop in the middle of the road. Paul's heart pounded so strongly he could feel its thumping all the way up his neck and down his abdomen. He looked at Ellen, who still held onto the dash, eyes wide.

"I'd better see if there's a spare," he said with a nervous chuckle. He opened the door, walked around the car and popped the trunk. Underneath the trunk liner, he found a small spare, tire iron and jack in perfect condition. He felt dizzy. He placed his hands on the bumper and hunched forward. For an instant, he felt he would wretch, but the feeling dissipated. Instead, he laughed, laughed hard, harder than he had in a long time. He couldn't stop himself. He laughed so hard that his eyes squeezed out tears. He dropped down and leaned against the back bumper, wiping tears from his face.

Ellen stepped out of the car and looked down at Paul sideways. "Are you okay?"

Paul nodded vigorously. "Yeah, I'm fine."

"You sure?" She raised an eyebrow.

"What are the chances," he chuckled and pointed over his shoulder with his thumb, "that a twenty year old car is going to have a spare kit in perfect condition?" He shook his head and smiled, "what are the chances?"

Ellen showed a sympathetic smile, one that said *well at least you're still able to see the light side of things*, and sat on the road next to him. She took his hand and placed the side of her face on his upper arm. She ran her thumb along his fingers and gazed up at the night sky. "Remember when we went on our first trip to the Red Sea and we went to that beach?"

"Gurgussum," Paul nodded.

"Yeah," Ellen smiled, "the sky looks the same as it did that day."

He shrugged. "The sky doesn't change."

Paul turned his eyes up, so they looked at the sky together. He felt better. The dizziness and shakes he had experienced earlier in the day had dissipated. *Amazing what adrenaline could do*, he thought. A feeling crept through him, one of relief and of calm. Energy ran between them, one that he hadn't felt in a long time. Strong, maybe stronger than it had ever been. Ellen turned her head and looked at him grimly. "It's my fault, what happened today."

Part of him agreed with her. The sour, betrayed part. He hesitated, turned his head towards her, and gazed into her dark almond-shaped eyes. "No, it's not," he shook his head. "I pulled you into this situation by not telling you the truth about who I am. Please believe me when I say that I never meant for you to get wrapped up in this world. I thought I could keep it separate from us." He stood and leaned on the bumper. "But something bigger is happening here. We're pawns in whatever this game is."

"Maybe it's over," a look of relief flashed across her face. "You've informed the people at Langley about the stolen weapons, so that's good. Maybe once they track them down, they'll stop looking for us."

That made Paul laugh again. "As far as the U.S government knows, I gave nuclear weapons to terrorists. I killed a U.S. operative. I don't think they'll *ever* stop looking for me."

"But I was there, Paul, you had to kill him. There was no choice."

"They're not going to see it that way." Paul shook his head.

"Well, maybe you'll have to explain it to them."

"How am I supposed to do that? My only connection to them is dead."

Ellen reached out and touched his thigh. Instead of feeling her soft fingers through his cargo shorts, he felt a hard block press against his thigh. The cell phone in his pocket. "Langley was the last place James called," she smiled.

Paul stood up, removed the phone from his pocket and held it in his palm. Some part of him realized that dialing would be useless. There wasn't enough time to explain; he didn't even know how he would begin. But it was the only option left. By now, a comprehensive, organized search was undoubtedly underway. He could almost feel the search party circling him like a pack of wolves, and then converging. He pressed the REDIAL button and gripped the phone tightly to his ear. The phone began dialing.

The pitch-black desert around him suddenly seemed congested. The small, low-lying shrubs that were a tinge darker than the rest of the landscape crept almost imperceptibly closer. A sudden breeze kicked a spray of dust into Paul's eyes. An operator came on the line and he said his name was James Wright and she promptly patched him through.

"Hello?" a woman's voice came through on the phone.

By this time, his heart had reached a full out gallop and sweat tracked down his face. He felt a large, unmovable lump in his throat.

"Hello? Hello? Is anyone there?" the voice cut in and out.

"Who is this?" he forced out.

A long, staticky pause, then, "Who is this?"

"This is Paul Alban."

An even longer pause. "Doctor Alban, where are you?"

"I've left Garowe, you can stop looking for me there," Paul said. "Who are you?"

"M-my name is Officer Clarke," papers shuffling and then a thump on the other end, "N-national Clandestine Service," fuzz through the receiver, "how did you get this number?"

How did I get this number? What was he doing calling Langley anyway? Did he expect them to say *oh, yeah, you killed an operative, no worries*. He should have changed the tire, hit the road and kept on driving. "This is James Wright's cell phone. You were the last person he called," came out matter-of-factly.

"How did you get his phone?"

"Because he wanted to kill me and I had to defend myself."

"You killed him?"

He glanced at Ellen sitting on the bumper, her face dark, lit only by the small trunk light. But in her eyes he saw hope, enough to give him the strength to be truthful. "It was self defense."

"We need to get more details on what happened," Officer Clarke's words suddenly came out smoothly. "The best way is for us to meet. Where can that take place?"

"I don't think that's a good idea."

"No?"

"No."

"How come?"

"You want me dead," he said evenly.

"That's not true," the tremble returned to the voice, "we just want to sort this out."

Sort it out. His mind retrieved the image of the last time an agent at Langley had told him they would help him *sort it out*. He could count the strands of hair covering the shiny bald patch on the man's head and still see his moustache bounce up and down as he read off of the clipboard on the table in front of him. What was his name? Crighton? Chichtlow? Crippy? Crilley? Yes, the agent was Crilley. Crilley had given him the option: *Either you go to trial where you will likely be convicted of torture or you make a statement that Sargeant Sidwell ordered the torture of Kadar Hadad and then we can help you move on from this. Put it all behind you. Start over in a new life. Let Joan live thinking you died nobly, instead of hanging her head in shame while you rot in prison. Let Peter grow up to be proud of his father.*

Behind Crilley, in the background, he saw his own reflection in the one-way mirror, with less gray and fewer wrinkles. But far more naïve.

"Sort what out?" Paul snorted, "three of your men already tried to kill me today. Forgive me for thinking you want me dead."

"All we know is that you provided a detailed ship's manifest containing nuclear materials to a group of pirates. If we meet—"

"It was a manifest the National Clandestine Service provided. I did my job according to protocol. Someone sent that manifest to me, with a decryption code."

"But we have several checks and balances that—"

"I'm telling you it came through the same way," Paul shouted. "Something went wrong on your end of things."

"Do you have evidence of this?"

Paul pressed his teeth together, closed his eyes and took a deep breath in through his nose. His initial impulse was to scream, but instead he lowered his voice so that it was almost robotic. "How am I supposed to have evidence when according to the procedures that were set out by the NCS, I'm to destroy the information as soon as I pass it on?"

"So you can't prove it," her voice rose, as if to say *Aha! Gotcha!*

"Listen, Officer Clarke, if I wanted to give nuclear weapons to terrorists, why would I immediately inform the NCS of the situation?"

"I don't know what your motives are, Dr. Alban. But I do know that, after you informed Officer Wright of the situation, you proceeded to murder him."

"They had no intention of letting me leave alive and you know it."

"You were in custody and you escaped."

"Officer Clarke, does it make sense to *you* that I would have set something like this up?"

"It doesn't really matter what I—"

"To you personally, does it make sense?"

"It doesn't really matter what I think."

"Look at the facts, objectively."

There was a heavy sigh on the other end. For a moment, Paul felt hopeful. Had he made a connection with her? He bit down on his upper lip and held his breath, waiting for her to continue. But when she did, her voice assumed a professional and distant tone. "The facts are that you're a wanted man. Look at the situation. A stock of nuclear weapons is missing in the hands of terrorists. You are the only connection to them. You escaped custody and killed an intelligence officer. The truth is that it doesn't matter what I think. Full resources are being put towards recovering these weapons right now. What I do know is that once they are recovered, the next priority will be to bring those people responsible to justice. And you are number one on that list. Unless, of course, you have evidence that someone, as you claim, somehow interfered with the lines of communication."

She paused and her question lingered. Paul dragged his gaze over to Ellen. She stared intently back at him, unaware of what Bailey Clarke had just said. The thought entered his mind to tell Officer Clarke that Ellen had switched the SIM card on his phone. That someone posing as an INTERPOL agent had convinced her to do it. But then what? Would they hunt Ellen instead of him? She didn't have anywhere to run, at least nowhere that the NCS wouldn't find her. And where would that leave him? Alone. Again.

After the moment of silence, she continued, "In that case, Dr. Alban, I suggest you get some proof. Or run."

Twenty-one

When Bailey Clarke opened the door of her one bedroom condominium and tossed her car keys and laptop case onto the kitchen counter at 10 p.m., she realized she couldn't really remember the drive home. She remembered leaving the Langley complex and smiling politely when the cute, blonde guard at the security checkpoint asked if she needed help carrying her laptop bag to her car. She remembered that when she started the Honda, the volume control was turned up and the radio blasted a Coldplay song. But any memory of the drive home had dissipated like a puff of smoke.

All she thought of on the ride was Paul Alban's angry voice. Their conversation ran through her mind like a looped tape. She remembered herself sitting at her desk, mulling over Alban's file when the call came through and the operator told her it was James Wright. That struck her as bizarre: James Wright had been confirmed dead in his Garowe apartment less than an hour earlier. Then he came online: Paul Alban, the suspected murderer. Her heart fluttered as his voice came through the receiver. Predictably, he claimed his innocence. Even more predicable was that he attributed James Wright's death to self-defense. But why was he calling her? That wasn't predictable; a guilty man would have fled as fast and as far as possible. By now, he could have been on a boat heading to the Arabian Gulf. Instead, he called her. *Look at the facts, objectively,* kept playing on her mind. Questions kept floating through her head. If he set this up, as Crilley had said, then why did he warn them about the missing weapons?

But one question kept flashing like a fluorescent billboard: *could Paul Alban be telling the truth?*

She put her hand on the kitchen counter, stared at the vase of daffodils above the stove and tried to force the thought from her head. But she couldn't. *Pursuing these questions won't get you anywhere*, she reminded herself. Crilley had made it clear there would be no discussion of Paul Alban's possible innocence. When he had said it, it had come out almost as a warning, hadn't it? Even though his assumption that Paul Alban was guilty seemed hasty, Crilley had far more experience than she did in managing these situations. And where would challenging Crilley get her? Fired. No transfer this time. Just fired.

Bailey slid one of the kitchen chairs over to the fridge, stood on it and opened the cupboard that hung above it. She reached inside and felt with her fingers through the bags of pita chips until they found the unopened glass bottle of spiced rum. It had collected dust at the back of the cupboard ever since she returned from her vacation in Jamaica four months ago. Sherri Banks had driven down from New York and presented Bailey with two all-inclusive tickets to a singles resort in Montego Bay. *It's been six months, Bailey, we're going to go down and have a great time and forget all about Chris, okay?*

She twisted the cap until it snapped open and poured several lugs into a glass. She poured a tepid can of diet Coke over the rum that fizzed, took a big gulp and grimaced as it went down. She stood there with her esophagus burning and looked over the kitchen counter, past the beige microfiber sofa and the floral printed ottoman, to the large living room window that overlooked Vernon St. Parkway and the all-night Chinese food restaurant across the street. She thought that the vague nausea she felt was probably because she hadn't eaten since lunchtime. That's all she needed: a good meal and a good sleep. She turned and opened the refrigerator, looked inside at the shelves half filled with potatoes, carrots, soggy celery and orange juice and decided that preparing anything would take too long. She picked up the phone and ordered a ginger beef plate over chow mein noodles, for delivery.

She crossed the room, tossed the phone on the sofa, sat down and put her feet up on the ottoman. She leaned forward and rubbed her feet with her fingers, trying to press out the soreness that had developed from being in uncomfortable heels all day long. She picked up the remote control, turned on the flat screen that hung on the wall and clicked through the channels, not resting on a single one for more than a second before she decided there was nothing on worth watching anyway. She leaned forward and picked up the magazine that rested on the ottoman. The cover read *How to Win Future Wars* and featured an article discussing the merits of working with internal resistances in countries rather than full-scale invasions as the U.S. had done in Iraq.

It was as if Crilley had written the article himself. She remembered what he had said earlier in the day about the warlords in Somalia: *If we help them fight these extremists and stabilize the country, things could settle out. This is the future of warfare.*

But the fact was that as a result of this strategy, a stockpile of man portable nuclear weapons was in the possession of terrorists. And they had no leads. Their only connection to them was now on the run. And she had told him to do that.

But why would the NCS want to kill their only connection to a missing stockpile of nuclear weapons? Guilty or not, Paul Alban was the only person they had on the ground in Somalia. He was their best chance at recovering them.

Look at the facts, objectively.

The similarities between Paul Alban's situation and Bailey's own experience at her last job in the paramilitary division didn't escape her. It hadn't been her fault that Roger Blake was drinking scotch that night anymore than it was Paul Alban's fault for receiving a transmission with a doctored manifest. She did her job that evening, punching numbers on her keyboard just the way Paul Alban had worked passing the information to pirates. Maybe Blake had mistaken the times she flashed a smile at him in morning meetings or the times she touched his shoulder when he teased her as flirting, but it was not her fault; she had said 'no' when he pressed her on the desk that night. She was a victim of the situation, just like Paul

Alban. She had told people about what happened—she had told Chris Hanson—but he didn't believe her, just like no one believed Paul Alban. Sure, she had waited three weeks before she said anything, but what could she be expected to do? Even when she told Chris and he confronted Roger and then Roger's wife found out and accused Bailey of being a home wrecker, no one thought of her as a victim in the situation. Instead, she was shoved aside until she transferred and 'the problem' in paramilitary was gone. Just the way Crilley planned to eliminate 'the problem' by killing Paul Alban.

She got up, took another sip of her rum and Coke and grabbed her black leather laptop bag. She thumbed through a stack of papers stuffed inside the back pocket until she found the printouts of the *Steblesky's* official manifest that she had obtained from port records in Odessa. She read through it again, all one hundred and twelve pages, part of her hoping in vain that she had somehow overlooked an entry for man portable nuclear weapons when she had scoured it earlier. As she squared the papers into a pile, her eye was drawn to a series of entries. The majority of cargo was registered to multinational corporations such as *Odessa Arms, Markov Factory* and *Tomahawk Manufacturing*. But four containers had *A. Senechaux* listed as the registrant. It seemed odd that four individual containers would be registered to an individual rather than a corporation. All the containers registered to A. Senechaux contained small arms, mostly AK-47s and hand grenades. She flipped her laptop open and once it booted up, she accessed the NCS remote access server and typed in her passwords. She searched the name A. Senechaux and came up with a one line entry: *Armand Senechaux — suspected alias for small arms dealer or group of dealers — probable French or Russian national.*

Disappointed that she didn't find anything more substantial on A. Senechaux, she pulled up the files on Paul Alban. She had been through them a half dozen times during the day, but part of her hoped that if she looked through them, she would find a clue to support her suspicion that Alban was set up. Three quarters of the paramilitary staff were at Langley planning a recovery mission for the missing weapons. Once recovered, they would go after Alban. If she was going to find evidence of his innocence, she had to find it soon. Or maybe, she would find something that convinced her that he was lying. Either way, her mind would rest.

The files on Paul Alban appeared onscreen. The first folder contained basic identifying information page she had seen in Crilley's office. Forty-eight years old, Caucasian, single. Born in Massacheusetts but on a French passport. Fluent in English, French, Spanish, Somali, comprehends Arabic. There was a poorly scanned copy of a medical degree from Université Francois Rabelais in 1985, with a fellowship in internal medicine. Bailey assumed the degree was a fake. Alban spoke perfect English and the accent she detected in his voice was New Englander, not French. She figured he likely received his degree somewhere in the U.S. Active operative in Somalia since 1999. Working under the cover of a foreign aid worker in Bosasso, Autonomous Republic of Puntland,

Somalia. James Wright was listed as the contact point for Paul Alban.

She scanned through the long list of folders in Paul's file. There were hundreds. She needed to find out more about him and didn't have time to go through it all. She double-clicked on a folder named *Background*, but it was empty. Not a single file was inside the folder. Bailey rubbed her eyes with her palms. The agency typically recorded massive amounts of history on their operatives. It was common to find exhaustive transcripts of screening interviews documenting social upbringing, psychological or behavioral problems, family members, significant relationships and education history. Results of psychological testing and history of mental health problems were usually documented. Sometimes, the names of pets could be found in the files.

But nothing on Paul Alban.

It was as if he had not existed before 1999.

She sat staring at the computer screen on her lap when her apartment buzzer went off. She didn't react initially, but after a few seconds, the buzzer went off again and she hauled herself off of the couch. She had forgotten all about the Chinese food and only when she realized it had been twenty-five minutes since she called her order in, did her hunger return. In fact, she felt weak and close to vomiting. As she stood up, she felt the alcohol course its way to her head. She staggered to the doorway and didn't bother asking '*who is it*' before pressing the button beside the intercom to let them in. She pressed her hand against the wall for support, as the black rings in her vision threatened to expand. When the delivery boy arrived, she snatched the paper bag from his arms, pressed a twenty-dollar bill in his hand, and muttered for him to keep the change. She made her way to the kitchen, peeled open the foil lid on her ginger beef noodles and dumped it into a white bowl.

She sat on the couch, plopped the bowl beside her and shoveled the noodles into her mouth faster than she could chew. She leaned on her elbow and scrolled through Paul Alban's files with her free hand, ignoring the food that slipped out of her mouth and onto the couch.

Then she stopped chewing.

MR-14406.

It referred to another file. Bailey had heard that when Langley started converting from paper to computerized records, some operations officers refused to give up the files on some of their operatives. They said that they didn't trust the confidentiality of computerized records. But the skeptics thought they just didn't want people privy to the operations they were conducting. Was *MR-14406* referring to a paper file? Immediately, her mind flashed to Crilley's office. He had hundreds of manila folders stored away in boxes on the floor in his office. Could one of those be *MR-14406*?

She slurped up the last of her noodles when she heard her blackberry vibrating inside her laptop bag. She put the bowl on the ottoman and scrambled to get the phone to her ear.

"Bailey Clarke here."

"Clarke," Crilley's voice boomed through the receiver. For a moment that seemed longer than it probably was, he didn't say anything. Bailey sat up straight and suddenly felt alert, sober. *Does he somehow know I was snooping through Paul Alban's file?*

When Crilley continued, his voice had sharpened, "I need you to come back to Langley, meet me in my office. And you can forget about that report for the meeting."

"Yes, sir." She closed her laptop and stood, making her way to the door. "You don't need the report?"

"No. Things have changed. We have a lead on the weapons."

Twenty-two

It was his first dream in a decade.

It began with Paul running down the main drag in his hometown of Beverly, Massachusetts. The muscles in his legs strained to propel him forward. *Faster*, he thought, *it's gaining*. He didn't turn his head. He couldn't risk the split second hesitation that turning would require because it was close, too close. Whatever *it* was. He could feel its hot breath on his neck. He flew past the hardware store where he had worked in the summer helping stack two-by-fours in the lumberyard. The tubs filled with cut roses and tulips in front of Mr. Johnston's flower shop were nothing more than a blur of colors in Paul's peripheral vision at this pace. Only when he screamed for help and the words came out so shrill that the sound almost tripped him up did he realize that this wasn't the Beverly he grew up in. Sure, the set was a perfect match: the parking lot in front of the Tom Boy Foods' massive window was full of parked cars, paper napkins were laid out in the take-out window of Country Ice Cream, Graham Decker's blue ten speed was tied up in front of the arcade and water dripped down from the freshly watered hanging baskets that hung from the light posts. But the actors were missing.

Then he heard a horrible, savage, gnawing sound that reminded him of a Doberman tearing a slab of meat to shreds. He fell over, his face smacking into the pavement and realized it had him clamped by the ankle. He tried to free his leg, but it dragged him along the pavement. He tried to turn around so he could get a look at it, but each time he swiveled his torso, it flipped him face down onto the pavement. He kicked at it with his free leg and he heard his heel crack into its head. He hit it three more times and then the gnawing stopped.

He scrambled to his feet and didn't bother looking back. He looked down at his ankle: remarkably, it was intact. He darted to the left through the deserted Texaco fill station, jumped the Robichaux's eight-foot fence and landed on all fours in their backyard rose garden. Thorns tore deep scrapes into both his forearms and a second later blood seeped out of them. Searing pain traveled up his arms. He dabbed the blood with his shirt.

He kept moving forward and when he got to the Robichaux's front gate, he looked behind him and saw no sign of it. He passed their driveway and stopped in front of the barn-shaped house with green shutters. A plastic sheet duct taped to the window that Eddie Mitchell had knocked out with a baseball flapped in the breeze. An old sycamore cast a large shadow over the front yard and its branches just touched the roof. Moss grew between the red brick path that led up to the front door.

His childhood home.

He ran to the front door so quickly his feet nearly slipped out from underneath him, turned the brass knob and pushed simultaneously, but it didn't open. Locked. He knocked and knocked, beating his knuckles against the door until they turned red and angry, but there was no answer. He pushed his fingers through the mail slot in the door, looked inside and asked if anyone was home. No answer.

He stepped off the landing, pushed through the cedar bushes to his left, and stopped in front of the living room window. He banged on the window with the inside of his fist until he thought the glass would break. He stopped and then put his hands beside his face and looked through the window.

His eyes tracked through the dim interior, along the marble fireplace to the wood staircase. He made out a long figure lying face down with one of its legs twisted in the newel posts. Paul strained his eyes so he made out the face mashed against the hallway rug: a graying beard ran along the jaw line, broken eyeglasses hung off the man's ears and his eyes stared out at nothing.

Paul's father, Peter Ramsey.

He banged on the window again, even harder this time. He had to get inside to help him. He dug out a landscaping rock the size of a basketball from beside the cedar bushes and held it on his shoulder. He heaved it at the front window like a shot put, but it bounced off and dropped onto the ground. He returned to the window and screamed.

Then he saw movement inside. A young boy with his father's blonde hair, in beachwear, swimming shorts and flip-flops, stopped at the sight of his dead father. The towel dropped from under his arm and he ran towards the corpse, his flip-flops flying. Paul immediately recognized the boy in the window as himself, as Marshall Ramsey. He watched Marshall drag his limp father's corpse off of the stairs and untwist his father's leg from the railing. Tears ran down Marshall's face as he attempted chest compressions, just like he had seen on television. He tried and tried, but his skinny six-year-old arms couldn't press hard enough.

Paul placed his hand palm flat against the window and stood motionless. Agony at seeing his young self try to bring his father back to life in vain tensed him up inside. Tears filled his eyes. He wanted to get in, to protect Marshall from the pain that was etched on his face. He wanted to break the seemingly impenetrable barrier between them, hold Marshall and tell him he would be okay. But he was stuck outside looking in.

Suddenly, flames burst out from the kitchen and burned up the walls and curtains. Flames surrounded the entire scene. Flaming beams fell from the ceiling and crashed down on top of his father's corpse. But when he looked down at the corpse, it wasn't his father; it was Dennis Hildebrand crushed underneath the beam, screaming agonizing screams.

Then the flames disappeared again and the man underneath the beam was again his father.

Young Marshall got up from his knees and stared at the corpse like he was looking at a stranger. The emotion in him had vanished. Paul remembered that moment. It was the instant when his father turned into nothing more than a vague memory of a man who had made sandcastles with him in the summer and read stories to him when his mother felt sick. His head turned slowly, imperceptibly, towards the window and Paul swore they made eye contact. In that moment, he saw fear, sheer terror in his young eyes. And then he knew what Marshall was about to do.

Paul moved quickly through the cedar bushes to the front door. It swung open and Marshall ran out in an all out sprint. Paul dove over a bush and reached for Marshall's foot but it passed right through it, like a hand through smoke. As he thudded onto the landing, he saw Marshall round the house to the backyard. Paul scrambled to his feet and ran after him. *You can catch him, Paul, he's just a kid.* As he rounded the house, he saw Marshall jumping over the fence barefoot. Paul climbed the fence and at the top he saw the field of tall grass that seemed to go on forever. Since then, an entire suburb of modern homes had popped up in this field, but this wasn't today, this was 1966. Marshall cut through the open field at full speed. Paul remembered where Marshall was heading. On the opposite side of the hill, far in the distance was an abandoned shack. Marshall would stumble upon it and sit inside for two days until a local search party found him. The first day he would sit on an old upturned barrel inside, clutching his knees and telling his six-year-old brain that maybe it didn't happen. He would fall asleep and the next day wake up and realize it was not all a dream and spend the rest of the day torturing himself with thoughts that he had killed his father. Later, his mother would tell him that he died from a heart attack and that it wasn't his fault. But part of him would continue to think that if he had done things differently, maybe called for help instead of running away, his father would be alive.

His father's death had changed everything, though, hadn't it? A month after his father's ashes were tossed into the sea, his mother, Annette Ramsey, put the house up for sale and three weeks later, they were on a plane to Paris. Marshall's protests fell on deaf ears. His mother didn't seem to take into account the fact that summer camp was less than a month away and Marshall had been practicing his J-strokes and U-strokes every night in preparation for the weeklong canoe trip. One thing about Annette Ramsey (or Annette Perrot as she soon changed back to her maiden name) was that once she had made a decision on something, no amount of begging or pleading could turn her mind around. *Headstrong*, is how Marshall's father had once described her, *like a mob of Marxists*. She had decided she could not raise Marshall alone and wanted to be closer to her parents and sister. And he didn't like Paris from the minute he got there. There were too many people and those that were there were too skinny and spoke too softly and no one had heard of baseball. Worst of all were the nights. The memory of his father expiring on that staircase haunted him each night until he returned to Beverly sixteen years later during a weekend off medical school in Boston.

Paul jumped off the top of the fence but instead of landing in tall grass, he landed in cool white sand. In front of him, waves broke on a beach and water submerged his feet. Sea spray felt cool on his face. He looked down at his bare feet and saw that he was wearing a tuxedo. He looked down at his watch and saw that he was late for his wedding. He started running again, fast, and this time he turned around to see dark clouds chasing him. *Rain on your wedding day means the marriage is blessed*, Joan had said to him smiling. *Then this marriage is as holy as holy gets*. Rain poured down behind him in torrents and slapped against the sand. He managed to stay just ahead of the clouds, but then he realized he wasn't running from the storm. He turned his head towards the sea, which had become choppy and black, and saw waves smashing against the shore. Offshore, in waist high water, his Joan stood in her wedding dress. She did not look beautiful. Her eyeliner was smudged on her high cheekbones and her long blonde hair was matted down against her forehead. Her black veil whipped in the increasing wind.

Paul veered into the water as the rain finally caught and poured all over him. He slogged through the water towards her and stretched his arms out in front of him to grab her, but his hands passed right through her again and he lost his balance and tumbled into the water. He resurfaced, and heard screaming, but it wasn't Joan, it was coming from atop one of the sand dunes on shore. He turned around and saw Ellen, standing alone atop a sand dune screaming. A ray of light poked through the angry black clouds and illuminated her. He had to go to her.

He bulldozed his way through the massive waves that crashed all over him and ran towards Ellen. As he sprinted closer, the sand dune she stood on moved farther and farther away. She kept moving backwards as quickly as he ran towards her.

He sped up, his feet barely touching the ground, but then his foot caught something and he fell, skidding along the ground, getting the black suit covered in sand. He scrambled on all fours and crawled back to see what he had tripped over.

He immediately recognized Sami's nephew Ali lying on his back among the grasses in the sand dunes, bringing a cigarette to his mouth. As he inhaled, smoke floated out of the three holes in his chest. He kept taking drag after drag.

"Where is my uncle?" he finally said.

Paul said nothing.

"It's okay," he held out a pack of cigarettes, "would you like one?"

Paul shook his head.

"I know where he is, you know," Ali raised his eyebrows and smiled.

"Who?" Paul said.

"Hadad."

"What? Where is he?"

Ali pointed over Paul's shoulder, "Behind you."

~ * ~

Paul opened his eyes and drifted back into consciousness. He rubbed his eyes and saw that he was still in the old beater Benz with the spare tire on the front driver's side wheel. It had become even darker than it had been before he drifted off, inky black. Ellen looked over from behind the wheel, her knuckles turning a little white at ten and two. One thing about Ellen was that she was terrified of driving, especially at night. Something that Paul had always assumed had something to do with her brother having been plowed over by a taxi at a crosswalk at midnight on his twentieth birthday.

She took her eyes off of the road for only a second, enough to flash a smile at him. "You were dreaming."

"Yeah," his voice came out a little crackly so he cleared it and sat up straight, "haven't slept much in the past couple of days."

"Tell me about it," she said. But to Paul she didn't look tired; in fact Ellen never did.

They were driving through a small town. Small dwellings with corrugated metal roofs and walls made of a patchwork of fiberglass sheeting stretched out on either side of the road. The leftover embers of daytime cooking fires provided the only visible light in the town. No one was out at this time.

"Where are we?" Paul asked.

"We're in Xidda," Ellen said, "where do you think we should go from here?"

"I think we should go back to Bosasso."

"Bosasso?" Ellen snapped her head over towards Paul. "They'll definitely be looking for us there."

"Maybe not. We've been driving almost two hours and they haven't followed us. And they'd just as quick assume we wouldn't head back to Bosasso because it's so obvious." Paul paused and stared out the window, appraising the shanty land around him. He opened the glove box, found a pack of cigarettes and lit one up. "And the agent I talked to said they're focused on recovering the weapons. But that's not why I think we should go there."

Ellen glanced over at him, expecting more.

"I think the patient I worked on two days ago might know something about the weapons."

"The pirate?"

"Yeah," Paul nodded, "he might know where they are."

"How do you know that?" Ellen asked with a hefty portion of skepticism in her voice.

"Just a feeling," Paul said and took a drag on his cigarette, "but it's all we've got to go on at this point."

Twenty-three

Darkness still resisted giving way to sunlight when they pulled into the deserted clinic parking lot. Their feet crunched along the gravel as they crossed the parking lot to the front door. Paul stopped Ellen two times on the way over by grabbing her arm because he thought he heard a third set of footsteps approaching. Each time they unconsciously held their breath while the little hairs on their arms stood up. Paul blindly scanned the pitch-black parking lot for anything out of the ordinary before they started walking again. Did he truly believe the CIA wasn't going to look for him in Bosasso? When he really thought about it (and he tried not to), agents could have already encircled the clinic as well as his home. They could already be waiting inside the clinic or in a car down the road, waiting for the first sign of the drug-dealing doctor.

When they got to the front door, Ellen placed her hand on the handle, hesitated and looked at Paul with her wide eyes asking, *are you sure about this?* Paul turned around and squinted through the darkness, part of him expecting a mob of agents to rush through the parking lot, holding flashlights and guns, screaming at him to get on the ground. Part of him expecting to not see anything at all, just hear the pop of a sniper before he fell to the ground and everything turned black.

But there were no men. No guns and no snipers. All he heard was the sound of his own breathing and the faint chirping of crickets in the thicket at the edge of the parking lot.

Paul turned and nodded towards Ellen as she unlocked and opened the door. They stepped inside and Paul let the door shut gently behind him to ensure that it did not make a sound. A nurse, a ward aide and a guard played cards in the far corner of the room, under a dim table lamp. He couldn't quite make out what they were talking about because of the hum of the overhead fans, but they hadn't broken their conversation when Paul and Ellen walked in. Paul pushed the small of Ellen's back to nudge her forward. His mind kept repeating: *in and out*. He wanted to avoid Ellen getting them bogged down in small talk with anyone. How would he explain where they had been? It was easier to get in unnoticed.

They swept forward through the main aisle between the patient beds, taking soft, deliberate steps. When Paul had left the clinic two days ago, he had left Ali in the bed next to the surgical suites at the back of the clinic. Ali was in stable condition at the time and breathing on his own and already asking to be sent home. They slipped through the canvas curtain that divided the clinic in half.

Through the darkness in the back of the clinic, Paul saw a figure lying wrapped in a blanket in the bed where he had left Ali two days earlier. He moved in until his face was inches from the person's face when he heard a voice whisper behind him.

"Doctor."

Paul whipped around, startled. He was surprised to see Ali sitting up in the bed behind him, half covered in a white blanket. Paul could barely make out his features in the dark. But he saw that Ali's once glassy, empty eyes were now alive. His breathing too had improved; no longer was it labored and wheezy. Yet, somehow, he looked older, like he had aged overnight. His face had the drawn expression of an old man reflecting on a life complete.

"Ali," Paul said, "I've been looking for you."

Ali looked at Ellen and then at Paul again. "Where is my uncle?" he said, his face tightening, anticipating his worst nightmare coming true.

Paul considered for a moment. Saying, *he's lying face down on the side of a cliff, as far as I know*, flashed through his mind. But the words came out eventually, slowly, against a resistance in his throat. "I'm sorry," he said and his voice became softer and trailed off, "he was killed."

The words lingered in the hot, sticky air. For a moment, Ali's expression didn't change; he just kept his eyes locked on Paul's. Then, he let out a few stuttering sighs and brought his trembling hands to his face.

Ali hunched forward crying. Ellen sat down on the edge of the bed and put her arm around him. Paul thought of how Sami had considered Ali his son and how Ali was now once again fatherless. He cried the way a son would cry about his father's death. Part of him wanted to tell Ali he knew how it felt to lose a father and that he knew the agony that came with losing someone that filled that void. An agony that faded but never died. He wondered if Ali blamed himself for Sami's death, the same way Paul blamed himself for Dennis' death. If Ali would let himself drown in guilt.

The truth was that he didn't squeeze a single tear out when Dennis died. When the coroner unzipped the bodybag and asked Paul to identify Dennis' charred remains, he nodded and walked away feeling numb. But no tears. Way too late for tears. Another month would pass before he allowed his mind to ask himself whether he could have turned back for Dennis. Whether he could have saved him.

"How did he die?" Ali gathered himself and turned his red-rimmed eyes towards Paul.

"He died saving my life," Paul said. His voice sounded calm and reassuring. "The ship that you hijacked had important weapons on it. Asabiyyah found out about them and tortured me to get information about the ship. They tried to get me to lead them to Sami so they could steal the weapons from the port. We went to stop them and that's where he was killed. It was a firefight."

Ali nodded rhythmically, absorbing the information. Then his head stopped bobbing, his brow furrowed and his gaze met Paul's. "Why would they torture you?"

Paul sighed, and explained how he had been providing shipping manifests and routes to pirates and how the *Stebelsky* had man portable nuclear weapons aboard. Ali listened closely as Paul described Hadad plucking his fingernail and then trying to capture Sami. Ellen filled in the details that Paul left out about their encounter with James and now being on the run.

"And Hadad has the weapons now?" Ali said.

"I think so."

"Then you should find them before he uses them. Kadar Hadad is a crazy man."

"That's why we're here. We need your help finding him."

Ali shook his head and laid back down on the gurney. "My uncle is dead, it is too late to do anything."

"It's not too late," Paul pleaded, "but the longer we wait, the farther he could have taken them." Paul stared at Ali who had his head turned away towards the curtain. Paul threw his arms up in the air.

"Ali," Ellen said gently, "we need you to help us. You know people in the Puntland. At this point, Asabiyaah either are moving the weapons or have already taken them out. But I know that you know people who work the docks, and the border crossings. You're our only hope."

Ali didn't move. Paul cut in, "Ali, this is a disaster waiting to happen. Asabiyaah are taking over your country. Imagine what they can do with thirteen nuclear weapons." Paul's voice rose and part of him hoped that anger would build inside Ali. He grabbed Ali's chin in his hand and turned his face towards him, stared directly in his eyes, and spoke deliberately "*Your uncle* wanted to stop them."

Ali shot up in the bed, smacked Paul's hand away and pointed a finger in Paul's face. "*You* created this problem. *You* gave us the fake manifest. *You* went with my uncle to those docks. He died because of *you*."

Ali's finger trembled and his eyes were wide. Paul ignored the finger and returned the gaze. "He helped me because I saved your life. He felt he owed me something for saving his 'son.' So he came with me to the docks, to stop Hadad and stop the weapons from being stolen. He did it all for you."

Ali eyes darted around as his mind reeled. He lowered his finger, sighed and lowered his shoulders. The tension left his body.

"Ali, we can stop them together."

Ali nodded and placed his palm on his forehead. "There's a man who works at the docks, his name is Salaam. His cousin is in Asabiyaah, maybe he knows where they have gone."

Twenty-four

Only once during the one hundred mile drive across the desert did Paul consider the foolishness of what he was about to do.

He sat in the backseat of a speeding top-down Jeep, next to Ellen, gripping her hand. Ali sat behind the wheel, the tails of his black bandana whipping in the wind. He spoke over the wind to Habib, a young looking, wiry member of Sami's group, who sat in the passenger seat. A half dozen rifles, four handguns and four grenades were wedged behind Paul and Ellen's seats.

Ali wasn't following a road of any sort, just the tire grooves in the gritty sand made by vehicles that had previously crossed the desert. The sun was setting ahead of them, turning the white landscape red. Angry rain clouds grew on the horizon. The air felt swollen and heavy.

Paul couldn't be sure whether it was a sense of purpose or sheer vengeance that came over Ali after Paul had convinced him to help track down the weapons thirteen hours earlier. But from that moment on, it was clear that Ali was in charge.

Without hesitation, Ali had pulled out the intravenous catheter from his hand and then instructed Paul to reinforce the bandages on his chest. By the time they left the clinic, Ali had three rolls of bandages wrapped around his torso.

Ali took the keys to the green Benz and drove them to Habib's coastal home, on the outskirts of Bosasso. It was really more of a Spanish villa than a house, complete with grape vines climbing up to the second floor balcony and a bronze fountain spewing water in the central courtyard. Apparently, piracy was good business.

As soon as Habib let them inside the opulent main foyer, Ali explained the situation to him. The two of them spoke quickly in Somali and Paul strained to keep up with the conversation, but the next thing he knew, Habib was passing AK-47s to them from a shelf in the cellar. Then, the four of them piled into Habib's Jeep, stocked with weapons.

Ali and Habib decided that they would pay a man named Salaam, their contact at the ports, a visit. Salaam had worked at the port for over fifteen years and was by all accounts a loyal worker. However, his eighteen-year-old nephew had become swept up in Asabiyaah ideology and had joined their ranks several months earlier. Habib and Ali suspected that while Salaam likely had nothing to do with the stolen weapons, he probably knew something about where they were.

Salaam's home was modest. White paint was flaking off of the concrete walls of the single floor house. Two rusted bicycles with flat tires leaned against the sidewalls. They parked in front. Ali and Habib each tucked handguns into their belts and Habib handed one to Paul who did the same. Ali and Habib didn't bother knocking and pushed through the front door that hung on by one hinge and Paul followed. They moved to the kitchen where Salaam sat at a small folding table across from an elderly man shoving torn pieces of flatbread into his mouth. They both wore loose-fitting white shirts and pants. Salaam's wife hovered over the stove, stirring a strong curry. As soon as he saw the three of them enter the kitchen, Salaam stopped chewing and his expression turned serious. He promptly excused himself from the table and led them to the living room. He sat down on a chesterfield, wrung his hands and picked at the grey hairs on his neck before Ali and Habib even opened their mouths. Ali didn't waste any time, and immediately pressed the muzzle of the handgun into Salaam's forehead. Salaam shook his head when asked where Hadad was, saying he didn't know. Then Habib grabbed Salam's wife and brought his two young daughters into the room. He forced his wife to her knees facing Salaam and held the pistol tight to her skull.

It worked. Salaam knew everything. He knew Hadad had taken six men with him and they were transporting the weapons to a beach near Maydh. From there, they would take them to a ship anchored off the coast. They were destined for Yemen. He knew they had left the Puntland less than two hours earlier, which would put them at Maydh shortly. Paul watched Salaam closely as he spilled the information. When he decided he would talk, Salaam stopped wringing his hands, his breathing slowed and he looked Ali in the eye. He didn't waiver or trip over details, rather he described them soberly. He was telling the truth.

They left Salaam's and Ali sped through Bosasso to a main road heading west towards Maydh. The trip was nerve-wracking. Paul quietly held his breath every time they passed a military vehicle or checkpoint. But Ali and Habib managed to traverse these obstacles seamlessly. At each roadblock, they seemed to know one of the guards and engaged in friendly conversation before they were let through. But they eventually decided it was best to avoid any potential hassle from the soldiers at the checkpoints. So, they took an alternate route through open desert to Maydh.

Only when they were past the halfway point to Maydh did doubt start to poke through the exhilaration Paul felt at having a lead on the weapons. What were they going to do if they found the weapons? Did they really expect to stop Hadad with four assault rifles? Hadad would certainly be well prepared and guarded. Paul just hoped that Ali and Habib knew something more than he did.

Ali downshifted as the silhouette of the houses in Maydh came into view. They were simple dwellings: concrete walls and straw roofs. They joined the main road between the houses and drove towards the beach. The whole seaside town had less than twenty homes, all built at varying angles in relation to the windy gravel road. The place seemed deserted aside from three boys playing soccer barefoot with a ball made of tied up rags.

Rain began misting as they approached the beach. The sun had already set and the moon had taken its place. Silver moonlight poked through the rain clouds. The surf crashed gently and the sound of small rocks rattling around as the water receded could be heard over the hum of the Jeep's engine.

There was a row of a dozen small abandoned beach houses about two hundred yards from the shoreline. Ali parked the Jeep between two small beach houses on the end. They took care not to make a sound as they stepped out of the vehicle. Ellen swung her leg over the vehicle's door, but Ali put his hand out to stop her.

"You stay here," Ali said and pointed at Paul and Habib. "We will go, but it will be safer for you here."

"I'm not going to stay here alone," Ellen grabbed an AK-47 from the backseat, her voice raised, "in the dark, in the rain while you guys go with guns. How do you know it is safe here? They could be anywhere."

"Ellen, listen," Ali smiled then snatched the rifle from her hands and tossed it over to Paul who fumbled it, "you will do what I say. And I am saying that you stay here."

Ellen sat back in the passenger seat and sulked. Ali reached in his holster and handed her a Glock pistol, smiling. "For protection."

Paul slung the AK-47 over his shoulder and followed Ali around the beach house. The windows were broken out and the inside was empty save for two overturned stools.

At the corner of the house, Ali crouched down and looked towards the sea. Paul followed suit. The beach was at least two hundred feet wide, as the tide was out. It was an empty, untouched stretch of beach that stretched well past the horizon.

Paul scanned the beach on the left. He barely made out the silhouette of a convoy truck, parked in the middle of the sand. Beside it, he saw the orange glow of two cigarettes moving. Guards talking.

"Over there," Paul tapped Ali's shoulder and pointed, "the truck."

Ali pulled binoculars from his backpack and had a look. "I see four men," he passed the binoculars to Paul, "but I do not see Hadad."

Paul put the binoculars to his face and saw three soldiers, each with an assault rifle hanging crossways on their shoulders surrounding the truck. Another sat in the driver's seat. The passenger door of the truck swung open and a long, thin, almost lanky figure jumped down onto the sand. As he turned his head, his face caught the light and Paul at once recognized the image that was etched into his memory. Kadar Hadad.

"He's there," Paul said without moving the binoculars from his face.

He watched as Hadad made his way towards the water. He heard the faint sound of a powerboat approaching. A white skiff skipped along the water and right up on the beach, where two of Hadad's men dragged it onto the shore. Hadad greeted one of the men with a handshake.

Paul stood up to stretch his legs, which cramped from crouching down. "A boat just arrived," Paul whispered, "two men are on it."

Ali looked again. "They are going to load the weapons onto it. They can take the skiff across the Gulf to Yemen."

The mist was turning to hard rain now and Paul was drenched. Ali and Habib told Paul to stay at the first beach house while they moved forward to the next one over, which was closer to the convoy truck. They left Paul to provide cover for them. From his vantage point, he could see Ali and Habib crouched in the wet sand beside the beach house, pointing their guns towards the transport truck. The moon was behind them, casting their thin shadows towards the beach. Hadad's men carefully heaved the weapons off the truck bed and carried them over to the skiff.

Paul still wasn't certain how Ali and Habib planned to stop Hadad. Hadad's men outnumbered them two to one and Paul knew that Hadad's men knew how to handle themselves.

It didn't really matter to Paul, though. This was his chance to clear his name. He found the missing weapons and he could now stop Hadad from taking them out of Somalia. If he notified Langley and managed to get out of this situation alive, it would all be over. Maybe he could even get out of Somalia for good.

He placed the AK-47 down in the sand and pulled James' cell phone from his pocket. He dialed Officer Clarke's phone number and held his breath as he prayed he wasn't out of range of a transmitting station. He let out a quiet sigh when it started ringing.

When the operator answered, he asked to be connected to Officer Clarke. The static increased on the phone as he waited for the line to connect.

He needed to speak to Clarke. She knew about his situation and Paul felt she believed him. Something about the way she had tripped over her words, that she had let him speak rather than dismissing him immediately, made him think, or at least hope, that she believed him. She was his only hope.

"Officer Clarke speaking," she came on the phone, her voice barely audible through the static.

"I have a location on the weapons," Paul said. "A man name Kadar Hadad is loading them onto a ship as I speak."

"We already know that. We're in the middle of—"

Suddenly, a blast shook the entire beach, knocking the phone out of Paul's hand. He looked up and saw orange flames shooting up from a crater in the sand less than twenty feet from Hadad's transport truck. A cacophony of gunshots clanged off the transport truck and thudded into the sand. Hadad's men scrambled and took cover under the transport truck. The gunfire seemed to come from the open sea. They aimed their guns towards the black water.

Paul looked over at Habib and Ali, who had fallen on their backsides after the explosion. They looked as surprised as Paul as they watched Hadad's men react to the onslaught that came from some invisible source. Hadad's men faced the water and had their backs to Ali and Habib. They righted themselves and then opened fire on the transport truck, catching Hadad's men off guard.

Rain fell even harder, pattering into puddles on the beach.

Two of Hadad's men swiveled around and peppered shots towards Ali, sending fine dust spraying off the beach house's concrete walls. A shot zinged past Paul's ear into the wall behind him. Paul instinctively dropped down into a small divot in the sand, grinding his chest into the ground to get as low as possible. All he heard was his own heavy breathing.

For a moment, he lay there paralyzed. Maybe they wouldn't see him. But he heard another two cracks in the concrete wall behind him and realized he had to return fire. He poked his head out a couple of inches from the divot, grabbed his rifle and pointed it at the truck. He pulled the trigger, sending a series of rounds towards the truck. The kickback hit his shoulder like a punch from a heavyweight.

More gunfire. Paul couldn't tell where it was coming from anymore. Some from Hadad's men. Some from the invisible force in the water.

Ali and Habib retreated in a crouch, ran to Paul's position and fired at the truck.

"It's the Americans," Ali spat out, catching his breath, "we have to go."

"Is Hadad dead?"

"It doesn't matter. We have to go. They will finish this."

Ali grabbed Paul's shoulder as they moved towards the Jeep. Paul pushed Ali's hand away. He didn't want to leave. He couldn't. He had spent ten years brooding over the fact that Hadad had gotten away. He needed to know it was over.

Suddenly, Paul heard a flurry of gunshots across the beach and saw two of Hadad's men drop dead on the beach. The fire seemed to come from the far end of the beach, more blackness.

Then it became quiet. Too quiet.

Paul scanned the beach. He counted the silhouettes of five bodies lying motionless around the truck. Embers smoldered in the hole where the explosion had been, sizzling as the rain fell down. The canvas on the transport truck whipped in the breeze. The white skiff floated around the shoreline.

Something in the black water drew his eye. Three dark figures, completely black, emerged from the sea, and slogged through the water to the shore. Each held a gun in hand. Paul knew who they were.

"Navy SEALs," Paul said, pointing at the water.

"Go back to the truck," Ali nudged Paul with the tip of his gun, "now."

"No, you don't understand," Paul stood upright, raising his voice, excited, "they're with us. I called them to tell them we're here. That Hadad was here. They're on our side."

"We have to go." Habib grabbed Paul's arm with force and dragged him towards the Jeep.

Paul resisted but Habib was too strong for him. Why didn't they understand that it was over? Then Habib completely released his death grip on Paul's arm. He went limp and fell to his knees. A red spot on Habib's temple expanded. A single gunshot to the head.

Paul suddenly heard the echo of Bailey Clarke's voice in his head. *Full resources are being put towards recovering these weapons right now. What I do know is that once they are recovered, the next priority will be to bring those people responsible to justice. And you are number one on that list. So I suggest you get some proof, Dr. Alban, or run.*

Ali pushed Paul onto the ground and took a position next to him, prone on the sand. He fired towards the three SEALs, his automatic rifle making a heavy staccato with each round. The three SEALs landed on the beach and crouched, taking aim at Paul and Ali, each of their rounds causing a slick whizzing sound past Paul's ear.

"Shoot at them," Ali glanced over at Paul and then sent a series of bullets towards the beach.

"I can't do it. They're with us," Paul said, "they're American."

"They're going to kill us if you don't shoot them."

He picked up Habib's rifle from the sand and fired at the SEALs on the beach. He had barely shot off ten rounds when the transport truck's headlights flicked on and the engine roared to life. The gunfire between them and the SEALs stopped momentarily as they all looked towards the truck.

It started up the beach, directly towards them, increasing in speed. Ali was the first to react, firing at the truck. Paul followed his lead and soon the SEALs were also firing at the truck. Bullet holes punctured the gas tanks and tires along its side and it swerved hard trying to keep its course. The driver overcorrected and it swerved, crashing into the beach house about fifty yards in front of them, knocking the concrete wall in and sending a plume of smoke up from under the hood.

It was silent other than the sound of steam from the engine and a broken wheel left spinning. Paul and Ali didn't move, just stared at the wreckage. No more bullets were fired from the other side. Presumably, the SEALs were just as interested in the truck as they were.

Paul waited to see if the driver survived the crash. He needed to know who the driver was. A sinking, sick feeling coursed through him. Part of him knew it could only be one person.

Then, the driver's side door creaked open and a groan came from inside. The door swung open and a hand clenched the doorframe. Then, the driver's free hand appeared, clenching a pistol. Bullets flew towards Ali and Paul. A bullet found Ali's right shoulder, sending him to ground, writhing in agony.

Paul crouched down to look at Ali and in that instant, the driver jumped out of the truck. He carried a large duffel bag on his back. As the driver ran past the truck, Paul caught a glimpse of his face: Hadad.

Paul fired at the truck. He sprayed waves of bullets towards Hadad. They clanged against the truck's metal frame. A series hit the gas tanks and the truck exploded into bright orange flames. The blast sent metal pieces flying in all directions and its sheer force knocked Paul back several feet.

He got up and stared wide-eyed at the smoldering wreckage. Flames illuminated the pitch-black sky. When he looked for Ali, all he saw was a flaming truck door. He scrambled in closer and saw Ali lying motionless underneath. Paul pushed the door aside with the butt of the AK-47. He checked for a pulse and for breathing, but there was none. He tore Ali's shirt off and felt the bandages around Ali's torso. They were soaked. Then his fingers found a massive gash along his chest, his ribs poking out. Paul paused for a moment, one that felt like an eternity. His mind tried to refute the reality that Ali was dead.

Then he heard the SEALs firing shots again, but this time they weren't directed at Paul, they were shooting at Hadad. Hadad was in a full sprint, not slowed down at all by the weight of the duffel bag on his back. He sprinted along the backside of the beach houses right past Paul.

Paul traced Hadad's trajectory with his eyes and saw where he was headed. The last beach house.

The Jeep. Ellen.

Paul jumped up and ran along the sand, chasing after Hadad, who was less than fifty yards ahead of him. He saw Hadad get to the Jeep and throw the duffel bag inside. Ellen tried to jump out, but Hadad grabbed her hair and swung her down into the passenger seat. Then he elbowed her in the face and she fell back into the seat.

The Jeep started up. Paul broke into a sprint. He pushed himself, straining his muscles, to get to the Jeep. When he was less than ten feet away, the Jeep started moving away from him. Paul gave another burst of speed and lunged forward, but his finger slipped off the back bumper.

Paul picked himself up and focused. The Jeep was turning around to head away from the water, towards the open desert. The wheel spun in the sand and momentarily the Jeep stopped.

Paul ran, and pushed even harder as the Jeep got going again. He was gaining on it. He took another step and lunged forward, stretching his arms as far as he could towards the Jeep. His fingertips hooked onto the spare tire on the back of the Jeep and then he swung his palm and clenched the back frame of the vehicle. The Jeep sped up and he briefly lost his grip and slipped down, his knees scraping as they dragged along the desert sand.

Paul glanced behind him to see where the SEALs were but all he saw was darkness, the beach no longer in view. Hadad accelerated.

Paul propped himself up and looked to the front of the Jeep. Ellen was now awake and looked back at Paul, motioning for him to come forward. Hadad's arm then struck her in the back of her head, knocking her face first into the seat back.

Paul gritted his teeth, heaved himself up on the tire and tried to swing his foot up onto the bumper. The Jeep swerved and Paul lost his footing, slipping down again. Hadad kept swerving the vehicle back and forth as they drove deeper into the desert. Paul focused on his hold to the Jeep, each swerve loosening it by millimeters. The rain made the Jeep surfaces slick, even harder to hold on to.

Then Hadad took the Jeep into a sharp turn going around in a circle. The force pulled Paul from the Jeep, his grip unable to hold on any longer. He flew from the Jeep and skidded along the wet sand, tumbling end over end until he thumped into a sand dune. He landed hard on his shoulder and the wind was knocked out of him.

Paul tried to get air in through his mouth, but he couldn't manage more than a wheeze. He looked out at the desert and made out the Jeep's headlights not more than one hundred yards from him.

Paul focused on his breathing, heaved himself up and started towards the Jeep. It was at most a brisk walk, he couldn't run.

Then a *thwoosh - thwoosh - thwoosh* came from above.

Paul looked up and saw a helicopter approaching, spinning the desert sand into a mini-tornado. There were no lights on the helicopter; it blended in with the dark sky perfectly. It hovered briefly above the Jeep, partially obscuring Hadad and Ellen. Paul tried to walk towards them but sand flew into his eyes, making it impossible to see.

The chopper touched down and Hadad dragged Ellen towards it. She thrashed at him but he easily subdued her and dragged her onto the aircraft.

Paul kept moving towards it, trying to get a view of the helicopter through the spinning sand. It rose up. The helicopter was huge, at least five times the size of the Jeep. It was sleek and dark with a light blue stripe along the side. There were no weapons of any kind on it. A civilian helicopter. Along the tail, he saw a serial number, *VO4-66A*.

The helicopter rose back up into the blackness.

Then things became quiet again. Paul plopped down on the sand, ignoring the pain from his scraped, burning skin.

Thoughts swirled in his head. Thoughts that came so quickly he couldn't finish one before the next one pushed it out of the way. Thoughts that could be best summarized as *what the hell is going on here?*

Then, he lifted himself off the sand, started the Jeep and drove into the black desert.

He had to find out what was happening.

Twenty-five

The central situation room at the NCS was exuberant. It had quickly filled up with a dozen or so senior officials in perfect suits. They stood around the large conference table in the center of the room and congratulated each other with smiles and firm slaps on the back. They had just received the call from General Kaczmareck, the head of AFRICOM.

The operation was a success; all the man portable nuclear weapons were accounted for. It was a well-coordinated effort. The intelligence on the location of the weapons had come in, paramilitary officers were immediately notified and they activated a special operations force stationed in Yemen. AFRICOM commanders coordinated the attack and extraction of the weapons. Time from intel to extraction: twelve hours, forty-two minutes.

It had all of the features of a well-run clandestine operation. There were no casualties and all objectives were completed. Most importantly, they managed to recover the weapons before the Ukrainians started asking questions and no one in the media got wind of it.

At the center of the backslapping was a beaming Jim Crilley. He accepted the accolades from all around him, laughing boisterously at the simplest joke. It was he, after all, who had obtained the intel on the weapons.

Removed from the crowd, Bailey Clarke leaned against a desk in the corner of the room with her arms crossed sipping Red Rose from a Styrofoam cup. She hoped the tea would ease the slight headache that lingered after the rum and Coke she had at her apartment.

She had hoped that any thoughts of Paul Alban being innocent would dissipate as the alcohol left her system. But it didn't. Her mind kept flashing back to the missing file. *MR-14406.* She told herself it was a footnote, that was all. It didn't prove anything. Objectively, Crilley was right. Was it more likely that the NCS was somehow infiltrated? Or that Paul Alban botched an intelligence transfer? *But why did he contact us? Twice?*

Bailey knew that asking these questions wouldn't get her anywhere. The National Clandestine Service mandate was first and foremost to keep the United States safe from outside threats, through intelligence. They had done that. They had stopped twelve nuclear weapons from disappearing into terrorist hands. Case closed. It was now time to move onto the next threat, the next mission.

But her mind couldn't let it go. There were too many unanswered questions. Paul Alban had called to notify them about the location of the weapons. And where did Crilley get the intel on the weapons anyway? All Crilley said was that the intel had come through her old workplace, the paramilitary operations division, the place she had left less than two months ago to start fresh in clandestine operations.

Bailey slipped out the door and went into the women's washroom across the hall. She checked under each stall for ankles and when she satisfied herself that it was empty, she took her cell phone out of her jacket pocket. Before dialing, she took a deep breath and ran the tap to muffle her voice.

"Officer Christopher Hanson here," he always answered his cell phone that way, punctuating each syllable. She had once thought it was a cute quirk, but it irritated her now. Only when she heard his voice did she decide that calling him was a bad idea. If Crilley found out what she was doing, she would lose her job altogether. But if she could just speak to someone in paramilitary, maybe she could find out where the intelligence on the weapons came from. Chris would know. And he would tell her what he knew.

"Hi," she swallowed hard, "it's me." A long moment passed before he spoke.

"Bailey?"

"Yeah," she said, but it came out as a grunt.

"What is it?" his voice turned cold, icy.

"I need to meet with you. As soon as possible."

"What?" she had caught him off guard, "I don't have time for this, Bailey. I'm busy, we'll have to—"

"Chris it's not about that," Bailey said, "it's about this Somalia thing. I can't tell you everything over the phone, but it's serious. It needs to be sorted out right away. I need to speak to you, someone I can trust. You're the only one I can turn to right now."

Chris exhaled into the receiver. "Come to my office in fifteen minutes."

"No, that won't work," Bailey shook her head, "it needs to be off site."

"What've you gotten into?"

"Starbucks on Chain Bridge in fifteen minutes." She hung up before Chris could protest.

~ * ~

Thirty minutes later (fifteen minutes late), Bailey parked her entry level Honda Civic in front of the Starbucks on Chain Lake. A random car search at Langley's North parking lot exit had caused a fifteen minute delay. No amount of horn honking or steering wheel smacking could speed up a search. Bailey was relieved that she had made it out so quickly. She just hoped Chris had waited for her.

She scurried across the parking lot, shielding her head from the pouring rain by lifting the jacket collar over the top of her head.

She opened the door, shook the rain off and scanned the coffee shop. On the surface, this Starbucks looked like every other Starbucks. Customers sat around the bistro tables. The staccato of baristas frothing milk and background jazz music drowned out any conversations. The difference was that this Starbucks was a quarter mile up the road from the CIA headquarters in Langley, Virginia. Men and women in suits and long coats regularly made the trip down for coffee runs, returning to work with trayfulls of coffee for their department. The excuse was that the coffee at headquarters was sub-par and stale. And while there was some truth to that, many people drifted in to discuss matters off the record.

She saw Chris sitting at a table by the window across from two cups of coffee. He stared out the window at merging traffic on the highway and hadn't noticed her come in. The first thing Bailey felt was relief that he waited for her. The second thing was a wave of apprehension. It had been five months since Chris asked Bailey to leave the apartment. Six months since she had told him about the sex with Blake. Up until then, in their three years together, they had never had what Bailey would have considered a real argument. Bailey knew that a large part of what had kept them together during those three years was her ability to keep Chris' ego inflated and his ability to make her feel safe.

Chris was what her father would have labeled as *silver spooned from the cradle*. His upbringing couldn't have contrasted more with Bailey's. He was the son of a state senator and heiress to a mining corporation, while she was raised by a widowed, unemployed alcoholic father. He used trust funds to go to boarding schools and then attended West Point while Bailey earned scholarship after scholarship to get an education. After West Point, Chris joined the Army Rangers and within two years, the CIA's paramilitary division recruited him.

It was at a morning intelligence debriefing that Bailey had first seen him. He stood up and delivered a report on rebel activity in Southern Armenia. He immediately gave her the impression of being a strong, loyal person. Someone who made her feel secure. To her surprise, later that day, he stopped her at the elevator and asked her point blank if she would go to dinner with him. She agreed. While she realized that many women would take offense to a man ordering for them, she loved it. Shortly thereafter, she moved in with him and a year later, he proposed at the foot of the Washington Monument at night. Two years of bliss followed.

But that all changed. After she told Chris about the incident with Blake, they both agreed they would *work through it.* But in the month that followed, they had arguments that Bailey could only describe as vicious. The arguments would start benignly enough, with her going out with some girlfriends and Chris repeatedly asking her what time she would be back. And she would become defensive and even hateful. And Chris was not the kind of person to let things go. The arguments quickly spiraled out of control. Yelling, screaming, a broken picture frame, a broken vase.

For months after he had asked her to leave the apartment, she couldn't recall a night where she didn't burst into tears. In time, she wasn't sure what she was even crying about. Was it losing Chris? Being alone? The rape? But the one thing that crept in and grabbed hold was her disdain for Chris. She wondered what she had ever seen in him. How had she not recognized his porcelain ego before? How had she allowed herself to love a man who couldn't get past the blow to his own self-esteem when his fiancée was raped?

But the thought that troubled her most right now was that he looked good.

His blonde hair was freshly trimmed and he had finally gotten rid of the goatee. He was just over six feet tall, with a lean frame that filled out the trench coat he had unbuttoned underneath which he wore a perfectly pressed navy wool suit. The ensemble was complete with a pair of polished caramel-colored loafers.

He noticed Bailey standing at the entryway of the coffee shop and half raised his hand, acknowledging her. She walked over and lowered herself into the chair across from him.

"It's for you," Chris motioned to the coffee on the table.

"You remembered my drink," Bailey smiled.

"It's hard to forget extra foam, non-fat, extra hot, vanilla latte with cinnamon sprinkles."

They both let out a nervous laugh but it quickly faded and the awkwardness returned. Bailey shifted her eyes to her coffee cup.

"You look good," Bailey offered.

"Thanks." Chris furrowed his brow. "Don't take this the wrong way, but you kind of look like hell."

"Thanks, Chris. Let's just say it's been a long, long day. And I don't think it's over."

"The Somalia thing? Sounded like it's over to me."

Bailey looked him straight in the eye. "Is it?"

Chris shrugged.

"So, what happened on your end?"

"Bailey, those things are classified internally. You know that."

"I'm looking into something here. There's some inconsistencies that my department needs to sort out. It's a bit outside of protocol. Can you help me?"

Chris leaned back and crossed his arms, looking at Bailey sideways. "Sure," he said. "But first, can I ask you something?"

Bailey nodded.

"Are you seeing anyone?"

It took a second to register. She let out a sound of disbelief and looked out the window. "Are you kidding? I can't believe you're asking that," she looked at Chris, his face unfazed, "No, I'm not."

Chris took it in and exhaled, relieved.

Bailey stared back, her eyes burrowing holes into Chris'. She was processing the information, the way he was sitting, relaxed, pompous, entitled. "Do you think I called you here to get back together or something? To come crawling back?"

Chris shrugged.

"The fact you showed up, the coffee, the small talk." She shook her head. "No, Chris, it's over, it's been over. I'm sorry if I somehow misled you."

His face turned red. He was angry. Chris drummed on the table for a few beats, stood up and made for the door. Bailey rose, leaving the coffee behind and followed him into the parking lot outside. Rain was pouring over her as she galloped and grabbed Chris by the arm.

"I need to know about what happened today," she shouted over the rain pounding the asphalt. "Where did the intelligence come from about the location of the weapons?"

"I don't know." Chris tried to pull away, but Bailey held his arm.

"I can tell when you're lying, Chris. What do you want from me?"

Chris considered for a moment, then smiled. "Come over tonight. I want to see you."

Bailey curled her lip and snarled, "You asshole. That's what this is about?"

"You're the one who needs something, Bailey." Chris was serious and she could tell that this was his final offer. The last thing she wanted was to get back together with him. But she needed to find out more about what happened in Somalia.

"You can call me sometime." She was totally drenched from the rain. "Now tell me who got the information about the weapons. It came from your division."

"No, it didn't," Chris pulled away from Bailey's grip, "we just acted on the intelligence once it was passed on to us. We didn't gather the intel. I don't know where you got that from."

"Where did it come from, then?"

"I should be asking you," Chris started up the parking lot, "because it came from your boss. Jim Crilley."

Bailey stood drenched in the middle of the parking lot and watched Chris drive away.

Twenty-six

Paul drove across the desert and eventually reached a broken up road that he followed for over an hour. Most of the roads in this part of Somalia hadn't been repaired since the 1969 *coup d'etat* that many felt knocked the nation onto its downward trajectory.

Bullet holes dotted the Jeep's driver's side and the nylon roof cover was torn to shreds. Something rattled around under the hood and Paul thought the Jeep would either stall or burst into flames.

To his surprise, it stayed in one piece the whole sixty miles to the town of Ceerigaabo. By the time he parked the Jeep, it had cooled off considerably. He walked across the street to an Internet café that was open until 10 p.m. Decals in the front window claimed they not only had the best Internet and phone rates in Somalia but all of Africa. While Paul didn't pay much attention to their advertising, the lights were on inside, so he entered, paid the worker behind the desk enough for two hours and a pack of Italian Marlboros and sat in front of the computer closest to the back wall.

He pushed the computer's power button. As it booted up, he lit a cigarette and didn't mind the smoke drifting into his eyes. He thought of Ellen being dragged up into the mysterious helicopter. What troubled him most about his current situation was that he didn't feel much of anything. Numb. He believed that most people, when faced with a desperate scenario like his own, would (*and should*) feel emotions ranging from anger to sadness to confusion. He was somehow set up to look like a terrorist, he was considered an enemy to his own country and the one person he truly loved had been abducted. He realized then, that when the stress of a situation stretched far beyond the limits of which one could cope did the mind do the only thing it could still manage: denial. That had to explain the numbness, the emptiness. He was in denial.

He took another drag on his cigarette and stared at the monitor. His only lead at this point was the helicopter serial number. He took the chewed pencil resting on the keyboard and wrote the number down on the pack of cigarettes so he wouldn't forget: *VO4-66A*.

The thing he couldn't understand was that the helicopter was a private one. The kind that billionaires owned. It couldn't have belonged to Hadad. That meant Hadad had to be working with someone, or *for* someone.

Hadad worked with many different businessmen, mafia, politicians and military officials over the years. He had a history of carefully manipulating each deal to suit his own needs. In 1992, Hadad had controlled a mercenary force of retired Senegalese soldiers and made a large backroom financial deal with the United States government to invade the Liberian capital Monrovia and restore order after warlord Charles Taylor had taken over the government. Instead, he funneled the funds into a personal bank account, informed the Taylor regime of the planned invasion and essentially sent his own men into slaughter. Then he went off the grid for six years, occasionally mentioned in relation to terrorist activities, until he carried out the Nairobi and dar es Salaam embassy bombings.

Paul searched the Internet for two hours, trying to match the serial number with a helicopter. By that point, he had already popped open his second pack of cigarettes, polished off two stale pastries and a cup of tea. The Internet connection was dial-up and slow as hell, but he searched a series of photographs to try and match the helicopter.

He learned that Sosnovsky, a large American Aircraft Corporation, manufactured the helicopter. The image of the massive helicopter in his memory most closely matched Model S-42A, a fourteen-passenger commercial helicopter. The company webpage listed that it had a range of nearly five hundred miles and that it could land in any open area. The helicopter could have come from any nearby country to pick up Hadad.

He subsequently searched the model number and found that forty-four were currently in commercial use worldwide. Forty-four possibilities, assuming it was registered. Large aeronautical and military corporations often made a surplus of weapons and vehicles that never got registered and sold them at huge profit on the black market. While government agencies tried to crack down on this, the truth was that there were likely as many unregistered helicopters as registered ones. If the helicopter was unregistered, Paul knew it would be impossible to trace.

He scrolled through the list of registered helicopters and came across the serial number he was looking for.

It was registered to an American petrol company named VeritOil. He immediately asked himself what on earth an American oil company was doing with a high level terrorist like Hadad.

He kept searching for information about the company. According to wikipedia, the company was initially founded in 1958, and bought up reserves in Columbia and Peru. It had later discovered reserves in the Gulf of Mexico and by 1997 had grown to be the third highest producer of natural gas and fifth highest producer of crude oil among United States-based companies. A new CEO had been introduced in 1996 and since then, a combination of political unrest and failed explorations lead to major decline in profit. The company's credit had become so poor that in 2004, it unsuccessfully applied for a $240 million government loan for exploration in Atlantic Canada. It had apparently stayed afloat by introducing new technology for clean fuel processing. It became a leader in clean fuel emissions and last year was the only U.S. petrol company to have met new government emissions standards.

He found the answer to their connection to Somalia in an archived BBC article from 2006. He rested his cigarette on an ashtray and stared at the screen. *VeritOil signs contract with Somalia's transitional government.* According to the article, VeritOil had signed a contract with the transitional federal government granting them exclusive drilling rights to seventy percent of the Puntland as well as any oil reserves they found in the Gulf of Aden. In exchange, they forwarded the Somali government five billion dollars and would pay a twenty percent tax on all profits.

Paul shook his head in disbelief. He had heard that Somalia was considered one of the few untapped oil reserves left on dry land. Only ocean and arctic deposits were bigger. But from a strictly engineering perspective, Somalia's reserve was considered more accessible. No one had drilled, though, because the country was far too unstable for major projects to begin. But for a company to exclusively own that proportion of the reserve was incredible.

The company's CEO, John Daniels, was pictured on an insert in the article shaking hands with the then Prime Minister of the transitional federal government. They stood in front of a group of men and women in suits on the steps of the Puntland parliament building. At one point in time, Daniels had likely been a handsome man, with a strong jaw and gentle eyes. But by the time this picture had been taken, he was at least fifty pounds overweight and balding. His graying temples and full beard suited his olive complexion. The BBC report quoted him as saying, "*we hope this contract can help bring about stability to this region and prosperity to this country. This is not a contract just for today, but for the future.*"

No doubt, the contract hadn't worked the way Daniels had hoped. Somalia was in worse shape that it had been two years ago. And there was no drilling to speak of.

But Paul was still missing the link between VeritOil and Kadar Hadad. Had they made a deal with Hadad for something? But they already had a deal with the transitional government. If anything, they would want to eliminate Hadad; he was a part of the reason for the unrest in Somalia. But there had to be a reason. He had to find it out, if he was to have a chance of finding Hadad. Of finding Ellen.

Paul popped another cigarette in his mouth. He stared at the slightly blurry picture of Daniels, wishing that the answer would somehow come to him just by looking at the man. A woman standing just to the right of Daniels caught his eye. He zoomed in on the picture, on the woman. She wore a tight fitting black skirt and a red sweater. He immediately recognized her. As his mouth gaped open and he let out a little gasp, the cigarette fell onto the floor.

She didn't look much different than he remembered her. She didn't seem to have aged at all. Her blonde hair was shorter, but she was still trim and in shape. She still wore too much eye makeup. He read the caption carefully; her name was Joan Daniels, John Daniels' wife.

She was also Marshall Ramsey's widow.

Twenty-seven

Whenever a letter was sent home from Peter Daniels' school because of truancy, his mother blamed it on the fact that his biological father had died suddenly in a head-on collision when Peter was six. It also, in her eyes, explained his chronic marijuana and alcohol use, his angry outbursts, his general disrespect for authority figures and his stealing cash from her purse on a regular basis.

Even though Peter didn't believe that to be the case, he found it a convenient enough excuse to avoid any lasting punishment when he misbehaved. Rather, he thought his anger stemmed from having an asshole for a stepfather, a mother who agreed with any stupid thing that came out of his mouth and having grown up in a sheltered, gated community in Virginia.

The truth was that Peter thought very little about his real father. That man was reduced to little more than a series of fuzzy memories in his head that Peter was pretty sure every kid had experienced with their old man: building sandcastles and laughing as the tide came in and swallowed them up, playing airplanes in the living room and having wheelbarrow races across the front lawn.

He had gone through a brief phase when he was fourteen where he wanted to learn more about his real dad. It came on the heels of his first suspension at school for spraying a fire extinguisher at another student. His step-dad John decided (and his mom agreed, as usual) that he not be allowed to go to camp at all that summer. Maybe because he felt such anger, hatred, towards John, part of him hoped he would learn that his real dad—the man he should have grown up with—was a good guy.

Less than two hours of research suggested that was not the case. His father was a war criminal. Peter searched out archived articles on the Internet from all the news sources he could manage: *Time, Vanity Fair, The Washington Post,* etc. His father had been part of a team charged with finding the people responsible for bombings in Kenya and Tanzania. His dad was the doctor on the team. But the whole investigation turned into a debacle and his father was charged with permitting torture. But he was never convicted. According to the *New York Times* and *Washington Post* articles, the only reason he got away without a conviction was because he testified against the other men on the team.

For Peter, that was the worst part. This meant that his father was not only a war criminal; he was a backstabber.

That was enough for Peter to conclude that to him, his father would remain no more than a montage of pleasant, generic memories.

Peter sat on a futon in his bedroom on the third floor of John Daniels' Victorian home. The curtains were drawn shut and a lava lamp on a nightstand next to an unmade bed provided the only light in the room. A tangle of dirty clothes lay strewn across the floor and empty soda bottles stood next to bags of chips on the nightstand. Peter's hair touched his shoulders and was in need of a good wash. His clothes hung off his spindly frame.

His best friend, Wayne Robinson, who was onto his second stepfather, searched the Internet on Peter's computer in the corner of the room.

Peter lit up a joint, took a long drag and coughed a little bit afterwards. "You should try some of this." Peter stood up, passed the joint over to Wayne and took a sip of Dr. Pepper.

"Smells good," Wayne took a drag, sending him into a brief coughing fit. "That is good."

Wayne passed the joint back to Peter. "What'd you tell your mom about why you're not at school?"

"I said I was sick," Peter laughed.

"Sick with what?"

"I said I felt depressed."

"She believed you?" Wayne said.

"Oh yeah" Peter bit into a ketchup chip, "she's big time into that. Takes it super serious, she's on like two medications for it herself."

"This is my antidepressant," Wayne said, taking another toke on the joint. Then he waved for Peter to come over. "Come check this out, man. Have you seen this?"

Peter walked around the computer and saw a YouTube clip opened. He read the title, "*Spy torture*? Haven't seen it. What is it?"

"Craziest shit, man. It's these terrorist guys in Somalia—they torture a guy in it. They say he's a CIA spy."

"Play it, play it, man."

They watched the two-minute clip intently. It was a poor recording, and there was no audio, but there were two blurry men on the clip. The black man stood and spoke to the white man who sat tied to a chair. Both Peter and Wayne groaned when the interrogator ripped the man's nail out. Their eyes widened when the interrogator pressed the circular saw on the man's neck.

But before anything else happened, the clip ended.

"That's crazy," Peter said, his eyes still glued to the screen. "Did they kill him?"

"I don't know. I checked it out on some news sites but all they say is that there was a bit of audio at the beginning that someone translated and the interrogator refers to him as 'doctor'."

"All I'm saying is that's a good cover for a spy."

"You think the clip's real?"

"Probably," Peter said. "Look at the way he just stared through the whole process. Man, he barely flinched. That guy's trained. Imagine if you were being tortured, you'd be shitting your pants, not sitting there making eye contact with the guy."

Wayne nodded slowly, considering. "Yeah, you're probably right."

"The guy's probably dead by now."

"Maybe the whole thing's fake," Wayne threw his hands up, "as if the government would let something like this happen."

"It happens man, trust me."

Wayne abruptly stopped, nodded his head slowly and grinned. "Is this you talking? Or is it Leah?"

"Oh, give me a break, man, I have my own opinions, okay?"

"I'm just saying, man, ever since you met dreadlocks hottie you've become this political activist slash conspiracy theorist."

Peter waved his hand in the air to suggest he didn't care and then took a drag on the joint. He wasn't about to admit that his friend had a point. He'd met Leah at a Smokes and Chains concert two months earlier. Afterwards they went to a house party on a beach outside the city, got drunk and went skinny-dipping. They'd been seeing each other ever since. Peter wasn't exactly sure what the word love meant, but he figured that if it meant it was a person you wanted to spend every second with, then he was probably in love.

Leah was three years his senior, beautiful with a narrow nose, blue eyes and a wide mouth. She had her blonde hair in dreadlocks and had multiple rings in her ears, nose and lip. She was a Poli Sci major at university and one day while he was waiting for her to get ready at her apartment, he picked up a book by an author named Noam Chomsky. It took him two days to read through the whole book but it was enough to light a fire inside him, one that raged with thoughts of injustices in politics. A flame he shared with Leah.

"That reminds me," Peter said, "are you going to come with us to the rally tomorrow?"

"What's she got you protesting against this time?"

Peter ignored the dig. "It's an anti-war rally. It's going to be huge, maybe a hundred thousand people down at the National Mall." Wayne didn't seem impressed. "Her friend Jessie's going."

"In that case, I'm all for peace," Wayne lifted two fingers up, "hopefully some free love too."

There was a knock at the bedroom door. "It's my mom," he whispered to Wayne, then louder towards the door, "just a sec." Peter put the joint out in the ashtray and threw it into the nightstand drawer. He grabbed the bottle of cheap cologne from the shelf and sprayed it around the room.

"Your mom?" Wayne flattened his hair with his palm and ran his tongue across his teeth. "She's hot, man."

"Shut up."

~ * ~

Joan Daniels stared at Peter's bedroom door wringing her hands. She needed to know her son was safe in his room. The feeling had risen up in her slowly and then expanded until she could no longer stand it. She knew her son found her intrusive and she did her best to give him space. She had already gone for a forty-five minute jog, had a shower, blow-dried her hair and did her make-up. She couldn't distract herself any longer; she just needed to know he was okay.

Lately, Joan spent most of her time worrying about her son's mental health. High school had been a difficult transition. He had made a few friends, but he was constantly in trouble. At home, he barely spoke a civil word to her or John. Rather, he stayed in his room and listened to angry music. She asked her therapist about it and they concluded that Peter likely had depression and would benefit from seeing a professional. Peter, of course, refused.

Joan knew all about depression. She had stabilized her moods on a cocktail of several antidepressants. She knew that some people with depression ended up committing suicide. The thought that he may not answer the door always flashed through her in the seconds after she knocked.

Joan blamed herself for Peter's problems. She had tried her best, but she was always bothered with the idea that she could have done things differently. Sure, he had lost his father when he was six, but she had quickly remarried, largely so Peter would have a father. And John tried to treat Peter like his own son. For some reason she could never comprehend, Peter never took to John and they ended up growing apart. She couldn't help but think that maybe she shouldn't have remarried; maybe then Peter would be happy.

The door swung open and the smell of marijuana and cheap cologne instantly hit her. She decided not to say anything. She suspected the only reason that Peter still spoke to her was that some deep down part of him knew she really loved him. And although she sometimes felt like she should have a talk with him about drug use, she just couldn't risk rocking the boat and alienating him completely.

Peter stood in front of her, resting his arm on the doorframe.

"What is it, mom?" he said, enunciating each syllable.

"Just wanted to see if I could take some dishes downstairs," Joan smiled. She always managed an excuse to enter his room.

Peter shrugged and let Joan walk inside. She waved at Wayne and collected the dirty cups and plates that lay around the room. She could feel Wayne's eyes examining her as she did this but tried not to pay it much attention. Peter stood near the entrance with his arms crossed, making it clear to Joan that she was not welcome to stay.

"What are you boys doing?"

"Nothing much," Wayne said, "just watching T.V."

"Shouldn't you be at school, Wayne?"

Joan picked up a mug sitting near the computer.

"I have the afternoon off."

"What's that you guys are looking at?" Joan pointed at the fuzzy screenshot on the computer.

"It's a YouTube clip of a guy being tortured," Wayne said. "In the clip they say that he's a CIA agent."

"You two shouldn't be looking at that stuff," Joan smiled, "it'll give you nightmares."

"Mom," Peter motioned for her to leave. Her time was up.

"Wait a sec, Mrs. Daniels," Wayne cut in. "Look at the clip, do you think its real?"

Joan smiled and half rolled her eyes and decided to play along. "Okay, play it." She heard Peter huff behind her.

At first, Joan only half watched the clip in a halfhearted attempt to be closer to her son. But when she saw Marshall tied to the chair, her eyes fixed on the screen. She didn't drop the dishes or gasp. Rather, she stood motionless. Her heart sped up but didn't race. She would later tell herself that it was only her overactive imagination, like one of those weird perceptual experiences like hearing footsteps while alone in an old house in the dead of a summer night. But at that moment, her mind grasped for an explanation. Long after the clip had ended, she stood there staring right through the computer screen.

"Mom... Mom?" she heard Pete's voice through the fog, "what's wrong?"

But she couldn't break from her trance.

Then she felt a stiff hand grab her shoulder. "Mom?"

She managed to turn her head slowly towards Peter. He looked relieved. "Jesus, Mom, you look like you saw a ghost."

And she had. She was certain she had.

Twenty-eight

Although Bailey told herself to turn back a dozen times, once she got off the elevator on the fourteenth floor of the CIA headquarters, she knew she was going to go through with it. She had systematically planned out each component of what she was about to do. First, she kept herself up until one in the morning by sipping strong coffee so she would be sure the floor of the NCS was deserted. As she tiptoed up the aisle, all she noticed were two cubicles with desk lights on, where a couple of keen analysts were buried in paper work. Behind the cubicles, at the far end of the floor, a cleaner ran a vacuum. She had managed to slip in without raising any suspicion. The first part of her plan had gone smoothly. Next, she would enter Crilley's office using the key he had given here two weeks ago, quickly scan all of the folders and once she found *MR-14406*, she would quickly scan through it. She would read it quickly, just enough to make sense of the inconsistencies. She would replace the file, maybe make a few key photocopies, slip out of the office and be on the road back home. *I'll be out in fifteen minutes,* she said to herself.

That, of course, was the best-case scenario. The analytical part of her mind, the part that constantly weighed the risks and benefits, that annoying part that wouldn't shut off, kept going through worst-case scenarios in her head. If she were caught breaking into her boss's office, her career in the CIA was over. That much was a certainty. More likely, she would be charged with treason, made an example of in court, and sent to a military prison for five to ten years.

But those scenarios required someone to walk in on her. The chances of that happening were low.

She needed to make sense of what was happening. A clandestine operative claimed to have been given a ship's manifest that conveniently had the nuclear weapons aboard omitted. Then, he tracked the weapons down and notified her about them. All the while, her boss somehow managed to locate the weapons in the middle of a Somali desert and arranged a swift recovery operation in record time. And half of the operative's file was missing. It didn't take someone with Bailey's attention to detail to sense there was more to the story.

Bailey stood in front of Crilley's office door and glanced from side-to-side one last time. She read the engraved plastic sign on the oak door bearing Jim Crilley's name and title and thought, *what on earth is the Deputy Director of the NCS up to?*

She unlocked the door, walked in and closed it carefully behind her, conscious of not making a sound. She closed the Venetian blind covering the small hallway window before turning the desk lamp on. It cast a dull orange glow over the sea of files in stacked brown banker boxes against the walls. There were more boxes on a bookshelf next to the window and Bailey assumed the locked metal filing cabinet opposite his desk contained even more.

Bailey lifted a box up onto the desk and flicked through the files, reading each label looking for any combination of *Paul Alban* or *Somalia* or the *MR-14406*. After thumbing through a couple of boxes, she realized Crilley had no apparent order to his filing. Finding *MR-14406* was a needle in a haystack proposition. She looked through box after box of files, placing each one in their original position, just to make sure Crilley didn't notice that someone had been in his office.

Her fifteen minutes came and went without her noticing. She went through each box systematically, but found nothing. A second perusal was fruitless. She tried the filing cabinet, but it was locked.

She sat in Crilley's leather chair and rubbed her eyes. She calculated she hadn't slept for forty hours. That probably explained the nausea. Maybe the sleep deprivation led her to believe that Marshall Ramsey's file would be in plain sight in Jim Crilley's office. Maybe it was what led her to believe that Jim Crilley was at the center of some sort of conspiracy.

She decided she had to look through the filing cabinet. Most of the files out in the open were non-specific intelligence reports with very little sensitivity. If he had a sensitive file on a clandestine operative, he would have it under lock and key.

Bailey searched Crilley's desk, felt around the bottom of the drawers, and around the keyboard but couldn't find a key. She got up and looked at the filing cabinet. It seemed like it had a fairly standard lock. Nothing special. In college, Bailey had chronically locked her keys in her dorm room. And as her roommate was almost always out late partying, Bailey had to learn how to pick the lock on the front door. It had been awhile, but she still remembered how to go about it.

She grabbed a uniball pen from the keyboard on Crilley's desk, popped off the top and bent the clip off. Then she removed a bobby pin from her hair. She inserted the pen clip into the lock and pressed down. All the while, she shimmied the bobby pin into the lock until she felt it release. Then she carefully turned the lock.

Bailey looked at her watch and saw that she had been in Crilley's office for an hour and twenty minutes. She told herself that she would look through the filing cabinet once and then leave. If she didn't find anything, she would forget all about Paul Alban. She would wake up in the morning, shower, put extra make-up under the developing circles under her eyes and come back to work in five hours, looking fresh and ready for the next assignment.

But that didn't happen. *MR-14406* was the first file in the top drawer.

Any sleepiness that had accumulated in her disappeared. Her eyelids felt light and her mind became sharp. She sat in Crilley's plush leather office chair and smoothed the dossier out on the desk.

She flipped open the dossier and saw that the *MR* were the initials for a deceased man named Marshall Ramsey. A red stamp across the front sheet of the file identified that he had been *KILLED IN ACTION* in 1998. The first page had basic identifying information: born in Beverly Massacheusetts, the only child of Peter and Annette Ramsey, on June 29, 1960. Peter Ramsey, according to the file, died in 1966, when Marshall Ramsey was six. Fluent in English and French. Married Joan Elridge in 1989 and had one son in 1991. He obtained his medical degree from Harvard in 1985 and then specialized in emergency medicine at Johns Hopkins University.

Bailey didn't have to wonder about the relationship between Marshall Ramsey and Paul Alban for very long. As she flipped the sheet over, the answer stared her in the face. A passport- sized photo of Marshall Ramsey was stapled in the top right corner. He was slightly younger in the photo and sported a beard, but it was undeniable.

Marshall Ramsey is Paul Alban.

Bailey felt flushed. Her heart galloped. She had the feeling that she was about to make a major discovery. She quickly read through the files in the dossier.

The *Operations* section of the dossier outlined Marshall Ramsey's activities in the agency. She learned that Ramsey worked as a military physician in Fort Worth after he completed his residency in emergency medicine. He had gone as medical support on a number of covert missions to Central America and West Africa. According to the file, the CIA had tried, unsuccessfully, to recruit Ramsey for a number of years. Ramsey was apparently involved in the development of a proposal to establish a joint psychiatry-medical clinic in refugee camps in Africa with a military psychiatrist named Dennis Hildebrand. The project never came to fruition. While they were about to present their proposal at the Nairobi embassy in 1998, terrorists bombed the building, killing Hildebrand in the process. It was only after that, that Ramsey applied to join clandestine operations as medical support. According to the file, he specifically asked to be part of the investigation into the Nairobi bombing. Bailey found that odd. Why would the CIA allow him to join an investigation when he obviously had a personal axe to grind? Apparently, she wasn't the only person to question that. The files made reference to a potential personal conflict of interest, which Ramsey vehemently denied. Extensive psychological reports concluded that there was *no objective evidence that M. Ramsey's judgment is compromised in this matter*.

Bailey screwed her eyes tight and then opened them, focusing on the papers in front of her. She kept reading. It seemed Ramsey became part of the FBI-DND team interrogating suspects implicated in the bombing. Towards the end of '98, he worked exclusively with interrogators Sgt. Steven Sidwell and Special Agent Bruce McCormick.

The documents outlined the evidence that the team uncovered, the confessions and the leads. The evidence led to a man named Kadar Hadad; a terrorist on the most wanted list for the better part of a decade. Summaries of forty-five days of interrogations showed that although Hadad was likely behind the attacks, he never confessed.

Then she saw reports of the internal investigation. According to the file, Agent Bruce McCormick leaked information to an international magazine that they were close to obtaining a confession but also discussed some of their interrogation techniques. It led to an article being published entitled *American Torture*. Consequently, an internal investigation was launched which concluded that *Sgt. Steven Sidwell, Agent Bruck McCormick and Dr. Marshall Ramsey used heinous interrogation techniques and engaged in prisoner abuse*. It specified that *Dr. Ramsey, while not directly involved in physical punishment, delayed medically necessary treatment and had permitted medically compromising interrogation strategies. A number of these acts are in direct violation of the Geneva Convention and the Hippocratic Oath.* This led to a trial for courts martial.

As a result of the torture, the court also ruled that all information provided by Kadar Hadad was invalid. As well, the court ruled, that the team's techniques resulted in forced confessions, so all material they obtained from collateral sources was also invalid. The case fell apart.

And Marshall Ramsey was found guilty and was about to be sentenced to up to ten years in federal prison.

And then, prior to sentencing, he died in a major car crash in Washington D.C.

But he didn't; he became Paul Alban.

Just as Bailey flipped the page, the overhead lights came on.

Bailey froze. Only her eyes widened. She slowly craned her neck towards the door.

Jim Crilley stood in the doorway, arms crossed holding and jaw clenched. His eyes pierced.

Bailey's elbows shook as she leaned over the file. She didn't say anything. Her mind stopped working. All that registered was fear.

He only said one word, "Explain."

Bailey stared at the ground. "I, was just getting background… on Paul Alban." She looked up, eyes wide, hoping for mercy. "I'm sorry, I didn't mean to…."

Crilley nodded, stepped into the room and looked sideways at the file on the desk. "I see you've got *all* the background now. Because that's Marshall Ramsey's file."

Bailey didn't say anything.

Crilley walked around the table and patted her on the back. "Good investigating, Clarke. Not a lot of analysts would piece it together the way you did. That's why we took you from paramilitary," he tapped her forehead with his index finger, "we wanted that brain of yours."

Bailey sat frozen, unsure of how to respond.

"Relax, Clarke." Crilley sat down in the chair across from her and interlocked his fingers behind his head. "I'm not going to do anything to you. There will be no firing, no reporting and no court martial. Okay?"

Bailey furrowed her brow. Was she hearing him correctly? She had broken into his office, read confidential files and he didn't care? "Why?" came out softly, her thoughts forming into words.

"Why?" Crilley laughed, "Do you want to go to jail or something, Clarke? Don't get me wrong here. I know after this you'll never break into my office again. And you have my word that if you do, I won't have the same reaction. Okay?"

Bailey nodded.

"The reason is because I understand," Crilley said. "Things weren't making sense to you, so you went digging. That's good judgment. That's why your work is going to save American lives. And I wasn't totally honest with you about everything that was going on. I kept you on a 'need to know' basis. But clearly, you needed to know more. And you're working for me, so you might as well know what I know. So I'm here now, Clarke, what do you want to know?"

Bailey had to collect her thoughts. She still felt as though this wasn't happening, couldn't be happening. She glanced at Crilley, who looked somewhat amused but inviting. Bailey shuffled through the papers in the file. "It says Marshall Ramsey died. But he didn't, he's Paul Alban."

"He certainly did not die. We just made it look that way. Marshall Ramsey was a good man, a good doctor and he and his team were on their way to getting a confession from a big time terrorist."

"Kadar Hadad."

Crilley nodded. "They took things pretty far, all kinds of torture, to get a confession. I tell you, Clarke, this team got things done and they would have got the confession. But there was this FBI agent on the team, McCormick, a real fuckin' lush. He gets drunk in a bar one night and gets conned by an undercover reporter and tells her all about what they're doing in the black site. It gets out into the media and boom, it's all over."

"What do you mean?"

"Optics. It's all about optics. People hear of the U.S. government torturing anyone, there's an outcry, and they want justice. They don't care about justice for the terrorists. And well, these guys were it. Their names were mentioned in *Vanity Fair*, exclusive report, one of those ten page ones you know? We had no choice but to prosecute him."

"But he was working for the CIA, under orders of—"

"Optics, Clarke. Let me ask you, what's worse: that we had someone working outside of protocol or that the whole CIA is involved in what the public perceives as barbaric torture? So we hung him out to dry."

"But he didn't serve time. It says he died."

"He cut a deal." Crilley rubbed his moustache. "A military man who was the team leader, name was Steve Sidwell, who was a real crazy fuck to be honest with you, was causing all sorts of problems inside our black sites. He consistently worked outside of protocol. He was such a loose canon that prisoners would give false confessions all the time just to avoid any further abuse. He caused us to follow a bunch of bogus leads costing agents' lives, not to mention millions of dollars."

"So why did you keep him?"

"It was hard to get concrete proof of all this. We keep surveillance of interrogations minimal for obvious reasons. And Sidwell kept things pretty hidden. That's what we used Ramsey for. Ramsey monitored the prisoners while they interrogated them. He witnessed everything Sidwell did. Ramsey's testimony gave us enough information to put Sidwell away."

"Where is Sidwell now?"

"Sidwell was a well connected man. He spent years running interrogations all over the world, met a lot of people. He disappeared before we could arrest him. Probably sipping pina coladas on a beach in the Canaries or something. As long as he's not under my watch," Crilley shrugged, "I don't really care."

"What happened with Ramsey?"

"Ramsey got to work for us some more. In exchange for the testimony and his continued work with us in clandestine operations, we gave him a death certificate."

"That doesn't make sense." Bailey shook her head. "It says here that Ramsey was about to be sentenced to ten years. Why would he leave his family forever to go live in the most dangerous country on earth?"

"Think about it," Crilley smiled, impressed with Bailey's questions, "if you're alive, the guys you tortured are going to come for retribution."

"So his death ensured his family's safety," Bailey said, more to herself than to Crilley. She thought about Alban, who had been little more than a voice on the phone to her, faced with the decision to leave his family and his past behind. How could a man put all that behind him?

Crilley sat with his arms crossed. The edges of his moustache curled up just a bit and the corners of his eyes puckered underneath his glasses. Bailey had initially thought he was amused at her interest in the case, but a feeling flashed through her and then disappeared. In that instant, she sensed that something about the situation wasn't right. Her mind tried to grab hold of the thought, but it slipped away.

"So you used him as an operative in Somalia," Bailey said and Crilley nodded in agreement. "But why embed an operative instead of obtaining a local asset?"

"Good question, Clarke," Crilley raised his eyebrows, surprised. "We'd been trying that for some time, but the problem was getting an asset that would stay loyal. We'd been through hundreds of assets in the nineties, but they'd either get lazy or sell intelligence off to the highest bidder. We couldn't get a foothold and frankly, we couldn't compete with the offers they were getting from the warlords down there. So, we used Alban. He had a good cover, Doctors Without Borders, and we knew he'd stay loyal. On top of it, we could always hang the carrot of coming back to the United States over his head if he ever mentioned quitting."

"Did he ever mention it?"

"Not once. Not once in a decade. He was as reliable as you could pray for."

"Until now, when he's been working on his own," Bailey said, pursing her lips, wondering if Crilley would bite.

Crilley looked at Bailey knowingly. "Bailey, Chris called me. I know you know I gave the intel on the location of the weapons."

Bailey didn't react. She looked blankly at Crilley.

"You don't have to pretend. We're on the same side here."

Bailey cleared her throat and looked at him with suspicion. "Who gave Alban the manifest?"

"We did," Crilley nodded.

Bailey leaned back, thinking. "Why?"

"Because we needed to get things done." Crilley let that sit in the air for a moment and continued. "Somalia is fucked up politically, Clarke. Diplomatically, politically, hell even militarily we haven't been able to make a lick of difference there. For the past decade, we've been doing this business of aiding pirates and warlords to try to establish some government from the inside. How far has that gotten us?"

Bailey nodded her acknowledgment.

"Nowhere. And Somalia is a powder keg. It's a hotbed for terrorism. Every CIA report shows that in the next ten years, terrorism from Somalia is going to be ten times a bigger threat to the U.S. than terrorists from Iran, Syria and Iraq all put together. The only solution, Clarke, is a full scale war. An invasion to establish a stable government. Do you know how easy it is to get the U.S. government to start a war?" Crilley didn't wait for an answer this time. "Almost impossible. Look at what it took for us to go into Afghanistan. Thousands of dead American civilians. And why won't the U.S. government act without a disaster?"

"Optics?" Bailey offered.

"Right. Unless there's a clear threat coming from a country, the public, the media will never get behind it. And neither will the government. So we create the threat."

"What?"

"We cause it. We make it happen. We get it done. If we show a real threat coming out of Somalia, one that we can control, it becomes a lot safer than if we let it happen on its own."

"How did you control this?"

"The general at AFRICOM received intel about a shipment of illegal nuclear weapons that were going to be passing through the Gulf of Aden. We go through our channels, using Paul Alban, to get pirates to hijack the ship. We then also inform, through different channels, terrorists about the shipment. They try to smuggle the weapons out and we stop them and recover the weapons, demonstrating the threat."

"It was all staged?"

Crilley nodded. "The pirates and the terrorists didn't know about it. But we did."

"So you planned it all?"

Crilley shook his head. "General Kaczmareck did. All I did was provide him with the channels to Paul Alban."

"Now that the weapons are recovered… What now?"

"We wait for the machine to move. Once the media create a stir and the government pulls out of Iraq, then Somalia will be next."

"What do we do with Alban?"

"His work is done," Crilley smiled, "he's done a great service to the country. Let's get him to come back for a debrief."

Bailey let out a sigh. "I can let him know on his cell phone. I'll arrange a flight for him."

Crilley nodded. "Let's bring our boy home."

Twenty-nine

While Bailey was finishing up her midnight chat with Jim Crilley, Paul cooked underneath the morning sun. After leaving the Internet café, he climbed into the Jeep, and drove around looking for some shade to park under. After a few minutes, he gave up. Ceerigabo seemed like a village built out of the desert sand. There were no trees to speak of and the buildings were all one-story concrete structures.

He ended up parking the Jeep across from the Internet café. He found a towel in the backseat and put it over his face to shield the sun. He reclined his seatback and closed his eyes. He planned to give his mind a rest and sleep.

But all he did was think. He had been able to dismiss the doctored manifest as a set-up, a way to smuggle weapons into an unstable country. On the balance of reason, even James Wright's reaction to arrest him as a traitor made some sense. He even managed to dismiss the resurrection of Kadar Hadad as a strange coincidence, but a coincidence nonetheless.

But he couldn't chalk this up to coincidence.

The fact that a helicopter registered to an oil company, whose CEO was his ex-wife's current husband, tipped the scales. First Hadad, now Joan. It felt unreal, as though his mind were making connections that couldn't possibly exist.

Up until the picture had loaded on the screen, the situation involved Paul Alban only. He was being used as a pawn for some political game. Yet, the feeling that something deeper lay beneath was always present. And here it was, a connection to him, personally, one that he could in no way ignore. A connection to Marshall Ramsey.

It felt like someone was toying with him.

Ringing broke the silence in the Jeep.

He shot up and threw the towel off of his face. He turned and rummaged through the contents of the back seat and found James Wright's cell phone. He put it to his ear and waited for the caller to say something.

It was a woman's voice. "Paul," she began. The voice was soft and gentle, barely louder than a whisper, just like Ellen's. Paul let out a sigh of relief. "Is this Paul?"

"Ellen?" he said, a smile forming on his face.

"Excuse me?" the voice turned curt and professional. "This is Officer Clarke." Paul rubbed his eyes, taking a moment to register. "From Langley."

He closed his eyes and put his hand on his forehead. It wasn't Ellen. His mind was playing tricks on him. He gave himself a second to regain his composure. "What do you want?"

Her voice was almost cheerful. "We've got good news for you. You can come back."

Paul stared out at the road in front of him, wishing Ellen would walk up to the car, enter and they could drive away together.

"Where?" he finally said.

"To the United States," she said. "Your posting in Somalia is done. You can come back home."

He didn't say anything.

"We have a ticket waiting for you at the airport in Garowe," she said. "A passport will be waiting for you there and we'll be at the airport in Washington to welcome you back."

He had always expected to feel sheer exhilaration when he was done in Somalia. He had been waiting for this news for a decade. It had meant so much to him, but now he felt indifferent.

"Are you still there?"

"Yeah," Paul said. "I'm here."

Why were they taking him back? Twelve hours ago they were trying to kill him, chasing him through the streets of Garowe. What changed?

"What about Ellen?" Paul said.

"Who?"

Paul then realized that she didn't know who Ellen was. He hadn't told her. Maybe it was best for Ellen that the CIA didn't know about her.

"Why are you taking me back?" Paul said. "You were trying to kill me."

"Because," she answered as though she had been expecting the question, "the mission is over. We've recovered the weapons and you've done your job. We know that you were set up."

Paul held the phone to his ear, turned on the ignition and the Jeep's engine heaved to a start, sending a plume of diesel smoke into the air. "Where's Hadad?"

"We don't know. But Paul, rest assured, we're going to find him and bring him in and prosecute him."

"I'll believe that when I see it." Paul started up the road. "We had him in custody a decade ago and your people let him go."

"That was then. Things are different now," she said.

Paul rolled his eyes. Hadad had gotten away again. Another crime unpunished. As far as the CIA was concerned, they had the weapons back and nothing else mattered. They didn't care about Hadad or VeritOil for that matter. Did they know about the helicopter in the middle of the desert? Did they care?

"What about John Daniels?" Paul said. "You know anything about him?"

"Who?"

"John Daniels, the CEO of VeritOil."

Paul's initial impression of Bailey Clarke was that she didn't fit in. She wasn't like any of the men and women he had met in the CIA. She listened to him; she hesitated when he made an argument instead of toeing the official line. He sensed that she believed him. And part of him suspected she was in the dark, just like he was.

"What are you referring to?" she said.

Paul smiled. She had no idea about the VeritOil connection. "Nothing, Officer Clarke, don't worry about it."

"Your flight leaves in six hours. You should get moving."

"I'm already on the road. I'll be there in four." Paul accelerated. "Officer Clarke, what's your first name?"

She hesitated. "Bailey."

"Bailey Clarke. Do you have a number where I can reach you?" Paul said, waiting for an answer, then realizing he needed an explanation. "In case something goes wrong."

"Sure," Bailey said, "I'll give you my cell number." She recited the number and Paul wrote it on a piece of scrap paper against the steering wheel.

"Great," Paul said, "so I'll call you when I get in to D.C."

"No need. We'll be waiting for you there."

Paul chuckled to himself. "Bailey, trust me, I'll call you when I get in."

Paul ended the call, threw the phone in the backseat and drove to Bosasso.

Thirty

Ellen sat at the back of a fishing boat as it coasted into a port, looking desperately for something familiar to orient her. The line of overhead night-lights on the shore reflected off the black harbor water as gleaming orange lines. A row of cranes plucked containers off three cargo ships at the far end of the port. A couple of forklifts beeped below, while a couple of men with hardhats barked orders.

No one seemed to notice the dark, forty-foot fishing boat slipping through the darkest part of the harbor. Two men clad in all black played rummy at a small table beside her, under the light of a small lantern. A third man, also in black, crouched on the edge of the boat, his elbow lodged in his knee and his chin resting on his palm, staring out at the black landscape around him. In the dark, she could hardly make out their features. They spoke English, with American accents. They didn't speak to her, though; they didn't even do as much as sneak a glance. Yet, she sensed, they were painfully aware of her at all times. Any sudden movement and they would be on her in an instant.

She tightened the itchy wool blanket that lay over her shoulders, leaned over and craned her neck, looking to see where the boat was heading. She saw a seemingly endless row of rickety old boathouses in front of them. Most of them were open and the insides looked like black tunnels.

But nothing was familiar.

She hadn't seen Hadad since he dragged her onto the helicopter in the middle of the desert. Before she managed to get a look at anyone inside the cabin, a black hood was thrown over her head, bindings snapped onto her wrists and she was buckled into a seat. Earmuffs kept out any sound. The sensory deprivation robbed her of any sense of time. She sat in complete silence and pitch-blackness with her thoughts. Waves of sheer terror alternated with waves of hope. *Maybe*, she thought at times, *maybe they'll let me off when we stop*.

The helicopter landed and took off two times, presumably to refuel. The third time, they boarded an airplane and flew for a long time. When the helicopter landed, a strong arm grabbed her shoulder and herded her out of the cabin and onto the tarmac. A warm, brisk wind whipped around and she felt a cool misty spray on her skin. She heard the faint sound of waves crashing in the distance. They had landed somewhere tropical, coastal. But before she could make any more speculations, she took a brief ride in a vehicle before being moved to the fishing boat.

Only when the boat had been moving at a tremendous pace for thirty minutes or so did one of the men slip the hood off her head. It barely took any time at all for her eyes to adjust. Blackness all around. The moon was almost invisible behind clouds in the sky. A desk light inside the wheelhouse provided the only light.

In the helicopter, she had trembled badly. It had felt as though her organs were vibrating. She alternated feeling cold and then hot. Each time she felt a shift in the helicopter, or the elbow of the person next to her, she tensed up, expecting the lights to go out. She thought of how she had betrayed Paul by switching the SIM card on his phone. If she hadn't listened to the man with the bad pockmarks who had approached her on that scorching hot afternoon two months ago, she wouldn't be here, waiting to be killed. While Paul had lied to her, for some reason, his lie seemed more defensible than hers. He hadn't betrayed her personally, the way she had done to him. He was simply trying to move on with his life. Was there really anything wrong with that?

She wondered how many times he had lied to her. He had been in Bosasso for over six years before she showed up and that would have given him plenty of time to polish his story. Three months after she started working at the clinic, they made love for the first time in his bedroom, and a month later, she moved in. Any personal items—photos, jewelry, letters—that may have connected him to an earlier life had been purged from his place. When she used to lie on his chest for hours after they made love, she tried to slip in the occasional personal question about him but he always responded with the *Coles Notes* version of his life before skipping onto the next topic.

What bothered her the most about his lies was that she felt comfortable in Somalia. She had spent seven restless years after medical school searching for a place she could settle down and feel as though she were part of something. She loved her time working at clinics in Bangalore and Dakar and Mwuanza. Even her two years in an Inuit village near Iqualuit were well spent. Growing up in Montreal—ever since Haz was put in a coma by the drunken cabbie when she was fifteen—she felt like an outsider without a place in the world. But when she came to Bosasso, that all changed. The people needed her as much as she needed them. And they accepted her. And Paul. She had had lovers in the past, ones with whom she had fallen hopelessly in love, but Paul made her feel safe. He made it possible for her to settle. And that restlessness that had grabbed hold of her when her brother died had left. But what was she supposed to do now, now that all that was taken from her?

At some point on the journey over, Ellen recognized that the feeling of terror, the one that had seemed to infiltrate her bones and spread, had slowly dissipated. She had felt a vague sense of anxiety, which lingered for some time and then stopped. She stopped conjuring up what-ifs and what-nows. Her mind slowed from its Ferrari pace to one that stopped on a single thought: she was going to die.

She remembered a psychiatrist who had asserted during a lecture in medical school that fear is simply a physiological response. *It's evolutionary, the flight or fight response.* Fear or anxiety, he had said, was nothing more than wide-scale release of neurotransmitters in the fear centers of the brain. Once all of the neurotransmitters were released, the brain was no longer capable of experiencing anxiety in a given situation. *It's called habituation. No one can stay in a state of fear forever.*

The vessel coasted into a boathouse and its headlight came on. By the look of the place, a boat hadn't ventured inside for a long time. Soot coated the walls and its two small windows were broken. Several planks were missing on the dock that lined three sides of the boathouse. Someone had spray-painted *Who Watches the Watchmen?* on the wall to her left. Along the far wall, two stacks of crates nearly touched the ceiling. Immediately beside the front door were two empty Budweiser crates. The inside smelled of mildew and rotting garbage.

The two men at the table collected the cards and tied an elastic band around them before jumping onto the dock and securing the boat. The third man walked over to the table, picked up the lantern and held Ellen's gaze for a moment before walking to the bow.

It took a second longer to register than Ellen would have thought, but when the part of her brain that recognized faces put it all together, she was jolted out of her sense of calm. Her face went white and her fingertips covered her mouth. She hadn't recognized him in the dark, but the lantern gave her a clear snapshot of the man's pockmarked cheeks and bushy eyebrows. It was unmistakably him: the man who introduced himself to her at *Café Americka* as the man who works for a general. The man who was convincing enough to make Ellen trick her boyfriend into giving a forged shipping manifest to pirates.

She stared as he stepped off of the boat and onto the dock. Her eyes followed him as his figure melted into the darkness of the boathouse. That tremble in her hands came back. It wasn't terror she felt now, no, it was fury. She had been duped and the man with the pockmarks knew it. He seemed pleased at the confusion she wore on her face. That look in his eyes said it all, didn't it? *Thanks,* it said, *we couldn't have done it without you.*

Ellen blinked her eyes tight and let her mind ask: *how could you be so naïve?* When she opened them, Hadad sat at the table across from her.

"She will wait here with me," Hadad called out to the men on the dock. "Tell me when he arrives."

The three men responded with quick 'okays' and walked up the dock. Their footsteps creaked against the old wood planks and became softer as they disappeared at the boathouse entrance. Hadad rested his elbows on the table and stared at the ground. He didn't look up until their footsteps stopped.

Not for the first time, the thought of how this man was capable of such evil crossed Ellen's mind. He looked fragile; he was slightly taller than she and his bones seemed to jut out of his skin. His skin seemed paper thin, stretched taut over his cheekbones. This was an internationally wanted terrorist? She had heard stories of Kadar Hadad before. She had heard of the bombings he orchestrated and his involvement in military operations across Africa. She had heard Paul describe Hadad's torture. She had envisioned a taller, stronger man. But somehow, at this moment, he looked human.

"I will not hurt you," Hadad said, his eyes easing, reassuring.

"What are we doing here?" Ellen said.

"Waiting."

"For what?"

"I am meeting someone," Hadad said, resting his cheek in his palm. "I will let you go soon. Don't worry."

Ellen gave a weak nod.

"You have done great work for Africa, Dr. Al-Hamadi," Hadad said, leaning forward. "I respect that. And I know you hate me, Doctor, and you have reasons to hate me." Hadad leaned back and squinted. "A lot of people hate me because of what I have done. Horrible things. It is okay to hate me because of the things I do. But nobody can hate me for who I am because no one knows me. They only know my actions, not the reasons behind them."

"People are defined by their actions." Ellen shook her head, "How do you justify killing innocent children?"

"We want the same thing for Africa, Doctor," Hadad continued, unfazed, "peace, prosperity, equal opportunity. Am I correct?"

Ellen nodded, suspicious.

"And you came to Somalia to help people get there. But let me ask you, how long have people been doing this in Africa?" Hadad paused for a moment, then continued, "A long time; centuries. And what has it done? Nothing." Hadad snapped his fingers sharply in front of Ellen's face. She didn't flinch.

"I like to think I make a difference," Ellen said, arms crossed.

"You do, Doctor. I know you do." Hadad nodded, knowingly. "To one, or two, or even one hundred. I know that. I was born in Sudan. My parents were killed in the civil war there when I was six years old and I went to Ethopia into an orphanage. The Child Benefit Fund. There were people there just like you, helping children like me. I remember a man named Rick, he worked there. He was a very nice man. He was from North Carolina. He taught me to speak English, to write, he told me about America, about the Tar Heels," Hadad said and laughed. He stopped only when he met Ellen's sharp stare. "We even made a business—we would go to the river nearby, pick up shells, make necklaces and sell them to earn money for the orphanage. It was a happy time." Hadad looked away and his voice roughened. "But one day, rebels came into the village again when we were picking shells, and wanted Rick to give them the money we had. He wouldn't give it to them. He looked them right in the eyes and said that it was for the children in the orphanage. So they shot him dead." Hadad made a pistol sign with his hand. "Then they destroyed the orphanage. Everything gone in one day. All the work all of those people did was gone like that."

Ellen looked at Hadad. His mouth was half-open, his eyes downcast. His mind was still there, thinking about that time in his life.

"And that's why I do what I do," Hadad said, snapping out of it. "Because to make a change, we need to stop those people that don't want peace."

"By killing more people?" Ellen said, her tone sharp.

"I learned that the only way to stop them is for someone stronger to come in."

Ellen furrowed her brow. "What do you mean?"

Hadad smiled. "Someone who can fight and squash them. Not a rebellion or peacekeepers. We need someone to invade to restore order so that you people, you humanitarians, can work safely."

"You mean an army of some sort?"

"The United States army, to be exact. If they invade, then order can happen and we can have a peaceful country in Somalia. But the U.S.A. will only invade if they see a danger to themselves. So, I create the danger. Like Nairobi. But that wasn't big enough for them." Hadad waved his arms in the air. The look in his eyes suddenly seemed disconnected, his voice louder and his words sharper. "They need something bigger, something more dangerous. So that is what will happen."

"What?" Ellen said. "What are you planning?"

"Something that has never happened on U.S. soil." Hadad beamed a grin that sent a chill slithering down her neck. "A nuclear explosion. Caused by pirates in Somalia, and a terrorist from Sudan."

"You have a nuclear weapon?" Ellen said airily, the wind taken out of her.

Hadad nodded, his whole face smiling. "It is taken care of. We will both have what we want when this is over."

"I don't want that. I don't want innocent people killed so you can cause a war," Ellen said, reaching out and clutched his arm. "Please don't."

Hadad took her forearm and released her grip. He rose and moved towards the edge of the boat. "Tomorrow, it will happen. The world will change."

Before Ellen could form any words, Hadad turned and stepped onto the dock. She noticed her fingers were clenched white against the edges of the blanket she had wrapped around her. Her back was wet, not from the slight mist that had started when they entered the harbor, but from sweat. For some reason, she heard her father—the Syrian immigrant, the armchair politician, the man whose opinion she rarely took without a heaping portion of salt—in her head: *it is a dangerous woman who believes that killing is ever justified.*

Ellen threw the blanket off her shoulders, stood and watched Hadad walk up to the front of the boathouse. She craned her neck around the wheelhouse and saw all four men standing at the boathouse entrance. Their cigarettes glowed in the dark.

Satisfied that she had a second, she swiveled around and stepped onto the stairs that led up into the wheelhouse. She grasped the railing, but her hand slipped on the wet metal sending her face down on the deck. She rubbed her elbow and her arm ached all the way to her shoulder, but she got to her feet and slowly climbed the stairs into the main wheelhouse.

It was dark inside. She felt around with her hands, sending papers and clipboards and pens to the floor. Her fingers stumbled upon a radio and she picked up the receiver. Her hands were so clammy it slipped out of her palm twice before she managed to press the transmit button.

"Mayday, mayday," she whispered, "help!"

No static, nothing. The radio was dead. She twisted the knobs and pressed switches but nothing changed. The indicator lights stayed off.

Ellen dropped the receiver and pounded down the stairs, not bothering to hold onto the railing. She rounded the corner and stopped at the top of the ladder that led below deck. She swept her sweaty hair off her forehead and stepped down into the blackness below. She felt around for a light switch or a flashlight but found nothing. She felt around the walls, spilling a can of something wet and slippery onto the floor. She knocked a couple of heavy items off their hangers and they crashed on the floor. Her hands came across a rough metal item. She ran her hands along it: it was heavy and it hooked into a sharp point at the end. She carefully lifted the hook off its hanger.

She gripped the end of the hook in her palm, between her middle and ring fingers and held it by her side. She caught a glimpse of her shadow when she stepped on deck and it brought up a soft giggle, the kind that always bubbled up at the wrong time. *Here comes Captain Hook*, she said to herself. She bent down by the edge of the boat and jumped over onto the dock. A streak of yellow from the security light outside ran along the dock, so Ellen made straight for the shadows by the wall. She pressed herself tight against a joist, hoping she was shielded from view. Her heart thudded against her ribcage.

She poked her head out and looked towards the entrance. The four men had moved outside and faced the road that ran in front of the boathouse. Immediately, Ellen stepped out and walked along the wall until she reached the front door. She crouched behind the stack of empty Budweiser beer crates. She heard mumbling outside, but couldn't make out what the men were saying. She turned her head and stared through a small gap between the planks on the walls. The two men who had played rummy smoked cigarettes less than five feet away, while the pockmarked man and Hadad paced, crisscrossing in front of the boathouse.

Then, a loud engine and blinding light came up the road on the left and Hadad put his forearm over his eyes. A black SUV pulled up in front of the boathouse, killed its engine and the headlights went off. Three doors swung open in synchrony and three men wearing sleek leather jackets stepped out. They walked up to Hadad and his men, motioned for them to spread their arms and legs and then quickly frisked them. Hadad's men exchanged glances and rolled their eyes. The pockmarked man initially refused, so one of them spread his arms out for him while the other efficiently patted him down.

When they had finished, they nodded towards the SUV and a large, barrel-chested man pulled himself out. He wore an open fishing vest and Ellen guessed he probably couldn't zip it up if he tried. His thick beard nearly reached his eyes, obscuring most of his facial features and a baseball cap worn low cast a shadow over his eyes. He walked up to Hadad and offered his hand, which Hadad took. Ellen strained to hear what they were saying.

"I didn't think you'd be here on time," the man said in a gruff American accent. "That's a hell of a journey to make across the pond."

Hadad nodded. "Navy SEALS came sooner than you said. All my men were killed, I barely escaped."

The man stepped towards Hadad. He was a half-foot taller. "I don't give a shit what happened to your men. Where is the weapon?"

"I have it. It's on the boat."

"Go get it." The man pointed towards the boathouse with his thumb.

Ellen shifted behind the crates, jangling the beer bottles slightly. Her heart pounded all the way to her neck. She gripped the hook tightly.

But Hadad didn't move. He stood in front of the man wearing the fishing vest, shaking his head.

"What the fuck is this? You don't understand English?" The man pointed at Hadad and emphasized each word. "Go and get it."

"You owe me money for it."

The man bellowed a laugh. "You think I have a suitcase with two mill in the trunk? What do you think this is, Kadar? You'll get your wire transfer once I see the goods. Go and get it."

Hadad quickly turned and walked towards the boathouse. Ellen rose just a bit so she saw the doorway. She held the hook in her hand. She thought of the young boy who had died after being blown up by a land mine three days ago in Bosasso and felt overwhelming hatred. Her veins seared through her arms and legs. She trembled with anticipation. She kept thinking, *you justify killing anyway you want. You are the murderer.*

All Ellen Al-Hamadi saw before she lifted the hook high above her head was a large shadow cast against the wall, but she still didn't miss. The power with which she swung it down surprised her. Even more surprising, when she would look back later, was that she didn't have an ounce of hesitation as she did it.

The hook cracked through Kadar Hadad's skull and lodged itself inside his brain. He let out a horrible shriek and collapsed onto his side on the dock. His face winced, teeth clenched and the left side of his body jerked a few times. Blood streamed out of the hole in his skull into a puddle around him that dripped off the dock into the black water.

The men ran in from outside and two of them grabbed Ellen's arms and pressed her to the ground. She didn't struggle; rather, she kept her eyes on Hadad. His eyelids fluttered slightly then rested half open. But the gaze was vacant.

The two men lifted her to her feet and the husky man with the vest walked inside. He glanced down at Hadad's corpse like it was road kill on a highway shoulder, then smiled at Ellen. "I guess I should thank you for that. He's a liability." He put his hand on her soft shoulder. "To be honest, if you didn't do it, one of us would have had to." He motioned for the men to let her go.

"So tell me, sweetie, why are you here?"

"He kidnapped me." Ellen pointed at Hadad with her foot.

"No wonder you killed him," he said nonchalantly. "Why on earth did he kidnap you?"

The man with the pockmarks spoke up. "She was at the beach with Paul Alban. Hadad wanted to take her in case she would be of some use."

"Paul Alban?" he said and then grabbed her face painfully between his thumb and forefingers and turned her head towards him. "I barely recognized you. You look so different from the pictures I've seen. It is a pleasure. Dr. Ellen Al-Hamadi, right?"

Ellen nodded.

"Armand Senechaux." He held out his hand.

"How do you know me?" she swallowed.

"I know you through Paul. Your boyfriend, right?" He smiled and put an arm around her. "Or do you know him better as Marshall Ramsey? That's how I know him."

"You know him?"

"Yes, I do. We can talk all about how I know Marshall." He squinted. "I think we should hang onto you. 'Cause he's going to come looking for you, isn't he? And he and I have a lot of catching up to do."

Thirty-one

At ten-fifteen the next morning, John Daniels scanned the crowd of over five hundred shareholders, businessmen and prospective investors seated in front of him inside the modern glass structure of the Arlington Convention Centre. Beside him was a large screen that projected his PowerPoint presentation. The room was quiet; only the occasional throat clearing was heard. They were all there waiting to hear what he had to say.

Daniels adjusted his collar and cleared his throat. He had hoped that by wearing a cotton suit, he would stay cool, but beads of sweat were already forming on his bald head. *This is it*, he thought to himself, *my last chance to convince them we're making progress*. It had been a poor year for VeritOil. A poor year on top of a poor half-decade. Three consecutive quarters with negative earnings had caused the company's stock to tank. They had lost two bids for drilling rights in the North Atlantic; a major pipeline through Panama was shut down by guerillas and virtually every investment analyst was advising people to sell the stock. In a month, he would be on the podium again giving the annual report. Unless he could convince these people that things were turning around, the company would be sold.

Part of him knew he should have been giving this speech over twelve months ago, when Mark Hatfield, VeritOil's Chief Financial Officer and Art Williams, his Chief of Operations, had come into his office wearing grim expressions. They laid spreadsheets in front of him, highlighted the important sections, the ones in red. Mark's assessment was that within twelve months the company's downward trajectory (as evidenced by the steadily dropping line on the graph titled *Capital*) would mean that over a third of shareholders would pull out. He used the words *bankruptcy protection*, and suggested they start the application process. Art suggested they shut down four major oil fields in northeastern Texas because they could no longer keep up their maintenance costs. *We have to do this before the shareholders lose all confidence in us.* But John decided to do nothing. The whole time he knew that what they had urged him to do made sense, but it was his pride that chose to ignore them.

He had started working for VeritOil before it was even called VeritOil. At seventeen, a fresh high school dropout, John landed a job working as a roustabout for Gorland Oil. He painted the rigs and kept the platforms clean. They paid four dollars an hour, unheard of for a kid without higher-level education. He worked his way up, learned to operate cranes, and even briefly worked as a welder. He made friends—the kind that made a smile crack his usually serious demeanor whenever he thought of them—hared laughs and some of the best times of his life out on the rigs. By the time he turned thirty-two, upper management came looking for him. *The boys in the yard respect you, John, they look up to you. How'd you like a move up to manager?* And he did. They even paid him to finish high school and then paid for him to complete a commerce degree by correspondence from University of Northern Texas. He still remembered the beaming pride on his mother's face—on pass from the palliative care unit—when he stepped up onto the podium to accept his diploma. If there were ever a proud momma. This company had handed it all to him. And things had been going so well for so long.

Bankruptcy.

We have to do this before the shareholders lose all confidence in us.

First Mark resigned and then Art let his contract expire before taking a mid-level position with Shell. *Disloyal bastards*. Disloyal to him and disloyal to the company. He reshuffled the upper echelons of VeritOil and made his personal assistant Craig Lynch Chief Financial Officer. Craig was young, quick as a whip, newly out of the Ivy League and most importantly, had stuck with the company despite poachers from all of big oil coming up with offers for him. But he was committed to the company.

The two had worked sixteen-hour days over the past seven months. They had racked up over seventy-six thousand air miles trying to seal contracts and make new deals. They turned out to be a good team; Daniels would charm potential investors and Craig would do the research and crunch the numbers. They'd slowed the decline and bought themselves a couple of months. At most.

But it all had come down to this.

He immediately noticed that most of the people in the audience had their arms crossed. A few already had their eyebrows raised. The only empty chairs he could make out were in the last two rows. The room felt stuffy and tense. Daniel massaged the PowerPoint remote in his palm.

"Three quarters of negative growth," he boomed into the microphone and deliberately accentuated his Southern drawl as he had practiced. "It's no secret and it's nothin' to be proud of. This recession has hit us, and it's hit us hard. Harder than most. The numbers over the past eight months speak for themselves."

Daniels clicked on the presentation and a graph came up. An animated red line traced across the screen, steadily declining. He stared out at the crowd for a moment and counted to five in his head, just as he'd practiced. He took a deep breath.

"But that's not why I'm here today talking to you all. I'm here to tell you that we're turning her 'round, we're righting the ship. We've all lost in this company the past year or two. Hell, I think I've lost just 'bout as much as anyone else. My savings are all invested in VeritOil and not to mention my job is resting on my convincing you to buy more of these stocks."

Nervous laughter bubbled through the crowd. He smiled and felt a slight sense of relief.

"But there's more for me in this company than just money. I've been here since I was a teenager working the rigs. I've worked in nearly every position in this company and I can tell you what it's about. This company is about..."

"...character." Craig Lynch whispered in concert with Daniels. Lynch sat alone in the middle of the last row with a pen and a pad of paper on his lap, listening for every word and every inflection in Daniels' voice. So far, Daniels had got the speech bang on. Every pause was perfect. Daniels was inspiring confidence with his words. His southern demeanor and salt of the earth persona were connecting with the investors, who nodded along, captivated.

He had coached him well.

Lynch had been the personal assistant to the CEO of VeritOil since he graduated with his MBA from Northwestern University six years ago. He had worked as an intern for the finance department at VeritOil for three months before his cost-benefit analysis of South American Oil Reserves raised eyebrows around the department heads for its clarity and accuracy. Before long, he was hand-picked by Daniels to be his advisor on everything from picking out suits to contract negotiation. He had stayed with VeritOil despite every one of his university professors urging him to leave before the company went bankrupt. But he didn't. He stayed on and Daniels rewarded him by promoting him to CFO.

The thing was that Craig Lynch liked John Daniels. He was a down-to-earth kind of guy. After only two weeks of working at VeritOil, Daniels had invited Craig for a round of golf. Five and a half hours and countless beers later, they closed down the Norquay Country Club members-only club and staggered out to Daniels' car. Somehow, Daniels (Lynch still wasn't sure how Daniels managed to drive so well after so many drinks) got them both home in one piece. Then Daniels took Lynch fishing out on Lake Nippising and told him stories about working the rigs. Then they grabbed a few pints at the end of the workday. It became routine.

It always struck Lynch how naturally their friendship had grown. It was by no means a typical friendship; Daniels was in his early sixties and Lynch was just turning thirty-six. But it was the kind of relationship that Lynch had always imagined he would have had, if his father hadn't died at thirty-eight of liver failure. And he suspected Daniels viewed him similarly; the son he always wished he had.

So how could he leave the man who treated him like his own? After Hatfield left the company, Daniels and Lynch really tied one on at Tug's Pub in downtown Arlington. After his sixth or seventh pint, Daniels wiped the foam from his moustache and suddenly looked sober. He put his arm on Craig's shoulder and said evenly, *It's okay if you want to leave. I'm going down with the ship, no matter what, but you, you can move on if you want.* Daniels' jaw had quivered just the slightest bit, betraying his brave front. The fear in Daniels' eye in that moment frightened Lynch. It seemed surreal that this man, larger than life, was scared. It was then that Craig Lynch decided he would do whatever it took to keep the company alive.

"... at our current rate of extraction, combined with projections that the cost of oil will rise by six percent a barrel by January, means that VeritOil will turn a profit by February of next year. That's five months away." Daniels continued speaking, using a laser pointer to draw attention to graphs and charts onscreen. Lynch smiled to himself and followed along with the script. "That's the short term story. But we are always looking ahead at this company, and there are exciting things coming. The hot topic these days is Arctic oil exploration. More oil is under the ice than the rest of the world combined and it's a gold rush. Good luck, I say. It's a hundred years before we have the technology to make anything of that. Let the rest of big oil have it. 'So what about the future, John?' you might ask. Well, we have a plan. This, my friends, is the future location of VeritOil exploration."

He clicked the remote control and a stylized world map popped up on the screen. He clicked again and it zoomed in on Africa and then on the eastern side. "The Horn of Africa. The largest accessible, untapped reservoir left in the world. The Puntland, a region in what was formerly Somalia, alone has eleven million barrels. We have reached an agreement with the Transitional Federal Government of that region that gives us exclusive rights to drilling. Exclusive rights."

Lynch looked around as people in the audience leaned over and whispered to the people next to them. He had expected it. Somalia was unstable and drilling there was a crapshoot. But that wasn't important at this point. All people needed to know was that Somalia was theirs to drill. Stability would come later. And the stock would skyrocket when the rest came into place.

"...But Somalia's a dangerous place," Daniels said over the babbling in the audience. "We're taking care of it. Twelve percent of all revenue from oil extraction goes directly into developing a security force...."

Lynch felt a firm hand pat him on the shoulder and he turned around just long enough to see General Robert Kaczmareck sitting behind him in a golf shirt and shorts before he swiveled back around. Kaczmaeck got up and sat right next to Lynch, his arms crossed, wearing a massive smile.

"What are you doing here?" Lynch said through his teeth, keeping his eyes on the podium.

"Me?" the general huffed. "Coming to congratulate you on a job well done."

"We don't meet in person."

"It's all over now, those precautions aren't necessary." The general waved his hand dismissively.

"That is not the point." Lynch turned and pointed his pen at the general. "We can't be connected."

"Relax," he said, "I'm just a concerned shareholder."

Lynch turned and faced the podium again, unsure of where he was in the speech. He took a deep breath, hoping his pulse would settle. "Did you recover them all?"

"I thought you couldn't talk in person."

Lynch sighed. "Just tell me."

"Twelve warheads, all in the possession of the greatest military force in the world."

"Now who would that be?" Lynch teased.

Kaczmareck ignored him. "When are you going to go public with the story?"

"Soon," Lynch nodded. "Real soon. You just keep your mouth shut until I tell you."

The general put his thumb and index fingers together and ran them along his pursed lips before he stood and made for the exit. As he squeezed out of the row, he turned to Lynch. "Out of curiosity Lynch, what are you getting out of this?"

"If Somalia is stabilized, we get to drill. It's simple."

"No," the general said and shook his head, "I mean you personally, what are you getting out of it?"

Lynch turned his head back to the podium and found his place in the speech. "That's it. Nothing else."

The general shrugged, turned stiffly and walked away.

Lynch looked back at the podium as Daniels finished his speech. A contagious applause spread through the crowd and Daniels looked proud. Although Daniels had delivered the speech that won the investors over, Lynch knew it was really his own work. Daniels had no idea the impact his words would have on his company. Ultimately, Daniels was a figurehead; there for public relations, not for brains or business savvy. The one thing Daniels did right through this debacle, Lynch knew, was that he surrounded himself with intelligent people, like Craig.

Lynch's blackberry vibrated in his jacket pocket. He glanced at the caller ID, tiptoed between the row of chairs and answered it in the hallway.

"It's me," he said, glancing around the empty hallway, "what's going on?"

"We're good to go. Tomorrow, eleven a.m., the party starts." It was Senechaux. He was in the country. Things were moving ahead like clockwork.

"Good. We need this to happen soon. The general was here asking questions."

"What an idiot. What doesn't he understand about no face-to-face meetings?"

"As far as he knows, it's over."

"Does he know anything more?"

"No." Lynch looked up. Investors were filing out of the room into the hallway around the table with catered breakfast food. He walked into the bathroom at the end of the hall. He ran the water in the sink to muffle his voice.

"Let's keep it that way," Senechaux said. "That being said, I need the wire transfer before anything else happens."

"I'll put it through as soon as I get to the office. I guess our man came through and delivered the goods, so he's probably looking for his payment, too."

"I wouldn't worry about that," Senechaux said, "he didn't quite make it."

"What?" Lynch raised his voice and the echo off the bathroom walls startled him a bit so he lowered his voice to whisper. "You killed him? Why?"

"It was a strange turn of events. He brought along a lady friend who was pretty disgruntled. She drove a shipping hook right into him. And, well, he's gone, my friend."

"What are you going to do?"

"Nothing changes really. But it is interesting, you know. The girl might be of some use to us because she's Paul Alban's girlfriend."

"Are you kidding? And where's he?"

"He can't be far behind. I'd love to see him."

Thirty-two

As the Boeing 747 started its descent into the Thurgood Marshall Airport at seven minutes past eleven in the morning, the attractive blonde flight attendant touched Paul on the shoulder, startling him awake, and asked him to bring his seat back up. As the fog from his sleep lifted, he pressed the button on the inside of the armrest. He swept at his eyes with his hands and then checked his watch and realized he had slept through the entire six-hour flight from London to Baltimore.

He craned his neck, looked across the man in the grey suit next to him, out the small cabin window, and saw the emerald green eastern coast of the United States come into view. He could even make out the movement of a few waves building their way up to the shore. He felt the corners of his mouth curl up, and then, as though he were afraid someone would notice, he bit down on his lower lip to stop himself from smiling. It was hardly the homecoming he had hoped for, but for a brief moment, a feeling of hope came over him. He let himself entertain the idea that there was a possibility he'd get through the situation unscathed. *You've made it this far, Marshall.*

But the feeling didn't last long. He couldn't pretend that a dozen federal agents weren't likely waiting for him to step off of the jetway and escort him to an interrogation room. And there he would be charged, likely with a list of offenses so long it would take an hour to read through. And he couldn't ignore that somehow the *Stebelsky's* manifest was meant specifically for him and it somehow connected to his ex-wife and to his life as Marshall Ramsey. And Kadar Hadad had kidnapped Ellen. Was she even alive? Yes, she had to be. Hadad would think to use her as leverage of some sort. But to have any chance at getting to Hadad, Paul had to get through the airport and find out what was happening.

He had taken all the precautions he was capable of. But the truth was he probably wouldn't manage to get through the cabin doors before handcuffs were snapped on his wrists. After getting off the phone with Bailey Clarke, Paul drove two hours to his home in Bosasso. He parked the Jeep several blocks from his front door, slipped through the gate and walked around the building, looking to see if anyone was waiting for him. From what he could tell, no one had been in the home since the men from Asabiyaah had kidnapped him. He climbed the stairs and carefully pushed the door open and hesitated briefly before deciding that it was safe to go inside. He stepped into the shower and cleaned the wound on his finger before wrapping a clean bandage over his nail bed. Afterwards, he changed into a beige suit with a light blue shirt and made himself a sliced tomato and salami sandwich that he ate over the sink. He then went down to the basement and picked up the flashlight at the top of the stairs. He flicked the light around, over damp boxes and crates that smelled of mildew. He put the flashlight between his teeth, moved several boxes over and opened one stuffed full with papers and folders. He found a brown envelope, reached in, pulled out a stack of passports and flicked through each one. He had accumulated passports in a variety of pseudonyms that he had used for different missions over the past decade. He lifted up the one he was looking for. Underneath a picture of Paul Alban, the passport read:

Joshua Allistair Borden

Place of Birth: Hadleigh, England

He had acquired the British passport eight years earlier when James Wright had asked him to investigate an American fertilizer plant in Kenya, which had been suspected of manufacturing explosives. Paul had purchased the passport on the black market in Mogadishu for two thousand dollars but the company shut down before he started the investigation and the passport went unused. But he held onto it, never knowing when he may need it.

He figured the CIA would likely trace the other passports in the envelope in case he tried to run. They would likely cross-reference all of his known aliases to ensure he checked in for each flight. The Joshua Borden passport was the only one Langley wouldn't have on file.

He placed the passport in his inside jacket pocket and went back upstairs. He then drove to Garowe and got on the flight to Cairo and then the connecting flight to London using tickets purchased in Paul Alban's name. He suspected that Langley would have an agent follow him at a distance, as added security that he got on the flights to Washington, where they could safely take him into custody. In Heathrow, he drank a pint of beer at a bar and then purchased a striped tie at Paul and Shark, keeping his eyes peeled for a tail, but saw no one. Afterwards, he boarded his Washington-bound flight as Paul Alban but just before the cabin doors closed, he pressed the call button for the flight attendant and told her that he had to get off the flight, that he had a family emergency. He then went across the terminal and purchased another ticket for a Baltimore-bound flight leaving in twenty minutes. He hoped that by the time Langley realized he never got on the Washington-bound flight, he would be out the airport doors.

~ * ~

Forty-four miles away, Jim Crilley paced across the floor of the customs control room at Dulles International Airport. In rows on either side of him, border control officers sat in front of monitors that displayed real time images from the security cameras that filmed the ten thousand passengers that walked through customs each day. To detect forgeries, the customs officers at the counters manually examined each passport and then scanned them through an electronic reader designed to detect their passport footprint. Any forged passport, or more importantly, a flagged one, would instantly notify the customs officials in the control room and the individual would be taken into custody.

Crilley had briefed the border control officers and flagged all of Paul Alban's passports. The second that he stepped up and handed that little book of stamps over the customs counter, four big boys with Department of Homeland Security badges would be escorting him into a windowless interview room.

Crilley glanced at his watch. Paul Alban was scheduled to land in fourteen minutes. He had monitored Alban all the way from Cairo to ensure he got on each flight. Alban had done as he was told, and had checked in for his last flight from Heathrow. Having Bailey Clarke talk to Alban was a perfect move. She was new and had a genuineness about her. More importantly, she believed Crilley when he told her they were going to release Alban, and that all they would do was debrief him and let him go. Discharge from the NCS. Honorably. If Alban was going to trust anyone, it was going to be Clarke. And he had followed her instructions to a T.

Of course, there was no way Crilley could let Paul go. He had given detailed cargo ship information to a pirate that was given to terrorists who ended up with a nuclear weapon in their possession. If a mission like this were traced back to the agency, they'd have another Bay of Pigs to deal with. They had to pin it on someone, and Alban had been the one all along.

The nagging part of his mind wouldn't stop. *What if you don't get Alban in custody? What if the manifest is traced back to you? Courts Martial, Jimmy, your only retirement's gonna be on death row.* No, he refused to let his plan unravel in his mind. Hadn't really done anything wrong, had he? Two months earlier, General Robert Kaczmareck had contacted him with an off-the-record proposal to stage a serious threat coming out of Somalia. All he needed from Crilley was the name and contact of an operative in the Puntland. Was that so grave? Hell, some good might even come of it. If this somehow managed to get the men and women on Capitol Hill to send some forces down there, would anyone complain? And if it ever came back to him, he could always claim ignorance; *the head of AFRICOM asked me for my contact in the Puntland for a classified mission, so I gave it to him.*

But then there was the issue of the money transfer. In exchange for the Paul Alban information, a total of $750K had been wired to three separate offshore accounts that Crilley had opened. If someone ever made that link, what would he say? Looking back on it, he realized it had all gone wrong fifteen years ago when he'd poured all his retirement savings (and sons' college funds) into what turned out to be a Ponzi scheme. He had been set to retire in 2000. But he got greedy. Why retire in Arizona when you can retire in the Hamptons? And then it all went to shit. He'd been duped. And he probably could have dealt with it, but people kept rubbing it in his face. His colleagues at work saying *tough luck, Jimmy, there's no way you could've known* and then snickering behind his back. His wife taking every chance she had to go off to her sister's cottage. His two boys working at drive-thrus to pay to get into a local community college. His best friend, Brian MacInnis, inviting him to his Florida beach home every winter.

Yup, this was his last chance to salvage the ounce of pride he had left.

"Ten minutes, gentlemen." Crilley glanced at the flight arrivals information screen, "Our man lands in ten minutes."

~ * ~

Meanwhile, at the customs counter in Thurgood Marshall Airport, a citizen of the United Kingdom named Joshua Borden was having his passport examined at the customs counter. He stood calmly, giving a slight comfortable nod to the female customs official who didn't return the glance. She lifted the passport up into the light, carefully examining it for what felt like an eternity. Then she stared directly at him. He worked hard to control his breathing and hoped the officer didn't notice his carotid pulse bounding. She swiped the passport through the reader and glanced at her screen. Paul swallowed hard, hoping she didn't notice. Something beeped and she pressed a few keys on the keyboard in front of her and looked back at him.

"Welcome to America, Mr. Borden," she flashed a quick smile and placed the passport back on the counter in front of him.

He grabbed the passport, his hand trembling slightly and walked through the doors, past the customs control room and down the escalator into the main terminal. He looked around at the scene before him. People raced around, dragging luggage and children up escalators. Others jostled for position around the baggage carousel. A lineup for a coffee looped around a corner. Large flatscreens displayed flight information. Computerized overhead voices delivered announcements over the buzz of passengers trying to make their flights. It was chaos. But he was home.

Paul made his way out of the terminal and hailed a cab. He stepped inside and told the driver his destination.

"Arlington, Virginia."

Thirty-three

Paul stared at his ex-wife's house from the street. He stood behind one of the large willows that marked the boundary of the massive property. He estimated the house was set back from the road by nearly two hundred yards, a distance that ensured no one could see inside. But the bronze lion statues that flanked the driveway, the massive black iron gate that blocked entry from the road and the fountain that spit water fifteen feet in the air in front of the home begged for attention. Undoubtedly, it was a home featured in magazines, showing the latest in suburban living and comfort.

The distance from the road troubled Paul. He couldn't simply hop the fence, saunter across the finely manicured grass and knock on the door. There would certainly be a maid or a butler in the home, if not a security guard. And he couldn't press the buzzer on the gate and announce *hey, honey, it's your husband, back from the dead!* He needed time with her alone, time to explain. She would want to know where he went, why he left. Most of all, she'd want to know why he was back.

He leaned against the trunk of the tree, rubbing his palm against the soft bark. He had spotted four security cameras so far. A U-shaped driveway connected the two entry points from the street. An opulent gate stood at each entrance, each with two surveillance cameras pointed in opposite directions. An eight-foot iron fence surrounded the entire property, which was likely an acre or more, but he couldn't be sure how far back it stretched. He assumed that cameras covered the entire perimeter. He doubted anyone actually monitored them; rather, they were likely used as a deterrent for trespassers. John Daniels was the head of a big oil firm, who knew how many disgruntled environmental activists tried to invade his home to make a statement.

He decided his best chance would be to find a blind spot in the cameras and hop the fence there. He walked towards the west flank of the property, which was lined by a row of tall ash trees surrounded by low-lying brush. He walked through the brush, sweeping branches away from him as he passed. He saw cameras perched on top of the fence, every twenty feet or so. Halfway along, he realized there were likely no blind spots in the cameras and he would have to create one.

He dug through the brush, and ignored the thorns that tore at his skin, looking for a solid branch. He came across one wedged deep in the ground, as thick as a scrawny man's wrist and pulled it out. He gripped the branch in both hands like it was a fishing rod and reached up towards the security camera, standing on the balls of his feet. The tip of the branch touched the camera and his forearms strained as he pressed on the camera and it swiveled about an inch. He tried several times, the branch bending each time, but it wouldn't budge. Sweat ran down his face and neck. He stopped for a moment to catch his breath and let his shoulders rest. He wiped his face with his forearm and tugged his collar a few times to cool himself. Then, he took the branch and swung with all the force he could manage and connected with the camera, swiveling it around one hundred and eighty degrees.

Paul tossed the branch aside and jumped up onto the fence. He gripped the top bar and pushed his feet into the vertical iron bars, trying to get some traction with his loafers. He managed to wedge his foot between two of the vertical bars and pull himself up at the expense of stretching the muscles in his ankle. At the top, he avoided the black spears that marched along and dropped over onto the other side.

He fell hard onto the grass, rolled over and scrambled to his feet. He glanced up at the cameras along the fence and calculated the trajectory of the blind spot he had created and ran, half-crouching towards the mansion across the open field of grass. He headed straight for the patio at the back of the house.

He stepped up onto the deck, careful not to make a sound and peered through the back kitchen window. Sparkling stainless steel appliances sat between black granite countertops. They looked unused and that brought a smile to his face, as he could count on one hand the number of times Joan had cooked when they were together. Strange, for a woman who always dreamed of having a designer kitchen. He remembered one time, when Peter was just over a year old, Joan had decided to make him a sweet potato/broccoli purée instead of the jarred stuff. An hour and a half later, the kitchen counters and floor were peppered with potato peels and a film of puree coated the stovetop, three dirty pots were stacked in the sink and the kitchen somehow smelled of smoke. When she proudly spooned the first dollop into Peter's gaping mouth, his nose wrinkled, his lips folded backwards and he spit it out all over Joan. Ever since then, Peter had refused to eat sweet potato of any kind. And then it struck Paul that he didn't really know that. *Maybe he started eating sweet potato after he heard his daddy was killed in a car accident. Maybe after he started eating sweet potato, he grew tall, agile and excelled at basketball and football. Maybe he studied hard and got on the honor roll at high school. Maybe he's planning on going to Harvard just like the stories he heard about his daddy. But you don't know about any of that shit, so maybe he does eat sweet potato until it comes out his ears!*

Paul felt the blood vessels around his temples swell with each heartbeat. His rapid breaths felt dry as they came out his throat. His eyelashes suddenly felt wet; his vision became blurry and he realized that he was crying.

It wasn't quite regret that he felt, because regret required that he had a choice in the matter. And he hadn't after all, had he? No, he took the deal offered to him at the time. Was he supposed to go to jail? Let his wife and son live in danger because Hadad would come looking for them to get to him? He couldn't feel regret, because there was no decision, no choice. *But Marshall, couldn't you have...*

His mind swatted the thought away like a mosquito buzzing in his ear. For the first time since he hopped in the taxi in front of the airport terminal, he thought to turn around and leave. It had been too long and they had moved on. He had no business coming to the house. He could have tracked John Daniels down at his office and confronted him there. He had no business disrupting her life. Joan had probably cried for a week straight after she received news that Marshall had been killed in a head-on collision on the interstate that was so severe his body could not be positively identified because of charring. She had probably seen Dr. Ellis and he prescribed her Ativan to help with her nerves and her sleep. After the funeral, she probably went to her parents' cottage on the Cape for a few weeks to *let things settle out*. Eventually, she would have accepted one of the invitations from her single friends (Roberta, most likely) and gone out to a coffee shop on the corner and then maybe dinner. At some point, she decided it was okay to date again. And somewhere along the way, she was introduced to John, an older but well off man and eventually would decide it was okay to love again.

Peter's six-year-old brain probably couldn't fully process it all. He would have seen his mommy cry and that would have made him sad, too. People would say things like *your daddy's gone away* and he would be left with questions like *for how long?* and, *where did he go?* He would miss playing hide and seek with daddy most of all, especially being picked up and tossed playfully into the air (*almost touching the ceiling!*) when he was found.

But then he would have learned new games. Joan might have signed him up for soccer and he would have asked why all of the other boys had daddys there while he didn't. Maybe Grandpy would have driven down from the cottage for a few games, but then Peter would wonder why all the other boys had daddys and he only had a grandfather. But as time passed, he would have learned that was the way things were. John would have come in and taught him how to throw a knuckle ball, gone to parent teacher, maybe even took Peter fishing out in an old rickety boat. He probably even went to a few bad school plays. *But would he have got up and whistled and cheered so loudly that Peter would feel kind of embarrassed but also feel good that his daddy was so proud of him that he remembered the lines he practiced in his room for three hours each night and asked how to pronounce words he couldn't quite sound out, would he have done that?*

"Marshall?"

Paul jerked as though waking up from a nightmare and slowly turned his head. Joan stood in front of the open patio door. She looked bewildered, like he was an apparition. Her face was pale. Tears streamed down her face, leaving black mascara trails on her cheeks. She cupped her shaky hands over her mouth and drew her elbows together over her breasts. She slowly shook her head while staring at him through red-rimmed eyes.

He edged closer to her, touched her right wrist and slowly lowered her hand to her side. She shook even more and her tongue made a shuddering noise that would have made Paul think she was freezing if it wasn't ninety degrees in the shade. Shock. "You're alive," she said between the shudders.

Paul nodded slowly, still holding her hand. "Let me explain." He looked in her eyes, which were still beautiful, the way he remembered.

He led her into the house by her arm, feeling her tremble beside him. They walked to the living room and sat down on the couch underneath the oil painting of an eastern seaboard fishing village. Joan took deep stuttering breaths and wiped away the tears on her face. "I thought they killed you," she said.

He nodded along, a big part of him relieved she didn't run at him with a knife, yelling that he ruined her life.

"I thought they killed you," she said again and exhaled, shaking her head.

And he sensed relief in her voice. Then he realized that what she was saying didn't quite make sense. Marshall Ramsey had officially died in an accidental motor vehicle collision. He was not killed. "You thought who killed me?"

"The men in the video," she said at last. "The men with scarves on their faces."

"What are you talking about, Joan?" Paul's grip on Joan's wrist tightened.

"I saw a video on the Internet. You're sitting in a chair in a cellar or something like that. You look scared in it, really scared. They tore your nails off. Then they held a saw to your neck. Oh my god, I thought they killed you."

Paul's mind flashed back to the camera running in the basement in Bosasso, with cords winding up to the laptop on the table. They had posted the video on the Internet.

"I got away, Joan, I got away," Paul said reassuringly, and put his arm around her. Joan wept on his shoulder and eventually he felt it safe enough to put his hand on her back. She looked up at him again.

"I just couldn't believe you were alive when I saw the video and then to see them do those things to you." She ran her hand through her hair and held blonde clumps between her fingers. "I thought you died. All those feelings came rushing back. *Rushing* back, Marshall."

Marshall. He was still Marshall to her.

"And I looked at Peter's face and I had to hide my reaction because if he saw it, he would have known."

"Wait a minute… Peter," Paul interrupted. "Peter saw the video?"

Joan nodded quickly. "But he didn't recognize you. He doesn't know and I couldn't tell him. He'd gone through so much alre…"

Joan stopped mid-sentence as though someone had plucked the words out of her mouth. The relief on her face disappeared. Her eyes narrowed and she turned her head to the side slightly. He saw hurt flicker in her eyes. Her voice softened. "Where did you go, Marshall?"

Paul held her gaze and collected his thoughts. How could he explain abandoning his young family, never saying goodbye, never sending them an anonymous letter so they could at least wish he were alive? Could he justify the pain he caused them? Yes, he had to run, not only for his sake but for theirs.

He managed to keep his voice calm as he told her about the Kadar Hadad trial and the courts martial. He explained that he took the deal offered to him so he could avoid jail time and protect his family. He described working in the clinic in Somalia and his role as an operative. He told her about the forged manifest he had given Sami and the stolen man portable nuclear weapons. He told her about Ellen being kidnapped by Kadar Hadad. He described how he could no longer trust his contacts at the National Clandestine Service.

When he finished, Joan stared not *at* him, but *through* him and said: "What on earth are you running from Marshall?"

His mind slipped to those tall grasses behind his house. He could feel their tops slapping against his shins as he ran towards the barn over the hill. His little legs burned but he kept running. And all the while, he saw that beard mashed against the hardwood at the bottom of the stairs. The image he just couldn't purge from his mind.

Paul looked her squarely in the eye. "I'm done running. That's why I'm here."

"Really?" He nodded and she continued. "Well maybe it's too late for all this, Marshall. I dealt with your death already. Peter dealt with you being dead."

"I tried to do the right thing for you," Paul said, his voice rising. He felt electricity course through his arms. "I was involved in horrible things and I was going to jail. The men I interrogated would come back for revenge. They would do anything to get to me, including going through you. They had to think I was dead, it was the only way to keep you safe."

"Ever since Nairobi, you were different," Joan shook her head with disdain. "Angry. So you chose to run away. And you didn't leave it behind, did you? It just stayed with you. What happened that changed you so much? What happened that made you stop caring?"

Paul's fists were clenched and tension built in his chest, he couldn't breathe. "I never stopped caring," he exploded and slapped his palm onto the wall. Joan jolted backwards at the sound. He took a deep breath and slipped his eyes closed, and then opened them. He lowered his voice. "I got sidetracked with this thing, the investigation. I had to get the people who killed Dennis. It eats away at me, every day. But I can't let it go. And now it's back. The man in the video torturing me—that was Kadar Hadad, the same man who killed Dennis. He's framing me, Joan. And I need your help. Then I'll leave and never come back. I promise you. Peter doesn't need to know I'm here."

"He never asks about you anymore," Joan said. "He's packed you away, Marshall, in some deep place inside of him. But he never forgets you, I can see that. You're always with him." Her lips parted slightly and the corners of her eyes puckered. "He's a lot like you. That's why I worry about him."

Those tears rose in Paul's eyes again like a tide coming in. A hollow cavity opened up inside his abdomen. He could not recall a time in his life when he felt so excluded, so alone. "So," Paul bit his lower lip, "what's he like?"

"He's a good kid," Joan shrugged. "A bit of a rebel phase the past couple of years, finding himself, I guess. He's all about political activism now."

"Activism?"

Joan nodded and smiled. "I think it's because of a girl, though. He's gone to Washington for a two-day anti-war rally on the National Mall."

She stopped and nothing was said for a long time. Part of him wanted to know more about his son and what he had missed when she broke for her trance: "You said you needed my help. What do you want?"

"I need to talk to John."

"About what?"

"He might be able to help me," Paul said, staying intentionally vague. "Someone's trying to frame me and he might have some answers."

"What would John have to do with any of this?"

Paul sighed. "I think someone inside VeritOil is involved."

"You think John set you up?" Joan snorted. "He thinks you're dead, just like I did."

"No, not necessarily him. Look, all I know is that a helicopter registered to his company picked Hadad up in the middle of the Somali desert. So someone within his company has to be involved."

She stared at him, considering for a moment and nodded.

He heard a door slam and then footsteps approach from up the hall. Paul froze and looked at Joan for a cue. She motioned for him to stay sitting.

"Hello?" she called out.

"Sweetheart," a booming voice and more footsteps approaching. "Got done a bit early so thought I'd come home and spend some time with the fam.."

John Daniels turned the corner and stopped abruptly in the doorway as soon has his eyes met Paul's. He was considerably taller and fatter than Paul had imagined from his photo; his frame filled the entire living room doorway.

A bolo tie hugged his neck, a neck that was craned to the side as he sized Paul up. “Who are you?”

Joan stood and held her hands up indicating that it was safe. She swallowed hard. “This is going to sound strange, but this is Marshall.”

“What?” John’s voice raised an octave. “Your dead husband?”

“It’s a long story, John. But he needs our help.”

“Well,” he folded his arms, “someone’d better start explaining things right now.”

Daniels hadn’t broken his stare with Paul the entire time. He opened his eyes very wide and had his mouth open, running his tongue against the inside of his teeth.

Paul shifted in his chair and rubbed his neck, wondering where to start. Joan seemed to sense his hesitation and began reciting the details of the story that she could remember. Daniels listened the entire time, not moving, not reacting. Paul cut in, summing up the conclusions of what had happened.

“Someone connected to your company is involved in this. Whoever it is has used NCS channels to feed me information that I gave up to Somali rebels. Now, the NCS suspects me of having conspired against the United States. I need to show them I followed protocol. If we can track down who it was in your company, then I can sort this out.”

“My company?” Daniels snarled.

“Yes. There’s got to be a money trail, a money transfer or something. Flight logs, someone who authorized the flight into Somalia two days ago.”

"You've just told me you're a wanted fugitive. You're running from the U.S. government. And you want me to help?" Daniels snickered and then looked at Joan. "And you believed him?"

Daniels turned and picked up the telephone sitting on the small end table beside the couch and started dialing.

"Who are you calling?" Joan said.

"The police."

Paul sprung up and reached for the phone Daniels had to his ear. Daniels twisted and lifted the phone high in the air and then recoiled, the point of his elbow connecting with Paul's nose. Paul fell onto the carpet, catching himself on his palms. The blood instantly poured out like an open faucet. He scrambled on all fours and then felt Daniels foot come up into his solar plexus, sending the wind out of him. Paul crawled to the doorway, each breath sharp and hurting his stunned abdominal muscles. When he got to the doorway, he ran into the kitchen and pulled a chef's knife off of the magnetic strip that ran above the countertops. He sprinted back into the living room holding the knife in front of him. Daniels saw him coming, turned and tried to side step out of the way. Paul grabbed Daniels' forehead from behind with his free hand, yanked back, touched the blade to his neck, and told him to drop the phone. Daniels did so.

"Listen carefully to me," Paul said. "You're going to help me. We're going to drive to your office and you're going to go through all records until we find who is involved. If we don't find anyone, I'll assume it's you and I'll kill you."

Thirty-four

At Dulles International Airport, Bailey Clarke flashed her identification badge at the airport security officer and then passed through a set of double doors with a sign, which read AUTHORIZED PERSONNEL ONLY - ALARM WILL SOUND. She walked to the end of a dimly lit hallway and stopped in front of the customs control room. She placed her hand on the door handle and let her fingers dance nervously on the cool metal. Crilley had been short on the phone when he called her to meet him at Dulles immediately. He didn't give her any further details. Earlier, in his office, he had told her he would debrief Paul Alban and she could take the day off. But now he was pulling her back in. The only conclusion she could come up with was that something had gone wrong. She thought of Alban's last words to her, *I'll call you when I get in.*

Part of her knew Paul Alban wasn't going to get on that plane and she chose to ignore it. Her instincts told her Alban sensed a noose being wrapped around his neck and slipped away before Crilley could tighten it. And she had the feeling Alban was right. Crilley wasn't going to let him go free, she was almost certain about that. But what she couldn't understand was why Crilley was doing all of this and leading her along.

She took a breath, turned the handle and slipped quietly into the room. Inside, Crilley was in full tirade mode, standing in front of a group of customs officers, screaming. His forehead had turned red and sweat rings had formed through his white shirt. File folders and papers were spread across a desk in the middle of the room. Two men sat in front of a monitor, reviewing security footage.

"I don't understand this," Crilley yelled and pointed at the papers on the desk. "We have records that have him confirmed for the flight from Somalia, from Egypt and from London! And then what? Poof! He's gone. Someone explain what the fuck happened to him?"

Crilley stared at the officer nearest him, huffing, expecting a response. The man put his head down uncomfortably. Bailey hid behind a group of officers trying to stay out of Crilley's line of sight.

"Um, sir?" One of the officers in front of the monitors raised his hand. "I think I have something here. It's footage from Thurgood International."

The group followed Crilley and huddled around the monitor on the far side of the room. Bailey followed and stood on the balls of her feet looking over the shoulders of the men in front of her. On the monitor she saw Paul Alban, a man she recognized from the file. He was standing at customs, handing his passport over and walking right through.

"Shit!" Crilley yelled, breaking through the crowd and moving back towards the table "We've just let a wanted criminal back into the United States." Crilley kicked the table with the side of his foot, sending it sliding across the room.

Bailey stood frozen. She had sensed Crilley had lied about Alban being allowed to come back to the United States freely. And now he was referring to him as a wanted criminal.

"You," Crilley looked at Bailey and stomped over, "you talked to him last. What did you say?"

"Exactly what we had talked about," Bailey stumbled over her words. "That he was coming home. That it was over, the weapons recovered."

"Well he must have got spooked. Cause he got on a different flight and now he's gone."

"I, I don't know why he would do that sir," Bailey lied

"Well, you find him and bring him back."

And Bailey Clarke knew that she had to find him. Because Jim Crilley was up to something and it didn't take a genius to know that.

Thirty-five

By the time John Daniels inserted his pass card in the elevator panel and the doors slid closed whisking Paul, Joan and John Daniels up to the executive suites inside the VeritOil headquarters in downtown Arlington, Paul felt a flame of hope light inside him. His heart thumped with excitement. He felt as though he were on the verge of making the breakthrough that would lead him to Ellen. But it didn't escape him that part of his excitement was the chance for revenge on Kadar Hadad. A *second* chance. An opportunity to eliminate the man who had killed Dennis Hildebrand a decade earlier.

The elevator beeped and the doors slid open, revealing the plush carpets and mahogany furniture of the executive suites. Soft classical music played in the background. Paul followed Daniels into the office marked OFFICE OF THE CHIEF. Daniels walked in and twisted the floor lamp on. The office was well over a thousand square feet. Two perfectly arranged bookshelves stood on either side of Daniels' carved mahogany desk. An enlarged black and white photo of what Paul assumed was a young John Daniel in overalls, beside a dozen or so other men sitting at the foot of a tall oil rig hung on the wall behind the desk.

The office had a full one-hundred and eighty degree view of Washinton D.C., which was on the opposite side of the Potomoc River. From that height, it struck Paul how still everything seemed. The Washington Monument stood tall, a bright white sliver against the dark night skyline. Streetlights marched along the riverbanks, reflecting off the water as shimmering white streaks. Traffic trickled by gracefully on the overpass below.

But Paul knew he didn't have much time. The NCS were likely already looking for him. It was only a matter of time before they tracked him down and took him into custody.

Paul motioned Daniels to turn on the computer that rested on the desk. Joan walked up to the window and stared outside. Daniels sat down in the leather armchair at the desk and Paul hovered over his shoulder as the computer booted up.

"What do you want me to look at?" Daniels glared up at Paul.

"Budget information. Your spreadsheets. If your helicopter was in use, that means someone paid to use it. We're looking for any unusual money coming in. Or out."

"Out? What are you talking about?"

"Come on, John," Paul smiled. "Your company stands to get a lot if the U.S. takes over the Puntland like Iraq. With VeritOil owning the rights to its oil."

Daniels looked up at Paul expressionless.

"You think I didn't check it out?" Paul patted Daniels on the shoulder as if to say *there, there*.

"I had nothing to do with this whole thing, if that's what you're suggesting."

"No, I'm not. I don't think you have a hot clue what's happening in your company."

Paul looked over Daniels' shoulder as he opened up a series of Excel spreadsheets. He scrolled through pages and pages of budget information. Paul's eyes became sore and his vision blurry as he tried to keep up with each row of money transfers. Each transaction had a label for the money source, destination and the amount. Each was coded, from what Paul could tell, by country of origin.

"Who codes this?"

"The CFO, he codes the material."

"And you double check it all."

Daniels flashed a crooked smile and then returned to his screen and kept scrolling down the page.

"I think he means to say that Craig looks through it all and John doesn't bother." Joan broke from her statuesque position by the window.

"What?" Paul said.

"Nothing," John waved his hand dismissively.

"No, not nothing." Joan walked over solemnly. "Craig Lynch is John's advisor. He looks over all the finances because John doesn't like to. And he trusts Craig with everything." Joan stood at the edge of the table with her arms crossed and her face suddenly flushed. "And this wouldn't be the first time Craig shuffled some money around. But John overlooks all that. Because Craig is, how did you put it, John? Oh yeah, *the son you never had.*"

Paul didn't say anything, Joan had said enough. He could tell by Daniels' expressionless face that he had no idea what he was looking at when he examined the spreadsheets. He was a figurehead, pure and simple.

For the next hour, Daniels scrolled through the spreadsheets, stopping when Paul pointed something out onscreen. They searched by date and then searched the spreadsheets by dollar amount, including only transfers between $1-and $15 million. Paul estimated that if there were a transfer related to nuclear weapons, it was unlikely to be larger than 15 million as that would draw attention, but couldn't reasonably be less than one million. But even with a narrowed search, there were a dizzying number of transactions each day, and there were no guarantees the transaction was recent.

Paul rubbed the corner of each eye with his fingers, trying to refocus. Daniels kept scrolling. Then an entry caught Paul's eye.

"Stop. That one." Paul pointed at an entry onscreen.

It was a fourteen million dollar outgoing transaction from a VeritOil account to an account number which was not coded by country.

"What does that mean? There's no country code."

Daniels made a *hmpf* sound, shifted in his chair and then shrugged, putting his palms up as he did so. Then he continued scrolling. Paul put his hand on the mouse and walked around the table so he was facing Daniels. "John, what is that? I know you know."

Daniels rubbed his lips together and then sighed, shaking his head. "Offshore."

"In which name?"

Daniels glanced at Joan and then at Paul and then at Joan again. He placed his elbow on the desk and touched his forehead to his palm. “Mine.”

“You’re stealing from the company, John?” Joan said with her head cocked sideways.

“I borrow to invest from time to time,” Daniels spoke slowly. “Blue chip stock. I take the investments and put all the money back in a month later. No one loses.”

“I can see it coming back right here.” Paul pointed at an entry lower down on the spreadsheet. “How often are you doing this?”

“A couple of times, *ever*.”

“What do you have in there now?”

“Nothing from the company.”

“What about this one, then?” Paul pointed at another entry. It showed a transfer of eight million dollars to the account, a day earlier.

Daniels stared at the screen, mouth gaping. “This isn’t me.”

“Well, its going to your account.”

“I had nothing to do with it.”

“Who else knows your account information?”

Daniels looked up at Joan, who shook her head and had her hand over her face. “Lynch.”

Daniels immediately picked up the telephone on his desk and dialed a long distance number. He recited his account number and identification code. “Yes, I was wondering about any transactions made from my account in the past forty-eight hours… Yes, the transfer of eight million yesterday… Is that it?... No?... How much?... I see." Daniels was white. He fumbled placing the phone back in the cradle.

"What is it?" Paul said.

"The money. It's gone." Daniels slumped into his chair like he'd been sucker punched.

"Where'd it go?"

"An hour after it was transferred in, it was transferred to another account."

"A payment."

Daniels sat slowly shaking his head side-to-side. "You were right, Joan. You were right about him all along."

"You have to call him in now," Paul said.

"Why?"

"Because he knows who he transferred the money to. He knows the people behind this. John, you have to track him down."

Thirty-six

The next hour crawled by. Daniels, Joan and Paul sat in silence in the chief executive officer's office as they waited for Craig Lynch to arrive. Daniels sat in his leather armchair at his desk, rubbing his chin repeatedly, his face made visible by the dull glow of the incandescent desk lamp. Joan sat on the window ledge at the opposite end of the office, staring out at the Arlington skyline. Paul paced across the plush grey carpet, stopped occasionally in front of the tall, elegantly carved bookcases, and ran his hand across the books, squinting to read the titles in the dark.

Daniels had called Lynch an hour ago and asked him to come and meet in his office under the pretext of setting up a press conference to discuss the state of the company stock. It was the best story they could come up with. Daniels assured them that nighttime meetings between himself and Lynch were common. Lynch had agreed to come without any hesitation, saying he would break dinner plans with his fiancée. Daniels was satisfied Lynch didn't suspect that anything was out of the ordinary.

But something didn't sit well with Paul. If Lynch were involved, he would likely know Paul had entered the country and it wasn't a stretch to assume Paul would have contacted Joan. And Daniels' voice sounded wooden and rehearsed on the phone. If Lynch had been listening to the way Daniels was speaking, his back would be up.

There was a confident knock on the door and then it opened. Craig Lynch poked his head through the door. "Sitting in the dark, John? That's somewhat creepy. Mind if I turn on the lights?" He stepped in and flicked the light switch beside the door. Lynch looked younger than thirty-six. He was clean-shaven and Paul suspected that was because he didn't grow a lot of facial hair. He wore a striped shirt and khakis. He looked around the room and as he saw Joan and Paul, his confident smile melted away. He gave a limp wave towards Joan and then turned back to Daniels.

"What's going on here, John?"

"Have a seat, Craig." Daniels pointed at the armchair in front of the desk. "We need to talk."

Lynch stepped over to the chair and flashed a quick glance at Paul, who sat down in the armchair next to him. Lynch sank in the plush leather cushions and placed his leather briefcase on his lap.

"Go ahead," Craig said, eyes wide.

"Do you know this man?" Daniels pointed at Paul.

Craig looked at Paul for a long moment and then shook his head, frowning. "I don't believe I do. I'm Craig Lynch—how do you do?" He offered his hand. Paul stared at it until Lynch withdrew uncomfortably.

"I didn't think you'd say 'yes'." Daniels picked up a stack of printed spreadsheets from his desk and put on a pair of reading glasses. "Can you explain this transaction?" He drew a circle on the paper with a red pen and pushed it across the desk.

Lynch lifted the paper off of the desk, placed it on his lap and carefully followed the entry with his finger. He looked up at Daniels "I don't know if you want me to say in front of this guy." He pointed at Paul with his thumb. "IRS, I assume?"

"Go ahead, it's okay." Daniels nodded.

"Its what we've been doing for years: borrowing to invest." Lynch turned towards Paul. "We take money from the company and invest it briefly, then cash it in. We then return the money to the company. Illegal? Technically, yes. Uncommon? Definitely not."

"It's not the same. I called the bank and that amount has already been withdrawn. Not by me, but by someone else with another numbered foreign account. And you authorized it." Daniels folded the arms of his glasses and then hung them from his collar. "Please tell me that you had nothing to do with one of our helicopters plucking a terrorist from the middle of a desert in Africa. Please tell me this transfer had nothing to do with funding terrorism in Somalia."

"Wait just a minute here." Lynch showed his palms. "Where is all this coming from? I made a *transfer*, that's it. I don't know where it went."

"The transfer was made by you, Craig, the bank confirmed it." Daniels rose from his seat, walked around the desk and faced Lynch. "They're looking into who the recipient was. We'll know in a few hours. We've contacted the authorities." He reached down and patted Lynch on the lap. "Son, it's best you come clean now."

Lynch didn't say anything. He eyes fixed straight ahead, at nothing in particular, trancelike. His breaths became deeper and faster. He made a guttural sound and little specks of saliva clustered at the corners of his mouth. His face turned pale. He brought his hands up to his head and squeezed a clump of hair in each fist until the pink drained from his knuckles.

Daniels leaned forward and placed a hand on Lynch's shoulder.

"No!" Lynch jolted back in the chair. Daniels recoiled as though he'd just frightened a wounded animal. Lynch shook his head back and forth, sending his hair flying to the sides. "No, this is not right. This is not how this is going to go!"

All at once, Lynch flipped open his briefcase, pulled out a Glock pistol and pointed it at Daniels. His eyes were livid and the veins in his neck distended. He rose slowly and stepped backwards, nearly tripping over one of the chair's legs as he moved.

Paul rose, lifted his hands up and spread his fingers apart. He sidestepped gradually towards the window beside Joan who stood frozen at the sight of the gun. Daniels raised his hands as well and moved towards the back window, farther away from the crazed gunman.

Lynch's hand trembled and he kept changing his target: first John, then Joan and then Paul. His eyes darted around the room. He pulled his shirt cuff over his wrist and wiped the sweat from his forehead.

"You listen to me," Lynch cried. "I've watched you wait for this company to right itself, to *come back* from near bankruptcy. Waiting, waiting, waiting. But no action.

You're just about finished, John, the company's almost dead." He gave Daniels a cunning look. "One more quarter and we're done. And your plan was to wait it out. I couldn't watch you do it anymore. Someone had to do something. So I did it. To help you." His eyelashes were wet and saliva sprayed from his mouth as he articulated his words. He waved the gun around indiscriminately, taken over by anger and fear. Paul could see Lynch's bony finger tense on the trigger.

"What did you do, Craig?" Daniels suddenly stood straight with his chest pushed out and moved towards Lynch. "Who did the money go to?"

Lynch stepped backwards until his heels hit the doorway. He kept the gun pointed at Daniels. "It went to funding a project that's going to bring our company back from the dead."

"Did it go to terrorists?" Daniels inched closer to Lynch whose back was now pressed against the back of the door.

"No," Lynch said, "it went to a contact of mine. He liaised with men in special forces and the NCS to set up a mission."

"What was the mission?" Daniels kept closing in on Lynch. His voice lowered and he stared sideways at him. "Was it to get nuclear weapons smuggled into Somalia?"

"Nuclear weapons?" Lynch scanned the room, surprised. "What are you talking about?"

"I think you do, Craig." Daniels was only a few feet away from Lynch. "How could you do this to me? I've treated you like a son."

"I did this for you, for us, for our company. You said it yourself in the speech today: Somalia is our only hope. I did what you didn't have the guts to do. I made the tough decision." Lynch spoke through his teeth, breathing heavily. The gun's muzzle was two inches from Daniels' sternum.

"A decision to smuggle nuclear weapons into Somalia?" Daniels boomed. "And then into the United States?"

"I don't know what you're talking about," Lynch shook his head, grinning.

"I think you do, Craig." Daniels pointed at Paul, who stood beside the window. "This is Paul Alban. I think you know who he is."

Lynch's eyes widened at the sound of Paul's name. He extended his trembling arm and took aim. In that instant, Paul recognized that Lynch had made the decision to fire, to kill him and eliminate the evidence. Paul instinctively lunged to the side, falling face down on top of Joan. He saw a white flame flash out of the gun's muzzle twice and then the window behind him shattered. Glass showered down over him and he felt warm trickles of blood running down the back of his neck. Wind rushed in through the twenty-ninth floor window, sending the glass shards that clung to the window frame on top of them and the papers on Daniels' desk spiraling through the office.

Paul looked up and saw the blur of Daniels run across the office and pummel Lynch, putting the smaller man in a bear hug on the floor. The size of Daniels almost completely obscured Lynch. They jostled for position and slammed into the wooden bookcase beside the desk, tipping it over beside them, sending books flying. Daniels pinned Lynch's wrist to the ground and tried to wrestle the gun out of his hand. He swung Lynch's hand against the wall, sending the gun skidding a few inches along the carpet.

Paul exploded to his feet and dove for the gun, which was a mere inch from Lynch's extended fingertips. Daniels straddled Lynch's abdomen and tried to get hold of his thrashing upper arms. Paul bent down and placed his fingers on the gun. Suddenly, Lynch explosively rolled out from under the two hundred and forty pound Daniels, sending him crashing through Paul's legs. The gun slipped out of Paul's hand. Daniels now lay on top of Paul, crushing his sternum.

Paul's face was pinned to the ground underneath Daniels' shoulder. His cheek rubbed against the carpet. With his free arm, he stretched for the gun. The tip of his middle finger slid across the sleek metal handle. He tried repeatedly, but it was too far. Daniels rolled, freeing Paul but as he reached for it, Lynch's hand scooped it up. He stepped on Paul's wrist and put his full weight down on it, sending pain shooting up Paul's arm.

Paul winced when he saw Lynch point the gun at his head.

"You weren't supposed to get this far," Lynch smiled wryly at Paul.

Paul's heart thumped away in his chest as Lynch's finger curled around the trigger. Paul squished his eyelids together. Then he heard a *thud* and then a *pop*! The pressure on his wrist was gone. He opened his eyes and saw Daniels lying face down on top of Lynch. Paul rolled over onto all fours and rose slowly, hearing his knees crackle a bit. He stared at Daniels' back for a long moment. Then, Lynch slithered out from underneath Daniels' body, panting, with a dark red circle on his shirt. He swallowed hard and ran his hands over the red circle. His eyes darted towards Paul and then to Joan.

Joan let out a shriek at the sight of the blood and ran to Daniels, kneeling beside his body.

Lynch looked at Paul, his eyes the size of saucers, briefly paralyzed, as if to ask *what do I do now?* Then, he snapped out of it and ran out of the room.

Paul pulled Joan off Daniels and then rolled him over. His blue shirt had turned purple and wet. Paul tore it open and ran his fingers along Daniels' chest and abdomen, finding the dime-sized hole in his belly. Blood leaked out onto the floor. Paul took off his blazer, bunched it together and pressed it over the hole in Daniel's belly. "Put pressure," he said to Joan and placed her hands over the jacket.

He put his fingers just below Daniels' jawbone, put his head down and closed his eyes. After a few seconds, Paul felt a fast, thready pulse and breathed a quick sigh. He put his hand on Daniels' forehead and lifted his eyelid with his thumb. Daniels didn't have much time left. He ran to the phone and dialed 911. They would be there in ten minutes.

Paul pulled a stack of books off the floor and piled them in front of Daniels. He lifted Daniels' feet on top of them, allowing some blood to return to his brain. Joan's arms vibrated as she pressed on her dying husband's abdomen. Slowly, Daniels' eyes opened, life barely left inside them.

"Where'd he go?" Daniels barely got the words out.

"He ran." Paul shook his head. "Ambulance is coming right away. You'll be okay."

"Go get him," Daniels said.

"What?"

"Get Lynch. Get whoever is behind this. You can't stay here. When police arrive, they'll take you in."

Paul looked at Joan. Through wet eyes, she looked at him and nodded fiercely. Her nod was more of a command than permission. But Paul stood paralyzed. He wanted to tell her he was sorry. Sorry for having left, but now, even more for having come back. If he hadn't, her husband wouldn't be dying in front of her.

"It's okay," Joan said softly as if she had read his mind.

Paul nodded and picked up the Glock that Lynch had left on the floor and clicked off the safety.

He sprinted out the door through a narrow hallway and turned the corner towards the main foyer, his momentum nearly sending him into a mahogany end table where a massive bouquet of tropical cut flowers sat. There was an elevator on either side of the leather sofas in the middle of the room. He scanned the flashing numbers above the elevators and after a few seconds realized that none of the elevators were moving. Both were parked on the fifteenth floor. Lynch didn't have more than a ninety second head start and it would have been impossible for the elevator to have traveled all the way to the bottom and then back up halfway which meant Lynch must have gone down another way. Or he was still hiding on the twenty-ninth floor.

Paul walked past the couches, gripping the pistol with both of his bloodstained hands, to the other end of the foyer where an empty walnut reception desk sat. Behind it, a dark corridor split into opposite directions. Beside one of the doors, a red fluorescent sign hung marked STAIRS. On the door itself, he saw four red fingerprints.

Paul pressed the push bar gently, poked his head into the stairwell, saw that it was empty and stepped inside. He heard faint footsteps, but because of the hum of the air vents above, he couldn't be sure they were coming from above or below. He held the gun by his thigh, walked over to the railing and looked up and down. About ten flights below, he saw the blur of a hand sliding across the railing.

Paul jumped down the first flight, skipping all of the stairs, his knees nearly buckling under him as he hit the landing. Sharp pain shot up from his knees to his hips. He gathered himself and ran down the stairs, taking four at a time. He held on to the metal railing to keep his balance and swung himself onto the next row of stairs. As he moved, Lynch's footsteps became louder and clearer. He could hear Lynch panting over his own heavy breathing.

Paul kept sprinting down the stairs, ignoring his aching knees and burning lungs. He had the target in his sights; he was only a few flights away from him. He circled down two more flights and then heard a door on the bottom floor squeak open and slam shut behind Lynch.

Paul arrived at the ground floor landing a moment after Lynch, flung open the door and stumbled out into the dark atrium. The massive chandelier that hung from the ceiling was turned off and the atrium was only lit by the orange streetlight coming in through the wall of fifty-foot windows that overlooked New York Avenue. The green marble floor looked almost black. He heard footsteps click up ahead of him and saw Lynch racing up to the gold-framed revolving front door. Lynch turned and yelled to the security guard in the corner of the room, "Stop that man."

Paul was halfway across the atrium when the security guard jumped up from his station in the corner of the atrium and ran directly at him. Paul tried to twist out of the way of the large guard's tackle, but his guard's shoulder rammed into Paul's hip sending him twisting to the ground. The gun flew out of Paul's hand and skidded along the ground towards the windows. Paul lifted himself up, his thigh already tightening up from the impact, as the security guard stood up ready to charge again. Paul turned around and ran for the gun as the security guard ran at him. Paul made for the window and slid, scooping up the gun. The guard slammed into him, sending the two of them crashing into the front window, making an audible thud. Paul righted the gun in his hand and pointed it at the guard, who lay on the floor, holding his hands up.

Paul kept the gun pointed at the guard while he looked out the window and saw Lynch descending down the front steps towards New York Avenue. He turned back to the guard. "Call the police, tell them what happened, now!"

Paul spilled out of the VeritOil building. His muscles burned, starved for oxygen. He spotted Lynch crossing the road, narrowly avoiding an Escalade. At the other side of the street, a crowd of minimally dressed women and well-dressed men stood in front of a building where a flashing sign advertised *Coconuts Nightclub.* Bass thumping music spilled out. Lynch weaved and pushed his way through the crowd, handed the large bouncer a wad of cash and walked into the club.

Paul ran down the stairs to New York Avenue, wincing with each step. He put the gun inside his belt, the handle still showing. He ran closer, winding through the crowd, saying *excuse me* as he passed each person.

Then something hit him. If the bouncers got to Lynch, he wouldn't be able to pry him out of their hands. The police were on their way and they would certainly follow the commotion to the club. He needed to get Lynch away to a different location where he could interrogate him alone. And he needed time to do that.

At the entrance, the bouncer pointed for Paul to get to the back of the line. He looked back; some people cursed at him for cutting them in front of them, others invited Paul to make love to himself. The bouncer put a hand on Paul's shoulder and squeezed. Paul turned quickly and took a step back. He pulled the gun out of his belt and aimed it towards the line-up. Some people hit the deck, lying on the cold pavement. Others ran into the street and took cover behind parked cars. Paul fired a round into the brick wall of the building so people would know he was serious.

The bouncer had his hands up and Paul walked right by him into the club. Red, pink and yellow lights spun around the room. Music blared. People inside had heard the gunshot and a crowd flowed out into the street, right past Paul. As he fought his way upstream, he scanned the faces funneling past him and didn't see Craig Lynch. That meant that Lynch had to be inside somewhere.

He saw Lynch slipping into a hallway at the back of the nightclub. Paul followed him and saw Lynch slide through another narrow hallway and slam through the VIP door. Paul caught the door before it closed and burst out into a back alley. A motion sensor above the door provided the only lighting. Rotting garbage overflowed from bins that lined both sides of the street. A cat cried in the distance. But it suddenly felt very silent. He didn't hear footsteps or any doors opening or closing. That meant Lynch was close, very close.

He walked slowly out into the middle of the alley where a small puddle formed around a sewer drain. The motion sensor light went off and the alley was almost completely dark. Paul stared up and down the street, giving his eyes time to adjust to the darkness.

Then he heard the hollow sound of an empty can rolling along concrete. The light came back on above the door and there was a rustle behind the garbage bins. Lynch burst out of the shadows and ran up the alley. Paul ran after him and when he was less than twenty feet away, stopped, raised the gun and took aim. His forearm tensed but he couldn't pull the trigger. He couldn't be sure that the shot would only injure Lynch. If a stray bullet ended up in Lynch's head, his only lead would become a dead end.

Instead, Paul went into a full sprint, his toes skimming the surface of the crumbling pavement. Lynch turned the corner at the cross street and went right through a large puddle that wrapped around the corner of a building. His foot skidded out from under him, sending him splashing into the puddle. Paul stood over Lynch who lay in the puddle on his back, propped up on his elbows, panting.

Paul tucked the gun in his pants and lifted Lynch up forcefully by his skinny arm. Paul glanced around and saw a gas station up the street, half a block away. The orange GULF sign wasn't lit, but all he needed was a semi-private venue to get information from Lynch. He kept a tight grip on Lynch's upper arm and directed him forwards.

"Where are you taking me?" Lynch said, his body rigid.

"To that gas station over there," Paul pointed.

"Just do me in already," Lynch said, with a false bravado in his voice, "put one in the back of my head."

"Not yet. Not until you tell me what I need to know."

Paul reached in his pants pocket and pulled out James Wright's cell phone. He dialed the number he had written down on a piece of paper in Ceerigaabo and put the phone to his ear. Bailey Clarke answered.

"I told you I would call you when I got in."

"Alban?" her voice squeaked as she said his name, "you weren't on the plane."

"I didn't think I'd be let in the country so easily. It sounded like a set-up to me."

He heard a long, relieved sigh on the other end. "You're right, it was a set-up. Paul, you have to believe me when I say I didn't know that at the time. But they are looking for you. I should say, they're *scouring* the eastern United States for you."

"I had a feeling." Paul steered Lynch towards the gas station kiosk. "But Bailey, I have information about what is going on. I have a man named Craig Lynch with me. He's involved with this whole thing and he's going to tell me who's behind all of this. I'll call you back in fifteen minutes. You need to record the call. Have someone you trust there with you, because if I'm right, someone inside your department is involved."

There was a long pause on the phone and then Bailey lowered her voice. "Paul, you cannot torture him. I've read your file; you can't do those things anymore. Tell me where you are and bring him in and we'll put it together."

"You've read my file? Then you know the last time we let someone go before getting a confession, my whole life fell apart." Paul gritted his teeth. "Get the recording equipment. Be by the phone when I call back."

Paul turned the phone off. They were in front of the gas station kiosk. The lights were off inside, except for a small desk light at the counter under which an elderly man in a ball cap read a paperback book. He hadn't noticed them at the door. Paul tugged the cold metal door handle, but it was locked. He knocked loudly, startling the man who rose from his chair and squinted at the window. He put a pair of thick-rimmed glasses on and looked at Paul.

The intercom by the door came on and the old man spoke through the static. "Can I help you?"

"My friend here is injured," Paul said. "Can we come in?"

"You want me to call an ambulance?"

"No, but can we come in?"

"Can't let no one in after hours."

Paul pulled the gun from his belt and punched the glass door twice with the gun, shattering it to pieces. He pushed Lynch underneath the handrail into a rack of potato chip bags and pointed the gun at the old man. The old man stepped back from the counter and raised his hands. His eyes were wide and they looked even bigger through his thick-rimmed glasses.

"Take whatever you want."

"I'm not taking anything from you," Paul said, lifting Lynch up to his feet. "Do you have a back room?"

The old man nodded and opened a small metal door beside the counter. It creaked on its hinges. Paul grabbed Lynch and pushed him into the room. The old man flicked the light switch. A single, solitary forty-watt bulb that hung from a wire on the ceiling flickered. The room was tiny, eight by ten feet at most. It felt even smaller because of the stacks of boxes and palettes of canned soda along the watermarked walls. A splintery wooden chair was against one end, likely used to reach the highest boxes. Paul slid it to the center of the room. It was wobbly, but it would do. He grabbed a roll of packing tape from atop one of the boxes and found the end. He looked at Lynch and pointed for him to sit.

Paul pulled Lynch's arms back tightly and wrapped them in the tape, using multiple figure eights before cutting the tape with his teeth. He then worked around Lynch's ankles and after securing them to each other, taped them to the chair. He then wrapped the tape around Lynch's torso and the chair back, making it impossible for Lynch to move. He would be able to breathe, but barely.

Paul looked up at the old man, who stood in the doorway aghast at what was happening in his store. He had removed his ballcap, showing his thin white hair and liver spots. He turned to leave the room.

"You stay here." Paul pointed to an upturned crate in the corner. "The last thing I need is you calling the police."

The old man took a deep breath and sat.

"What was that?" Paul said. "Did you already ring it in?"

The old man said nothing but his face betrayed him. He looked close to tears.

"Did you ring the silent alarm?" Paul yelled.

The old man nodded. "I did," he put his hands up, asking for mercy, "when you broke the glass, I pushed the button."

Paul saw Lynch smirk when he heard that the police were called. He knew the police were minutes away. He knew whatever pain was going to come would be time limited. All he had to endure was a few minutes of physical pain and then Paul Alban would be taken away in cuffs. Paul knew he had to make this happen quickly, no games.

Paul dialed the phone and Bailey picked up. He turned the speakerphone setting on and placed it upright on a box beside the wall.

Paul slammed the door shut and turned the deadbolt. He moved the palette of soda cans and stacked them against the door, six feet high.

He turned to Lynch who still smirked. Without hesitating, he pressed the gun's muzzle into Lynch's kneecap and fired. Blood shot up from the hole in his knee. Lynch's face squished together and he screamed.

"I know what you're thinking, Craig," Paul grabbed a clump of Lynch's hair in his fist and held his face inches away, "all you have to do is put up with me for a few minutes."

"Isn't that the case?" Lynch sputtered.

"You will talk in the next five minutes, I guarantee it."

"You might get me to say something. But there's no way you'll know if I'm telling the truth."

"Let me tell you something about me. I've already lost just about everything in my life. You're the one person keeping me from the *possibility* of getting the one thing left in my life back. But I am at my end. So help me god, if you don't tell me what I need to know, I will kill you and then I'll kill myself. There is no way that both of us are leaving this room alive without you giving me some information."

"Try what you want. I'll put up with it."

Paul fired a bullet into Lynch's other kneecap. Blood sprayed up and kept spraying, "That's the popliteal artery, in case you're wondering. You have," Paul shrugged and looked at his watch, "about twelve minutes before you bleed to death."

"I'll be in an ambulance before then." Lynch smiled through the pain, his eyes wild. "And you'll be in jail where you should be."

"You've read my file?"

"All of it. I know what you're about. You're a thug, you should've been in jail long ago. But you made a deal and ran with it, forgetting about the mess you left behind."

"So you know what I'm capable of then?"

"Nothing I can't handle."

"You know I can get you to talk."

"I might talk, but how will you know it's the truth?"

"I'll know."

"I'm trained to make people believe what I say," Lynch smiled, pain still etched on his face.

"Big talk for a scrawny businessman," Paul smiled. "But a smart one. Put one over on Daniels, that's for sure. I kind of enjoyed it on some level, to be honest, seeing my ex-wife's new husband being duped."

"Wasn't hard," Lynch said.

"Who'd you give the money to?"

"What money?"

"You know damn well what I'm talking about." Paul felt hot sweat was dripping down his forehead. "The money you transferred to John Daniels' account. We're tracing it, Lynch. That much we know."

"I don't know who it went to."

"My file, you got my file from somewhere. Who gave it to you?"

Lynch shook his head. He was turning pale; he was losing blood. It pooled underneath him. He needed a tourniquet. Paul took the packing tape, wrapped it tightly around his thigh and tipped him over onto his back so blood would return to his brain. His eyes opened slowly, weak, but alive.

"Who is your contact in the NCS? Who is it? Give me a name!" Paul stepped on Lynch's neck, pressing as he gagged. He tried to yell out but only a faint wheeze came out. He tried moving his head back and forth but Paul kept his foot firmly on his trachea. He waited until he was almost unconscious before he released his foot a little.

"Look, I know you paid someone to orchestrate this. Someone gave me a fake manifest for the ship and gave that information to Kadar Hadad. So, someone inside NCS is involved. You already told me that. And someone in Special Forces, you mentioned that too. Who'd you give the money to?"

"I won't say," Lynch's eyes rolled, "Police will be here any minute."

There was commotion outside the door. Two voices yelled for him to come out. They repeatedly pushed at the door, causing the deadbolt to rattle. He didn't have much time and Lynch knew that. Paul didn't have any leverage to use against him.

Except pain. Fear.

Paul grabbed the metal mop bucket from the corner and slid it beside Lynch's head. It smelled of ammonia. He tossed the mop against the wall, narrowly missing the old man. Lynch turned his head to the side, trying to see what Paul was up to.

He heard a metallic crack at the door and more rhythmic thuds. The deadbolt had cracked. Each one of the police officers' body checks slid the stack of cans over a sliver. By now, the door was open a crack, enough for a gun to fit through. He saw the face of one of the officers. Paul raised the gun, deliberately making sure the policeman saw it and had enough time to get out of the way and then pulled the trigger, firing two shots at the now empty doorway. Paul shut the door and slid the stack of drinks back over.

Paul turned Lynch's face down so each knee and his forehead touched the ground. Paul slid the bucket next to Lynch's head and then rocked him up just enough to get his head above the rim before dropping his whole head in the bucket, gravity holding him underwater. Paul held the bucket between his hands as Lynch thrashed around, trying to rock himself out of a shallow drowning.

Paul stared at Lynch as he progressed through the stages of drowning. He stopped thrashing and had a moment of calm. Then, the muscles in his neck contracted, followed by his chest wall expanding and further bubbling inside the mop bucket. He inhaled the water. Then his neck stiffened.

Paul lifted Lynch's head out of the bucket. He gasped for air, limp and weak. Lynch opened his eyes. Small, red dots formed on the whites of his eyes, signs of extremely forceful breathing. Paul knelt down and looked at Lynch.

"That was a test. One more time and then I leave you in there."

Lynch's eyes moved towards the door. The police were again banging on the door. There were more of them and they had already opened the door a crack. As it was now, they had no angle to shoot at him, but if they opened the door any wider, they might manage a shot. That's what Lynch was waiting for.

"You think I'll let them get to us. We're both going to die before they lay a hand on me. First you, then me."

Lynch sneered.

"You don't believe me?"

Paul turned the gun and pointed it at his thigh, making sure it was pointing away from his femur. He fired it. He groaned as the shot tore through his flesh and into the muscle, exiting the other side. A searing pain radiated up to his spine, like electricity.

Lynch's sneer disappeared.

Paul didn't give Lynch a chance to say anything. He forced his head back in the bucket and let him progress through the stages again. The second go 'round was many times worse. His body was still depleted of oxygen and he had less reserve. Everything would happen more quickly.

And Paul needed it to.

He lifted Lynch out and turned him over.

"Who is your contact?" Paul yelled. The shouts from the police outside the door were intensifying. *Put your hands up! There's no way out! We have the building surrounded!*

Lynch's eyes rolled in the back of his head, but he formed words. "Armand Senechaux."

"Who is that?"

"An arms dealer. I never met him. He contacted me." Lynch looked exhausted, his face was pale, as he drifted in and out of consciousness.

"What did he say?" Paul slapped Lynch's three times.

"That he could stage a problem in Somalia. Make it look like a threat. Another Afghanistan. Get the U.S. in a war again."

Paul nodded. "Because your company owns drilling rights there."

"It's good for business," Lynch said.

"You gave him the money?"

"Yes. Once it was done. I paid him."

"What about the weapons? Where did they go?"

"You know that. We arranged it so they'd be picked up, never get to U.S. soil. All we wanted was a threat."

"Who got me involved? Who's working for you in the NCS?"

The police were hammering at the door, louder and louder; the opening was nearly big enough for them to fit through. Lynch was almost unconscious. Paul slapped him awake. "Who is the NCS contact?

"Jim Crilley."

Police swarmed the room, knocked Paul to the ground and placed cuffs tightly on his wrists.

Thirty-seven

At 6:00 the next morning, Bailey Clarke sat on a stone bench in front of the koi pond in Langley's memorial garden. She sipped green tea from a paper cup and read through the morning's intelligence summaries that were in the folder on her lap. A stack of papers sat on the bench beside her. She decided to avoid the NCS floors as much as possible while internal affairs combed through Jim Crilley's office, gathering evidence of his role in the Somalia fiasco. She had told herself it was out of respect for her old boss, but she knew that part of her reluctance was to avoid the gossip that would be going on amongst the workers in the NCS. The rumor mill had already begun. Bailey heard that in the early hours of the morning, internal affairs came to Jim Crilley's office and knocked three times. After he didn't answer, they broke in and found him hanging from the doorknob with his belt tied around his neck, his face as red as a beet. He was then sent to the hospital for observation and psychiatric evaluation.

But part of her felt sorry for him. She had heard that Crilley had been given almost one million dollars for his role in the conspiracy and he had already used the money to purchase a 1200 square foot condominium in Palm Springs in preparation for an imminent retirement, one that would never come.

Bailey put down the folder and picked up another one, marked P.A. Inside were the key pieces of the Paul Alban investigation. She skimmed the eleven-page transcript of Craig Lynch's testimony and a copy of agreement of immunity against any charges related to the case. As a result of that document, both Jim Crilley and General Robert Kaczmareck were in custody. The only man still at large that Lynch had implicated was Armand Senechaux, a relatively unknown figure.

Bailey put the folder down, took a sip of her tea which had cooled down, and stared as a white and black spotted koi fish sucked fish flakes off of the water's surface. She was filled with a feeling of calm, one that relaxed the tightness in her shoulders, one that made her breathing slow. It was a feeling so foreign she briefly felt uncomfortable.

She got up and collected the folders into a pile under her arm. She walked through the cafeteria, past the lineup of people picking up their morning coffees to the main elevators and went down to the second level basement. She walked into the area marked INFIRMARY and stopped at the end of the hall in front of a large one-way mirror.

Inside, she saw Paul Alban lying on a gurney in a Johnny gown with his head slightly elevated and his wrist handcuffed to the bed. A heart monitor beeped slowly and a nurse inflated the blood pressure cuff around his arm.

As Bailey looked through the window, her heart raced. She noticed how the passport-sized photo stapled to the corner of his file didn't do him justice. The dirty brown hair in the picture was now sun-bleached blonde with a touch of gray around the ears. His deep-set brown eyes offset his coarse features. In so many ways, she felt like she knew Paul Alban. She knew all of his demographics, his age, his place of birth, his favorite foods, his relationship history, his IQ. There wasn't a detail in his file she had not committed to memory. But now, he was in front of her, in the flesh, alive.

Bailey turned to leave to get to the debriefing scheduled with internal affairs in fifteen minutes. Alban was no longer an active operative, so her professional relationship with him had ended. But a wave of curiosity came over her, one that pulled her towards the closed door.

~ * ~

"Blood pressure's good." The nurse flashed a smile at Paul, removed the cuff and recorded the number on a chart at the end of the bed, then left the room.

Paul tried to smile but it quickly turned into a wince, as any movement felt like needles being jabbed under his skin. His left thigh throbbed, pulsated. But his hand was the worst. His hand had ballooned to the point where it felt like his skin was going to explode. The doctors had examined it, saw the spreading redness and pus and immediately ran antibiotics through his intravenous. They said he was close to losing his hand and at this point the pain was so severe an amputation seemed merciful.

Lying on the gurney, alone in the room, Paul was forced to think. He thought of Hadad, the man who had re-entered his life, teasingly, and escaped again. And while Hadad was free, Paul was the one handcuffed in the basement of the NCS. Even though he had obtained Lynch's confession, Paul knew there was a labyrinth of red tape to get Lynch's admission used in any court. It could easily be dismissed as a forced confession and if Lynch had a half decent lawyer, it would be thrown out immediately. Which meant that Paul was still the number one suspect.

It was as if all of the actors from a decade ago had emerged for an encore to implicate him in an illegal weapons transfer. All working together to conspire against him. While he sensed this was true, he couldn't put all the pieces together. And while he would have most wanted to pack all of it away and forget about it, there was one piece with which he couldn't part.

Ellen was still missing.

Hadad had taken her onto the helicopter, presumably to be used as some sort of leverage. *But what leverage? Paul, you're going to jail. Maybe you should just accept the idea that Ellen's go—* Paul refused to entertain the idea that she had been harmed, but a niggling doubt crept in with more force after each passing minute.

The door swung open and a woman entered, carrying a stack of folders under her arm. She wore a grey pantsuit with a white collared shirt and her glossy brown hair touched her shoulders. She walked over slowly, her eyes wide, wobbling on her heels a couple of times. She stopped a few feet in front of the bed and bit her upper lip but didn't say anything.

Paul looked at the identification badge hanging off the lanyard around her neck.

"Bailey Clarke," he smiled, the pain suddenly less intense.

"Hi, Paul," she said, her voice shaking. "How are you feeling?"

"I've been better. I could do without these, though." Paul raised his hand that was cuffed to the bed.

"Sure." Bailey unlocked the cuffs. "Are you okay to talk?"

Paul nodded and sat up in the bed. Pain shot through his stiff joints. He pointed towards the one-way mirror. "Who's watching?"

"No one right now. I was behind there for the past few minutes."

Paul nodded. "Well, I guess you're here to get my statement or something like that."

Bailey shook her head. "I think," she hesitated, unsure of what to say, "I just wanted to meet you. Thank you for that." She stood for an awkward moment and looked as though she wanted to say more, but didn't know where to start. She turned abruptly and started towards the door as though she'd made some sort of mistake. Then she stopped, clicked the pen in her hand for a moment and turned her head around. "I'm not sure what to call you."

"What do you mean?"

"Do you go by Paul, or Marshall?"

Paul stared back blankly.

"I don't know..." Paul trailed off, then frowned. "I guess I'll go with Paul."

"Okay." She smiled. "It was nice to meet you, Paul."

She turned and walked to the door, lighter in her footsteps, at ease.

"Officer Clarke," Paul stopped her. "Can I ask you something?"

She gave a quick nod, her fingertips resting on the doorknob.

"What happened with Craig Lynch?"

"He's at the hospital right now, in custody. But he'll be in the hospital for awhile." She sighed. "You did quite a number on him."

"I had to." Paul shook his head, hardly looking like a man who had nearly tortured Craig Lynch to death six hours earlier. "Any truth to what he said?"

"Unfortunately I can't confirm or deny—"

"Please, Officer, tell me what happened. Don't give me the official line." Paul stared intently at Bailey. "I've spent a decade working for this organization. Now I've been framed by a man with a vendetta against me. My life's been torn apart, again. And yes, it's largely my doing, I know that. But I need to know if anything's going to come of this. I need to feel some sort of justice."

Bailey let her eyelids come together, inhaled deeply through her nose and then walked back over to the bed. She looked down at him with sympathetic eyes as if to say *go ahead, what do you want to know?*

"Was Craig Lynch telling the truth?"

"It appears so. We were able to get a signed statement and confession from Craig Lynch and that—"

"In exchange for what?" Paul sat up an inch.

"Immunity against charges for conspiracy or treason." She saw Paul's scowl and continued. "He was our key to getting details on people in our own department. We had to."

"So he goes free?"

"He does."

"And what did he give you?"

"He gave us information on people in the NCS and special forces. We've used his statement to issue a search warrant against high level men in my department and D.O.D."

"Anything turn up?"

"It did. We have two men in custody. We have evidence linking them to you, phone records, money transfers. They're being brought to justice, Paul."

"So the guy, um," Paul snapped his fingers jogging his mind for the name, "Crilley. He's one of them?"

"Yes, he was involved. The other is a General Robert Kaczmareck at AFRICOM."

Paul nodded, thinking about all the people involved. He felt some relief, but a weight still sat on his chest. He exhaled deeply.

"Internal Affairs is working out a deal, Paul. You'll be honorably discharged. You've done amazing work. They just have to clean up a few things you did."

Paul nodded, barely relieved. He thought of James Wright looking up at the ceiling in his apartment.

"What about Kadar Hadad?"

"He's dead. His body was found floating off the New Jersey coast."

Paul froze like he'd been hit by an arctic wind. Something inside him shattered and left a hole inside his chest. He had fantasized about Hadad's death ever since he had been released in 1998. Every time he thought about Dennis burning alive in the embassy, he countered it with a thought of the relief he would feel when Hadad died.

But for some reason, the excitement and vindication he had expected was nowhere to be found. It just felt empty.

"Are you sure the body's his?" Paul said, realizing the stupidity of his question as it came out of his mouth.

"It's been verified."

There it was: *verified*. He didn't want to believe but it was there. The anger that lived in a deep place inside of him rose up from his abdomen but petered out. Then a thought popped up, covering him like a wet blanket.

"Were any other bodies found?"

Bailey furrowed her brow. "What do you mean?"

Paul shook his head slowly and his eyes drifted towards his toes.

"Are you asking about Ellen?"

Paul nodded and brought his hands to his face.

"We have not located her, Paul. But at this time we presume that—"

"Okay," Paul cut her off and gave her a stone-cold look. He didn't need to hear what she presumed. They hadn't found Ellen. There was still hope. A chance. A *possibility*.

"Were yourself and Ellen," Bailey stuttered over the words and seemed to rest on one, "an item?"

"Yes."

"I'm very sorry."

Paul ignored her. Ellen could still be alive and he clung to that. That was all he needed.

"Do you know why they did this? The general, Crilley?"

"We still haven't been able to finish our interviews with them."

Paul stared, expecting more.

"It looks like they were conspiring to create a perceived threat coming out of Somalia. They used you to get the pirates to capture the ship. They tipped Hadad off about the ship so he would hijack the hijackers. Then, they told Hadad they would provide an escape route from Somalia via boat but ambushed him instead and recovered the weapons. Then, they figured they could use the situation to show that nuclear weapons are coming out of Somalia. But this is all conjecture at this point."

"You recovered the weapons?"

"All twelve accounted for."

"But what about the helicopter, Hadad getting away?"

"That part we don't know. Perhaps they were going to capture him and bring him in as the terrorist plotting against the United States. Show him to the media?"

"That doesn't make sense," Paul frowned.

"Like I said, they haven't finished the interrogations yet."

"What about Senech-something?"

"Armand Senechaux. We have very little on him. He's an arms dealer and he's popped up every now and again. Only one known photo of him and it's not of very good quality and it's a couple of years old." She pulled an eight by ten photograph from the files under her arm and held it between her fingertips.

"Lynch said Senechaux planned it all."

"That's what we're thinking. He may have known about the Ukrainian shipment and somehow contacted these guys on the inside. Money was transferred to an offshore account that we can't trace yet. So it might be his."

"Can I see the picture?"

Bailey hesitated and then handed the photo to Paul.

Paul glanced at the blurry black and white picture. Three men surrounded a small private jet, which had the stairs down. The three men wore all black and looked like bodyguards. He assumed that Senechaux was the burly white man, walking up the steps. His face was almost completely obscured by large aviator sunglasses and a thick goatee. He wore a khaki vest and shorts.

As he passed the photo back to Bailey, his eye was drawn to Senechaux's hand that gripped the railing. He followed Senechaux's wrist to his forearm where he saw a tattoo of a spider web tracing up to his bicep. A tattoo he had seen before. Paul felt dizzy; the bed felt like it was rocking under him. His heart raced and that seemed to make his hand throb more.

"What is it, Paul?" Bailey put her hand on his shoulder.

"This man, I know him. Senechaux." Paul swallowed hard, his tongue felt tied. "It's Sidwell."

"What?" Bailey looked at him, not understanding.

"My old partner from Addis Ababa, the Hadad interrogations. You've read my file. That's him," Paul said, tapping quickly on the photo.

"The sergeant that you were prosecuted with? Are you sure?"

"I know that tattoo, I know that profile. It's him." Paul looked at the photo again, holding it close. "No question about it. It's Steve."

"That's not possible." She shook her head and took the picture back, placing it in the folder.

"You're the one who gave me the photo. I'm telling you that's him."

"That would be quite a coincidence."

"Really, would it?" Paul said rhetorically. "You read the file. Steve and I didn't leave on such good terms. I testified against him. You said that Senechaux set it all up and Senechaux *is* Steve Sidwell. He must have had me in mind."

Paul started making connections. Crilley had given up Paul's name and contact information and Ellen switched the SIM card on his phone, so Sidwell would have been able to send Paul the manifest while making it impossible to recognize that it came from a different source. The man portable nuclear weapons were likely an illegal arms deal so they never would have made it onto the manifest. Hadad was brought on as the errand boy. Lynch provided the funds to make it all happen.

He painfully swung his legs over the side of the bed so they dangled while he tried to place all of the events in a logical and coherent sequence.

"Look at the facts, Bailey," Paul's voice rose; he spoke quickly, "I unknowingly give detailed information on a ship secretly carrying nuclear weapons to a group of pirates. Somehow, the man I had interrogated for the

Nairobi embassy bombings ten years ago is tipped off and steals them. Then, my ex-wife's new husband's business partner is making huge money transfers to fund the whole operation. And the man I used to work with, my ex-partner, is behind it all. This is no coincidence. This was all done to set me up."

"Paul, relax," she spoke calmly. "We have all the weapons. Hadad is dead. All the responsible people are in custody. Senechaux, or *if* it is Sidwell, is gone, we don't know where. What we need to do right now is to get you healthy and build a case against the men we have in custody."

Paul didn't relax. "How did he get away?"

"Excuse me?"

"Sidwell. I testified to the things the team did in Addis, the torture. They thought he'd be in for twelve to life. How is he out?"

Bailey stared back at Paul blankly. "He went underground before a trial even started, he was still at large. By that point you were already embedded in Somalia."

A part of his mind was suddenly activated, one that sent cold dripping down the back of his neck and made the hairs on his arms stand stiff. His heart thumped against his ribs. But he didn't know why. Paul narrowed his eyes as his mind groped for something, something Bailey had said.

"You've saved a lot of lives, Paul," Bailey continued in her steady voice. "By helping us get the nuclear weapons back."

The weapons! Something in the back of his cranium screamed so loudly that he thought he heard it echo. He turned stiffly and squeezed Bailey's arm so tightly she let out a squeal.

"Wait a minute. How many weapons did you say were recovered?"

"Twelve," Bailey winced, trying to get out of Paul's hold.

"No, that's not right. There were thirteen."

"What?"

"Thirteen weapons. I'm sure of it." Paul noticed his knuckles turning white around Bailey's arm and released. The image of Hadad running from the Navy SEALs, carrying a duffel bag rose in his mind.

"There's another weapon?" Bailey said.

"Yes. Hadad had it. When he got into the helicopter, he was carrying a bag. I remember that now."

"You saw him with it?"

"My own eyes. I didn't put it together, but he had it with him."

"And Hadad washed up in a New Jersey harbor which means that…"

Paul's eyes widened. So did Bailey's. "The weapon is in the United States."

Bailey nearly fell into the plastic chair beside Paul's bed and then reached for the cell phone in her jacket pocket.

"Who are you calling?"

"The FBI. We need to report this." Bailey began speaking into the phone, describing the information they had about the nuclear weapon.

Paul sat up on the stretcher with his head in his hands. What could the FBI do? A single weapon the size of a college student's backpack somewhere in the United States was next to impossible to find. Sidwell had arranged this for him. Paul was certain of it. He wanted Paul to do something, to figure it out. Lynch's words ran through his head.

I'm trained to make people believe what I say.

Did Lynch know more? Did he know where Sidwell was? Did he know where Ellen was?

"I need to go and debrief on this." Bailey placed the cell phone back in her pocket.

"We need to go to the hospital."

"We can treat you here."

"No, we need to see Craig Lynch. He knows more."

"I don't think he knows anymore than you got out of him. Let the FBI meet with him."

"You listened to the whole thing. At the beginning of the interrogation, he told us he was going to lie. He said he could lie and no one would know the truth. He knows more."

"Even if he does, we can't go. He's in custody, surrounded by guards." She looked at Paul, incredulous. "*You're* in custody right now. You can't leave."

"I need to interrogate him. He's scared of me. He'll talk the second he sees me because he knows I have nothing to lose. You've already given him immunity from prosecution; the only thing left to threaten him with is his life. And I'm the only one he believes will deliver on that threat. You know I'm right." Paul slid off the gurney, pain searing through his leg and up his right side as his feet touched the cold floor.

Bailey took a step back. "You're here. We have to leave it to them."

"You can help me get out of here, I know you can." Paul started walking toward the door, holding the ends of his Johnny shirt closed behind his back.

"If I let you out of here, I'm going to jail myself."

"The quickest way to figure this out is to go through Lynch. He knows where the weapon is." He stared, his eyes piercing. "We've come this far, Bailey. Let's finish it."

Thirty-eight

Thirty miles away at the Lakeview Motor Inn on Highway 214, Steve Sidwell sat in a flimsy plastic chair outside of room 104, sipping a Dunkin Donuts coffee while looking at the parking lot in front of him. It was deserted, aside from the orange Dodge Charger at the far end of the lot beside the Coke dispenser and his grey van parked in front of him. The hotel sign flashed VACANCY in red. Morning traffic was picking up on the twisty highway to his right, leaving the smell of exhaust in the air. It was still a bit crisp and the fine dew on the van's windshield hadn't burned off yet. The sky was clear, save for a few wisps of cloud.

It was going to be a fine day.

He could almost see the protestors carrying their signs over their shoulders and converging on the tall phallic structure fifty miles away. He could almost hear their cheers when the man on the megaphone called for the withdrawal of troops and when he screamed with his fist punching the air: *bring our boys home!*

The problem, he always knew, was that protestors didn't really know what they were fighting. They didn't believe the threats against their country were real. They'd never been on the ground and looked into the enemy's eyes. They'd never felt the risk of their military sitting idly by and doing nothing.

And the worst of it was that the politicians couldn't make the tough decisions. They caved; they always caved to popular opinion.

He thought about Kadar Hadad.

He had a terrorist in his hands, one who had blown up thousands of Americans in Nairobi, chained inside a four-by-four foot cell. He was building the case and was close to having enough evidence for a conviction. And what happened? Popular opinion. People heard the word 'torture' and started protesting against clandestine activities and the politicians gave in. Next thing he knew, Hadad was set free and he was the one charged with torture.

Ingrates, bunch of fucking ingrates.

The very people he was protecting had turned on him.

But he'd been able to move on. After he got wind of the investigation in 1998, he changed his name to Armand Senechaux and moved to Tbilisi, where he lived for three years earning a living importing small arms and selling them to Chechen rebels. Over time, the trade grew larger, and two years later, he was transporting decommissioned Soviet tanks across the Turkmenistan-Afghanistan border. He had regular trade routes to Mozambique and the Congo. Things were going smoothly. He had left America alone; he didn't need them anymore.

Until it all happened.

Marshall Ramsey happened.

After Somali pirates hijacked three of his shipments in the Gulf of Aden in less than four months, Sidwell decided to do some digging. He couldn't chalk it up to coincidence. It was as if the pirates already knew what was on the ships. He was unsurprised when he discovered that a physician working in the Puntland was feeding shipping information to pirates. The physician was likely an undercover operative for the United States government.

He was surprised, though, when he saw the photo of the operative. He could hardly believe it. Marshall Ramsey, back from the dead.

Ramsey, of course, was worse than all of the protestors, politicians and terrorists combined. A man of no morals and no loyalties. He was the man who had put the final nail in Sidwell's coffin when he testified to the interrogation techniques used in the Kadar Hadad trial. There he was, a man who should never have even been part of the investigation in the first place, testifying that Sidwell was using extreme methods to extract information. Ramsey was a snake, only trying to save his own skin. He had been truly disappointed when he heard Ramsey died in a car accident because he wished he could have had the chance to kill him himself. But the damage was already done. Ramsey's testimony was admissible in court.

But when he learned Ramsey was alive and well, not to mention causing his shipments to be intercepted in the Gulf of Aden, Sidwell seized the opportunity. He smelled a chance, a chance for revenge, not only on the nation that turned its back on him, but on the man who betrayed him.

Shortly after he discovered Ramsey working in the Puntland, Sidwell heard of a "sensitive" shipment of illegal weapons heading from Odessa to Nairobi on a ship named the *Stebelsky*. Sidwell purchased several boxcars on the ship in order to have a pretext on which to investigate what those sensitive materials were. He paid three of the dockworkers in Odessa handsome amounts to give him some information on the nature of the weapons. What he learned brought a smile to his face. Man portable nuclear weapons. These were thought to be unattainable and were worth an obscene amount on the black market.

But he had no intention of selling them. He just needed to get his hands on one.

Soon the plan fell into place. He immediately contacted General Kaczmareck at AFRICOM to inform him of the shipment and his idea to stage a hijacking under the pretext of making a perceived threat coming out of Somalia. Unsurprisingly, the general immediately agreed and contacted his man in the NCS to give contact information to his operative in the Puntland. Then he told Kaczmareck they would recover the weapons before they left Somalia, leak the information to the press and hopefully build a case for at least a small force in Somalia.

He didn't tell the general the rest. He didn't tell him that he would hire Kadar Hadad to steal the weapons at the docks in Bosasso or that he intended to smuggle one out of the country and set it off in the United States. He didn't tell him that, once the nuclear weapons exploded, killing thousands of protestors and civilians, the investigation would eventually trace the weapon back to Somalia. He didn't say that investigators would conclude that Kadar Hadad, the man who was released from U.S. custody, was the man responsible for the bombing. He didn't say the investigation would also find out that the man to whom the United States gave amnesty had conspired with Kadar Hadad to steal the weapon.

Of course, he needed funding for his plan and VeritOil became the obvious choice. Marshall Ramsey's widow's husband was the CEO, after all. He had dropped the final hint to Lynch earlier that day. Now Sidwell hoped Ramsey would piece it all together in time. It was all for him, after all.

The only piece that didn't go according to plan was Ramsey's girlfriend. His man had convinced her to switch the SIM card on Paul Alban's mobile so he wouldn't recognize that the manifest had not come from the National Clandestine Service. He never thought she would come along with Ramsey. He never thought she would kill Kadar Hadad. But in every misfortune, Sidwell saw an opportunity, and this was no different. Ramsey would come looking for her.

Sidwell had heard from his contact in the FBI that Ramsey had entered the United States and interrogated Craig Lynch. Ramsey was getting close. A smile spread on Sidwell's face. He felt excited, almost exhilarated. Ramsey was falling right into the trap.

Ah, he could see the explosion…the whip of the wind just before the van burst open in a violet-orange fireball shooting up to the sky like lava. The people around it would disintegrate. And the fireball would grow wider and taller, breaking anything in its path. The tall stone spear on the national mall would crumble, and chunks of granite and marble would rip through the air at a hundred miles per second, slicing anything in their way. And everything would be aflame; the trees like torches, the grass alight like wildfire. A four-block radius in ashes, eight blocks infected with radiation poisoning.

Burn baby burn!

Sidwell lifted himself out of the chair, took another sip of coffee and put his hand on the doorknob to room 104. He jiggled the handle a few times before he managed to get the door opened (what could you really expect for $59/night) and walked inside. The flowery curtains were drawn shut on the window looking out on the parking lot and even though all three floor lamps were turned on, the room was still dim. The room smelled of mothballs, a smell that reminded Sidwell of his grandmother's trailer home.

Razman worked at a long desk opposite the two double beds, underneath the desk lamp. He was busy twisting wires together and securing them to a larger device with a screwdriver. Razman wore a red and blue tracksuit and sandals, so he looked more like a local mobster than an explosives expert. But Sidwell had known Razman for well over a decade and knew there was no one he could trust more to build a detonator quickly and efficiently. Now Razman was putting the finishing touches on the electrical detonator that Sidwell could activate from four miles away, using the keypad on his blackberry device.

Sidwell stood there watching Razman work for a good minute and then went through the connecting door to room 105. The television was on inside and a meteorologist was calling for sun and seventy-two degrees. Ellen Al-Hamadi sat on the edge of the bed nearest the door with her elbows on her knees and glared at Sidwell. Her leg was handcuffed to the bed frame.

He had to admit Ramsey had done well for himself. She was more than ten years younger than Ramsey, curvaceous and had beautiful exotic eyes. Eyes that were piercing at the moment.

"Why are you doing this?" Her head shook as she spoke. "To get back at Paul or something?"

"This isn't about him. He's a symptom of bigger problems, that's all." Sidwell sat down on the bed beside her and took a loud sip of coffee. "It's because of this country. It's changed. A bunch of protestors can get together, chant for something they know this much about," he put his thumb and index finger close together, "and make the policymakers back out of tough decisions. They have all the power in this country, this democracy. They protest war without ever having held a gun, or ever had a gun held to them. They've never seen the destruction some of these dictators or terrorists are capable of. They only care what their government does in return and they fight them every step of the way. For what? A principle? Because war is bad, because torture is morally wrong?" He smirked and looked at Ellen. "What they don't realize is that when we go to war, or interrogate someone, we're doing a tough job, but we're *saving* lives. Their lives. And they don't even realize it."

"So you'll blow up one protest. There's millions of anti-war activists out there."

"There sure is. But it's not even about these ones. America needs to see war on their doorstep, feel war, see terrorism and destruction so it can see why we fight abroad, why we do the tough job. Doing this here will only show what not fighting terrorism has done. A nuclear blast on American soil. Imagine."

"By an American, an ex-military official. That's not what we fight abroad."

"Is that what people will hear? Or will they hear that a notorious terrorist responsible for the Nairobi embassy bombings smuggled a nuclear weapon into the United States." He put his hand on her shoulder. "And that a man the U.S. was supposed to prosecute but instead sent to work as an undercover operative set the weapons off."

She squinted and shook her head. "Paul won't set it off. He's still in Somalia."

Sidwell shook his head and laughed. "No, he isn't. He's here. He's come looking for you, honey."

Thirty-nine

Before the Honda came to a complete stop between the yellow lines in front of the Virginia Hospital Center, Paul already had the passenger side door open and had his foot dragging along the pavement. They crossed the parking lot, passed a group of hospital workers in green scrubs that puffed on cigarettes and walked underneath the glass archway that covered the entrance to the seven-story complex. The overhead nighttime security lights were still on, sending fans of yellow against the sidewalk. Paul stayed in the shadows, hoping no one would notice his serious limp and the over-sized trench coat he had on. Underneath, he wore the pants and shirt that were stained with John Daniels' blood. Bailey had taken the coat from a coatroom in the NCS. According to the identification badge, the coat belonged to a man named Evan Rice.

They had left the NCS headquarters with relative ease. They had waited until the nurse returned to take another blood pressure and pulse, which she was doing every fifteen minutes. Once she left, they had packed up quickly and left the infirmary. Bailey had known that, although a security camera was filming him, no one was monitoring it. They left through the front entrance and Paul used the identification tag that was inside one of the jacket's pockets. It looked nothing like him. Rice was twenty years older, bald and had a beard. Paul signed out using his identification number and luckily, the security at the front did not check the photo. They estimated they had at least fifteen minutes before anyone noticed he was missing and another fifteen to review the security tapes. Then they would have to find out where Paul and Bailey were heading, which could take several hours.

The automatic doors slid open before them and they walked into the atrium. Against the far wall, a mural depicted a doctor sitting beside a patient's bed with his eyes closed and Paul couldn't tell whether the doctor was listening or sleeping. Below the mural sat an ebony veneered semicircle desk marked RECEPTION. Behind it, a large woman with a perm smiled at them.

"Can I help you?" She was far too perky for this hour.

Bailey and Paul approached the desk. Paul kept his hands in his pockets.

"We're looking for a patient," Bailey said, "his name is Craig Lynch."

"Certainly." The lady swiveled around in her chair and clacked a few keys on the keyboard in front of her.

The perma-smile on her face dissolved and she slowly turned back towards them.

"Umm. We're not able to give information about—"

"We're with the CIA," Bailey said, flipping open her badge. "We're here to speak with the prisoner."

"Oh, I'm so sorry," her eyes widened, apologetic, "he's on the fourth floor, room forty-three-fourteen. I can call upstairs so they know you're coming."

"That's not necessary."

Paul followed Bailey around the desk to the main elevators. Lynch likely had a note next to his file that he was in federal custody and no details on his condition were to be given out, Paul thought. Without question, no visitors would be allowed.

They stepped into the elevator and pressed the button for the fourth floor. The elevator labored its way up. Paul looked at Bailey, who ran her hand nervously up and down the metal railing on the elevator wall. The color in her face drained. Paul found himself wincing at the idea that Bailey was having second thoughts. That she would decide this had gone far enough and she wanted no part of it. *Don't you bail on me now, Bailey Clarke.*

But she didn't. The elevator stopped and before the door had completely slid open, Bailey had already walked out to the nursing station. She didn't waste any time and held her identification in front of the two nurses at the desk. One of them pointed down the end of the long corridor.

As they walked down the dimly lit corridor, Paul's thigh really started throbbing underneath the bandages. He kept moving forward at the expense of letting a grunt out with each step. Most of his mind was preoccupied with the fragile sense of hope that had washed over him when he concluded Ellen could still be alive and Craig Lynch could hold the key to finding her.

There was thick silence in the hallway, broken only by a beeping heart monitor and someone vomiting around the corner. To his right, Paul saw a medical cart stocked with intravenous bags and vials of medications parked in front of a room. He stopped and looked both ways and only saw one nurse with her back towards him at the end of the hall, penciling something onto a clipboard. He bent over and quickly rummaged through the cart, his hands moving until he found three vials of the cardiac medication adenosine, which he put into his pocket.

At the end of the hall, they found two middle-aged uniformed city police officers sitting in front of a closed door, sipping coffee. The two officers kept talking, sharing a good laugh and didn't notice Paul and Bailey until they were a few feet from them. When they did see them, the officers stopped talking abruptly and stood on either side of the doorway.

"I'm Officer Bailey Clarke, from the National Clandestine Service and this is Officer Rice," she said without pause. "Is this where the accused is? We need to speak with him."

"Yes it is. He's sleeping right now, though," the one who was already graying said. "But we need to check identification, is what we were told."

Paul exchanged glances with Bailey. If they looked at Paul's identification, they would instantly know he was an imposter. He looked over the officer's shoulder at the closed door, with a small PRIVATE sign on the front. A tall narrow window beside the door had the blinds drawn closed so no one could see inside.

Paul looked the officer up and down and inched closer to him. "How do you know he's sleeping?"

"We check on him every few minutes."

"Right. And you're concerned about identification, because you were *told*. I'm sure you were also *told* that high-ranking businessmen who get charged with serious federal crimes are at high risk of suicide and need to be constantly monitored. Or do we pick and choose what we do?"

The officer turned his eyes to the ground and Paul pushed his way between them and pressed on the door. He looked at Bailey out of the corner of his eye and saw the corner of her lips curl up slightly.

Inside, Lynch was lying on the bed with his eyes closed. Paul hardly recognized him. Nasal prongs fed oxygen into his brown-purple-splotched face and his finely styled hair was now matted down on his forehead. Bruises had formed on his neck. Both of his legs were covered in thick layers of bandages. Intravenous fluid dripped into each arm. Paul looked at the beeping heart monitor and then pressed the off button on the television that was playing a Red Sox game. He pushed the armchair next to Lynch's bed towards the window overlooking the playground at the back of the hospital.

He quietly turned the deadbolt on the door and then walked beside the bed. Bailey didn't move from her position next to the door.

Paul stared for a moment and then pressed his thumb into the bandages above Lynch's kneecap.

Lynch shot up and twisted in agony, letting out a weak scream. His eyelids flipped open and when he saw Paul hovering over him, he recoiled and brought his hands over his head like an injured animal.

"You lied to me, Craig." Paul smiled.

"What are you talking about?" Lynch crawled up the bed slightly, grasping the handrails.

"I know about the weapon."

"What are you talking about?"

"The missing suitcase, Craig. I know about it and you're going to tell me who has it." Paul pressed down on his kneecap again, eliciting another squeal.

"You monster," he cried through the pain. "You can't get blood from a stone."

"You're no stone and you've held out on me," Paul kept his voice steady. "You need to be aware that I will take this as far as is necessary to find out where that weapon is."

"What if I don't know anything?"

"There are three possible scenarios here, Craig: the first is that you cooperate and tell me who has the weapon and where it is. The second is that you lie and I torture you until you speak. The last is that you don't know anything and I torture you and you die." Paul shrugged. "I think all parties will be satisfied with the first scenario."

"She'll never let you torture me the way you did." Lynch let out a nervous chuckle and nodded at Bailey. "These are scare tactics."

Paul pretended to consider for a moment. "You're right in some ways. But we're not the FBI here, Craig. We're the National Clandestine Service and there's a nuclear weapon loose within this country's borders. So let's just say she's willing to break a few international treaties to let this happen. And I won't be torturing you the way that I did earlier. It will be much quicker."

Lynch stared at Paul for several seconds. His breathing became more labored. The heart monitor beeped rapidly. Suddenly, he began to scream, "Help, help, officers!"

Paul smothered Lynch's face with both of his hands and pressed his head down into the mattress. Lynch tried to twist free of the muzzle, but Paul only pressed down harder. Paul turned to Bailey. "Tell them that everything's okay."

Bailey nodded and opened the door a crack and whispered something to the officers outside. Then she shut the door.

"Now come over here and twist that blanket up and tie it around his mouth."

Bailey hurried over, her shoes clicking along the linoleum floor. She picked up the pile of extra blankets on the chair beside the window. She twisted one up in a roll, shoved into Lynch's mouth and tied it tightly behind his head in a double knot.

Meanwhile, Paul held Lynch's arms down as best he could. Lynch flopped on the bed, moving all of his limbs, trying desperately to get out of Paul's hold. He managed to free his right arm and he swung it wildly. The IV tubing followed his hand like the tail on a kite. He balled his hand and connected squarely with Paul's jaw, jarring him. Paul tightened his grip on Lynch's other arm and then swung the point of his elbow into Lynch's nose, stunning the scrawny man for a moment. Paul took the chance and pinned down his other hand.

"Tie his hands to the bed."

Bailey tied a blanket around each of his hands, again in a double knot.

"I can't waste any more time." Paul reached in his pocket and dropped the plastic vials onto the tray table beside him. He picked one up and held it between his fingers. "This is a twenty cc vial of adenosine. It's used to slow rapid heart rates. It's a life-saving medication. I have three vials here. To slow the heart, about one vial is usually needed, at most two. Three vials will stop your heart permanently."

Lynch's eyes darted around the room and he made a grunting sound through the blanket stuffed inside his mouth. His chest rose up and down in shallow little breaths. The heart monitor beeped wildly.

"I'll inject the first ten cc's." Paul pressed the syringe into the IV tubing and watched the rhythm strip on the monitor above Lynch's bed steadily decrease. The rapid beeping slowed to a crawl. Lynch's eyes fluttered closed. His chest became motionless.

Bailey's eyes grew and she slapped Lynch gently on the cheek. His eyes opened. He shot a glance at each of them and began groaning through the cloth in his mouth.

"Do you have something to say?" Paul pulled the blanket to Lynch's chin.

"You can't do this. I have immunity." Lynch looked over at Bailey, hoping for protection but she stared right through him.

"She might have given you a no-prosecution agreement but you didn't get one from me. And no one will protect you, not even the pretty lady from the NCS." Paul motioned towards Bailey and then leaned in, pressing his index finger on Lynch's chest. "And trust me, immunity agreements are void when you're dead."

"You can't let him do this," Lynch's voice raised an octave and pointed at Bailey. "You signed the paper, it's your duty to protect me."

Bailey darted a look at Lynch, her eyes furious. She nudged Paul out of the way, grasped the handrails tightly and leaned over Lynch. "My duty is to protect the United States. And that agreement was contingent on your full disclosure of the events that happened. So now that we know you withheld crucial information, for the security of this country that agreement is null and void." She cocked her head sideways and squinted. "So in the interest of the safety of the American people, I'm going to let him do his thing."

Lynch's brazenness wilted as Bailey spoke. His shoulders slumped to the side and he folded his hands in front of him.

"People are going to die if you don't help us stop this. The man who has the weapon will use it and he will use it to kill thousands of innocent people. For nothing."

Paul's words hung in the air.

"It wasn't supposed to be for nothing," Lynch exhaled and looked up at Paul.

"What was it supposed to be for?"

Lynch shook his head. "Our company wasn't doing well, it was on the verge of bankruptcy. An oil company in today's economy bankrupt, can you imagine? I couldn't fathom it. And the funny thing about it is that it was all because of deals and business decisions made thirty or forty years ago. And we were going down because of that.

I couldn't bear to see it happen. My career was on the line. So was John's. It was killing him, but he was a 'going down with the ship' kind of guy. I couldn't stand to see him that way. It was sad. I had to do something about it."

"You could have found another job," Bailey seethed.

"But I just had to make it work, for me and for John. So, this offer came up. They were planning on getting a stockpile of nuclear weapons into Somalia. At the same time, letting a terrorist group know about it, so they would steal them and try to smuggle them into the United States. It would create a perceived threat, so maybe the U.S. government would take notice and invade. The weapons were never going to get out of Somalia, but it would look like it. They had it all planned out. All they needed from me was money to fund it."

"And that's where the transfer came from."

"Right. And that worked for me, because if the U.S. ever came into Somalia, it would stabilize the region and our company could drill. And then we'd be back on top, the company comes back out of nowhere."

"Who were the people that planned it?"

"Well, there was the one guy in the NCS who gave us your information and General Kaczmareck, too. They had planned out the military side of things. You see, they had dealt with the terrorist on the side, keeping their identities secret so they could recover the weapons. But the guy who came up with the whole thing I never met. He's an arms dealer and he came to me with this offer."

"Senechaux," Bailey said.

"Yeah. All he wanted was a fee, a big one, too. But we took it too far. We figured: was the government really going to do anything because of a clandestine Special Forces operation? It took nine-eleven for the U.S. to finally go into Afghanistan and Iraq even though they knew they were involved in all sorts of crazy smuggling operations for decades. I needed results right away."

"So you smuggled the weapon into the United States."

"Senechaux wanted a helicopter because we knew of the planned ambush by the military. We tipped Hadad off and he managed to get a suitcase out. We were going to frame him, essentially. Get him to bring in the suitcase and then notify the authorities and media that a nuclear weapon had come onto U.S. soil."

"So where is it?"

"I think it's too late," Lynch frowned.

"What are you talking about?" Paul boomed.

Suddenly there was a bang at the door. Paul turned and the loud knocking at the door continued. "This is the FBI. Open the door immediately."

Paul exchanged glances with Bailey. They had come more quickly than they had thought.

"Why is too late, Craig?" Paul screamed.

"I lost contact with Senechaux yesterday. He has the weapon. He said he was going to set it off."

More banging. "We will break this door open!"

"Set it off where?"

"I don't know," Lynch shook his head, "he said he had to do it today, at noon. He said he was going to take out the people that prevent the military from getting things done. He was going to castrate the United States."

"What did you say?" Paul said.

"Castrate the United States."

"Did he use those words?"

"Yeah." Lynch looked at Paul sideways.

It felt like a hand reached up inside his abdomen and twisted his intestines. Something crept between the layers of his skin. He just heard something that his initial, split-second reaction was to dismiss as hallucination.

But instead, his mind was thrown back to Addis Ababa. Hadad's words: *castrate the United States* played on REPEAT in his mind. The protestors. The rally at the National Mall.

Peter.

"The Washington Monument," Paul blurted out.

"What?" Bailey looked at him.

"The target, it's the monument."

More banging at the door. "We're coming in."

"I have to go there," Paul said, "he's expecting me."

"Who is?" Bailey said.

"Senechaux, Sidwell. He talked about it when I used to work with him. He mentioned this. I know he's waiting for me."

"You're never going to get through them." Bailey pointed at the door, a door that was bending with each body check by the agents on the other side. "We're going to jail, Paul."

"Not yet," Paul said. "Car keys." Bailey stared blankly at him. "Give me your keys!" Bailey reached in her pocket and tossed her keys to him. "Bailey, you have to tell them to clear out the rally going on at the Washington Monument. He's going to set it off there."

"I'll be going to a holding cell when they come in."

"Then you'll have to convince them. Thousands of lives are at stake."

Paul turned and picked up the armchair beside the window and raised it high above his head. He launched it at the window, shattering it to pieces. In that instant, the door opened and FBI officers flooded into the room. Paul ran across the room and jumped out of the window, dropping the four stories onto the lawn below. As he landed, his knees buckled and he fell forward rolling three times. Pain seared from his ankle up to his lower back. He dragged himself along the grass and around the corner of the building so he was out of sight of the window.

He got to his feet, his left ankle already swelling. He dragged his ankle along the ground, nearly hopping on one foot to the car. He swung the door open, started the car and drove to D.C.

Forty

The FBI agent that arrested Bailey had placed the handcuffs on her wrists so tightly her hands were going numb. She looked up at the clock on the bland wall inside a basement office of the J. Edgar Hoover Building and realized she had been sitting alone for over half an hour. The only other item of décor in this room was a framed lithograph of the Counterterrorism Division seal, an eagle in full flight over which the slogan *PROTECTING AMERICA* was superimposed.

Bailey scanned the room, looking for any sign of life. The computer monitor on the desk across from her was turned off and the door was closed. The ceiling was devoid of any surveillance cameras. Why were they leaving her alone? She needed to tell someone there was a nuclear weapon at the Washington Monument.

She had tried, but so far, it had fallen on deaf ears. After the FBI agents had piled into Lynch's hospital room, she was promptly read her rights and herded into one of the black cruisers parked in front of the hospital. She had pleaded with the agents, begged them to put an alert out that the monument was an imminent terrorist target. But the agents responded to her the same way each time *you have the right to remain silent…* And why shouldn't they? As far as they were concerned, she had permitted an in-custody rogue clandestine operative out onto U.S. soil. She was an accomplice.

Bailey's only hope now was that her interrogator would listen, and he would get there soon.

The door swung open and a thin, middle-aged man in a dark suit with a slicked three-quarter part walked in. The musky scent of his aftershave followed him. He placed a can of 7-Up on the table in front of Bailey and dug into his pockets, removed a set of keys and unlocked her handcuffs. He sat on the corner of the desk and faced Bailey

"I'm Special Agent Mike Russo, state your name please." He pulled out a small digital tape recorder and placed it on the desk beside him.

"Bailey Clarke."

"Thirsty, Mizz Clarke?" He pointed at the can of soda.

Bailey shook her head.

"Okay, I have a few questions for you, Mizz Clarke. You have been arrested for aiding a suspected terrorist and are under suspicion of conspiracy to commit a terrorist act against the United States of America. Do you understand?"

"I understand that, but you have to listen to—"

"I'm sorry, Mizz Clarke, but the only words I need coming out of your mouth are those that directly answer my questions. Do you understand?"

"Yes, but if you just give me a second—"

"I'm not sure you do," he raised his voice and stood up with his arms crossed, "because what you say here will affect your prosecution. So it's in your interest to cooperate with what I say because the maximum penalty for the charges you face is death by lethal injection. Do you understand that?"

Bailey put her hands over her face. She was going to prison, if she was lucky. What else could she have done? She had uncovered a conspiracy and at least two high-ranking NCS and military officials were going to be prosecuted. But then she had learned more. A nuclear bomb was set to explode in the United States. Maybe she shouldn't have let Paul out of the infirmary. But they wouldn't have got the information from Lynch the way Paul did. Was she supposed to have sat idly by and pretended she knew nothing of the bomb?

She needed to convince this man. It could still be stopped. She had done nothing wrong. Tension filled up in her muscles, traveling up through her chest and down her arms; energy.

"No, I do not understand that," Bailey snarled at the agent, sending him reflexively two steps backwards. "What I understand is that there is a nuclear weapon loose out there set to go off at the Washington Monument and all you care to do is interrogate me while I was working to stop it. But instead of—"

"You lower your voice, you are in custody of the—"

Bailey got up and stared into his sunken eyes, inches from his face. "—Counterterrorism Division of the FBI and I'm warning you about a threat to national security and all you keep repeating are lines from your field manual. This is real, you need to shut down the Monument, the National Mall, send your agents there now."

Agent Russo put his hands up, half taken aback, half hoping she would calm down. "What evidence do you have of this threat?" he spoke gently, almost patronizing.

Bailey exhaled, letting the pressure escape. She relayed the events that had happened over the past two days to him. She told him about the pirate hijacking, Hadad, Crilley and the general. She talked about the recovery of the weapons and the missing suitcase. She told him about their interrogations with Lynch, about the wire transfers and Steven Sidwell, alias Armand Senechaux.

Russo seemed to be listening intently and nodded his head as she spoke.

"Quite the case you've built there." He reached for the can of 7-Up, opened it and took a sip. "But what evidence do you have?"

"I've just told you about it all." Bailey shook her head. "The transcripts of conversations, the wire transfers, signed confessions. It's airtight."

"That part sounds like it is. You have a lot of evidence that these people conspired to *make it look* like nuclear weapons were almost smuggled out of Somalia." Bailey's mouth gaped open as she listened to him, wondering where he was going with it. "But what evidence do you have that a weapon actually got into the United States?"

"I-I have information from Paul Alban who was on the ground level as this was happening, f-f-rom Craig Lynch, I was personally there when he said Sidwell managed to smuggle the weapon in the United States."

"And how did you come up with the Washington Monument as a target?"

"Umm, something that came up that Paul Alban remembered Sidwell talking about when they worked together, years ago..."

"Years ago." He let the words hang there, almost teasing Bailey.

"What are you getting at?"

"What do you think I'm getting at, Mizz Clarke?" He adjusted the lapels on his suit. "Paul Alban sold the whole story to you. *He* told you there was an extra weapon, *he* told you the target was the Washington Monument, *he* forced a confession from Craig Lynch."

"But why would he fabricate a story like that?"

"To be set free maybe? You said yourself, he killed one of your case officers point blank."

"That would have been exempted. It would take some paperwork, but it could be done."

"But did he know that? Or would it be safer to convince you there was an ongoing threat so he could escape your custody and be free, once and for all." He took another sip of 7-Up, looking smug. "Face it, Mizz Clarke, you've been duped. And now, you're in a lot of trouble."

Bailey's mind raced. Russo was right; it had happened that way. But why would Paul do that? What motivation would he have to run? She was there; she had seen Paul's reactions, his anger and his fear. There was no way he could have fabricated those emotions. But how could she convince Russo?

"Kadar Hadad is dead," Bailey blurted out. Russo furrowed his brow and Bailey continued. "His body washed up in a New Jersey harbor yesterday. He made it to the United States. So could a weapon."

Russo stared at her for a moment and clicked his teeth together. He didn't say a word. Then he reached for the phone on the desk and ordered an evacuation of the National Mall.

Forty-one

By 8:30 a.m., just over half of the expected 120,000 protestors had already gathered on the mile of grass between the Capitol steps and the Washington Monument. On a typical Wednesday morning, traffic would be flowing past on Madison and Jefferson Drives, joggers and women pushing strollers would dot the green space, and pigeons would waddle around park benches. But today, the police had closed the roads around the National Mall, so that no cars could come in, and those unlucky enough to have left their cars there overnight would have to wait until the rally was over at 3 p.m. to move their cars out. There was hardly a square of green left that wasn't already covered by the running shoes of a protestor. In several hours, the rally would be in full force and the people in the crowd would be rubbing shoulders. Several speakers were scheduled to speak on the stage at the foot of the United States Capitol complex, including Nathan Zeal, the controversial political scientist, whose attacks on U.S. foreign policy had begun to polarize the country.

Peter Daniels stood on the grass, his fingers interlaced with those of his girlfriend, Leah. Next to them was his best friend, Wayne and Leah's friend, Jessie. Peter was preoccupied with finding a spot closer to the stage, so he could hear the speeches. On some level, he hoped his enthusiasm would impress Leah.

Like the 65,000 people around him, Peter Daniels was oblivious to the fact that a faded grey van with rusted wheel wells, parked at the corner of Constitution Avenue and 14th Street, was going to explode in less than one hour.

~ * ~

The GPS that sat on the dashboard in Bailey's sedan directed Paul up Madison Drive, and as he approached the National Mall, the traffic swelled and reduced to a trickle, until he came up to the police barricade, which prevented vehicles from getting anywhere near the rally. Crowds of people, most carrying signs with phrases ranging from *OUT OF IRAQ NOW!* to *WHAT IF YOUR CHILD WAS COLLATERAL DAMAGE?* flowed up the sidewalk, underneath the row of elm trees to his left. Paul slammed his fist into the steering wheel, the honk joining the orchestra of car horns already blaring down the street. He thought to roll down his window, scream out for protestors to turn back, that there was a bomb set to go off. Panic vibrated inside of him; every second he wasted could mean the difference to stopping Sidwell.

The Washington Monument loomed in front of him, poking out behind the elm trees. The reflection of the rising sun made the obelisk look like an orange spear against the pink sky. Was that where Sidwell was? Paul realized he had convinced himself that the connections between the events of the past three days and Sidwell were real, but as time passed, the feeling that it all could have been wishful thinking gnawed at him. Would Sidwell really wait for Paul to arrive? Maybe all he wanted was for Paul to know he had set him up. Maybe the Washington Monument was a diversion, one used to set Paul marching along on the wrong path. Paul put his thumbs on his temples and shook his head, trying to shake the doubt out of his mind. Sidwell had left him clues, ones that only he could have pieced together. The Monument had to be the target. Sidwell had to be close. Ellen had to be there.

Paul's eyes traveled across the sea of protestors around him, stretching across the National Mall. He recognized that Peter was out there somewhere. Terror spread quietly under Paul's skin, all the way up to his head where a thought pulsated: *Am I too late?*

Paul put the car in park, took out the keys and flung the door open. He tried to take a step, but as his left foot touched the ground, a cutting pain shot up from his left ankle. He rolled up his pant leg to his knee and saw that his ankle had become scarlet and puffy to the point that he could feel the skin becoming tight around it. He pressed on his ankle and the joint felt intact underneath with no obvious deformity, which meant he probably hadn't broken it, but it was a bad sprain. The Washington Monument was at least a mile away and he wouldn't be able to get there with his ankle in this state.

He scanned the inside of the car and noticed the Club, a steering wheel locking device, lying in the passenger seat well. He dismantled it, placed the thick end inside his shoe, and fastened the top around his calf with the belt from his trench coat.

He stepped out of the car again, and his makeshift splint took a slight amount of weight off his leg, just enough to enable him to step through the pain. He headed for the sidewalk and ignored the people in the cars behind him, yelling out their open windows that he couldn't abandon his car.

He walked as quickly as he could with the pain in his thigh and ankle, and weaved and pushed his way through the hoards of people collected on the sidewalk. He passed a blonde woman with each arm outstretched, holding hands with two identical boys who couldn't be a day over seven. They each wore homemade T-shirts that read *WAR KILLS CHILDREN*. Paul saw the mother in his clinic Somalia before his eyes, crying hysterically after her two sons stepped on the landmine.

As he approached the Monument, the crowd became thick, with barely enough room to push through. He saw that crowd control barriers had been set up in a wide perimeter around the base of the Washington Monument, keeping people away from its entrance. Four police officers in riot gear patrolled the area. Paul weaved his way to the barrier, and put his hand on the metal fencing. He yelled for the nearest officer to come by. The officer turned and walked up to Paul with purpose.

"What is it, sir?" The man looked through the visor on his helmet.

"I think someone is inside the Monument right now."

"Impossible, it's closed today." He turned to walk away.

"But no, I think someone has broken in." Paul grabbed his shoulder.

"Do not touch me, sir." He took two abrupt steps back and put his hand on the baton on his belt.

"You have to listen to me for a minute."

Suddenly there was a loud *pop!* coming from the opposite side of the Monument. A young shirtless man held a glowing red flare high above his head, screaming obscenities. Three security guards converged and had him on the ground, in cuffs, in an instant. People in the crowd around Paul moved closer to get a look at the commotion.

Then a firm hand clasped down on Paul's shoulder, and something hard and blunt pressed into his spine.

"You are right on time," a voice in an eastern European accent whispered in his ear. "Do not try to run, or I will shoot you. We will walk in that direction, side-by-side." A large, hairy hand reached over Paul's shoulder and pointed northwest, towards a long building with a series of columns running around the outside.

Paul started walking and turned his head slowly towards the man with the gun. He didn't recognize the man with the dark, hairy forearms and pockmarked face who wore a slushy nylon blue and red tracksuit, but he knew the man must work for Sidwell.

As they crossed the street away from the Monument, they passed near a police officer in riot gear and the man with the pockmarks slipped the gun into his jacket pocket. Paul didn't think about running, or of telling the officer the man next to him had a gun. That would only cause a diversion and he estimated his best chance of stopping the weapon from exploding was getting to Sidwell.

Out of the corner of his eye, Paul saw half a dozen black cruisers with flashing blue and red lights pull up to the traffic barricades at the far end of the National Mall. Several men in trench coats ran out and spoke quickly and animatedly to the police officers at the barricades. Immediately, the police officers started waving at protestors nearby to move down the street, away from the rally. Paul assumed they were evacuating the site and that Bailey Clarke had managed to convince the FBI there was a real threat at the rally. It did little to reassure him, though; an evacuation of that size would take hours. He doubted they had that much time.

Any hope he might have had that the rally would be evacuated swiftly in record time died as he and the pockmarked man moved against the tide of thousands of protestors still converging on the National Mall.

They crossed Constitution Avenue and walked about two hundred yards down 14th Street Northwest, under the shade of oak and elm trees until they came upon a faded grey utility van with rusted holes around the wheel wells. The rear windows were painted. A worn sign on the side advertised *SUPER CITY ELECTRICAL INC*. The only things about the van that could seem out of place to someone passing by were the dark blacked out windows.

The man with the pockmarked cheeks pressed the rear door handle, swung it open and pushed Paul inside. The door slammed behind him.

"For god sakes, Marshall, for a minute there I thought you weren't going to show up."

The twang in the voice stuck in Paul's ears and took him back to last time he had seen Sidwell in Addis Ababa.

Paul stood hunched over at the edge of the van and let his eyes scan through the interior. The van had been hollowed out, so that only the front seats remained. Sidwell sat on a bench behind the front seats. A black Adidas duffel bag sat on the floor in front of him. Ellen sat next to him, her hands shackled to an eyehook in the floor. Her face puckered as her eyes met Paul's and she burst into tears.

Paul batted away every impulse he had to run over and take Ellen into his arms, to tell her he loved her, that he was sorry and to kiss her on the forehead. Instead, he shifted his eyes towards Sidwell, a much larger, rounder Sidwell than he remembered. Sidwell sat on the bench with his arms crossed, a grin beaming through his thick beard.

At that instant, Paul recognized that he had never felt such rage in his entire life. He unconsciously balled his hands into fists, until they turned white. His jaw clamped down to the point that his teeth hurt. He had the impulse to lunge at Sidwell, claw his piercing eyes out and choke the life right out of him. The man in front of him had manipulated everyone around Paul to set him up and smuggle a dangerous weapon into the United States. He had shattered everything in Paul's life. He had made Paul kill. And now this man was about to kill thousands of innocent people.

And he had a grin on his face.

But Paul didn't move. He stood there, fixated on Sidwell, part of him curious as to what this crazed man wanted with him.

"I thought I was going to have to blow this thing without you," he pointed at the duffel bag.

"You knew I'd come," Paul said. "You made it happen that way."

"Correction, I made it *likely* that you'd come." Sidwell stood up, his head touching the ceiling. "When it comes to Marshall Ramsey, one can never be certain whether he'll run away."

Paul didn't say anything.

"Come on there, Marshall, can you honestly deny that? First example: you leave your buddy Dennis burning alive in Nairobi." Sidwell rubbed his hands together and shuddered exaggeratedly. "That's cold, Marshall, real cold."

A chill ran up Paul's back and he looked in Sidwell's eyes. *How does he know about leaving Dennis behind? I never told him that.*

"How do I know about that, Marshall?" Sidwell said, as if he had read Paul's mind. "Remember Dr. Ross, the psychologist you saw before you joined the team tracking Kadar? Well I got the clinic letters. Second example," Sidwell continued, "young Marshall leaves his father dead on the stairs of his home and runs and hides in a field."

Paul suddenly felt as though the van were rocking underneath him. He put his fingers over his temples to stop the throbbing.

"And then internal affairs starts smelling blood in the Kadar Hadad torture. And what do you do? You run… Again. You testify against me and you run away from any consequences. You leave your family behind. But now it all comes crashing back on you, doesn't it?"

Paul saw his fist shoot out. He saw it touch Sidwell's jaw and send his head snapping to the side. He felt

Sidwell's coarse beard scratch his knuckles. Then, he felt two hands clamp down on his shoulders and twist him to the floor. A swift kick came up into his ribs sending a paralyzing pain through his chest, one that made his breathing shallow and wheezy. He heard Ellen scream something. The man with the pockmarks pressed his knee into Paul's back and forced Paul's face onto the cool metal floor.

"Get up, Marshall."

Paul turned onto his back, propped himself onto his elbows and looked up at Sidwell, who licked the blood dripping down from his upper lip.

"Kill me then," Paul said softly. "You did this for me, kill me. There's no need to go and set a nuclear bomb off and kill all those civilians."

"You think this is all for you?" Sidwell shrieked and then spit a gob of blood at Paul's feet. "It's about everyone out there right now!"

Paul didn't look up at Sidwell.

"Do you honestly think we went too far with Hadad?"

Paul's heart raced. He thought of Dennis collapsing under the pillar, burning alive. He thought of Sami lying on his back on the hill in Bosasso.

"Don't you think he deserved it? He was a terrorist that killed thousands of innocent people. He killed children and Americans. He almost killed you—"

"He deserved it," Paul said. "He deserved it and more."

"You're damned right! And the people down there got him released. Political pressure."

"You really think those are the same people? Most of the people out there weren't out of diapers in ninety-eight."

"They're the same, and this will show them."

"Show them what, Steve?"

"It will show them they cause their own destruction. The same terrorist that one decade ago they protested for has now smuggled in a nuclear weapon that is about to kill them."

Paul shook his head. "You've gone mad, Steve."

Sidwell laughed to himself and stared at Paul, his eyes seemingly floating above his cheekbones. He rolled his eyes as if to say, *you haven't seen 'mad' yet*. He shook his head, still chuckling, reached in his pocket and held out a blackberry device. He crouched down and unzipped the duffel bag. Inside, Paul saw a tangle of wires running between a large metal canister and a battery.

"Here's how this is going to work." Sidwell stopped laughing abruptly, and stared at Paul, a grave expression on his face. He reached out and put his right hand gently on the back of Paul's neck, as though he was going to pull Paul in for a hug. Paul could smell the coffee aroma emanating from his mouth as he spoke. "I'm going to activate the device on my blackberry once Razman and I get to our car. That will give it four minutes until the device explodes. I will be well out of the blast radius by that time."

"So what, then? Everyone dies?" the words came out calmly, even though his heart was pounding away.

"Not necessarily everyone." Sidwell smiled wide, like a game show host saying *let's see what's behind door number 3!*

"What are you talking about?"

"You might survive."

"How?"

"Four minutes is enough time to get out of the blast radius on foot," Sidwell shrugged, "if you run."

"What?"

"You can run, Marshall. You can save yourself again."

Before Paul said anything more, Sidwell patted him on the back of the neck, swung the rear doors open and he and Razman hopped out. They slammed the door behind them.

It took more than a second for Paul to process what had just happened. He stood at the back of the van, his hair touching the ceiling, dumbfounded. Sidwell had given him a chance to run. He could live.

His eyes slowly moved towards Ellen sitting on the bench. She cried hysterically, unable to bring her hands to her face to wipe away her tears because they were shackled to the eyehook in the floor. He recognized this would be the last image he would have of her, one that would be burned into his brain forever. A portrait of helplessness.

He moved to her and crouched down. He ran his hand down the side of her face and pressed his lips on hers. It only lasted a moment because by this point the tears were coming so fast that she sputtered. She tasted salty and her whole face was wet. Through her short breaths, she whispered something.

"It's okay, Paul. It's okay."

He didn't say anything. He slowly rose and any angst he may have felt at that moment didn't show itself on his face. He turned, swung the rear door open and ran out of the van.

He ran out into the street, ignoring the sharp pain in his ankle. He scanned the scene around him. Cars parked bumper to bumper lined both sides of the road. Protestors continued to flow past the van on the sidewalks and the middle of the street towards the National Mall. Sidwell and Razman were nowhere to be seen. He heard someone's voice through a megaphone far in the distance, over the cacophony of protestors chanting. He also heard a sharp thudding sound around the corner in front of him. A jackhammer.

Paul raced towards the sound. He darted through the crowd of people rushing towards him. On the sidewalk underneath a hanging basket, he saw two construction workers chipping away at a section of sidewalk. One of them ran the jackhammer in repeated bursts, while the other shoveled away the debris.

He ran at them and ripped the spade out of the worker's hand. Before the worker reacted, Paul already had a five second head start.

He ran back to the van, ignoring the pain in his leg and swung the door open. He jumped inside, lifted the spade over his shoulder and thrust it down into the eyehook at the bottom of the van, making a loud *clang!* He kept hitting the eyehook repeatedly: *clang, clang, clang!* His face had folded into a grimace at the sound, but he kept going feverishly. A spark shot out from the metal on metal contact.

The eyehook bent over slowly and he kept pounding away, harder and harder. The hook broke open a touch and he reached his fingers inside and pulled it apart about half an inch. He unhooked the chain. Ellen was free.

"Go," Paul commanded and pointed at the open door.

Ellen stared at him, confusion etched on her face.

"Just go!" he turned her around and pushed her out the door before he slammed it shut. He pressed the lock down and heard her slap on the door a few times.

Paul ran to the driver's seat and looked at the steering column. He needed to get the van started. Sami's words ran through his head: *First try to shove a screwdriver into the ignition.*

He leaned over and opened the passenger side glove box. All he found inside was a CAA map of New England and a flashlight. He swept his hands through the pockets inside the doorframes and found a rusty metal butter knife.

He stabbed the knife into the ignition and twisted. It did not move. He jiggled it frantically; his time was running out. He grasped the handle as hard as he could and twisted and the van sputtered to life.

Paul threw the van into drive and pulled out onto the road. He maneuvered the van through the sea of protestors, like a car pushing through a flock of sheep. As he passed, people angrily banged on the van, screaming for him to be careful. *You're going to kill someone!*

They had no idea how right they were.

People started making space for the van to get through and Paul took full advantage. He floored the gas and sped down the road, away from the rally. He saw Ellen in his side mirror, becoming smaller as he pulled away. The sea of protestors parted as the van ripped up the street.

As he tore up the road, Paul Alban tried not to think about what was set to happen in a few short minutes. At this point, the wheels were in motion. This was his last chance to end what had started over a decade earlier.

With each second that ticked past, the weight on Paul's chest became heavier. His eyes became wet and blurry and he burst into tears. He thought of Ellen and of Peter. He thought of how he would never see them again. *It's almost over,* he said to himself.

He took a left turn at forty miles an hour, and the van fishtailed erratically. The tires screamed. The duffel bag slid along the floor and slammed against the van's interior wall.

He pressed the ball of his foot down and watched the needle of the speedometer climb steadily. A seed of doubt grew in his mind as he started to recognize the craziness of what he was about to do. *Sometimes you have to go for a Hail Mary.*

He ripped through a stop light, narrowly avoiding three cars. He flew up an on-ramp, the van leaning as he went up the cloverleaf. Up ahead, he could see the glimmer of sunlight reflecting off water.

The river.

Even when the van reached the edge of the bridge with concrete railings on either side, Paul still wasn't one hundred percent certain he was going to go through with it. But at some point, he had decided it was going to happen. *No turning back*. And when that moment came, he felt calm.

He rolled down the window and pushed down on the accelerator. He put his seatbelt on with his left hand. When he reached the middle of the bridge, he turned the steering wheel forty-five degrees.

When the van hit the concrete railing, the front end crumpled. Paul felt as through the seatbelt was going to cut through his torso diagonally. The van lurched forward and the back end came up so the van was briefly standing on its nose. Then, the van slowly tipped over the rail and fell thirty-five feet into the Potomac River.

The van sank in ten seconds.

Forty-two

Three days later

Ellen woke up to the sun's glare through the dusty hotel window. She squinted and rolled over to the digital clock on the nightstand beside the bed and saw it was 10:23 A.M. She had overslept.

The place was a Holiday Inn Express, on the outskirts of Arlington. The FBI covered the bill while they continued their investigation into the botched attack on the Washington Monument. It wasn't a bad place; the mattress was soft, the linens clean but maybe a little scratchy and the bathroom was recently updated. The problem was they wanted her to stay until all the initial interviews were done, which could take up to two months. A long time to live in a hotel room.

She sat up in the bed, reached for the remote control and turned on the national news. Three former officials of Homeland Security debated about how Kadar Hadad managed to enter the United States, build a homemade "dirty" bomb and nearly set it off without the FBI getting wind of it. They hailed the *brave men and women* in the FBI who had stopped the explosion and driven the van off the bridge, short circuiting the detonator and saving *hundreds of lives*. Then they segued into a debate about the merits of preemptive strikes against countries like Iran and Syria and Somalia to stop terrorism.

There was no mention of Paul Alban, Craig Lynch or Steven Sidwell.

No mention of a nuclear bomb.

Ellen smiled a crooked smile and shook her head.

She turned her head towards the tangle of blankets in the space on the bed beside her, the side that Paul had slept on. She hadn't heard him get up, which was no real surprise since she had slept like a rock the past three nights.

She got up and walked to the bathroom. The door was open and the lights were off. She turned and opened the closet and saw that Paul's shoes and jacket were gone.

She initially felt a twinge of panic and thought maybe he had run away, that maybe he didn't believe he would be pardoned for any offenses he may have committed during the Somalia affair as the people at Langley had promised. *And why should he trust anyone?* But she quickly reassured herself that he had probably only gone for a walk, maybe to get a newspaper, maybe to get some food, maybe a coffee, maybe...

~ * ~

He couldn't really understand what had made him slide out of bed at 4:00 A.M., walk to the bus terminal and get on the Greyhound, but he felt compelled to do so. He'd been struck with a terrible case of insomnia and he swore he hadn't slept more than two hours in the past three nights.

And during those two hours, he dreamed. The same dream.

He realized that he should feel calm. He was about to be discharged from any active duty in the National Clandestine Service; he was given his identity back; he could continue living with Ellen and his son was alive and well.

But he felt more restless than ever.

After the two-hour bus ride, he got off at the bus stop in front of an Esso station. A mechanic's garage door was open beside the gas station and he asked the mechanic for directions. The man wiped the grease off his hands with a red bandana and said he wasn't a hundred percent sure, but he thought the place was three miles up the road, down a gravel path *quite a ways* and that he should come upon a sign.

He decided to walk along the shoulder of the twisty highway that was lined with tall spruce and oak trees. When the slight breeze picked up, he caught the scent of pine. Every few hundred feet or so, he made out small cabins through the trees.

Two trucks had stopped beside him and asked if he needed a ride, but he told them no thank you, that it was a beautiful day and he would prefer to walk.

After about forty minutes, he turned onto the gravel road that cut through the forest on his right. He followed the upward and then downward sloping road, avoided the major puddles in the pot holes until he came upon the sign that was partially obscured by a tree branch that read *Eden Cemetery*.

It was small, as far as cemeteries go, and he was alone. He slowly walked from headstone to headstone, reading the name on each one, because he had no idea where to find the one he was looking for. A few had fresh flowers beside them, but even more had fake ones.

Then he came upon it, read the name twice to be sure. He ran his hand along the cold stone. He knelt down and wept.

Epilogue

18 months later

The bus was packed. It rattled as it drove up the gravel road toward the eastern district. Bailey Clarke sat against an open window in the middle of the bus wearing long pants and long sleeves because the *Lonely Planet* guidebook had stated that one should wear modest clothing when traveling in East Africa, but it made the sweltering heat almost unbearable. She rested her backpack on her lap and grabbed her camera case off the seat next to her as two young boys squished into the seat, whispered something to each other and burst into laughter. She couldn't afford a broken lens on her first field assignment.

It had been over a year since she had resigned from her position at the NCS and, after a brief period of mental recuperation, Bailey applied for jobs around the country. She eventually took a job as a reporter for a small magazine out of Oregon named the *Cultured Nomad.* She had spent her first eight months working alongside a senior editor, mainly checking stories' references and correcting grammatical errors. Eventually she pitched a story idea to the editor and after a bit of convincing, she was given the okay. She already had a working title: *Developing world, developing medicine: cutting edge treatment in Somalia.*

When the bus stopped, Bailey fumbled with her bags, squeezed her way through the aisle and stepped off the bus. She walked across the road and stopped at the edge of the gravel parking lot. She dropped her backpack onto the ground and unzipped her camera case. She flicked through the four lenses she had brought with her and after a fairly long period of deliberation, decided to go with the 40 millimeter.

She took twelve photos of the patients sitting on long benches underneath the shade of a yellow and red tent in front of the concrete building. A waiting room.

She hooked her arm through the strap of her backpack, lumbered over to the entrance and took another set of photos of the small sign that hung beside the doorway. *The Dennis Hildebrand Medical Center.*

As two local women walked out the door, Bailey slipped inside. Three beds down, she saw Paul and Ellen busy at work. They hadn't noticed her enter. She watched Paul sew up a laceration on a young man's shin. Ellen was next to him, passing over bandages that he used to wrap up the leg. They were both smiling.

Yes, it was going to make a great story.

Meet

Daniel Rasic is a physician and lives with his family in Nova Scotia, Canada.